Fate and Tomorrow

ROSE DOYLE

Fate and Tomorrow

Hodder & Stoughton

First published in Great Britain in 2002 by Hodder & Stoughton
A division of Hodder Headline

The right of Rose Doyle to be identified as the Author of the Work has been
asserted by her in accordance with the Copyright, Designs and Patents Act 1988.

1 3 5 7 9 10 8 6 4 2

All characters in this publication are fictitious and any resemblance to real persons,
living or dead, is purely coincidental.

A CIP catalogue record for this title is available from the British Library.

Cased edition ISBN 0 340 77135 6
Trade paperback edition ISBN 0 340 77136 4

Typeset in Plantin Light by Palimpsest Book Production Limited,
Polmont, Stirlingshire

Printed and bound in Great Britain by
Mackays of Chatham plc, Chatham, Kent

Hodder & Stoughton
A division of Hodder Headline
338 Euston Road
London NW1 3BH

For Simon

My thanks, again, to my editor Sue Fletcher, who can work, encourage and have fun all at the same time. Thanks, too, to Swati Gamble, no longer a voice on the phone and a pleasure to work with. And thank you, Darley, for setting things up. Great thanks to Tom McGettrick, a Sligo man who knows his county and its history, for the loan of precious journals and books. Most useful among these were *The Sligo Champion Sesquicentenary* 1836–1886; *In Sligo Long Ago* and *Olde Sligo* by John C. McTernan; and *In the Shadow of Benbulben* by Joe McGowan. *Twilight of the Ascendancy* by Mark Bence-Jones, along with Valerie Pakenham's *The Big House in Ireland* told me much that I needed to know about the decline of the big house and old landed class in Ireland. *Dress in Ireland – A History* by Mairead Dunlevy helped me put clothes on characters. Adam Hochchild's superb book – *King Leopold's Ghost* – on the exploitation of the Congo and its people in the nineteenth century, was both an inspiration and a mine of information. Mary Kingsley's *Travels in West Africa* and *West African Studies* were invaluable – what a woman! In lieu of a trip to present day West Africa, *Congo Journey* by Redmond O'Hanlon filled the gaps about that country's flora and fauna. And for sharing their knowledge (and books), much gratitude to John Bannigan and Carmel Dinan. I'm grateful, too, to the writer Standish O'Grady who, as the nineteenth century came to an end, prophesied anarchy and civil war for Ireland. When he went on to say that this 'might end in a shabby, sordid Irish Republic ruled by corrupt politicians and the ignoble rich', he gave me a predictive quote for Jerome O'Grady.

I

If the storm hadn't happened.

If, knowing it was threatened, I'd stayed indoors.

If I'd listened, for once, and left the gun where it was. If I'd put it back. If I'd never used it in the first place.

Then the tragedy that started it all might never have happened. Things would certainly have taken a different course and life, at the very least, would have gone on its fretfully peaceful way.

In my own defence it must be said that I couldn't have foreseen events. No sane person could have imagined the insanity and horror to come.

The biggest *if* of all, of course, had to do with my date of birth. If I hadn't come into the world on 31 March, 1879 then my twenty-third birthday wouldn't have fallen on 31 March, 1902.

But I was and it did and, restless about the dinner party being given for me that night, I got up early on my birthday morning and left Kilraven, where I'd lived all of my twenty-three years, to go walking along the shoreline of the estuary. Finn the wolfhound, who in dog years was three times my age, went unwillingly along with me. He could feel the storm in the air. I'd have sensed its imminence myself if I'd been paying attention.

If . . .

When the rain came I ran for the trees. The winter had been long and bitter and the leaves slow in coming so they didn't offer much cover. But they sheltered me from the wind as I leaned against an old trunk to catch my breath.

Finn was the first to hear the cry. He moved closer to my skirts and stood with his ears back, making a small, moaning sound of his own. I shook the cloak hood from my head and heard for myself the low, dying cry of an animal in pain. It was quite close and I knew, as Finn knew, that the animal was a dog.

We found her quickly enough, an unhappy lurcher bitch without a name owned by a man called Barnie Kilgallen who lived alone at the edge of the village. The lurcher's hind leg was caught in the rusty, steel jaws of a trap and was all but severed. There was nothing left of it but a sodden, black-red pulpy mass of bone and sinew.

She'd been in the trap some time. The ground under and around her was blood-soaked and she was just about able to raise her scraggy head and give a feeble baring of teeth as we came near. The trap belonged to Fardy Quin, another villager, but in his case with a family to feed. He'd been told by my father, time out of number, to keep himself and his contraptions off our lands.

I crouched down and lifted the lurcher's tired head in my hands. Finn nosed at the blood on the ground.

'You didn't have much of a life,' I said softly and she sighed, 'and you're not having much of a death. I don't know either that there's a lot I can do for you.' I looked again at what the trap had done to her. 'You could get around on three legs, I suppose . . .' I lowered her poor head to the ground again '. . . but there's all that blood lost. You're half-dead, and you know it. Kilgallen's never looked after you before . . .'

She whimpered when I said his name, her eyes full of trust. She was a dog who'd never lost her faith in man. I got to my feet.

'. . . and he's not going to look after you now,' I said,

'whatever you may hope. I can't get you out of that thing and you're dead anyway, even if I did.' She lay without moving, pain-dulled eyes staring up at me. 'I'll be back,' I said.

Finn sniffed and moaned again at the bottom of his throat and dragged himself after me out of the trees. Although he was a wolfhound he'd never, even at the best of times, cared for the woods.

The door to the gun room was locked.

I found Mossie Hope in the kitchen. He had a bowl of maizemeal stir-about in front of him with griddle bread, milk and butter to follow. It was what he always had for breakfast, winter and summer.

'The gun room's locked and I need the shotgun.' I sat on the form beside him at the long table, keeping my back to Julia Hope.

Julia had been busy at the range when I came in but had turned to sniff at my sodden clothes in a way I thought would dislodge the nose from her face. She was now giving me one of her best glares. It burned through the wet cloak clinging to my back.

'What do you want the gun for?' Mossie said.

He didn't look at me but from the side his expression wasn't encouraging. Not that this bothered me. Mossie was a giant of a man, 6 foot 4 inches tall and with shoulders more than half that width. He wore his black-grey hair tied back in a tail and his brows, the same colour and thick, made his eyes difficult to see. The space between his top lip and nose was so thin he looked to have a permanent sneer but he was the kindest man on earth, and one of the gentlest.

'Kilgallen's old lurcher's caught in a trap.' I traced with a finger where a farm boy had carved his name in the oak of the table. It was a long time since we'd had farm boys at Kilraven, a long time since we'd had enough land to give

3

them work. 'Her leg's almost off. She looks as if she's been trapped and bleeding most of the night.'

'She's none of your business.' Mossie finished his stir-about and began to butter bread. 'Bring the child some milk,' he said to his wife.

Julia didn't move. I could have done with the milk, or even a cup of sweet tea. I wasn't looking forward to shooting the dog.

'You're wet through,' Mossie pushed his own mug of milk my way, 'you'd no business going out with a storm coming.'

'Give me the key to the gun room, Mossie, please.' I drank the milk and took the buttered bread when he gave it to me. 'I don't know why you've taken to keeping it locked anyway.' I bit into the bread. It was still warm. Whatever her faults Julia Hope still made the best bread in Co. Sligo.

'The dog's none of your business,' Mossie said stubbornly, 'the misfortunate bitch is most likely dead by now anyway, if she's as hurt as all that.' He'd stopped eating. Mossie's heart was very soft when it came to animals.

'And if she's not dead she's still dying.' I let him think about this before I said, 'Will you put her out of her misery?' I stopped again. Mossie had never used a gun in his life. I took his silence for a no and went on, 'Will my father?'

'Your father's not . . .'

'Not fit to shoot a fish in a bucket,' I cut him short before he could make the excuse that my father was not well enough, or too busy. My father was probably drinking. It was never too early for him to begin, these days. 'Please, Mossie, give me the key,' I said, 'you know I can do it, that I'm a better shot than the boys ever were.'

This was true. Even though it was my brothers who'd taught me to shoot I'd a better eye than either of them. I could ride as well as either of them too. Sadly, such accomplishments seemed of less and less value as I grew older.

4

'Doesn't take much of a markswoman to shoot a trapped animal.' Julia's sinewy, freckled arm came between us as she put a fresh mug of milk in front of Mossie. 'I'll have breakfast ready for yourself and your mother in the dining room in less than half an hour.' She wiped her hands on her apron, a sure sign she was moving into full, angry flight. 'It'd be more in your line to go and hang up those wet clothes instead of making work for me by going back out to shoot a useless animal. You needn't be expecting me to dry them for you. I've enough to be doing with the food for tonight. The beef I've had hanging for weeks has to come down and there's a hundred other things to be done too.' She sniffed and gave a mighty twitch of her nose. 'You've no thought for others, coming in here like that, dripping wet sand and mud all over the floor I cleaned on my hands and knees at five o'clock this morning . . .'

Julia's harping drove Mossie from the table and out of the kitchen. I followed him, my skirt hems still dripping mud and water on to the flagstones she'd scrubbed at five o'clock that morning. Julia was as regular in her habits as Mossie.

But Mossie was the one who knew everything there was to know about the land and house and the maintenance of both. Mossie could tend livestock, chop firewood, repair fences, clear ditches, earth potatoes, muck out, look after the stables and horses. He'd learned it all from his father before him, who had also looked after Kilraven. As a child I'd thought Mossie was God.

When he'd married Julia three years before I'd changed my mind. No god would have made the mistake of marrying a woman with flint for a heart, even if she was handsome and a good cook and he was used to working with her. Even if, as he explained to my father, he got lonely in the night.

Julia had been a childless widow looking after the motherless daughter of her dead sister. She'd been glad to move from

5

her small house in Ballycoole to Kilraven and had wanted appease the parish priest, Father Duggan, by taking her niece Ellie where she could no longer flirt with the village boys. This latter aspiration had fared no better than the marriage, however. Ellie came and went from Kilraven to the village as she pleased and the priest was still haranguing her reputation.

Julia feared God and the priest in equal measure. I think she'd thought to make a God-fearing Christian of Mossie, who didn't believe in anything, but she'd failed in that too. I pitied Julia, sometimes. I pitied Mossie more, all of the time.

'If you won't give me the key then at least open the door and let me get the gun myself.' I was shivering as I followed him up the stairs from the kitchen, my wet clothes beginning to soak through to my bones. 'It would be cruel to let me go through the whole of my birthday thinking and wondering about that dog.'

'There's no good in talking to you, I suppose.' Mossie stopped when we came into the great hall. He'd already got a fire burning there.

'None at all,' I affirmed.

Finn, always good at looking after himself, was stretched and steaming dry in front of the fire. Firewood was something we'd no shortage of at Kilraven and a fire burning in the great hall, which had a gallery and was the central well from which the rest of the house sprang, tended to warm the rest of the building. The wood crackled and the black polished hobs on either side shone red with the flames. I was tempted to lie beside Finn. I would have, too, if it hadn't been for the other miserably waiting dog in the woods.

Mossie opened the gun-room door. I got the shotgun from the wall and checked it was unloaded.

'Why're you keeping the place locked anyway?' I asked

Mossie again, aware he hadn't answered when I'd asked him this before in the kitchen.

'Signs,' he said.

'Signs?' I repeated. 'What signs?'

'You might need more than one.' He handed me a couple of cartridges.

'What signs, Mossie?' I persisted.

'Nothing you need concern yourself with.' He looked around the hall. 'I'll keep a good eye on them. Wind's slacking off a bit,' he could tell this from the sounds in the chimney, 'you'd best do what you have to do before it picks up again.'

There was no good questioning him any more, I knew that. Also, I trusted him. If Mossie Hope said he would keep an eye on 'signs' then he would.

'That poor animal will be dead before you get to her,' Mossie said from the door as I left. I hoped he was right just as much as he hoped he was right.

Kilgallen's lurcher was very still, but breathing. I loaded the cartridges, both of them, went as close as I had to and took aim quickly. Even at that I wasn't quick enough and she opened her eyes as I levelled the gun. She was looking at me when I shot her.

She died with dignity, as most animals do. In the lurcher's case she gave a small yelp when the shot struck, then turned it into a sigh as life left her. I told myself the sigh was one of relief. I made a grave over her with leaves and branches, said a quick prayer and left her there.

The rain stopped as I came out of the woods. Kilraven, sulking grey and ivy-covered in the weak sun, was not what it once used to be. These days it was a cause of many anxieties, and the burdens of keeping it in order and paying its taxes and rates and labour were heavy. House prices were poor and costs high and it was worn, impoverished and badly in need of new life. The value of an estate in Sligo was what you could get for it, according to Mossie.

Kilraven had been built by an O'Grady ancestor more than two hundred years before and a lot had happened in the country and to the house in those two centuries. A lot had happened, too, in the twenty-three years it had taken me to grow up there.

I'd been born the daughter of a visionary landowner. In the years since then my father had lost so much of the property he'd inherited to Land Acts and overdaring and bad management that, at twenty-three years of age, I was the daughter of an indebted, impoverished fantasist.

We were facing bankruptcy, racing headlong and uninterrupted and closer to it every day. It had begun with the famine, more than fifty years before, when the needs of a starving and destitute tenantry had all but bankrupted my grandfather. It was said of him that he'd died of heart ache.

My father inherited the land wars along with the land. The end of the wars, and the breaking up and selling off of the estate to the tenants, ended his dream of a Utopian community on Kilraven lands. In my father's dream, landowner and tenant ploughed the fields and gathered cattle and sheep and the flowers of May together.

But a dream was all it was and even as a child I'd thought it a simple-minded one. Without the tenants' rents, without leaving himself enough for us to farm, my father was left to watch the slates fall from the roof of the house while he drank whiskey and made wild plans about what he was going to do with the land he'd left. He was at the moment convinced that copper mining would save us all. Maybe it would too. Maybe there was nothing to be done now but dream and try for miracles, like he did, ignore reality, like my mother, or abandon Kilraven and the past, like my brothers.

I was trying to fulfil a dream myself, though nothing so extravagant as my father's wild imaginings.

In my dream I married the love of my childhood. Theo Howard was the son of the family whose lands adjoined ours. He was fair-haired and handsome and the only man I'd ever kissed, or wanted to. Marrying him would bring Howard and O'Grady holdings together, making Kilraven viable again. It would also fulfil a promise, made when we were children and by now a bit overdue, that we would marry when I was twenty-one. Most of all our marriage would put an end to my missing him, to the loneliness of wanting to be with him every day.

It was Christmas since I'd last seen, touched or talked to him but he would be at my birthday dinner tonight. He was to arrive on the afternoon train, along with my brother Hugh. They were studying law together in Dublin.

The sun shone stubbornly on my gloom as I took a short cut to the house through the gardens. Winter's havoc was everywhere; in the decay of the borders, the untilled wilderness beyond them, the heaving grey of the distant estuary waters. There was a mist on the mountains still, the end of it trailing like a veil over the lower boglands and the fields divided by grey dry-stone walls.

It would take more than a stormy spring sun to make it look any different. For that we needed summer and a summer sun.

Summer, with the trees in leaf and the estuary blue out as far as the cluster of islands where it opened to the Atlantic, was my favourite time of year. On very warm days you could see basking sharks in the sun-soaking waters.

And in the summer Theo would be home, his exams finished. We would make plans in the summer. This time for definite.

2

Finn hadn't budged from the fire but his coat had stopped steaming. He opened an eye and thumped his tail, once, when I threw the gun with my wet cloak on to a hob. I sat on the other to unlace my boots and take off my wet stockings.

'You've more intelligence than I'll ever have,' I said to him, 'you're the one didn't want to go out this morning.' He closed the eye. 'We should have stayed here, both of us, by the fire.'

The great hall, in spite of its size, was intimate as the kitchen. And the kitchen was a place people liked to gather together and often didn't want to leave. The dark polished wood of the walls could hardly be seen for the oil paintings of O'Gradys hanging there and the fireplace, high and wide as a small house, took up a good part of the wall facing the door. A wide staircase twisted its way to a gallery above, an architectural caprice which made Kilraven a house in which it was very hard to keep secrets. I'd never minded this. I'd always been one for openness. It made life less complicated.

My father, when playing cards or talking with Mossie and one or more of his other cronies, liked to sit in one of the throne-like wooden chairs to either side of the fire. I preferred the cosiness of the hobs myself. They were black as the hobs of hell and could, if you stayed there long enough, become hot as hell too. There was no danger of me burning that morning, though. Ellie Hope saw to that.

'I hear you've had a busy morning of it,' she called from the gallery, 'shooting half-dead animals and upsetting my step-uncle.' Her arms were filled with bed-linen.

'You can't have been too busy yourself,' I said, picking up my boots and starting for the stairs, 'if you'd enough time on your hands to be checking on what other people were doing.'

'Stay where you are,' Ellie piled the linen by the gallery rail, 'I'll get your slippers.'

The light from the long, vaulted skylight over the gallery caught the fiery red-gold in her hair as she ran back to my bedroom. I was a great admirer of Ellie Hope's hair and would have traded my own dark-brown locks for it any day. I sat back on the hob and put my long, cold white feet under Finn to keep them warm. He ignored me, too indolent even to open an eye.

'Give me your wet things.' Ellie, slightly breathless, put the slippers in front of me and her hands on her wide hips. There was pink in her cheeks and impatience in her green eyes. Depending on how you saw her, Ellie Hope was beautiful or overblown. My father said she was voluptuous. My mother thought her plump but pretty. The parish priest had been heard to call her 'a fleshy Delilah'. She was everything I wasn't and *I* thought her beautiful in every way.

The slippers were red wool with leather soles, made by Ellie herself and given to me at Christmas. I handed over my boots and stockings and slipped my feet into their warm red wool.

'Could you find nothing better to do on your birthday morning?' Ellie made a sling of her apron and put my wet footwear into it. They began to drip through immediately, making a puddle between us.

'I suppose I could have lain in my bed and waited for you to bring me champagne for my breakfast,' I said sourly.

'It might have happened, too, if you'd given me half a chance. You were up and gone before the fires were even stoked.' Ellie looked at the puddle, then at my wet skirts, finally at my bedraggled hair. 'It's time you grew up,' she said, 'time you decided to act like a woman.'

'I know,' I said, 'I know it is.'

I did too. Ellie and I had had this conversation before. At nineteen Ellie Hope knew more about being a woman than I ever would. Than most women ever would, if you measured womanhood in terms of an ability to beguile and tempt men.

Ellie had half the young men in Ballycoole village besotted, and some of the older ones too. She was fearless, able to dance and tease and walk away with her hips swinging. It was the best of sport, she said, a distraction from the one man she wanted but couldn't have. Father Duggan disagreed about its being sport. He denounced her from the altar, calling her an 'occasion of sin' and telling the young men that they should keep away from her.

It wasn't that I wanted to be like Ellie. It was more that I wanted to be less what I was. I'd grown up in a boys' world, doing the things boys did with my brothers Hugh and Manus and with Theo Howard. Apart from shooting a gun there were other things I could do as well, or better, than any of them. I could hold my own when riding a horse, walking the hills or fishing the river.

There had been a break in this when my monthly bleeds started and my parents packed me off to boarding school in Tipperary. I'd been sent home in no time. The misery of it, and the containment, had been more than I could bear. I'd spent the rest of my teen years living a boy's life.

It was different now that I was a grown woman, and had to make changes, for my own sake and for Theo's. He'd been coming and going from the university in Dublin for six years and I wasn't fool enough to imagine changes hadn't happened to him too. To make a wife and mother I would have to be more ladylike. Or be at least more womanly in my behaviour.

Or, at the *very* least, put a face on it.

'I'd stay in bed and have champagne, if I'd a choice,' Ellie said.

'Is there champagne in the house then?' I said. My father must have won at cards. I couldn't imagine where else the money for champagne would have come from.

'There is. Your father ordered it weeks ago. Half a dozen bottles were delivered on Wednesday last.' Ellie grinned, delighted I hadn't noticed, delighted with herself for keeping the secret. Ellie Hope had a lot to say for herself and wasn't renowned for curbing her tongue. 'I put it in a safe place,' she said, in a loud whisper.

'He wouldn't drink my birthday treat,' I said. But we both knew my father would drink holy water if he was desperate enough.

I was happy about the champagne, though. It meant my father was truly intent on a celebration, that forgiveness might be in the air.

He'd fought bitterly with Hugh, the first-born of us three O'Grady children, at Christmastime. Though he'd told Hugh he was no longer a son of his and that he would be disinheriting him, it had been hard to tell how much of this was drink talking. What was a fact was that he knew Hugh was expected home – and that six bottles was more than enough for a double celebration. I hoped the champagne was as much for Hugh as it was for me.

'I've a small present for you,' Ellie said.

'What is it?'

'Go up and take your wet clothes off. I'll bring it to your room.'

I'd changed my wet skirts and was lying on the bed, trying to plan my day and put Kilgallen's lurcher out of my head, when Ellie arrived. It was still only nine o'clock. There was a long day to go, and a long night.

'Your mother's downstairs.' She had a small package in her arms along with fresh bed-linen. The package was parcelled in newspaper and tied with one of her own blue ribbons. 'She's been to the kitchen looking for you and now she's in the salon, waiting.'

The salon, in another house, would have been called a parlour. Or a drawing room. My parents, who'd been to Biarritz for their honeymoon, brought the word back with them along with a ship's hold of *objects d'art*. The trip had accounted for every last penny of my mother's dowry.

I rolled to the side of the bed and sat there. Mossie had lit a fire while I was out and I stretched my feet in its direction. 'Is my father about yet?' I looked at Ellie when I said this. I didn't want her lying to me.

'He's gone for a walk with the dog.' She put the bed-linen on the couch by the fire and held out the package. 'The best of luck to you,' she said.

'I might be older than you, Ellie Hope, but I'm not senile yet.' I took the package. 'My father's no more out walking than the dog is.' I studied the neat bow she'd made with the ribbon. 'He's in the library, isn't he?'

'He is. Do I have to open that for you, or are you going to ignore it and insult me for another while?'

The library was where my father played serious card games and gambled, where he read and drew up plans for the salvation of Kilraven. It was also where he did his drinking and where, as a result, the plans he drew up went on to involve saving the world.

I pulled open the ribbon and sat looking at the embroidered linen chemise lying in the unfolded newspaper.

'Oh, Ellie,' I said, 'I don't deserve your being so good to me.'

'That's true,' she said, 'but you might see how it looks on you anyway.'

It looked made for me, which it was, by Ellie in her room late at night by candlelight. I like daisies, the way they resurface and open hopeful faces to the sun no matter how terrible the winter before. Ellie knew this and had embroidered daisies with green stems all across the white linen of the chemise.

I hugged her tight. Against her soft warmth I felt myself bonier and more angular than ever.

'I'll keep it for my trousseau,' I said, 'it's too beautiful to wear now.'

'You'll do nothing of the sort.' Ellie moved away. 'I didn't sit up making it so as you could wrap it in tissue for some man to enjoy.'

'Theo Howard's not just some man,' I said. Ellie gave me a hard look but said nothing.

I put on the chemise and looked at myself. In the long standing-mirror I saw a long, thin woman with curly dark hair and indigo eyes. 'Indigo' was my father's word for them. A 'warrior queen with indigo eyes' was how he described me in one of the poems he wrote. My brother Manus had inherited his gift and wrote a lot of poetry himself. Manus had also inherited my father's liking for strong drink.

Behind me in the mirror Ellie looked soft and golden. She was smiling again.

'Wear it for yourself,' she said, 'there's no good postponing life for a man – any man.'

'I'll wear it tonight,' I promised, 'and you're a one to talk about postponing life. You're the one keeping the men and boys of the parish hanging on because of my brother.'

'I know what I'm doing.' Ellie wasn't at all put out. 'And I'm *not* postponing my life. I'm living it.' She clasped her hands together and raised her eyes theatrically. 'But without the man I love.'

'Oh, Ellie,' I said, laughing, 'you'll have to give up loving him. He doesn't deserve you.'

'I agree. But he might, some day.'

My brother Manus was the fearless Ellie's weakness. He was the most beautiful of us all and Ellie had been unashamedly in love with him for three years now. She swore she would go on loving his 'soft brown eyes' until he married or was dead, and that if she couldn't have him she would 'settle for no one else'.

I sometimes wondered if our impoverished state was what gave Ellie hope that the divide between her and my brother might be bridged. What I knew for a fact was that it wasn't social conventions that prevented Manus loving her. It was just that he loved ideas more than any woman.

Manus was twenty-one years old and determined to be 'a remembered poet'. He lived for the Irish Ireland ideas of the time, inhabiting smoke-filled back rooms where the talk was of a reborn nation, a country free from 'the filthy modern tide' and saved by what was left of Gaelic civilisation. There were many who agreed with him. He was off at one such meeting now, and wouldn't arrive back until late evening. Some things, he'd patiently explained to me, were more important than birthday dinners.

'You deserve better than Manus,' I said, 'though God knows there's not a great deal of choice on offer around here.'

'I must get on with my work,' Ellie was brisk, 'you can help me dress the bed.'

She picked up the bed-linen and became businesslike and bossy, a role which came naturally to her. Ellie thought she knew better than most people how they should run their lives, even how life in general should be organised. She was sometimes right too. It was the only way in which she resembled her Aunt Julia.

16

We stripped and dressed the bed together before Ellie, carefully counting, laid towels across the hip bath.

'I'll be back to help wash your hair later.' She straightened the curtains, tut-tutting at a fresh tear in one. 'I'll put a stitch in that, when I've the time. The storm'll be back by midday, and in a worse temper too. Hugh will be wet through coming from the station so I'd best get his room made up. You'd be advised to get dressed and go on down to your mother.'

'And to my father,' I said. Ellie shrugged.

'If he was my father I wouldn't bother.' She pulled the door hard behind her when she left.

Ellie could only imagine how she would behave towards a father, or mother, for that matter, since she had neither.

Her mother, Julia's sister, had died giving birth to her in Tubbercurry workhouse, without once saying who had fathered her child. Julia, when sent for, had taken and reared Ellie in the cottage she and her dead sister had themselves grown up in, in Ballycoole. When Julia married Mossie, Ellie had come to live at Kilraven too. She'd had no choice since it was around that time Father Duggan had taken to declaring her an 'occasion of sin'. Ellie had been sixteen and had fallen in love with Manus on her very first morning in the kitchen.

I found my mother standing by a window in the salon.

'The storm will be back,' she said, echoing Ellie. 'What a pity we couldn't have sun all day, just for you.' She smiled, radiant and sunny as anything in the sky. As a child I used to do clever things just to make my mother smile. 'You've been out, I hear, sampling the day already.' Her face went on shining. The fact that her smile had become a mask for her feelings didn't at all diminish its splendour.

'It was bright, early on,' I said. 'I took Finn with me and . . .'

'What will you wear tonight?' My mother cut me short and returned to gazing through the window. She did this gently, but in a way you couldn't argue with. 'Blue is so pleasing with your eyes, Nessa. Perhaps your blue ribbed poplin with a satin sash at the waist?' Outside, the rain began to sweep in sheets across the mountains.

'A satin sash would be nice.' I tried to sound enthusiastic.

'You've breakfasted already, I'm told.' My mother picked idly at the heavy gold velvet of the curtains. 'I should put tassels on these,' she said, 'red, perhaps. They would brighten the windows, and the room.'

So would new curtains. 'Ellie says she'll repair the ones in my room,' I said.

'Things will be a lot more cheerful now that the spring is here.' My mother watched the rain coming closer. 'I have your present.' She turned, smiling. 'Why don't we sit for a few minutes?'

We sat together on the Chesterfield, the springs recoiling as they always did. The Chesterfield was where my mother and I had shared all of my life's landmarks so far. She'd brought it with her, from her home in Co. Wicklow, when she married my father. It was the most useful of all the things which had come from Wicklow; others, like the conversation sofa and the Bible box in Kilraven, had never really found a home. My mother hadn't wrapped my present. She could be practical enough in some ways.

'They're beautiful.' I took the hair combs she handed me and turned them in my hands. 'I remember you wearing them.'

What I remembered was their silver almost matching the pale cream colour of her hair. They would not look the same on me.

'I'll look after them.' I hugged her. Her arms fluttered for a moment on my shoulders, then she pushed herself away.

'Wear them,' she said, 'wear them tonight. Now you should go and visit your father.'

18

'Will he definitely eat with us tonight?' I said, putting words to a half-fear that he might not.

'Of course.' She hesitated. 'If he feels well enough. Your father has always been there for the milestones in your life.'

This last was true. He'd been the best of fathers to me. A friend, too, before the drinking. But hinting that he might not feel 'well enough' to dine was just my mother again refusing to accept that he'd become a drunkard

She stood and so did I. Standing together, we were as tall as one another. The difference was that my mother was delicate as a wand and as graceful.

'Be kind to your father,' she said.

3

The library was a long dark room at the back of the house. There was a billiard room adjacent to it and both rooms were used for the most part by the men – my father, brothers, their friends and Mossie. I played billiards myself, and played well, but couldn't abide the thick, smelly air when the men smoked cigarettes. These days my father liked to have the library to himself.

He didn't turn as I came in. The room was icy cold and in near darkness, the curtains unopened. My father said the cold helped him think. When my eyes adjusted I could see things were the same as any other day. But different too.

The unlit fire was a dark cavern under the black marble of the mantel. In front of it a round table and, a little to the side of it, my father's desk were, as always, littered with maps and plans and writing paper. The bookshelves were filled with accusing, no longer read rows of books behind dusty glass. But I knew there was something different.

My father sat very still in his chair.

'You'll damage your eyes, sitting in the dark,' I said, half-thinking he might be asleep. My breath made a small cloud in the icy air.

'I'm not looking at anything.' His arm moved as he lifted and drank from a glass of whiskey.

'You might want to, if there was light to see by.' I crossed to the window and pulled back the curtains, ignoring his groan.

'Or if you weren't seeing everything through the bottom of a whiskey glass.'

'You're such a wise young woman, my dear Nessa,' he lifted the bottle of JJ and refilled his glass, 'but you still don't have a right to talk to your father like that.'

'Is it right for my father to sit drinking himself into a stupor on my birthday?'

'You're hard on me, Nessa,' he smiled and raised his glass, 'and I deserve it, every word. But you're wrong, my girl, to accuse me of not singling out your birthday. It's early in the day yet and I didn't want to rush things. I knew you'd be along to see me. I've even got a glass here for you.'

He lifted a second glass from the slate hearth and filled it with a small measure of whiskey. My father didn't encourage his children to drink too much.

'I've got something else for you.' He looked dreamily into the fire that wasn't there. 'My plan for you . . .'

I'd heard enough about plans. 'All I want, Father, is for you to be at dinner tonight and to make friends again with Hugh. Please.'

My father handed me the glass. 'Sit down and be pleasant.'

I sat opposite him, whiskey in hand, in a second green high-backed leather chair. It was where Mossie sat each night, waiting for my father to finish drinking so as he could help him upstairs.

I leaned my head against the chair's back and looked at the ceiling. The drawings of Roman life there were the work of another, earlier O'Grady. They showed a great many cavorting semi-naked women and children, but no men. The contents of the bookcases, at least, were more representative of life in general, with books of Irish statutes, Dr Livingstone's last journals, the works of Charles Dickens and *1001 Arabian Nights*. Books of poetry, which my father read, were stacked on the floor along with the novels of such as George Moore.

'It would be nice if you and Hugh could be friends again,' I said.

'That depends on Hugh.' My father leaned across and touched my glass with his. 'Now let us drink to your birthday.'

I didn't often drink whiskey and it burned my throat as it went down. My father smiled and quoted, '"I sigh that I kiss you,/ For I must own/ That I shall miss you/ When you have grown".'

'I've been grown for a while now, Father,' I said. It seemed a very long time ago that he used to quote that same 'Cradle Song' of Mr Yeats' to put me to sleep at night.

'I suppose you have,' he said, 'I suppose you have.'

He drank from his whiskey glass, taking his time before he spoke again. I let him be quiet, and took a close look at him. This didn't bring me much joy. He was white as paper and paper-thin as well. His dark hair was too long and had more white in it than even a week before. It was oily and unwashed. His eyes were made blacker by the fact of their being sunk in purple hollows. He was wearing the long-tailed black coat he wore most days. There was a sour odour from it, from him.

'How is your mother this morning?' he said, and I knew then he'd been up all night.

'She's well,' I said, 'she gave me her silver combs for a present.' I took them from my pocket to show him.

'They'll look beautiful in your curls, Nessa,' he said, 'put them in for me.'

I did and he nodded and smiled, gently. Manus was gentle too. Hugh was different, he'd become a city person.

'Beautiful,' my father said, 'they were beautiful in Ada's hair too.' He adored my mother, every bit as much as she adored him. It didn't stop him from drinking. 'The package on the table is for you,' he added, 'open it.'

The red-leather-bound copy of William Butler Yeats' *The Rose* was the one from which he used to read 'The Cradle Song.' Inside its cover he'd written: '*For Vanessa, that she may know, in the dim coming times, how my heart goes with her*'. He'd packed a bundle of money inside the cover too.

'Thank you,' I said. For a minute it was all I could say. When I looked up he was watching me. 'There's a lot of money here, Father. What am I supposed to spend it on?'

'On getting away from here.' He got to his feet, wrapping the long black coat about him. He stood stiff and straight with his arms folded about him. 'I want you to go, Nessa,' he spoke quickly, 'I want you to see the world, become a travelled woman. An untravelled woman is a dissatisfied woman, and an ignorant one. You need to know about life and about yourself. You won't learn anything around here. The world is changing and, God help us, this country is changing along with it, and not for the better. The old ways are gone and the land's in the hands of a peasantry who're being idealised but who don't, and won't, know what to do with it.'

He put his hands on my shoulders suddenly. I thought he would shake me but he didn't.

'There's nothing for you here, Nessa. Nothing, nothing, nothing. That money will buy your fare to the Americas, or wherever you choose. You can stay there or not. But at least you'll have seen something. You'll know something of another life . . .'

He would have gone on but I began shouting. I had to stop him. 'Where did the money come from? Where did you get it?'

I took his hands from my shoulders and held them tight and looked into his frenzied face. None of what he was saying would mean anything until I knew where he'd got the money, what trouble he was in. There were hundreds of pounds in the book.

'Who did you borrow it from?' I shouted again.

'It's not borrowed money, Nessa.' He spoke quietly, removing his hands gently from mine and going to the table. 'It's family money. We're not completely without resources. I'm sorry you've so little regard for me as your father and as a provider, but I suppose I can't blame you. I've let you down. I've let you all down. But I'm redressing wrongs . . .' He began folding the maps on the table. 'No more of this. The world's looking to the rich copper ore being discovered in Spain and South America. Any mine I might set up here, on Kilraven, would only ever be low-yielding, no money in it . . .'

I'd have thought him sober if the whiskey bottle hadn't been seven-eighths empty on the floor. I hardened my heart; it ached with the effort.

'What resources did you fall back on, Father?'

'I sold the gelding,' he finished folding the maps, then moved to fold the plans, 'and a few unpleasant pictures. Amazing the lack of taste in people.'

I knew what was different about the room then. There were empty spaces where some indifferent animal drawings had hung. But the gelding . . .

'The gelding belonged to Hugh, Father.' The shock made me sit down. 'It wasn't yours to sell.'

'He won't be needing it,' my father said, 'he's given up on Kilraven and I've given up on him. He won't need a horse in the streets of Dublin. They've electrified omnibuses there.'

'Oh, Father,' I said.

'You must let me do this for you, Nessa.' He finished his folding at last. 'The boys will be all right. Even Manus. You're the one I worry about. Don't!' He held up a hand when I started to speak. 'Don't talk to me of marriage to Theo Howard. You might as well talk of marrying William of Orange. The idea is just as ridiculous and as long as I live I'll never consent.'

'I'm twenty-three. I can marry whom I choose.'

'Not from under my roof, my girl, not from under my roof.' Shaking his head, muttering and sighing, he picked up the whiskey bottle and sat at the table. 'Bird never flew on one wing, Nessa, bird never flew on one wing.' Refilling his glass, he seemed exhausted. 'I don't even want to talk about the Howard boy. Tell me you'll go travelling . . .'

He sat drinking the whiskey and looking at me, burst of energy gone and drunk as a lord. I'd never have believed it possible for a man to drink so much alcohol and remain conscious.

His difficulty with Theo had to do with religion. The Howards were Protestant and we were Catholic. My father liked Arthur Howard, thought the family the best of neighbours and considered them friends. But he saw himself still as a Catholic landlord, holding firm for a Catholic Ireland. He even stood by Father Duggan's mad zealotry about Ellie, saying the parish priest was guided by a vision of a severe God, no more. He saw my marrying Theo as a denial of the Church and Faith the O'Gradys had upheld for centuries. There was no talking to him about it but I knew he would neither deny nor throw me out when the time came for me to marry Theo.

'Tell me you'll come to dinner tonight and that you'll be civil to Hugh?' I stood by the table, looking him in the eye. He looked right back at me, the glass to his mouth, his eyes more bloodshot than they'd been ten minutes before.

'If that's what it'll take for you to put the money to use . . .'

'That's what it'll take for me to think about it.'

He grinned, drunkenly triumphant. 'I was going to make amends to Hugh anyway,' he said. 'His ideas are lunatic but he's entitled to hold them as long as he's not living here and I don't have to listen to them.'

I picked up the poetry book, and the money. 'Please don't tell Hugh about the gelding,' I said, 'not tonight.' I'd a hazy plan about buying it back, or buying another horse.

'Tonight, Nessa, will be a night to remember.' The alcohol fumes followed me to the door. 'There will be no talk of geldings, or of any other horse either. We'll be celebrating you, and only you, my unique and lovely daughter.'

He looked happy, and half-mad.

4

A two-horse car arrived with Hugh in the mid-afternoon. The driver, Peter Duffy, whipped and urged the animals to breakneck speed as they came down the tree-lined avenue.

Ellie joined me at the salon window. 'Wind's behind them and the storm's getting worse. Peter'll not have it so easy on the return journey.' She rubbed a circle in the fog made by her breath on the glass. 'Hugh's not alone.'

'I can see that for myself,' I said.

We watched the horse-car spin closer, spewing stones and mud as it came. The rain blew in sheets and Peter Duffy had the oil cloths up.

'How many would you say there are?' I said.

'Hard to tell with the covers.' Ellie put her face closer to the window and narrowed her eyes. 'Two,' she said, 'there's just two, counting Hugh.'

'We'll need to get an extra room ready.'

'There's blankets but no linen, so whoever they are they'll have to take things as they find them.'

The car rounded the low branches of a cedar and headed on the last gallop to the door. Ellie loosened her hair, tied back by Julia when she'd been helping in the kitchen. 'Could be he's brought a card-playing city man.' She shook it free.

'What do you know about card-playing city men?' I said.

'I know that they believe in free love. It's all the fashion in Dublin and London.' Ellie was lofty. 'Ruskin and those other poetic lads, they're all saying it's the natural and normal way for mankind to behave. I read it in the *Sligo Champion*.'

'Well, the fashion hasn't reached Sligo yet so he's in for a quiet time.' A thought struck me. 'It might be Theo. He might have come directly.'

'It will *not* be Theo Howard.' Ellie was firm. 'I'll go and waken your mother.'

I grabbed my cloak, steaming by the fire, and put it round my shoulders. It was damp and heavy. The gun was still on the hob, I would have to tell Mossie. The horse-car came to a mud-spraying halt in front of the steps as I went down them.

Mossie was already waiting, his hand on the door at the back of the car. One of the steaming horses reared, the other moved forward, and the door in Mossie's hand fell open. A gurgling scream came from under the oilcloth.

I ran down the last of the steps as Hugh's head appeared in the opening, then the rest of him, still wearing the black Melton overcoat our mother had bought him on his first going to Dublin six years before. He jumped to the ground with the car's footstep under his arm, waved and called something before reaching under the oilcloth. The woman who emerged, holding his hand, stood in the door of the horse-car for a full transfixed minute before getting down. Her wide-eyed, open-armed awe spoke dramatic volumes, as did her yellow Ulster, red gloves and the single black feather in her hair. Hugh had never, during all of the years he'd been in Dublin, brought a woman home to Kilraven before.

This one was an actress. Or if she wasn't then she should be. I'd never met one but the woman being helped from the horse-car by my brother was everything I imagined an actress to be.

When she reached the ground Hugh's actress, with a laugh, let go his hand and clapped both of hers together, in their wet red gloves.

28

'It's a castle,' she cried, 'and it's more magnificent than anything you described, Hughie, my sweet.' Her accent was English.

The horses might have gone on standing if the woman had kept still. But she spun, arms wide, and they moved nervously. With another gurgling scream she threw herself into Hugh's arms. The feather remained secure in her yellow hair.

'Hello, Hugh,' I said.

My brother disentangled himself from the woman and gave me a hug.

'I'm glad you're here,' I said into his shoulder, 'I was seriously afraid you wouldn't come.'

He held on to me. 'How is he?' he said, softly in my ear.

'The same,' I said, then corrected myself. 'Worse. He's drinking most of the night now as well as the day. He sold the gelding. For me. To send me abroad. I'm sorry.' Better I told him than our father.

'Don't be sorry.' Hugh pushed the hair back from my face. He was smiling, and it made him so very like our father to look at. 'The gelding and I had come to the parting of our ways. That old horse knew it too. Where are you going to?'

'I'm not going anywhere.' I was annoyed.

'How's Mama?' he said.

'The same. Mama doesn't change. Mama will never change.'

'Everyone changes, Nessa, *everyone*. Even you. What's my brother doing these days? He doesn't answer my letters.'

'He's joined the Gaelic Leaguers . . .'

'I'm all but drowned, standing here.' The actress's voice, interrupting, was right at Hugh's side.

She put her arm through his and gave me a friendly smile through chattering teeth. Her face was round-eyed and lovely but she was older than I'd at first thought. Definitely closer to thirty than twenty.

'Nessa, I'd like you to meet Bella Mulligan,' Hugh said,

quite formally, and the actress held out her hand to me, equally formal. The red glove was thin and silky and very wet.

'I shall call you by your given name, Vanessa,' she said, 'it suits you better.'

'I'm used to Nessa.'

'Then Nessa it will be.' She gave a shivering laugh and looked up the steps. 'I'd quite like to go inside, if that's the custom.'

Peter Duffy was paid and Mossie took their bags, of which there were a lot for a short visit, and I led the way up and into the house. Mama was waiting. She stood in the middle of the great hall, wearing a high-necked silvery-grey day dress, and opened her arms to Hugh as he stepped through the door.

'Hugh, my dear Hugh. I'm so glad you got here. We might be on the west coast of Africa for all the letters you've sent us since Christmas. You're wet,' she lifted her hands from his shoulders as he kissed her, looking at them in surprise, 'wet through.'

'It's raining, Mama,' he said.

'You shouldn't have delayed so long outside then. Your room is ready. Maurice has had the fire burning there since dawn and I turned down your bed myself.' She brushed at a raindrop as it fell from Hugh's hair to his collar. 'Go now.' Her smile was serene as she nodded at the stairs.

'I've brought a guest, Mama,' he said, gently, and brought Miss Mulligan forward. 'I'd like you to welcome Bella Mulligan.'

My mother's smile was heartbreaking. 'My apologies, Miss Mulligan, I'm far, far too preoccupied with my son. I didn't see you standing there.'

If it had been anyone else I wouldn't have believed this but in my mother's case her not noticing Bella Mulligan was the simple truth. She only ever saw what she wanted to see.

'I hope I'm not an inconvenience,' Bella Mulligan murmured, 'arriving unannounced like this. I did so want to see Hugh's home.'

'We're delighted to have you,' my mother said. She might have added shocked, too, which would have been true. She seemed unable to find anything else to say, however, and a small silence stretched.

It was by way of appeal to the Lord above that I raised my eyes and saw Ellie Hope, watching from the gallery, her arms folded and a frown on her face.

'She'll have to share a room with Nessa,' she called, 'there's no way we can get another heated and dry.'

She was gone before Hugh could say a word about this as an arrangement. Apart from anything else, my room was a long way from his.

I put my wet cloak on the hob again to dry, spreading it more evenly this time. When I turned Hugh was helping Bella Mulligan out of her caped Ulster. Underneath she was wearing a mauve S-shaped dress with a low, square bodice. Around her neck, on a mauve velvet band, she wore three large yellow stones. Next to my mother's cool elegance she looked vulgar. But she was still a very pretty woman.

'Nessa will take you to your room, Miss Mulligan,' my mother said.

'Please call me Bella, do.' Bella Mulligan looked around the hall, wide-eyed again. 'You have a wonderful home,' she said.

'Thank you.' My mother smiled and nodded and moved off. 'We'll meet in an hour.'

She would need at least that long to talk to my father, get some sort of promise of good behaviour from him. It wasn't that he was unwelcoming of guests, just that this was not a good time for Hugh to bring one home. Especially a woman, and without warning. Being English, Bella Mulligan was probably Protestant, so Father would have to be coaxed to be agreeable about that too.

The summer would have been a better time to bring a woman to stay. Maybe.

Hugh went to hang up the coats and Bella Mulligan followed me slowly to my room. Kilraven had a way of putting on a good show, even at the worst of times, and she professed enchantment with the stone walls, shining timber and vaulted windows. She seemed equally taken with the oils of horses and soldiers and battle scenes and, when we came to them, with the dark and dreary paintings of long-gone O'Gradys. But best of all she liked the watercolours in the gallery, pictures of rivers and lakes from all across Europe.

I left it to Hugh, when he joined us, to tell her they would be mostly sold off by the end of the summer.

Mossie had deposited the bags in the middle of the gallery. Bella Mulligan had three, made of tapestry and with Moroccan leather handles, which Hugh carried into my room. There was more gushing excitement here when she stood at the window taking in the windswept, darkening views of the mountains, sea and woods.

'I've had a wonderful idea for the gallery, Hughie.' She took my brother by the arm.

'You have?' He was indulgent.

'It's that it would make a one in a million music hall. The sound and the space . . . it's made for it.'

'And where would you put your audience?' Hugh laughed. Everything she said appeared to amuse and delight him.

'We could all be together, performers and audience,' she giggled, 'a sort of salon-cum-music hall.'

'Maybe you should discuss your idea with my father,' I said, 'he's forever looking for new ways to make money.'

'Perhaps I will,' Bella Mulligan said, 'at dinner.' She became all at once businesslike. 'Time now to rest and dry out. Will you be your darling self, Hughie, and leave us to repair ourselves?'

Alone with her I saw my bedroom as she must, a girl's room as opposed to a woman's. For the first time in my life I wished for something other than the ancient flowered curtains at the window, for a darker, more subtle canopy over the bed. But the hip bath and mirror were what interested Bella Mulligan and after an examination of one she let down her hair in front of the other. Just like Ellie's, only more golden-coloured, it fell in loose, tumbling curls to her shoulders. She caught me looking at her.

'What do you see then, Nessa?' She put her head to one side quizzically.

I saw a womanly woman with ivory-pale skin and violet eyes. I also saw, behind her smile, a worry about my answer. Or thought I did. She may have been acting.

'An actress?' I said.

'You're every bit as clever as Hugh said you were,' she said, softly. 'What gave me away?'

I laughed, and she looked hurt. I wished I could tell when she was acting.

'It wasn't so hard to see,' I said at last. She waited, head to one side, eyes on mine. She seemed really to want to know.

'The horse-car,' I said, 'it was as if you were on a stage.' I could have added that her clothes had a lot to do with it, too, but she was a guest, after all.

'Ah . . .' she sighed. 'The horse-car, of course. I can't stop myself. I've been acting all my life.'

'In play houses and theatres? Or just play acting?'

She laughed, loud and real and from her belly. 'Both. Life's a performance, don't you think?' She sat on my bed to unbutton her boots. 'We all perform . . . play act as

33

you call it . . . only some of us do it as an occupation too.'

She stood with her boots in her hand. In her bare feet she was quite small, several inches shorter than me.

'You're very forthright, Nessa,' she said, 'I like that.'

'You mean I'm plain spoken.' I shrugged. 'Country in my ways.'

'I mean you're artless, undesigning . . .'

'Which is to say untutored and unsophisticated?' I replied, with a touch of anger. 'Not given to play acting with people.'

'No, you're righteous and judge them instead.' She was angry, too, and this was no performance. I was shocked and silenced, not by her anger but by what she'd said. I'd never thought of myself in that way. I went to the window and looked out.

'You could be right,' I conceded.

'I'm sorry.' She came up behind me. 'We're none of us perfect.'

'I know that.' I felt childish and ignorant, more unaware of the world than ever.

'Let's start again, as if we'd just met,' Bella Mulligan proposed, 'and this time let's be friends.'

So we started again, with me determined to accept her for what she was. Maybe, in time, I would even come to know what that meant.

She was sitting with her skirts above her knees, unpinning her stockings, which were yellow, when she said, 'Your brother is life to me. He is the air I breathe, the man I've dreamed about all my life and hardly dared hope I would meet.' She peeled the stockings slowly down. 'I want you to be clear about that.'

'I'm glad of it,' I said, believing her. I wasn't so sure about the rest of the household.

'Another thing you should know is that Hugh will never

come back here to live,' she said, 'but this has nothing to do with me. He's not made for the life here. He's made for the city.'

'It's not me who needs to accept that, or his right to a life for himself,' I said, 'it's our father who must understand. Hugh told him as much at Christmas and they had a ferocious row about it.' I hesitated. She was folding the stockings. 'There will be disagreement at dinner, too, if the subject comes up. I'd prefer it if they were friends, for tonight.'

'I'll do what I can to keep the peace.' Bella Mulligan patted me on the arm. 'You deserve a good birthday.' She stood. 'A hip bath would be refreshing. Can your girl bring us some water?'

'I'll get it myself,' I said, 'Ellie is busy with tonight . . .'

'Of course she is.' Bella pulled open a tapestry bag, 'Hugh will get it.' She took out and slipped her feet into gold-tasselled slippers. 'You must show me which room is his.'

She put a paisley shawl around her shoulders and I led her to Hugh's room, not for a minute believing he would get the water. Unless he'd greatly changed.

Minutes later I was watching and marvelling at the power of love as he went obediently off to the kitchen.

While we waited Bella took out and put on a long-sleeved loose robe of green silk. With her gold hair she looked like the pagan Queen of the May but I didn't tell her so. She removed two rings from her fingers and examined her small white hands critically. My own hands, coarse and ringless with uneven nails, had never bothered me before.

'You're lucky to have a family.' She touched my hands. Not only was I artless, I was also transparent, it seemed.

'I wonder about that, sometimes,' I said.

'My father was born in Dublin.' She looked into the fire. 'He left for London with the police at his heels. His tenor voice made him a living, of sorts, in the music halls. My mother died when I was a week old but my father's women were always good to me, until they moved on. He moved on himself, four years ago. Caught pneumonia and died. That was when I came to Dublin.' She gave me a sideways look. 'So there you have it, my family story. Now we're even.'

Hugh came with the water and we began to dress for the night.

'You would be offended, I suppose, if I offered you help with your . . . toilette?' Bella Mulligan said, painting her face. I thought about it.

'I'm sure you've met Theo Howard?'

'I know Theo, from Dublin. He travelled on the train with us too.'

'And you know we're . . . promised?'

'Hugh said as much. Theo has never confided in me.'

'I'd like to look as well as I can for tonight,' I said, 'it's time he saw me differently.'

She laughed. 'Theo Howard will be at your feet. Man is not won by a good heart and scrubbed face alone, Nessa. Remember that.'

5

Ellie looked up as I came down the stairs with Bella Mulligan. Her eyes widened. The nostrils of her nose widened. She didn't say a word until I stepped on to the floor of the hallway.

'Given the day that's in it,' she said then, 'I suppose you can do what you like to yourself.'

'I can do what I like with myself any day of the year.' I touched my coiled hair with a cream-softened hand.

'There's no one to stop you,' Ellie said, 'more's the pity.'

'What's wrong with the way I look?'

'The way you look would be grand for Dublin society,' she walked around me, eyes narrowed, arms folded, 'but I can't say there's many of those waiting for you in the salon will be impressed with that sort of get-up.'

I was wearing green. My shoulders were on show above a pale-green duchesse satin bodice borrowed from Bella Mulligan. The dark-green velvet skirt was my own but the jade and jet earrings dangling from my ears also belonged to Bella.

Ellie's disapproval was all the reassurance I needed that I looked different, unlike myself. Part of it, of course, was that she was jealous of Bella Mulligan. She was unused to sharing me.

'Your mother's wearing grey,' Ellie said, proving me right by ignoring Bella, 'and Hermione Howard's in the blue she wore last Christmas twelvemonth.' Ellie herself was wearing the blue poplin dress she'd made a few weeks before with a cameo I'd given her around her neck.

'I've got the chemise you gave me on underneath,' I said, wanting her to approve some part of me.

'It's more what you're used to anyway,' Ellie sniffed. 'You might as well go on in. They're waiting for you, the lot of them.'

I thought of Theo and was suddenly unsure. 'Do I look so very wrong?' I said.

'You look very *grand*,' she said, 'you're transformed.'

'Is it the earrings?'

'They're not so bad as all that,' Ellie conceded.

But my confidence was ebbing so I took them off. 'They were beginning to hurt my ears,' I lied to Bella.

'What a pity,' she said, 'but keep them anyway, my angel. Your ears might become less sensitive as the night goes on.'

She looked dazzling herself in orange-tinted silk with a peacock feather in her hair. I knew that she didn't for a minute doubt that she was wearing the right thing and wished I could be more like her, in some ways. I slipped the earrings into my skirt pocket and squared my shoulders for the salon. Bella, behind me, gave a sudden small scream.

'Should that creature be in the house? It's going to attack . . .'

Finn, lazily curious, had come up from the kitchen and was sniffing at her skirts. He stepped back, affronted, when she went into a frenzy of arm waving. Unused to rejection, he stood looking at her in confusion.

'You'll frighten him,' Ellie snapped. 'This is his home, so leave him alone.'

'What is it?' Bella whispered and obediently dropped her arms. She was paper-white under the face paint.

'A dog,' Ellie said, 'a plain and simple dog.'

She took Finn by the collar and led him back to the fire. He threw himself down and gave Bella Mulligan a sad-eyed look.

Everyone stood as we went into the salon. Everyone but my father, conspicuous by his absence. Manus wasn't there either but no one expected him until late. Bella flitted to Hugh's side as Ellie, Mossie and Julia came into the room behind me. Everyone raised champagne glasses.

'Long life and happiness, Nessa,' Hugh called and they drank to my health, all of them golden and smiling in the light from the candles and fire.

Theo stared at me over the rim of his glass. He was wearing a spotted silk bow-tie. I wished I hadn't taken off the earrings.

'Thank you.' I raised my glass, smiled back and sipped. 'And thank you all for coming.'

My mother's social lessons might not have been a complete success, but they hadn't been entirely wasted on me either. I waited for Theo to come to me and he did, smiling and thinner than he'd been at Christmas. His hair was longer and there was a straggling growth across his upper lip.

'You're looking beautiful, Nessa.' He kissed me, very properly, on the cheek. 'Do I detect the lovely Bella's hand in your toilette?'

This wasn't the response I'd hoped for – but being too smart for his own good had always been a fault in Theo. 'You'll have to make up your own mind about that,' I said, 'though I see you've been busy with a toilette of your own. Is that a moustache along your lip?'

'A moustache it is.' He patted the hairs. 'You have not, I'm glad to see, lost any of your famous charm, Nessa.'

He was offended. It was going to take more than piled hair and a tight green bodice to make me a woman of allure.

'How are your studies coming along?' I looked at him over the rim of my glass, the way Bella, not three feet away, was looking at Hugh. My brother was returning her gaze in besotted fashion. I failed to similarly captivate Theo.

'Not as well as my tutors would like,' he said, 'nor my father, for that matter. I'm no Hugh O'Grady.'

Being in Hugh's shadow had never bothered him before. Something had happened.

'Have you failed an examination?' I said.

'I'm about to fail all of them in June.'

'You haven't studied then?'

'The old place is looking well for the night,' he said, clearly not intending to answer my question. I should have let it go, but I didn't.

'You're not lost yet. June is two months from now,' I pointed out.

'I'm lost to the law,' he gave a short laugh, 'and lost also to my father's notion of life in County Sligo.'

My mouth felt quite dry so I took a gulp from my glass. The sizzle had gone out of the champagne. 'Am I to understand that you've found something to replace the law and your life here?' I said.

He didn't answer. Instead he kissed me again, this time on the forehead, and guided me with an arm about my shoulders to where Hugh and Bella were standing.

'By God but that train journey gave me an appetite,' he said, grinning. 'Any chance we could get a bite to eat in this house tonight, Hugh?'

'We're waiting for my father,' I said.

Hugh shrugged. 'We're a hungry tribe and the wait might be long. I vote we go on into the dining room. Father will join us when he's hungry.'

'He won't like you starting without him,' Mossie, securing the iron clasps on the window shutters, turned slowly to face us.

'Can't be helped.' Hugh was determinedly cheerful. 'His guests can't wait any longer. We've been a long time on the road today.'

'It's not your place, Hugh, to say what's to be done.' Mossie was firm. His loyalty to my father was total.

'This house has always entertained and fed its guests,' Hugh was equally firm, 'and that tradition will not be broken tonight.'

I stepped between them. 'You know as well as I do, Mossie, that my father might not arrive to eat until midnight, if at all.'

'You want the food now then?' He looked disbelieving.

'I do. I want my guests fed.'

The candelabra was low over the dining-room table and had been filled with coloured candles, all of them ablaze. The table itself, which could take twenty diners, was filled with fruit, Dutch cheese and salt fish for the first remove. The sideboard along the wall, a relic of another century and covered in knotty animal carvings which had terrified me as a child, had more cheese and wine and all sorts laid out. The gelding had obviously sold well. We wouldn't go hungry.

Arthur Howard put himself to one side of me at the table. His son sat at my other side. Hermione Howard, with Hugh and Bella, sat opposite. My mother sat at one end and did her best to ignore the empty space left for my father at the other.

Julia and Ellie appeared to finish laying the first remove.

'You're the belle of the ball, Nessa.' Arthur Howard helped himself to fish as Ellie filled his bowl with white onion soup. 'The belle of the ball and no mistake.'

Arthur, being deaf and believing everyone else similarly afflicted, was inclined to repeat himself. Hermione, on the other hand, had acute hearing but could never be persuaded to listen. She was from England, from a place called Somerset, and I sometimes thought her incessant gabbling was because she didn't feel a part of things here. She started now.

'We're not at a ball, Arthur,' she shook a reproving head at her husband, 'though maybe a ball is what Nessa would have preferred. Would you, my dear?' She didn't wait for an answer but went on to the table at large, 'We're planning a ball ourselves, for later in the year, early in the month of October . . . wasn't that what we decided, Arthur? It'll be so nice to get everyone together on the cusp of winter, all the old friends as the nights draw in. Give us a chance to dress in our best and plan for the dark months. Always best to have plans, don't you agree, Nessa? Do you have plans for the year ahead yourself? I'm sure I had a great many plans when I was your age. When I was twenty-three I thought I would . . .'

'Has Bella told you, Mother, that she's to sing for us tonight?' Theo, interrupting her, put his foot over mine. It was an old conspiratorial signal we had.

'Oh, my goodness, how exciting!' Hermione would have launched herself into a rhapsody if Theo hadn't kept a rein on things.

'We're privileged to have her with us,' he said, ignoring Bella's prettily pouting protest, 'she's performed at the Lyceum in London . . .'

'As a witch in *Macbeth*!' With a tinkling laugh, Bella took over. 'And I'm sorry to say the Lyceum is no longer what it was. It's fallen on hard times since Mr Henry Irving gave up its management.'

'Nothing to do with Mr Irving.' Theo, pink in the face, leaned across the table. 'I refuse to believe the Lyceum's demise and your leaving are a coincidence . . .'

'White onion soup, Theo?' Ellie said at his shoulder. 'Or are you living on hot air and nonsense these days? You've grown thin as a whippet.' She gave me a sideways raise of her eyebrows. Ellie Hope was nothing if not loyal.

While she ladled soup into the bowl in front of Theo I clipped the earrings back on to my ears. They'd become a declaration of my womanhood.

'They look quite grand under the candles,' Ellie whispered

as she gave me my soup. But Ellie's capitulation, and Theo's captivation, became side issues as my father came through the door and stood at the top of the table.

'You're welcome, all of you.' His hair was swept back, but still oily, and he wore a red necktie with the long coat of earlier in the day. He looked, for him, respectable. In a half-hearted way. 'Stay where you are, man, continue with your food.' He waved an irritable, dismissive arm as Arthur Howard made to rise. 'Please continue with your meal, everyone. You were right to start without me.'

He put a bottle of his favourite ten-year-old JJ on the table, then ran a hand through his hair. He immediately looked as dissolute as ever.

'Some of you are more welcome than others,' he said, 'but my son knows that.'

'Will you have the soup?' Julia, by his side with a second tureen in hand, spoke loudly. 'The rest are nearly finished but it's still hot.'

'I will,' my father said, 'thank you, Julia.'

He sat and Julia gave him the onion soup. The table chattered loudly, as if to stave off what was to come. A dead man on horseback would have sensed the mood of apprehension my father had brought with him to the table.

'Jerome, my dear, you haven't welcomed our guest.' My mother didn't raise her voice. She didn't need to; my father always heard her.

'Forgive me.' He pushed his soup away and peered down the table at Bella. 'My wife mentioned you'd joined us. A Miss Mulligan, is it?' As Bella made to rise he waved his hand again, though less irritably than he'd done with Arthur Howard. 'We can forego the formalities.' Ignoring the wine, he poured himself a healthy measure of whiskey. 'You don't look to me, Miss Mulligan, like a young woman too concerned with life's formalities.'

'Nor am I. Please call me Bella.' She smiled and crumbled one of Ellie's wheaten farls in her plate.

'You're a citizen of our neighbouring island, from the sound of your accent,' my father said.

'I was born in London,' Bella said, 'but have made Dublin my home. There's great new life in the theatre there.'

'So you were drawn to Dublin by the outpourings of Mr Yeats and his kind?' My father sat back in his seat.

'I came to Dublin to find my father's family. My own family, if you like. My father left for London when he was a young man. He died without ever going back.'

'Has your search been successful?'

'Not for my relatives, no,' Bella shook her head, 'but my time in Dublin has been otherwise fruitful.'

My father choose to ignore the implication in this. 'Your mother is dead also?'

'She died when I was an infant.'

'You are alone then? An orphan with no one to guide and advise you?'

'I'm my own guide, Mr O'Grady, and take my own counsel too. In the times we live in, a woman must take her own life and independence in her hands.'

If she thought this would deflect my father she was wrong.

'That's as may be, Miss Mulligan.' He leaned forward. 'But being without family appears to have left you without caution in the matter of choosing male companions. A piece of advice: you would be unwise to consider my son as a future husband. You will find him feckless and unable to take responsibility. You're still young and lovely enough to have your pick of men. Leave him.'

Theo, beside me, had become rigid in his seat. Across the table I could hear Hermione Howard tut-tutting nervously. Without looking I knew Arthur would be mopping his brow and bald pate. What I didn't predict, but should have, was

Bella's reaction. Casually, and with exquisite timing, she took my brother's hand and held it to her cheek. She went on holding it as she spoke to my father.

'I love your son, Mr O'Grady. He's the only man I want and I am quite sure of my decision. If I am unwelcome in your home because of it, I will leave immediately.'

It was a perfectly pitched performance. Bella wasn't to know, or maybe she did, how my father felt about O'Grady hospitality. As children, he used to tell us stories of a thirteenth-century O'Grady who'd kept his kitchen fire constantly burning, with joints boiling in a cauldron, in readiness for the visits of strangers. We'd believed his tales. They may even have been true. Bella's threat to leave shocked him now into a brief sobriety.

'Of course you will not go, Miss Mulligan.' He became formal and kindly, something of his old self coming over him. 'You're more than welcome to any comfort you may find here.'

'Thank you,' she matched him for formality, 'but you'll make me feel much more comfortable if you call me Bella.'

'Bella it is.' My father picked up his glass and downed its contents.

The table burst into nervous chatter again, in the middle of which Ellie and Julia arrived with the second remove. What with the laying down and then the choosing from the leveret, turkey, quails and cheese cakes, there was hardly a sensible word spoken for fully ten minutes.

'You look quite the lady in Bella's earrings.' Theo, still filling his plate, was the first to attempt conversation.

I couldn't decide which made me more angry: that he knew the earrings belonged to Bella or the implication that without them I was no lady.

'It's a pity you couldn't behave more like a gentleman towards me then,' I said. I chose quail, my face burning.

45

'There's no pleasing you tonight.' Looking indignant, he played distractedly with his moustache. I moved clumsily to make amends.

'I like the moustache. It will fill out in time.'

Theo, spearing a leveret thigh, was spared having to answer this faint praise when my father, provoked by drink and Hugh's indifference to him, erupted again.

'Are you still in agreement with that highwayman Davitt?' he roared at my brother.

'Father . . .' I half-stood, but knew there was no chance of his listening to me. The case of Michael Davitt, land reformer, was an old, and sore, argument between him and Hugh. Even sober he'd have pursued it, though not at table.

'Michael Davitt hasn't changed what he believes,' Hugh replied calmly, 'so I see no reason to disagree with him.'

'The evidence of his wrongheadedness is all around you!' My father slammed the flat of his hand against the table. 'No more than two or three of the tenants I gave land to are making any use of it. It's the same all over the country. They have the means of livelihood Davitt and his kind said should be theirs, and what are they doing with it? They're wasting it, that's what they're doing, destroying the work of centuries. The woods . . .'

Words failed him and he sat, shaking his head and making circles on the table with his glass. He fuelled himself up with another drink.

'They're letting the land lie fallow and wet. We'll have a dead country soon, the land parcelled out into nothing but worthless postage stamps.'

'It'll take time to build a nation of small farmers,' Hugh said, 'but if this country is to move into the twentieth century, the laws, land, homes and government will have to belong to the people.'

He was still calm. But patience had never been a virtue

with him and I didn't see him holding on to his much longer. There would be a row, the evening would be ruined – and I found myself no longer caring very much. The heart for it had gone out of me. I told myself it had nothing to do with Theo's lack of warmth towards me, his interest in Bella, but knew it had.

'Without the landlords behind them, useless though many of them may be, your small farmers won't work and they won't learn.' My father shook his head as violently as a madman. His hair fell forward over his face. 'I see that now. I should have fought the Land Acts. Though, Christ save us, the landowning ascendancy knows nothing any longer, reads nothing, has nothing of the culture of their eighteenth century forebears. The Ireland of Swift and of Grattan is truly dead.' He thumped the table again, burned his guests with a glare. 'We must reshape ourselves in an heroic mould so that we may become again the real leaders of Ireland. There will be anarchy and civil war otherwise, which will end in a shabby, sordid Irish republic ruled by corrupt politicians and the ignoble rich.'

Full of impotent fury he swept the empty whiskey bottle from the table. It skidded, unbroken, across the floor. There was no masking chatter at the table this time.

'I did the fair thing by the tenants and what good did it do?' He was shouting now. 'The land is gone and soon the house will go . . .'

'It'll definitely go if you don't give up on the whiskey.' Hugh drummed his fingers on the table. 'But of course if you were sober you'd have to stop fooling yourself. You were fair with the tenants, Father, that's true. But you took the government's land money and pissed it to the winds . . .'

'Hugh!' My mother's protest was instinctive. So was Hermione Howard's rounding of the eyes and sucked in breath.

'Forgive me, Mama . . . Hermione.' Hugh put both his hands on the table. 'But there are things that must be said if we're to move forward. My father has wasted the money he got for our lands on madness of one kind or another. There's change all around us, and he must change. We all must.' He shrugged. 'But there was never any point in talking sense in this house. I shouldn't have come tonight.'

'In that at least you're right.' My father's face was sweating and grey. 'You should have stayed away. Tonight is Nessa's night.' His voice started to shake. 'Maybe neither of us should be here.' He began to shake all over.

Looking at him, I felt a sense of loss and emptiness. Not for the first time either. 'I'll leave.' I got to my feet. 'That should solve the problem for both of you.'

I walked quickly to the door, closing my ears to the hubbub behind me, to a voice calling me to come back.

Going up the stairs, I prayed Theo would come after me. He didn't.

In bed it took a long time for the bleak, chilly feeling to go away. By the time a thaw had set in Bella Mulligan was in the room. She hummed to herself as she undressed and got into bed beside me. I didn't open my eyes.

'You weren't the only one to lose heart for the night.' She didn't touch me and for that I was grateful. 'You'd barely left when Hermione Howard began to talk about gale-force winds, and how trees would be flying through the air if they didn't get home quickly.' She stopped, and sighed. She was lying on her back and I thought she'd gone to sleep when she said, 'Your father left right after you did. His friend Mossie went with him.'

I said nothing, just offered a fervent prayer that Mossie had managed to get my father to bed without his pouring any more whiskey into himself.

Bella was warm in the bed beside me and after a while I felt

48

myself drifting into sleep. 'My father will be better company in the morning,' I said, by way of a good-night.

'I'm glad you put the earrings back on,' she said.

In a minute, from her breathing and the way she folded herself against me, I knew Bella was asleep. I slept, too, for a short while. Two hours to be exact. I've never been able to remember if it was the sounds of a fight or the gunshot which woke me. But I've never been able forget the scene in the great hall when I looked down from the gallery.

Manus was there, on his knees with his head in his hands. Ellie was trying to hold him as he rocked back and forth, back and forth. Mossie was there, the shotgun I'd used on Kilgallen's dog in his hands. Julia was at the top of the steps from the kitchen, her rosary beads running like salt through her fingers. Hugh was running and tumbling down the stairs.

And my father was lying with the side of his head blown off, in a lake of blood on the flags in front of the fire.

6

The morning was a long time in coming.

When it did, at last, I watched the sun come up, beautifully pale and slow, from the bottom of the kitchen garden. I couldn't stay in the house. I didn't know either how I would ever go back in. Or watch another sunrise. All I was certain of was that my father was dead. Violently dead and gone for ever. I felt the cold of the day on my face, and the wet clay soaking through my boots, but felt nothing inside.

Poor Manus. He'd come home late, full of poetry and whiskey, to find my father in the great hall with the shotgun in his hand. He was going to do some late-night rabbit hunting, he told Manus, or maybe he'd get the fox Julia was complaining of raiding the hens.

'I'll come with you,' Manus offered, 'I wouldn't mind meeting that old fox myself.'

'This is a job for a man alone,' my father said.

'Two pairs of eyes are better than one,' Manus said.

'Go to your bed,' said my father.

Poor Mossie. In his bed downstairs he'd remembered the gun that I'd left it on the hob and that he hadn't locked it away. He arrived at the top of the stairs from the kitchen to see my father holding it and Manus arguing with him.

'Gun needs cleaning.' Mossie approached my father with outstretched hand.

'It's clean enough for my purposes.' My father stepped away.

'It's not working, I tell you.' Mossie kept on coming. As he drew close to Manus he said, out of the side of his mouth, 'When I grab him by the waist you're to take the gun from him.'

Manus, bemused, rubbed a hand over his eyes. 'I'll get him another,' he said, 'one that's working. There's no need . . .'

'Do as I tell you,' Mossie said, too loudly.

'Plotting! What're the two of you plotting?' My father held the gun away from him in one hand. He curled his finger around the trigger. 'This country was always and ever bedevilled by plotting and by deceit.' His voice rang through the hall. 'The clan chiefs were brought down by treachery and now we've been ruined again, the land given to a knavish people. We've been destroyed all over again by perfidious Albion . . .'

'Now, Manus, get it now!' Mossie pitched himself forward, arms spread like a great bat.

He wasn't fast enough, and anyway Manus hesitated. My father stepped away and, elegantly as he might have posed for a photographic portrait, angled the gun and put the muzzle to his temple. As Mossie's arms went around his waist he pulled the trigger and blew off the side of his own head. He fell to the floor with Mossie still holding on to him.

The gunshot and Manus's scream echoed together through the house.

Poor Manus. Seeing his father die because he was full of whiskey and hadn't been alert enough to do what was needed to save him would live with him for the rest of his life. He knelt and stared at the blood oozing from the pulpy ruins of Father's head until Ellie came and turned him away from it and into her skirts and held him while he cried, a sound like the wind in a ditch.

My mother could do nothing. She sat in a wooden armchair in the great hall and stared at the blanket-covered outline of my father's dead body without moving. She'd arrived on the gallery at the same time as myself and had started immediately down the stairs. In the hall she stood over my father's body with her hands in front of her, as if she would try to lift him up. Her face was as grey and still as the flags.

'His grandfather died the same way,' she said, 'though he had the kindness to do it away from the house, in the woods.'

This was the first I'd heard about my great-grandfather shooting himself. It was the first Hugh had heard of it, too, from the look on his face.

'Jerome would have done the job outside if he'd been allowed to have his way.' Mossie stared at the shotgun in his hands. 'But he wouldn't have done it at all if I'd done my job and locked things properly in the gun room.' He held the shotgun by both ends and with a strength more animal than human broke it in two. 'May I rot in hell if I ever forgive myself!' There were tears streaming down his face.

'He'd had no luck,' my mother said, 'not for a long time.' That was when she sank into the armchair, the one with eagles' heads carved into the arms. 'Cover him,' she ordered.

She didn't move or speak after that, even when I tried to give her hot whiskey and get her out of the chair.

Mossie brought a blanket and spread it so that it hid all of my father's body and most of the blood. A stain quickly soaked through it, in any event. Julia knelt at the far end of the hall, praying. Ellie took charge in the kitchen and brought Manus down there with her. Bella went down to the kitchen too and sat waiting with them while Hugh rode to Ballycoole for the priest and doctor.

I was in the kitchen garden again when Hugh rode back up the avenue, ahead of the carriage carrying the priest and doctor. He directed them to the front entrance and went on around the back of the house himself. Putting off the moment of having to look again at the red-soaked mound that was our father's body, I suppose

I left the garden and went to meet the new arrivals.

The parish priest, Father Duggan, made the sign of the cross over me before marching up the steps to the front door. What my father had done was a mortal sin in the eyes of the Church. There would be ecclesiastical difficulties about burying him and the priest's resolute stance was far from consoling.

Dr Fogarty put an arm about my shoulders. 'You will have to be strong for your mother, Vanessa,' he said, 'this will not be easy for her.'

He was a small man, and thin. As a child I'd always thought he had the look of a monkey and thought so again that morning, the way his face became a wrinkled puzzle as he looked at me. He had his medical bag with him but I couldn't for the life of me see what good any of the instruments inside were going to be.

'It will be hard on her,' I agreed.

'It will be hard on you all,' said Dr Fogarty, 'but you and your brothers will find a way of living without him. She may not.'

'I suppose we will.' I paused. 'His head is gone, Dr Fogarty. There's really no point your bringing the bag inside.'

'Oh, Nessa, my poor, unhappy child!' He dropped his bag and took me in his arms. They were relatively strange arms to me and I was glad of that, and of them. They were a comfort that did not bind. I sheltered for a few minutes then pushed myself away.

'There's nothing you can do for him but I'm glad you're here,' I said, 'you're more of a comfort than the priest.'

'Shh, Nessa. We all have our function around death, sadly. There are things I need to do.' He picked up the bag again. 'I must establish death for the police. They're following behind us. The coroner's court will want my report. I'll see to it that all's dealt with quickly.' He put an arm about my shoulders again and we went up the steps together. 'You *will* be strong. The alternative is to give up and you won't do that. It's not in your nature.'

My father gave up, I wanted to say to him, but didn't because I knew he was right. It wasn't in my nature. I would go on because I was a stoic and didn't know how not to go on.

'Tomorrow will be worse than today,' I said, 'and the days after that. Today is not so bad because nothing's real yet.'

My father's blood had turned oil-black in the time I'd been outside. Nothing much else had changed except that someone, Ellie most likely, had lit and placed candles at either end of his body. They were in the silver candleholders used on the table when my mother and father dined alone. The dog lay at my father's feet and my mother was still sitting in the armchair. Hugh stood behind her.

Father Duggan was talking to Julia, both of them a bit away from my father's body. Julia kept her head down all the while, her rosary cascading through her fingers as she relentlessly prayed on the beads.

'I will offer prayers for God's forgiveness for what has happened here today.' The priest turned and spoke as I came into the hall with Dr Fogarty. 'But I will wait until the household is gathered together and ready for God's presence amongst us.'

Julia scuttled off on her priestly mission. Dr Fogarty, who had severe differences of opinion with Father Duggan, patted me on the hand and discreetly withdrew to a seat by the door. I walked on alone to where my father lay on the ground.

The fire was burning well. There was no need for Mossie to throw extra logs on to it but he did, stepping back when they made a crone-like cackle and threw sparks on to the priest's

54

coat. Mossie, for reasons he never spoke of, attended neither church nor chapel. He didn't like Father Duggan either but I'd thought, until then, that he respected him.

The priest killed the sparks on his coat and turned coldly to Mossie.

'Leave the fire as it is,' he said. 'You'll be of more benefit to your dead master, and to yourself, on your knees.'

'Makes no odds to Jerome O'Grady what I do now,' Mossie said. 'When he had life and I could have been of use, I failed him.'

'He failed himself,' Father Duggan snapped, 'and he failed his God. The Lord our God gives us choices when he gives us the gift of life. Jerome O'Grady chose to fly in His almighty face and destroy that gift. He has diminished each one of us here by his deed.'

'It was unworthy of him, I'll grant you that,' said Mossie, 'a man like him should never have put an end to his own life.'

'He has diminished each one of us,' the priest insisted.

'We diminish ourselves when we lack understanding.' Hugh's voice was cold.

'To take a God-given life,' the priest insisted, 'is to belittle all life.'

Ellie, freckles dark in her white face, came ahead of Manus and Bella Mulligan up the stairs from the kitchen. Julia came after them but stayed well back as they knelt with me around my father's body. Mossie walked away. My mother and Hugh stayed where they were.

Father Duggan knelt and faced my father's feet, his hands raised above his head. His palms were blue-white, fingers long and delicate. 'We must pray together that the Lord Our God will help us find peace in our immortal souls . . .'

'What about my dead father's soul?' Hugh was stony-faced. 'Should we not pray for his peace and rest?'

If Father Duggan had even half-listened he would have

heard the controlled fury in Hugh's voice. But he was a man who was always closer to God than to anything on earth and heard only the words.

'We will ask Mary, the Mother of God, to intervene with Her Son, Jesus Christ, on Jerome O'Grady's behalf.'

Mossie, at the end of the hall, slammed the door as he left. In the draught the candles flickered and guttered out.

'My father had no use for you as a man, Father Duggan, and he was right not to.' Hugh's voice was low with fury. 'But he revered you as a priest, so you can bury him. It'll comfort my mother. We won't need you for anything else.'

'He cannot be buried in consecrated ground.' Father Duggan rose to his feet. 'It is the Church's law and as God's servant I must obey.'

'Be damned to your Church and its laws!' Hugh turned his back on the priest and went to meet the police, three of them including Sergeant O'Dowd, as they were ushered inside by Mossie. The sergeant, who had often played cards with my father and Mossie, spoke in low tones to Dr Fogarty.

I remained on my knees. My father needed someone by his side in the growing confusion. Ellie, Manus and Bella Mulligan stayed kneeling with me.

'Jerome O'Grady persevered in sin to the end.' Father Duggan, regretful but firm, turned to my mother. She gave no indication that she'd heard him, or even knew he was there. 'He was sadly without contrition,' the priest added.

'You refuse to bury him then?' Hugh, the policemen and doctor keeping their distance behind him, faced Father Duggan.

'God's will must be done, even in the saddest of earthly circumstances. I cannot bury him in consecrated ground,' the priest clasped his white hands in front of him, 'and the O'Grady mausoleum is, of course, on consecrated ground. I can, however, arrange to have him buried outside the

56

churchyard wall, where there is a special plot for such as he.'

'My father was many things, but he was faithful through it all to the Church.' Hugh's anger had turned cold. 'He gave more than his share when asked and supported the Church's every cause. He had no time for your craw-thumping hypocrisy, Duggan, but never went against you in public or with the tenants. For these things you are indebted to him, and the Church is indebted to him.' Hugh's voice rose. So did Bella, from her knees. 'You *will* inter him in the mausoleum,' Hugh insisted, 'or by God I'll do it myself!'

'I cannot.' Father Duggan shook his head. 'I am bound by canon law.' He seemed without emotion.

'There are ways around these things,' Hugh argued, 'it's well known how you look after your own. Sinful bishops, erring priests. They all get Christian burials, under church altars, some of them. There *are* ways.'

'You are grief-stricken, and so I will overlook what you are implying, Hugh.' The priest gave a sad smile. 'But you are right in one thing. There *is* a way your father could be buried in consecrated ground with the blessing of the Church . . .' He stopped, gazing into the distance. 'We should pray,' he said.

'Please continue with what you were saying, Father.' My mother's voice, heard for the first time since early morning, was cracked but clear. 'What must we do to have the Church bury my husband?'

'You must declare him mad.'

'But he was not mad.' My mother was patient, as if responding to a misguided child. 'He was unhappy that his world had been taken from him. There's nothing mad about that.'

'That he saw change in that way was clearly madness.' The priest adopted a similarly patient tone. 'The changes we're living through are the will of God. It saddens me to say it,

Ada,' he opened and spread his hands, 'but I'm compelled by a concern for the truth to tell you that your husband would have seen things that way had his mind been sound. There was a weakness there. The whole parish knows . . .'

'You take too many liberties, Father Duggan.' My mother closed her eyes and rested her head against the back of the armchair. 'Please don't ever again call me by my given name. You have overstepped your priestly duties.'

'It's best to face the past as well as the present, Mrs O'Grady.' Father Duggan shrugged. 'The past informs and guides . . .'

'Please leave, Father.' My mother opened her eyes and looked down at the blanket-shrouded body. 'I will make alternative arrangements for my husband's burial. Yours is not the only Church, nor the only way to follow God.'

There was a silence in which I could hear myself breathing. It was broken by the priest clearing his throat.

'This is a Catholic family, madam,' he said, sounding more incredulous than angry, 'a family fortunate enough to have found God's grace and been received into the arms of the one holy and apostolic Church.'

'I followed my husband's dictates, as a wife should,' my mother twisted her wedding ring on her finger, 'and now that he is dead I will not have his memory defiled.' She studied the ring intently. Dr Fogarty began to walk slowly towards her.

'What you mean, madam, is that you will not have the truth told.' Fathers Duggan looked, directly and for the first time, at the bloodied bundle on the floor. 'You would rather have a man who was the descendant of generations of loyal Catholic landowners buried a heathen than have his illness declared.'

'My mother has told you to leave, Father,' Hugh's face wore a look of revulsion, 'and now I'm telling you too. There will be no further discussion here today.' Bella took his arm. He pressed her hand to his side.

'The Church has compassion for the insane.' Father Duggan looked from Bella to my brother. 'You know, of course, that your great-grandfather died by his own hand, too, and by the same means your father chose. The Church, in Her infinite mercy, accepted your family's plea of insanity and he is interred in the mausoleum with his forebears. Why should it be any different today?'

'Because things *are* different, Father Duggan, and my husband was not insane.' My mother stood and held her hand out to Dr Fogarty. 'You're very welcome, Doctor, sad though the occasion is. Ellie will make tea.'

'Make it hot, Ellie, and don't spare the sugar.' Dr Fogarty eased my mother back into the chair. 'You might give her a helping hand, Julia.' He fixed a frown on the distantly hovering cook. 'I'm sure the lot of us would welcome some sweet tea.' Julia had begun to follow Ellie downstairs when the priest spoke. She stopped immediately.

'No tea for me, thank you.' Father Duggan spoke in measured, flat tones. 'I will finish my discussions with Mrs O'Grady, if you don't mind, Dr Fogarty, and be on my way.'

'Our discussion is over. My daughter will see you to the door, Father Duggan.' My mother had closed her eyes again.

I left my father's side reluctantly. 'I'm sure you've other souls to attend to,' I said to the priest.

It was all I could think to say and I didn't mean anything bad by it. He looked at me as if he couldn't credit what he'd heard.

'You're right, Vanessa, I do indeed have other souls to care for, though it's not your place to tell me so. Some of those souls are not so far away either.' He cast about with his cold eye, stopping when he came to Ellie. 'Eleanor Hope has been sheltered from her Catholic duties too long in this house.' He was breathing hard through his nostrils. 'I will await you at noon tomorrow in the presbytery, Eleanor. You'll see that she attends, Julia?'

When Julia bobbed and said said, yes, she would do that, the priest bestowed a brief blessing on us all. The studs on his black boots made a sound like nails being hammered home as he crossed the hall to the door.

7

We buried my father ourselves, in a grave in a far corner of the gardens with views of the sea and house. It was my mother's idea.

'We'll give him our own fine and Christian burial,' she said. 'It's the least we can do for him.'

She'd changed completely. She was purposeful and busy, up before cock crow to see to the house and kitchen and, three days after my father died, going with Mossie to an art dealer in Bridge Street, Sligo, to sell candlesticks and a salver of O'Grady silver. The dealer was a crook and if my father had been in his grave he'd have turned. But if she hadn't sold them, putting him there would have been a pauper's affair since we'd even less money than my father had told us.

My mother didn't go into mourning black. She didn't change a thing about her dress or hair and, the day we buried my father, wore the earrings and string of pearls he had given her when they married. I followed her lead. To wear black would have been to deny the person my father had once been. Even so, for decency's sake, I tied my hair in a black ribbon.

But the changes to my mother were on the surface only. In spite of the coroner's court finding that my father had died by his own hand, she spoke about his death as if it had been an accident. She wouldn't speak at all about my great-grandfather's end, even when my brothers and I asked her.

Father Duggan came calling but she refused to see him. I lied, telling him she was prostrate with grief and couldn't come downstairs. The dog, confused and lonely, circled the priest making small moaning sounds.

Father Duggan stepped out of his range and said he would pray for my mother, that God would not be pleased at what we were about to do, that he would pray we all might earn God's forgiveness, that His wrath might not be too great. I thanked him for keeping us in his prayers. He left without another word.

The priest himself would punish us, I was certain. He wouldn't wait for God to do the job.

Mossie was consumed by bitterness and anger and self-hate. In the days spent waiting for the coroner's court to release my father's body, I was fearful he would follow him to the grave. He slept in the stables and polished and shone the harnesses endlessly. When Manus and myself went to coax him back to the house he wouldn't come. He said he'd been forewarned and had failed, that he couldn't expect to sleep in his bed while my father was on the coroner's slab.

'I knew the signs to look for and saw plenty of them. I saw them for months past, and still I relaxed my vigilance. It was a bad day I let you off to shoot that blasted cur of Kilgallen's.' He puffed and polished and punished himself. His fingers were torn and bleeding. 'A useless cur it was too. I should have held firm and not given you the shotgun. Your father would be alive still if I'd refused you. I'd all of the weaponry locked safely away these months past on account of the signs.'

'What signs?' I was impatient.

I was angry with myself, too, in much the way Mossie was angry with himself. I was the one had left the shotgun on the hob, thrown it there with my wet cloak for my father to find.

'He was prowling,' Mossie said.

'Prowling?' I prompted him and waited. Blood fell from his chafed fingers on to the bit as he rubbed, then on the nose band. It was cold in the stables, the breaths of the two animals we still had making creamy clouds in the air. Manus stood leaning against one of them, a bay we called Oisin. He'd been unnaturally quiet since my father's death.

'Every night,' Mossie spoke at last, 'he went prowling all over the house. In and out of the rooms, up and down the stairs, in and out, up and down. Prowling and looking inside himself. The grandfather was the same way before he went into the woods and shot himself. My father often spoke of it. It was a warning and I failed him.'

'If you did then so did I,' I said, and walked to the door. A cold sun was bright on the stable yard; unbearable that my father would never again see it. 'I left the gun where he could get it.'

'You weren't to know,' Mossie said, 'the grandfather was kept a secret from you.'

True. But what had been unknown to us until my mother's revelation about my great-grandfather's death now seemed common knowledge in the entire parish.

'The last time I spoke to my father was in anger,' I said.

Behind me Manus erupted, shouting and throwing a saddle over Oisin's back.

'Why don't you both kill yourselves along with him? You'd at least spare the rest of us this craw-thumping, breast-beating self-pity!' He pressed his head, hard, against the animal's side while he tightened the girth. 'Father's dead because he wanted to die. It was his life and he saw nothing to live for, and maybe he was right. Maybe it's all the hell it had become for him. Maybe the rest of us are fooling ourselves.' He grabbed the reins and the horse went with him, high-stepping over the straw on the stable floor. At the door to the yard he stopped,

63

but didn't turn. 'He didn't think we were worth living for, that's the plain truth of it.'

Mossie and I didn't talk about blame, or even my father's dying, after that. Manus was right. Father had rejected all of us when he'd killed himself. But in a way, and most of all, he'd rejected the son who'd stood pleading with him in his last minutes. Manus had more to bear than any of the rest of us.

A Protestant clergyman my mother had known as a girl said the prayers over my father. He was an old man, white-haired and close to death himself by the look of him, but with a good heart and God-fearing.

Two of my father's ex-tenants dug the grave, then stayed to bury him. The Howards came and Theo stood beside me. He held my hand for part of the time and I saw Bella, on the other side of the grave, take Hugh's hand in her red-gloved one. Dr Fogarty was there, doubly sad because he'd come from the funeral of a child of ten who'd died of tuberculerosis. Ellie and Mossie were there but Julia stayed in the house.

My brothers and Mossie and Arthur Howard lowered my father in his coffin – oak, lead-lined and the best money could buy – into the ground. The dog looked worried and I turned his head away while the clergyman said the prayer in an old, cracked voice, the wind and the circling crows making him hard to hear.

'"The Lord bless thee, and keep thee: The Lord make His face to shine upon thee, and be gracious unto thee: the Lord lift up His countenance upon thee, and give thee peace".' It was short but it was enough.

The sun shone. Mossie played a lonesome air on the fiddle and Ellie sang a verse of *The Last Rose of Summer*, a song my father had loved to hear her sing. But the strong wind lifted music and words into the air and the crows cawed louder than before and we didn't hear much of them either.

It was all over in half an hour. It was long enough too.

Father Duggan's vengeance was swift. He arrived in a horse-car with the new young curate beside him. Mossie let them in and while the curate sat to one side on a bench, Father Duggan stood in the middle of the hall, black as one of the crow's outside in a long, double-breasted greatcoat, waiting while I went to get my mother.

Nothing I said would make her come down to speak with him.

'I never liked him and now I'm finished with him,' she said. 'Hugh can deal with him.'

But Hugh was out walking with Bella and Manus so there was only me.

'She's indisposed,' I told the priest, 'she's unable to see anyone.'

Mossie made a great show of building up the fire before sitting on a hob with his hands on his knees and his eyes on every move the parish priest made. The curate stepped into the hall, but kept out of Mossie's line of vision, studying the pictures around the walls. He couldn't have derived much comfort from them because his round face was flushed and unhappy-looking. The picture of my father had never looked more benign.

'I am your mother's priest.' Father Duggan's breath smelled of tea and bread. 'I am here to condole and pray with her.'

'She's talking to God in her own way,' I said.

He took a deep breath, drawing himself up like a turkey cock. Now that I was close to him he was much more like that farmyard bird than a bird of the air.

'Such arrogance will not lead to God's grace or forgiveness.' He looked as if he would move me aside but I stood my ground. Finn sat on his haunches beside me, looking at the priest with a surly expression. He hadn't been himself since my father died.

'What were we to do, Father Duggan?' I said. 'Your offer wasn't acceptable and we couldn't leave my father to rot above ground.' Finn gave a low growl and I put my hand on his head, afraid he might pounce on the priest. I was worried about Mossie as well, far too still and silent where he sat on his hob.

Father Duggan drew and held a breath for so long I began to worry about him also. When he let it go he was calmer.

'You don't know what you're saying, child,' he spoke softly, 'you are distressed, and understandably so. But I am distressed, too, and so is my curate, Father O'Brien. We are in particular, and more than ever, distressed about the welfare and morals of those you have working for you.' He turned to the curate. 'Perhaps you would fetch Julia and Eleanor Hope from the kitchens, Father O'Brien?'

The curate looked at me and then at his feet. He cleared his throat. 'Eleanor Hope is in the overhead gallery, Father. She's been there since we came in.' He looked up and smiled. It was a nice, shy smile and Ellie, her elbows on the gallery rail, smiled back.

'Is it possible, Father O'Brien, that she has turned your head along with that of every other young fool in the parish?' Father Duggan stared at his curate as if he saw the gates of hell opening around him. Father O'Brien reddened and coughed again and looked up at Ellie.

'The parish priest would like to speak with you, Miss Hope.' He was very polite.

'I'd better come down so,' said Ellie.

She came slowly down, dusting the bannisters and steps as she came. The curate left for the kitchen and Julia.

'You won't mind if I take a seat?' Father Duggan raised his thin eyebrows at me as he sat into the high-backed chair that had been my father's. Quickly as I could, I stepped between him and Mossie. I wasn't quick enough.

66

'You're not fit to put your backside where the man who's gone rested his!' Mossie stood over the priest with arms hanging. 'I'll have to ask you to stand or rest yourself elsewhere.' He gave his three-tooth grin. 'I find the hobs of hell by the fire comfortable enough myself.'

'You've been away from your church for too long.' Father Duggan didn't move. The dog gave another plaintive growl and I held his collar fast. 'You've forgotten the respect owed to your priest . . .'

'I've forgotten nothing. I remember too well.' Mossie's hands twitched at a level with the priest's eyes. 'I'm asking you to get out of Jerome O'Grady's chair.'

Father Duggan stood and clasped his trembling hands in front of him. His face was lifeless as a flat stone so it was hard to tell if they were shaking from fear or from anger.

'I am not proud,' he said, 'I am merely God's instrument, so it matters not whether I sit or stand. What I cannot do is allow your niece to be corrupted in this house and remain in your care any longer. I am here to return both women to the home they left. Your wife has agreed,' his eyes had expression in them now, of unholy triumph, 'and a husband has been found for your niece.'

Ellie, from the bottom of the stairs, made a small, strangled sound. She remained where she was. Her uncle laughed, a rare enough sound and never a joyful one.

'You're welcome to Julia. I hope she'll be happier in the village,' he sounded as if he meant this, 'but I wouldn't rate highly your chances of forcing my niece to marry any but the man she chooses for herself.'

Julia appeared at the top of the kitchen stairs as he finished speaking. She was wearing her best clothes, a quilted blue skirt with a black band above the hem and a white blouse with tucking, so must have been expecting the priest. The curate, close behind her with his round, country face perplexed and overheated, said something softly in her ear. Julia threw him a fast, dismissive look; her loyalty to Father Duggan might be based on fear but it was absolute. Father O'Brien was wasting his time acting as peacemaker.

Father Duggan, seeing his audience increase, raised his voice. He might have been at the altar.

'Do you think, Maurice Hope, that I am going to continue to allow your niece to lead the young men of this parish astray? To stand aside while she plays the Jezebel with one, then the other? She's an occasion of sin in the parish, with an evil in her that makes men mad. She must be saved from herself through the sacrament of marriage.'

Mossie snorted and made an impatient, fly-swatting movement with his hand. 'You may as well take yourself out of here, Duggan, because you'll never get her.' He looked at Julia. 'You can take her aunt with you.'

'You'll burn in hell, Mossie Hope.' Julia, in her rush to get between her husband and her priest, almost knocked the curate off his feet. 'Father Duggan is right about Eleanor and it's you has her the way she is. You never took a strong hand with her. You were always too . . .'

'I'll stay here if the O'Gradys will keep me and I'll marry the man pleases me most.' Ellie's voice, from the bottom of the stairs, cut Julia short and brought a sharp silence. Father Duggan recoiled without moving; you could see it in the stiffening of his neck inside its white collar. And in the disgust on his face.

The silence which followed, with the priest breathing heavily and everyone waiting for him to say something, was unbearable. I broke it myself.

'Ellie is a valued member of this household, Father Duggan,' I said.

He turned his head, slowly, and stared at me. It took all of my courage to meet those clay-cold eyes.

'She works honestly and well,' I went on. 'You're mistaken in thinking her brazen and of easy virtue.' I heard my own disbelief about the brazen bit in the wildness of my voice as I went on. 'She has a place here for as long as she wishes to stay . . .'

'It's not your place to come between Eleanor Hope and her priest.' Father Duggan's eyes blinked once. 'But since you and your family are not a little to blame for her being the way she is, I am not surprised, merely sorrowful.' He sighed deeply. 'The example set for her in this house would turn the head of any young woman. She will be removed, and married, for the good of her eternal soul. Would that I could do the same for you.' He sighed even more deeply before turning to give Julia a nod. She jumped in immediate obedience.

'Get your belongings together, miss,' she called loudly to Ellie, not moving an inch from her place by the priest. 'We'll go downstairs together. I'll pack my own bits and pieces for the road along with you.'

She managed to sound both triumphant and hard-done-by; but then Julia had always been both self-righteous and grumbling. There was neither sorrow nor regret in her voice and I knew she was certain Mossie would follow her. I was just as certain he wouldn't.

'Pack your own things, if you want to go so much.' Ellie, tossing her head, would have seemed carelessly defiant if you hadn't noticed the whiteness of her knuckles where they gripped the bannister. 'I'll be staying here, where there's work for me. There are laws in this land still. This is not Africa or some such place, and you cannot force me either to marry or to leave with you.' She began to walk backwards up the stairs. 'You won't see much of me around the village from now on.' She stopped after a few steps. 'You won't see me at Mass either.'

She turned then and ran, skirts gathered in front of her and yellow stockings I'd never seen before flashing all the way to the gallery. Her running footsteps went on until the door of my bedroom slammed shut.

'Leave her,' the priest said as Julia started for the stairs, 'she has decided her path. We will pray for her. It's all we can do now.'

He snapped his fingers at Father O'Brien who, head down and eyes on the floor, followed him to the door. I felt sorrier for that young priest than I did for myself or for Ellie. The dog padded after them, tail wagging sympathetically. Finn had a great deal of human understanding in him.

Father Duggan, before he went out of the door, turned back. 'Do you know where this household is headed, Vanessa? Do you know where you, a child baptised in my church, are headed?'

'No, Father,' I said, 'though I wish I did.'

He clicked his tongue and would have left on the turn of a heel had not Julia called to him.

'I'll be with you immediately, Father,' she said.

His hesitation was slight, but belittling. He'd forgotten her already. 'Of course,' he said, 'we'll wait for you outside, where the air is clean.'

Mossie went downstairs with Julia and helped her put her things into a bag. He helped her carry it to the carriage too. It was the strangest of endings to a marriage, for that's what it was. Mossie and Julia Hope never again lived together as man and wife.

8

The dog followed me everywhere. It was as if he knew things had fallen apart and feared for his future as much as I did. Wanted something to cling to as much as I did too.

Theo stayed for another two days after my father's burial. He was quiet, but so was I. There was much that needed saying between us but the time was not right.

'Hugh's worried about his exams,' I said on the second day to break a longer than usual silence.

'He's got less reason than I have to worry,' Theo said. 'But the truth is I'm gone past caring.' We were on the beach. He skimmed a stone across the first calm blue sea of the year. 'I made a mistake, Nessa, studying the law. Business is more my line.'

He said this with the air of a grandee, rubbing his lip growth and nearly making me laugh. Nearly, though I don't think he meant to.

'Where would you practise business then?' I said. 'In Ballymote? You could set about importing spices. Or maybe you could organise the gathering and distribution of seaweed here on the beach . . .'

'Oh, woman of little faith!' He shook his head good-humouredly. 'I could purchase wool and produce towels and blankets,' he put an arm about my shoulders, 'or open another corn mill. There's room for both in the county.'

'You sound like my father,' I said.

'There was nothing all that wrong with your father's plans,'

Theo said, 'it was the execution of them was the problem.'

I hadn't the heart to pursue this so I took his arm from
about me and, in a fit of sudden nostalgia, ran with him
to the water's edge. We took off our boots and watched
the small waves break over our feet, letting the sand run
between our toes and laughing at it the way we used to as
children.

I didn't think about the implications of what Theo was
telling me then. I was busy putting unpleasant things out
of my mind, trying to get used to the loss that couldn't be
put away. When Theo left the next day I went with him to
the station.

'Will you be all right?' he said, with his foot on the step to
the carriage. He'd said nothing until then about how I might
be feeling. I wished he hadn't said anything now either.

'I *am* all right,' I said, 'please don't worry about me. Try
for the exams and decide what you want to do with yourself.
We'll talk then.' The vapour from the engine, belching at
the far end of the terminus, made my eyes water. 'Please
don't worry about me,' I repeated and rubbed my damp
cheeks.

Theo took my hands and kissed my face. 'Things will
change for you, Nessa,' he said. 'They're bound to. It'll be
the summer soon and Hugh will be home.'

'I'm not so sure that he will,' I said, 'things are definitely
changing for him. But what about you? Will you not be home
for the summer?'

'It'll depend on my exams, and what I decide to do.' He
climbed into the train.

'We should talk together about what you'll do,' I said. 'We
should talk about the two of us, Theo.'

'We should and we will.' He leaned out of the door and held
my hand as a whistle blew and the train moved off. 'But not

with your father just buried. We'll do all of that the next time we meet.'

'Maybe I'll come to Dublin,' I said. The train was moving faster.

'I'll write.' Theo had to let go of my hand. He blew me a kiss.

'Goodbye!' I waved. 'Goodbye.'

The same unsteady passion that had driven my father's life seemed to grip Manus in the weeks following his death. He wore black and left his face unshaven. He drank whiskey, ate hardly anything and spent long hours in the library with the curtains drawn tight, writing by the light of several candles.

When he wasn't doing these things he wandered the house.

'Prowling,' Mossie said, 'prowling like the man that's dead prowled.'

Mossie himself was unsteady enough those few weeks. He spoke hardly at all and didn't sleep either, spending the nights by the locked door to the gun room. There was no good telling him Manus couldn't break it down, as Ellie did tell him, frequently. He drank a great deal from my father's store of JJ, though he never appeared drunk. He played cards alone and he cleaned and filled lamps in corners of the house unlit for years. He cut enough wood to keep fires burning to the millennium year. Finn, sighing a lot, kept him company.

'Leave him be,' Ellie said, 'talking will make him worse. He's well able to sort his devils for himself.'

She said the same about Manus but in his case I wasn't so sure she was right. She put food in front of my brother, often, but otherwise left him alone. She knew where he was, though, all the time, and was aware of everything he did.

Two days after Julia left, Mossie followed her to the village to fix the roof on her cottage. He fixed the door and windows too, while he was there. It was the last time he ever went there, in my time at Kilraven anyway.

My mother took to smiling a lot, her mask before the world. She talked a great deal, too, for two whole hours one day about what she might wear when the solicitor came to read us my father's will. When that day eventually came she dressed exactly as she had on the last night of his life.

Hugh and Bella Mulligan stayed on for a while. Hugh was quiet, his head buried in law books he'd brought with him. Bella spent the mornings in bed, the rest of the day making herself pleasant. She talked to me about London and the stage, and about Dublin and life there. I heard her without listening.

She slept the nights long, gently snoring beside me, and slept on when I got up in the mornings. My room was filled with her scents and plumage and bright wrappings and had never been so foreign to me. I envied her a great many things, most of all her freedom. It was Bella Mulligan that made me feel for the first time that I was a prisoner.

Ellie kept the house going until everyone learned to live again. She harangued Manus until he took her in the carriage to Sligo market. She got credit there on the strength of the family's 'great troubles' and filled the pantry when it became empty. She cooked and she baked bread, not as well as Julia but the continuity was reassuring. She filled the house with light, opening curtains in the mornings and windows, too, when there wasn't a wind blowing.

It was enough. The days passed, and the nights, and we all, in our different ways, began living life without my father.

I knew what everyone was doing because I wasn't sleeping a great deal myself. My head falling on the pillow at night had become a signal to my mind to start a race in which memories of the past chased dreams of the future.

In the memories, dust particles danced in rays of sun

74

through the kitchen window as I ate at the long table with the stable boys who used to work for us. In the mornings we ate maizemeal stir-about with plenty of milk and fresh bread; at midday I would go back for more milk and potatoes and dip.

Other nights, the memories were of the shadows made by my parents as they danced together in the great hall. I remembered a night, when I was eight or nine, my father had taken a pink rose from my mother's dress and pinned it to my hair and danced with me in his arms until Manus, jealous, had sent the dog to trip us up.

The dreams were also of a future in which I would be married to Theo and the world would be right again.

But it was the present, about which I couldn't put two consecutive thoughts together, which kept pushing these distractions from my mind and keeping me awake.

The solicitor, who'd been away when Father shot himself, arrived at the end of the third week. Valentine Beazley had smooth pink skin and an overweight body. He arrived an hour early, mopping his soft face with a ruby-coloured handkerchief. He'd been a card-playing friend of my father's and was full of regrets and talk of the weather and horseflesh.

My mother, her smile fixed on her face, led him wordlessly to the salon. Wordlessly, too, she gestured that he should sit. When he drew breath she smoothed the silver-grey of her dress and said, 'I'll send for my sons, Mr Beazley. I'm sure your time is as valuable as theirs. We would all like to be finished with this business.'

I'd never known she disliked him so much. The 'Mr Beazley' was what gave it away.

'No hurry, Ada, no hurry at all.' The solicitor assessed the room with his bulging, red-veined eyes, squeezing a tear from one of them and mopping it with the handkerchief. 'Jerome had great affection for this room. Great affection. He told me so, many times.'

75

He'd never before been in the salon. It was one of my mother's few rules that the card players keep to the hall and library.

'My husband held all of Kilraven in great affection.' She smiled at a point above his head and gripped the arms of her chair. 'Nessa, please tell your brothers to come at once and send Ellie with tea.' Her voice was a thread away from panic.

'Maurice Hope should be present also . . .' The solicitor's hoarse, breathy voice followed me from the room.

Manus was in the kitchen with Ellie so I left them to find Mossie and went myself in search of Hugh. Since it wasn't yet ten o'clock he would be working in his room. I knocked on his door and called his name and, when he didn't answer, went in. I couldn't bear the thought of my mother sitting any longer than she had to in the salon with Valentine Beazley.

In the dim, morning cool of the room I saw nothing at first. I would have gone straight to the bed to waken Hugh if it hadn't been for the sounds. And the way the room smelled.

First there was a soft laugh, then a whisper, then the kind of small gasp a person makes when surprised by joy. The smells were body ones, sweetly pungent and unfamiliar but instantly and instinctively knowable. There are some things we know because we are human, and animal.

Once my eyes adjusted I could see the room better, and everything in it. The bed coverings were on the floor and my brother and Bella lay entwined and naked as infants on the white-covered mattress. There was nothing infant-like about what they were doing.

I wasn't shocked, nor even greatly surprised. This was how Hugh and Bella lived in Dublin so why should it be wrong for them to make love in the countryside in Sligo? It was plain, too, that Bella's lazy mornings hadn't been nearly so lazy as I'd thought.

I was, however, paralysed, unable to take my eyes off them.

I heard my own gasp, like an axe landing on wood as it cut through the other sounds in the room. Hugh and Bella didn't hear a thing.

My brother's skin was palely white, the hairs covering his legs and chest thick and black. Bella Mulligan, curled over him with her limbs moving languidly against his, had skin the colour of pouring cream.

My own was the only woman's body I'd ever before seen and, compared to Bella's, mine was a mockery of the female form. Standing there I felt bony and mannish, the only clear thought in my head a resolve to never, ever allow Theo to see me naked as Bella was on that bed.

I'd never seen a man's body at all and it was scalding embarrassment at seeing my brother's that made me move at last. He murmured something that was smothered in the rampant tumble of Bella's hair. He murmured again and she moved back, her eyes lingering along every bit of him, slow and adoring and full of pleasure. Hugh made a low, brute sound and pulled her into him and they tossed together on the bed before beginning to kiss. The air became even thicker, the silence frenzied.

I backed out and closed the door softly behind me. I took a breath and knocked and called Hugh's name, loudly. I knocked twice and called his name four times before he answered. Through the door I told him about Valentine Beazley, then I went to my room and cooled my face in the water Ellie had left for Bella to wash with before going on downstairs. I was passing through the salon door when it occurred to me that Ellie, from making up the rooms, must know about Bella's morning visits to Hugh. I wondered what else she knew, and didn't tell me, about what was going on at Kilraven.

Valentine Beazley didn't take long to dispense with my father's last will and testament. He'd given up trying to be pleasing to my mother and was in foul and disappointed

77

humour by the time we'd all settled into various chairs in the salon. Hugh arrived frowning – an expression I now knew meant he was feeling good in himself.

Beazley stood by the mantelpiece and intoned like the undertaker his father had been: 'Jerome O'Grady made the will I will read to you one month ago. He died as close to bankruptcy as makes no difference.' He fiddled with a pair of spectacles which were too small for his nose, took a deep breath and went on. 'His estate and liabilities – in the form of this house and the lands remaining in his name – he leaves to his younger son, Manus. There are conditions. Manus O'Grady cannot sell or in any way break up the land and house without written permission from both his mother and Mr Maurice Hope. This will hold for a period of seven years. When, and if, the land and house are sold, half of the price achieved must be given to Jerome's widow, Mrs Ada O'Grady.

'To Maurice Hope is left ownership of the ruined gate lodge. To Ada O'Grady also he has willed the contents of Kilraven House, with certain exceptions. To Hugh O'Grady is left the library of books. To his daughter Vanessa, Jerome O'Grady leaves his watch and chain, silver snuff box and a sum of money,' the solicitor looked at me over the spectacles, 'this has been lodged not with the bank but in my own safe-keeping, as has a small sum to be given to Mrs Julia Hope. You would be wise not to speak about this outside this room. Banks have a way of gathering monies to themselves when they are owed.' He glanced briefly back at the paper in his hand. 'To Miss Eleanor Hope, Jerome O'Grady leaves a muff chain.'

That was it, give or take a few flourishes that were typical of my father. I didn't listen to these. Neither did Hugh. He left the room immediately, and Kilraven a few hours later.

Bella packed quickly. When I asked her if she'd hated

her visit so much she stopped, looking startled, and took my hands.

'It's been an experience I will treasure,' she said, looking sincere, 'in spite of the terrible sadness here.' She went back to packing her bags.

'It's understandable that you would want to be on your way . . .' I was remembering the scene in the bedroom and feeling awkward, not quite sure what to say.

'I pack quickly, out of habit.' She surveyed the diminishing chaos. 'I've spent my life on the move.' She picked up a pair of white stockings. 'Give these to Ellie, they're to go with a yellow pair I gave her already. And these,' she took the jet and jade earrings from her pocket, 'are for you. They look far, far better on you than they ever did on me.'

I took the gifts, marvelling at her generosity and thinking how cold the house would be without her. 'I hope I'll find occasion to wear the earrings.'

'You will,' she said firmly. 'You'll wear them in Dublin, if nowhere else, when you come to visit Hugh and me. You *will* come, won't you?'

'Perhaps. I don't go very often. I prefer the countryside.'

I sat on the bed and watched her packing small bottles of lavender water and the like. I might well go to Dublin, to see Theo if nothing else, but I needed to know first that there was going to be a summer at Kilraven, that everything wasn't going to fall apart. Hugh had always loved spending summers at home but now that he was disinherited, might not see the point. Which might mean Theo not coming home either. It would be a lonely, long summer without my father and Hugh. It would be unbearable without Theo too.

There were other reasons I wanted Hugh home. My mother, Manus and I needed him to help us create some sort of future for the place. Drink, grief and now responsibility had Manus in a continuing bad state and I wasn't sure

79

how much longer my mother would keep smiling if Hugh abandoned us.

I asked Bella outright: 'Will you and Hugh be coming here for the summer?'

'I'd like to.' Bella went to the window and stood there with her back to me. She was wearing the mauve dress she'd worn the first day. 'It would be nice to see all this with the sun shining on it.'

'In three days it'll be the first of May,' I said, 'the first day of summer. We'd like to have you to stay again, my mother and I. Manus too.'

'You certainly have room for us,' said Bella, avoiding answering me, 'the house is so big . . .' She turned. 'How will you live in it, you and your mother and Manus?'

'We'll shut up most of the rooms, live in the salon and kitchen and whatever bedrooms we'll need.'

'Close the whole blooming lot up and come to Dublin.' Bella spoke quickly. 'There's life there, and company and fun. Being here won't do you any good, Nessa my darling, no good at all. Hugh will worry about you all the time.'

'What about my mother? Is there no one to worry about her?'

'I'm sorry. I'm not helping.' Bella turned again to the window. 'It's an amazement to me that Hugh comes from a place like this,' her breath made a fog on the glass, 'he really is a creature of the streets and well-lit rooms of the city.' She cleared the fog with a finger. 'He's hurt, of course, at your father's rejection, which is how he sees his being disinherited. But he hates this place as well as loving it. It would have killed him, as it did your father, if he'd stayed here. He knows that.'

'It was sickness and history and drink killed my father,' I said. 'Hugh added to his misery, that's all.'

'True. Hugh loved his father. But he was afraid he would become him if he stayed here. "Each man kills the thing he loves . . ."'

80

'Indeed. I've read Mr Wilde too.'

The silence after this made me sorry I'd been so sharp. Bella left the window and began to tie up her bags.

'Forgive me for saying this, Nessa my angel,' she spoke with her head bent, 'but your childhood's well and truly over now, gone and not coming back. What are you going to do with the rest of your life?'

'You know, surely,' I said, awkward but wanting her response, too, 'that Theo Howard and I have an under-standing?'

'Hugh mentioned it.'

'It's the way we do things in the country,' I said, 'and of course Theo and I . . . care very much for one another.'

'I know you do,' Bella said.

'When he's finished his exams and knows what he's going to do, we'll settle things.'

'You've discussed this?'

'We have. At the train station, before he left.' I heard myself becoming strident and stopped talking.

'Perhaps your father was right and you should travel, Nessa, go away for a while before marrying.' She smiled. 'I'm a great believer in women as well as men having experience of life.'

'I've had all the experience I need,' I said.

'I'm sorry. It's not my place to tell you how to live your life.' She held up a hairbrush. 'Let me do your hair again. Then you can do it yourself when I'm gone.'

I sat at the mirror and she began to brush, then to coil and plait my hair. I watched my face change, become pale and high-boned, my brows darker.

'I'm both of them,' I said, 'I'm my mother and my father.'

'You're lovely,' said Bella, 'and intelligent and young. That's who and what you are.'

When she and Hugh had gone, rushing in the end to catch the 3.40 train from Sligo so as to get to Dublin by 9.30, I found she'd left me a small tub of orange-flower paste for rubbing into my hands. She'd written a note too: *'Three weeks, twice a day every day, and it will look as if you've never done a day's work.'*

Manus didn't want Kilraven. He fought the inevitable for fully a week. When he finally accepted, it was in a way that changed everything, for ever.

'I'll sell to the first man to give me a good price for it,' he announced at the beginning of the week. 'This whole house is a mausoleum, the land and woods fit only for the burying of the dead.'

'You can't do that,' my mother said, smiling, 'unless I sign. And I won't.'

Manus stared at her. 'Why? Why will you not sign?'

We were on the steps, my mother, Manus and myself, waiting for Mossie to bring round the carriage. He was driving my mother and me to Sligo to bring a pair of decanters, four goblets, a sugar bowl and teapot to the art dealer in Bridge Street.

'Because it's my home, and yours, too, and Nessa's,' she said. 'Ellie and Mossie must be considered also.'

'We're bankrupt, Mama, finished.' Manus sat on the wet cold of the steps and put his head in his hands. His hair hadn't been cut for weeks and fell forward, dark and oily in the sunlight. He was so very like our father in every way. 'Kilraven is finished.'

'You'll think of a plan.' My mother touched his shoulder. 'I have faith in you. Just as your father had faith in you.'

In the end we sent Mossie to the art dealer's to do the selling. My mother took tea in the Victoria Hotel while we waited and I walked the streets, passing shops I'd known for years and seeing my father in every one of them: the pawnbroker's and loan office, Johnnie Ward delph auctioneering on Market Street, the spirit store on Knox Street and the pubs near the military barracks, the courthouse, the barber shop . . .

I was glad when my mother didn't delay in the town after Mossie sold the silver.

Manus had made his decision by the time we got back.

'I'm going to join up with the Boers for the South African War.' He sat huddled and damp on the steps, looking as if he hadn't moved since we left. 'I'll fight their cause. It's a just one.' He stood as we came up to him. 'People have a right to their own land, and to fight for it. I'll be of use there. I'm of no value to anyone here.'

With a pale hand clutching the lapel of his long black coat, one leg thrust forward and his lank hair curling about his collar, he certainly looked the romantic revolutionary.

Except that the coat was wet, he'd no shoes on his feet and was blind drunk.

'Of course you're of value here,' my mother spoke absently, 'what would I do without you?'

'A lot better than you're doing now,' said Manus, 'I'd be one less mouth to feed.'

'You don't eat. All you do is drink,' I shouted at him. 'You're a drunken fool, Manus, and I'm ashamed to have you for a brother.'

'I'm sorry to hear that, sister mine.' Manus took a bottle from his pocket. It had a long neck and the liquid inside was clear. Poteen. 'Very sorry indeed.' He put the bottle to his mouth.

'You'll kill yourself with that stuff.' I grabbed the lapels of the coat and shook him. 'Haven't we had enough trouble? Maybe you *should* fight for the Boers. They're welcome to you. You might as well die there as drink yourself to death here. You'll be fighting neighbours – that'll no doubt please you. Charlie Martyn from Cliffmore is gone to fight with the Royal Irish Fusiliers and Robert Wilson from Ballingara was killed there a month ago. Others are dying of typhoid.' I shook him even harder, shouting even louder. 'But you know all this.

You know and you don't care, either who you die for or who you fight for . . .'

My voice had become hoarse with the shouting and when Ellie came running up and tried to pull me away I shook her off. I wasn't half-finished with Manus.

'The Boers don't need you. They've plenty of their own. You're needed here. Your mother needs you and this house needs you . . .'

'Leave him to me.' Ellie put both her arms about me from behind and pulled me away. She'd always had a great deal of strength in her arms. 'It's all lunacy and grief. He won't be going out to the Boers, or anywhere else either.'

She held me so tightly against her I could smell the kitchen from her clothes, the soap she'd used in her hair. When she dropped her arms from about me I sank to the steps.

Ellie sat with me while I wept. When I thought I could weep no more, I wept again. I wept for my father and brother; I cried plenty of tears for myself too.

'There's no harm in a few tears,' said Ellie when it was all over. 'I shed a few from time to time myself.'

'I never saw you cry,' I was interested.

'There's plenty you don't see,' said Ellie.

'The gardens will need work soon or they'll grow wild,' I said, to prove I saw some things.

But what happened next proved Ellie's point about my not seeing much. Manus didn't stop drinking that day. He didn't stop talking about the Boers and going to war either. He kept on at both pastimes for several more days, until word of peace in South Africa ended that as a topic. Ellie Hope ended his drinking.

'Ellie says she'll marry me if I give up hard liquor.' Manus was apparently reading the *Sligo Champion* by a window in the salon when he made his announcement. My mother was sewing tassels on to a curtain.

I took the paper out of Manus's hands and stared at him. There were lines like white threads around his eyes.

'What did you say to her?' I said.

I knew he wasn't joking. He'd cut his hair for one thing, and his gaze was steady. Most conclusive of all was the fact that it was ten in the morning and he'd had breakfast.

'I gave her the answer she wanted. I emptied the bottle in the yard where I stood. That was two nights ago and I haven't had a drop since.' He took back and opened out the paper. 'I'm on trial still but you won't see my mouth to a bottle again.'

'That's good news about your drinking, Manus,' said my mother.

I got him alone when he was saddling up for a ride. He looked terrible; his face white and his eyes sitting in two dark-blue hollows.

'Is it very hard?' I said.

'It's the devil. My head is bursting in several places, and the shakes . . .' He held up a hand. It danced at the end of his wrist like a puppet. 'Worse still is the craving, and the demons I can't get rid of without taking a glass. Or two.' He grinned, a painful sight in his blanched face. 'But I'll do it, if it kills me. And I'll marry Ellie.'

'Why?' I said. 'You don't love her. Mother won't accept her.'

'I love her enough. She's a fine woman, you know that as well as I do, and no matter what some people may think or say she's as much of this place as I am myself. I've great respect for her. I won't do wrong by her.'

He rubbed the back of his hand across his damp forehead and leaned against the horse's flank. He wasn't well, but he was better than he had been.

'I'm caught, Nessa, caught in a trap, and the truth is that I'm the happier for it. Before the will,' he made a gesture that took in the entire countryside beyond the stable, 'before

Father hauled me in and made me The O'Grady, there was everything and nothing to do with my life.'

He paused, fondling the horse's nose for a minute. Then he looked me in the eye. 'Ellie Hope is the only woman will stand by me while I make this place pay for itself again. I can't do it without her. She's a good woman and a strong one and she suits me. That's love, Nessa, love enough for me.'

I was used to Manus's grand speeches but this one, plain-spoken and shorter than usual, had more real tenderness in it than anything I'd heard from him in years. He meant every word he said, too, I knew that. I had to hope he would go on meaning it. I kissed his shivering cheek. 'I'll be glad to have Ellie Hope for a sister.'

'We get Mossie, too, don't forget.' He swung himself into the saddle and turned the horse's head. 'Continuity's what I plan for Kilraven.' He laughed to himself, heading slowly down the yard.

'Are you strong enough to be riding?' I called.

'The horse'll look after me.' He waved.

Someone, or something, would always look after Manus. Ellie certainly would. My own security was less certain. I said as much to Ellie in her bedroom that evening.

'You could have me out on the side of the road,' I pointed out, 'once you're mistress of the place.' She didn't think this funny.

'Don't you ever talk to me like that again, Nessa O'Grady.' Her nostrils dilated and she took a deep breath to calm herself down. 'I'll be a wife to Manus and that's all I want. I'll be with him in everything he does, too, because we both want that.' She smiled a slightly incredulous smile. 'I've been given the moon and the stars, Nessa. Please be happy with me, do.'

'I am happy.' I rocked myself in the chair beside her bed. 'I'm very happy for you, and for Manus. For all of us.'

My mother wasn't happy. But she would be, in time. Manus

was talking with her every day and Ellie was keeping out of her way. Only that day she'd said to Mossie that the twentieth century was proving very different from the nineteenth. It was a new beginning.

'It would never have happened without your father dying the way he did,' Ellie said, 'and that's the sad truth of it. Manus would have gone on the way he was for another ten years and there would have been no turning him back then. But every cloud, they say, has a silver lining.' She straightened from her sewing, looking worried. 'That's not to say I wished your father dead.'

'I know that, Ellie,' I said impatiently.

'Your brother's full of romantic nonsense.' Ellie put the sewing away and wrapped her arms about her knees. 'He thinks that by marrying me he'll bring the two Irelands together, gentry and serving girl of the poor.' She gave a short laugh. 'All he'll do is give scandal.'

'I suppose he will,' I said slowly, 'but we've always done that.'

'They're saying around the village and townlands that your father was a harmless fool from a line of harmless fools,' Ellie said. 'They're saying he was wrong to cause grief by ending his life the way he did. They'll never say the same about Manus. I know he doesn't love me as I love him, but what of it?'

She fondled the dog's head. He was lying on her bed and snorting, looking for attention as always.

'I'll wait,' she said, 'I've plenty of time. A lifetime, if it comes to that.'

The thing about Ellie Hope was that she knew what she wanted and wouldn't have anything else.

'I'm going to Dublin.' I said this on impulse, a sudden whim, and wished immediately that I'd kept the notion to myself until I'd thought a bit more about it.

'To be with Theo Howard?' Ellie said.

'To see the town, too.'

'It would be a good thing for you to get away for a while,' Ellie confirmed, and my fate was sealed.

If Ellie thought it a 'good thing' for me to go to Dublin then I would get no peace from her until I'd bought my ticket and was on the train. Maybe it *was* a good thing too. Maybe it was time for me to learn a thing or two from Ellie about putting my marrying affairs in order. In Dublin with Theo I could help him study for his exams. He would see how useful I could be to him, in the way Manus had seen how much he needed Ellie.

Things could be settled between us, at last.

9

I held Bella Mulligan's earrings to my ears. Above my white pleated blouse and blue poplin skirt they didn't look anything like they had on the night of my birthday. They looked gaudy. I wrapped them in a lace handkerchief and put them at the bottom of my travelling bag.

'Do you intend arriving in on top of Theo Howard without notice?' Ellie asked.

'Yes. I thought I'd surprise him.'

'You'll be a surprise for him all right! You might get a surprise yourself too.'

'If you're saying what I think you're saying then it's disgusting and shows how little you know Theo.' I stared directly, and furiously, into her eyes. She didn't so much as blink.

'It shows how little *you* know him,' she said, 'or any man.'

'I'll finish packing on my own.' I turned my back to her.

'I've other work to be doing anyway,' Ellie said, and left.

She was right, of course, and that was part of my anger. There was a lot I didn't know about Theo, about the world in general, if it came to that, and it frightened me. I ran after Ellie to the gallery.

'I'll telegraph him,' I called down the stairs, 'before I get on the train.'

'That'd be the best thing,' agreed Ellie.

Once I'd made up my mind to go to Dublin I wasted no time. I was packing to go the next day, which happened to be 1 June. A propitious date, I hoped. The weather had improved dramatically and a score of warm days was promised. The 6.45 train would get me to Dublin by noon, time enough to find myself lodgings close to where Theo and Hugh lived by late afternoon.

It might not be the sort of travelling my father had had in mind for me but it would be as good a way as any of spending some of the money he'd given me. Together with the amount I'd claimed from Valentine Beazley I now had nearly £2,500.

My mother had been surprised, and sat down quickly when I had told her of my plan. She was coming round to the view that Ellie would look after Manus, so the problem of their marrying was resolving itself. My going to Dublin gave her a new cause for worry, however.

'On your own?' she said. 'You're going to Dublin on your own? I didn't think you were so fond of the place. And in the summertime. The heat. The dust in the streets . . .'

'Would you like to come with me?'

'No, no. I have much too much to do here. No. Thank you, Nessa, but no.'

Surprised by such vehemence, I said, 'I thought you liked Dublin?'

'Not without your father,' she said, her mouth smiling and her eyes wide, as if she was afraid to blink.

'I want to be with Theo when he's doing his exams.'

'Oh, Vanessa,' she said, 'my lovely girl. What did we do to you?' A tear, just one, rolled down her face. 'We guided you badly. We gave you so little. It's you who should be getting married.'

The sun through the window picked out lines I'd never seen before on her face and made her skin look transparent and thin.

'Don't talk like that.' I went on my knees beside her. 'You were the best of parents. I wouldn't trade you for any others,' I gave a half-grin, 'even if I could.'

'You're so loyal, Nessa,' she said, 'you always were, even as a child. Ridiculously loyal. But your father was right to tell you to get away.'

I wrapped my arms about her knees, as I had when a child, and sat for a while with her stroking my head.

'I'm used to you being here, Vanessa,' she said after a minute, 'I like having you with me all the time. But you're right to go to Dublin. It'll do you good.'

Everyone thought it would do me good. Manus said so, too, when he heard, and Ellie had already said it would be 'a good thing'. They couldn't all be wrong.

Dawn was seeping into an inky sky when I left. You could feel in the air already that it would be another warm day; see it, too, in the way the morning mist was rolling back, like a spectre setting me free.

Mossie, with a good deal of grumbling, had agreed to drive me to the railway station in Sligo town. He saw no reason for anyone, ever, to go to Dublin. He'd been there once, thought it a 'black hole' and told me, as I climbed to sit with him on the driver's box, that I'd be better off taking a long car and going for a week to the 'peace and decency' of Rosses Point. I told him to be quiet and he grumbled on as Finn, with a great deal of barking, lolloped after us to the turn in the avenue.

Rounding it, there was enough light to see, quite clearly, as far as the hollow where we'd buried my father. The mound of his grave was already sinking and I was glad to be getting away.

I waved goodbye to Manus and Ellie from the turn in the avenue. Standing together on the steps, waving back at me, they looked as if they were already married and living happy, shared lives. I hoped they'd be as happy-looking when they *did* marry. My mother's tall shape waved behind them.

That scene, with the house grey and grand against the lightening sky and the dog making his lazy way back up the avenue, would stay with me for a long time to come. Whenever I needed a peaceful image to fill my mind I would close my eyes and call up that morning on the first day of June, 1902. It rarely failed me.

We were almost in Sligo when we came upon a motoring car, only the third such I'd ever seen. It was stopped by the side of the road with its engine uncovered. A large, over-dressed woman with a cross face sat in the back seat, a squarish man in top hat, with a pair of binoculars, beside her.

The driver lifted his head away from the engine and jumped into the road as we came along. He was in his shirt sleeves, a bearded, fidgety-looking man who seemed to think I should know him. So did the woman, who nodded to me. They were the kind of people the Howards were inclined to have for friends so maybe I had met them on some occasion.

'She's run out of motor spirit,' the driver called to Mossie. I looked at the fat woman, thinking for a minute that he meant her. The man in the top hat caught my eye and raised an amused eyebrow.

'That's not so hard to cure,' Mossie said, and raised the whip to move us on.

'I'd be obliged to you, my good man,' the shirt-sleeved man said loudly, 'for a drive to the nearest supplier.'

If the driver hadn't said 'my good man', Mossie might have been more inclined to be obliging. Might have. But it was one of Mossie's pecadillos that he wouldn't be the 'good man' of any other man, or woman. He didn't like motoring cars either. They were dangerous, in his opinion, to the health of both animals and humans.

'We're for the Dublin train. We've no time to delay.' Mossie lifted the reins and the horses moved on. The driver ran along-side us, brow frenziedly furrowed as he waved an oily cloth.

'We were making for the train ourselves,' he cried, 'I won't delay you. There's a supplier at the edge of the town . . .'

'We've got the time,' I said to Mossie, 'let him come with us.'

'After that he'll be wanting a lift back as well.' Mossie kept going and the man fell behind. 'He's fit enough to walk to the suppliers and catch the later train. Or drive to Dublin in his motoring car.'

I looked back. The driver was panting and mopping his brow with the cloth, leaving oily streaks and giving him a wounded as well as an anxious look. His male passenger was on the road now, too, binoculars trained on myself and Mossie.

'Stop!' I caught the reins. 'It's a small thing to give him a lift. They'll be there for a long time before anyone else comes along. We'll take him.'

Mossie, muttering under his breath, pulled up the horses but remained firmly in his seat after they stopped. I climbed down myself and began walking back, frowning into the binoculars. Their owner lowered them immediately. He looked apologetic as I came up.

'Forgive me,' he said, indicating the field glasses, 'there's so much to look at that I've got used to training them on everything I see.'

He'd taken off the top hat, revealing short, sun-bleached hair going a bit thin on top. The field glasses were encased in green leather and had the letters T.C. tooled on the side.

'May I look through them?' I said, in a burst of sudden curiosity.

'Of course.' He handed them over with an obliging smile and I put them to my eyes. The countryside and mountains appeared fuzzily.

'They need adjusting,' I said.

'We haven't the time for tomfoolery,' Mossie called. In the mood he was working himself into he was as likely to turn and

93

go home as he was to take me to the station. I handed back the field glasses.

'We'll take one of you to the supplier,' I said to their owner, 'but we can't bring you back or we'll miss miss the train. There's a horse-car at the suppliers, or a bicycle if you know how to use it.'

'I'll go. I'm grateful to you,' the driver said, his beard agitated as an ant's nest, 'I'll get my jacket.'

The day was going to be much too hot for the heavy jacket of home-spun tweed he got from the car. The woman, also overdressed, handed down to him a large white handkerchief and watched severely as he buttoned himself into the jacket.

'You've got a fine pair of horses there,' the man with the binoculars said to me, 'no danger of them running out of energy.'

I looked hard at him. He was neither young nor old. Something over thirty, I would have said, neither ugly nor plain, and of middle height. He had blue sailor's eyes, creased at the corners as if he was used to narrowing them at horizons, or into the sun. His moustache was neatly trimmed and a great deal bushier than Theo's.

'Old ways are usually best,' I looked briefly at the exposed engine, 'more reliable.'

I didn't particularly believe this but was too put out by the man's stare to think of anything more intelligent to say. He was half-smiling and didn't seem in the least put out by the collapse of the motoring car. Nor about the fact that Mossie and I were being delayed. My guess about T.C. was that he thought himself a great deal more important than the rest of the world.

'This morning is certainly proving your point,' he agreed. 'Motorised transport is a great deal more complicated than the horse-drawn kind.' There was something of the West of Ireland in his accent, but with edges of something else to it as well.

94

'Are you holidaying in County Sligo?' I said.

'Not any longer.' He smiled regretfully. 'My holiday is just ending. It's back to Dublin and work again, I'm afraid.' He brought his heels together and gave a small bow. 'My name is Thomas Cooper,' he held out his hand, 'and I'm grateful to you for stopping. I'd never have caught the train to Dublin otherwise. My friends are Redmond and Frances Mansfield.'

'I'm Nessa O'Grady.' I shook his hand but didn't encourage him to acquaint me further with his companions. 'And you're not on the train yet. None of us will catch it if we don't hurry . . .'

I half-ran to where the motoring car driver was making energetic, red-faced efforts to open the carriage door. Mossie, high on his seat and with his back to us, showed no inclination to help him.

'You need to lift it on its hinges,' I called, coming up to the driver, 'then give it a sharp tug.'

He lifted, then tugged the door so hard he was sent spinning backwards when it finally, and violently, opened. Mopping more sweat off his grease-streaked forehead, he climbed inside and pulled the door after him. His beard jiggled alarmingly from his exertions.

'We should go,' he said.

'Perhaps I should come too?' Thomas Cooper put a hand on the carriage door. 'I could continue on to the station and be sure of catching the train. You could bicycle back with the motor spirit.'

The beard dropped as his friend's mouth fell open. The man looked shocked.

'We couldn't leave Frances here on her own,' he squeaked, panic-stricken, 'not here. Not in the middle of . . . this place.'

I looked around. No savages, thieves or wild animals. No marauding peasantry.

95

'Your companion will be quite safe,' I said, 'she might even enjoy the sunrise.'

'But anything could happen,' the man's eyes darted nervously between me and the woman in the motoring car, 'anything. My wife isn't a woman used to the wilderness and would be terrified. Truly terrified. She cannot be left alone.'

'There would be hell to pay, right enough,' agreed Thomas Cooper.

Voices carry in a still morning, even low ones.

'You will *not* leave me here alone!' The waiting woman squawked like an enraged magpie. Even Mossie turned in his seat. 'I will *not* have it. I will not have my virtue and dignity endangered.' Impossibly, the squawk rose higher. 'Thomas will remain to keep me company, as already decided, and you, Redmond, will go with . . .' she stopped, tried to find a name, failed and went on '. . . these people to get the motor spirit. The oversight was yours. There's no reason why I should be the one to suffer the consequences.'

Bristling and swollen, her feathers well and truly ruffled, she snapped open a pink parasol.

'We've a train to catch,' Mossie lifted the reins, 'so you'd better make up your minds who's coming.' The horses, tired of waiting, jerked forward.

'He's right,' I agreed briskly, 'we must go.'

I swung myself up beside Mossie, folded my skirts under me and and, by way of discouraging debate, stared straight ahead. I didn't know Thomas Cooper was on the road beside me until I felt the hard curve of the binoculars against my hand.

'Take these, Miss O'Grady,' he said, 'I'd like you to have them.'

'There's no need.' I had to take them in my hand or they would have fallen, 'absolutely none . . .' But the carriage moved on, relentless as Mossie grumbling beside me.

'I'll be on the train,' Thomas Cooper called after us, 'I'll show you then how to focus them.'

'You may miss it,' I warned, and he shook his head, not even considering the idea.

What struck me, as we moved on, was that Thomas Cooper was evidently a man used to things going his way. I didn't want his company on the train. I didn't know him and didn't want to have to be explaining myself and making polite conversation all the way to Dublin. My own company would do me very well.

But Thomas Cooper, standing in the middle of the road with his legs apart and hands by his side, was fixed and resolute in the way of a dog that will not give up a bone. If he made the train he would seek me out, I'd no doubt about that. He was nothing like my brothers or father or Theo. He was a lot more like the women in my life, determined as Julia and Ellie were, in their different ways, to get and do what they thought was the right thing. I didn't at all fancy six hours of pleasing him on the train to Dublin.

'You'd be better off keeping to yourself and away from the likes of Cooper until you meet with your brother in Dublin,' growled Mossie. His reasons for thinking so might be different but at least we were as one on something.

'I don't think we need worry about Mr Cooper catching the train,' I said.

Redmond Mansfield didn't speak to us from inside the carriage until we were coming near to the motor-spirit suppliers. He stuck his head out of the window then, and his bawling voice, telling us to 'Stop – stop at once and let me out!' was full of the hysteria of earlier. The unfortunate fellow must have been in a state for all of the journey even though Mossie, for all his grumbling, had got a cracking pace out of the horses.

Our passenger hopped from the carriage even before we'd stopped. Before we'd started up again he was banging on the supplier's door loud enough to waken the dead. Or the sleeping, as was the case. From my perch beside Mossie I could see a bicycle in the yard. All going well, Thomas Cooper might indeed make the train.

Sligo station was awake and alive with passengers even at 6.15 a.m., men and women herded together and waiting like sheep for the employees of the Midland and Great Western Railway to open carriage doors. The Dublin train was drawn in to the platform and belching enough steam to shroud the engine. The atmosphere was choking after the clear air outside and once I had my ticket I waited near the end of the platform, as far as I could from the vapour-filled miasma.

'Dublin looks to be a shocking popular place these days.' Mossie's voice in my ear held more foreboding than usual. 'We'd best move or you'll have more company than you want for the journey.'

I thought he meant Thomas Cooper and turned, ready to hand over the binoculars and bid the man a polite good day. But it was Father Hubert Duggan he'd seen, bearing down on us with his hat low over his eyes and mouth tight as a trap. I dropped my head and turned away quickly.

'We'll find a carriage at the other end,' I said.

But Mossie was already ahead of me, forging his way through the crowd like a battering ram as he distanced us from the priest. Father Duggan had to have seen him, and me as well, a minnow in his slip stream. I didn't turn when I heard my name called, just kept going until we got to the head of the train, for once glad of the belching veil of steam. Mossie jerked open a carriage door and, ignoring an irate railway official in blue serge, threw my bags on to a seat and helped me aboard.

'Stay in that carriage until you get to Dublin,' he called from the platform. 'You'll be safe enough there from that black divil.' He slammed the door shut. 'Be sure to tell

Hugh the lake's full and signs good for the fishing this summer.'

'Miss O'Grady!'

The voice was the one I'd heard calling from the crowd and it didn't, after all, belong to Father Duggan. Thomas Cooper was smiling and sure as he'd been the last time I'd seen him, only now he was standing beside Mossie, a bag in each hand, ready to board the train.

'You made it then.' My heart didn't sink, but it didn't soar either. If I had to have one or other of them for company he was at least preferable to Father Duggan. I grabbed his binoculars from the seat. 'Thank you for lending me these.' I reached with them through the window; maybe I could still put him off. 'I'd prefer not to try and use them on the train.'

He smiled and turned to Mossie. 'I'd be obliged, sir, if you would open the door for me. My hands, as you can see, are full.' He was carrying a leather-handled bag in each, waiting so politely it would have been unnaturally uncivil not to open the carriage door.

Mossie looked up at me. A word, a nod even, and he'd have sent Thomas Cooper on his way. But life is full of fateful moments and that was one.

'Maybe you should open the door for Mr Cooper,' I said to him.

Mossie all but wrenched the carriage door from its hinges before wishing me a good journey and leaving Thomas Cooper to clamber inside unaided. He sank into the seat opposite, perspiring a little. His forehead, when he put his hat on the seat beside him, was beaded with sweat. He'd rushed along the platform then; finding my carriage hadn't been as accidental as it had seemed.

'You made good time in the motor car,' I said.

'I drove it myself. It's a mistake to allow a boy do a man's job.'

Redmond Mansfield was hardly a boy but I let it pass. Thomas Cooper, on the other hand, removing his gloves and planting both feet firmly on the floor, was now uncomfortably close and definitely a man. He had a clear, central crease down his trouser leg and looked much more of a first-class than a second-class passenger. The carriage seemed to have shrunk, now he was in it, as if it was too small to contain him and his energies.

His scrutiny verged on rudeness, his strange blue gaze reminding me of how countrified I was. I knew he could see very well that my bolero didn't match the green of my skirt, that a clump of hair had escaped from under my hat and that I was altogether less elegant than the women he would have seen getting into the first-class carriages.

When the hubbub and whistle-blowing of departure time started without warning I was glad of the distraction.

'We're underway,' I said.

'It would appear so.' He smiled.

We were clear of station and town before he spoke again. By then I'd remembered, with a sensation of panic that made me feel hot and bothered, that I'd forgotten to send Theo a telegram from the station. There was nothing to do but go with my original plan and surprise him. I was studying the window with a view to opening it when Thomas Cooper spoke again.

'You're not going to jump, I hope?' He'd folded his arms and was sitting straight-backed in his seat. Over his head there was a framed photograph of an hotel in Co. Kerry. It had palm trees all around it and was very grand.

'I find the carriage stuffy,' I said. 'Thought I might open the window a little.'

Afraid he might think I was accusing him of fouling the air, I added, 'Perhaps you don't find it so warm as I do?'

'You're absolutely right.' He unfolded his arms. 'We need some refreshing air in here.'

He got up, dropped the window leather by two holes and stood holding the belt while he took an extravagant breath of air.

'Should I go another notch or two?' He smiled down at me, competent and confident and solidly unshaken by the train's increasing speed.

'I think you've opened it enough.' I was prim, torn between gratitude and a sense that my journey was no longer my own. He secured the belt and sat down.

'An open window should ensure we keep the carriage to ourselves.'

'I hope so,' I said, and immediately began to wonder how I could get him to close it again. Another passenger would at least give him someone else to talk to.

'Would you like me to help you focus the binoculars?' he asked politely. 'You might enjoy the views of the mountains before we leave them behind.'

I handed him the glasses and he showed me what to do, then handed them back. I put them to my eyes and, following his continuing guidance, worked at making more of the mountains than blurry dark-blue humps. He was patient, and I was slow, but the mountain ridges had just become sharp-edged fortress walls when the carriage door ground noisily open behind us.

'I am glad to see, Miss O'Grady, that you've found yourself both amusement and company.' Father Duggan stepped into the carriage. 'I worried that you might be travelling alone when I saw you on the platform. You and your family are a constant worry to me since your poor father . . .'

He sighed, letting the sentence go unfinished as he closed the door behind him. Without so much as a glance at Thomas Cooper, the priest sat beside him and raised his eyebrows at the field glasses.

'Are you going all the way to Dublin?'

'All the way', I echoed, 'and you?' The carriage might have felt small before but now it felt like a cage.

Father Duggan nodded. 'For a conference of religious. The Church gathering the troops together, you might say.' He gave an involuntary smile, then coughed and straightened his back as if embarrassed. 'It's rare enough for me to have the opportunity to meet my fellow priests.' He sighed. 'Or visit Dublin, for that matter.'

'Then I hope you enjoy it,' I said. Just my luck that his opportunity to visit Dublin should coincide with my own.

'You will be staying with your brother Hugh?' He draped his hands over the sharp, high peaks of his knees. He hadn't taken off his hat and his long black coat was still buttoned to the neck. His face and hands were the blue-white colour they always were, and my mother's view that he had thin blood seemed suddenly optimistic. Water was the more likely component.

While he waited for my answer I thought about lying. Where I stayed was none of his business. It wasn't Thomas Cooper's business either, listening just as hard as the priest while pretending to study the passing landscape. Only I couldn't think of a lie. Even if I did, I would be caught out, so I told the truth.

'No,' I said, 'I'll be staying in lodgings near by.'

'You have a place in mind?' Father Duggan was relentless.

'Yes.' The lie hung in the air, blatant as the flush on my face. The priest waited for me to recant or say where I would be staying. Thomas Cooper waited. I picked up and put the field glasses to my eyes again. We were going much too fast for me to see anything.

'The views are not half so interesting now,' I said.

'Dublin is not Sligo.' Father Duggan, speaking in a loud voice, announced this as if it were a new and startling piece of information. 'It's not a place for a young woman alone. There are not the same safeguards on morals as exist in country places.'

I turned in time to catch his eyes sliding towards Thomas Cooper. It was the first time he'd acknowledged the presence of anyone else in the carriage. Cooper gave him a pleasant nod.

'Indeed, Miss O'Grady,' Father Duggan frowned my way again, 'it would be fair to say I'm surprised at your mother for allowing you to travel alone in the first place, and so soon . . .' He cleared his throat. 'The poor woman is obviously distracted and doesn't know what she's doing of late. I pray for her. I pray for all of you. Even so, I must emphasise again how surprised I am to find you travelling alone like this. It's unwise of you, highly unwise. We live in wayward, Godforsaken times. Might I also say how surprised I am . . .'

He paused, leaned forward and lowered his voice to a whisper which made not a whit of difference so far as Thomas Cooper's hearing everything was concerned. All it did was fill the carriage with a hissing sound.

'. . . that you yourself should wish to leave your home, and unfortunate mother, so soon after the sad tragedy of your father's death.'

'But I'm not travelling alone, Father Duggan,' I said. 'As you've already remarked, I have Mr Cooper for company and his binoculars to amuse me.'

'I'm privileged to have Miss O'Grady as a travelling companion.' Thomas Cooper rose slightly in his seat, half-smiled at Father Duggan, and sat down again. 'You are, of course, welcome to join us, Father . . . ?'

'Duggan. Father Hubert Duggan. I am Miss O'Grady's parish priest and confessor, and confidant to the sadly deceased Jerome O'Grady, her father. Are you a friend of the O'Grady family, Mr Cooper? Or even an acquaintance?'

'I'm an indebted acquaintance of Miss O'Grady's.' Thomas

Cooper smoothed his moustache with two fingers. 'It's thanks to her I'm on this train at all.'

'And how might that be?' The priest's voice was dry with disbelief.

I explained to him, with as little elaboration as possible, what had happened in the early morning. As I did, I had an appalling vision of the day ahead, the three of us trapped in this swaying carriage, the priest intoning about God and the parish, the hours and miles unrelenting. The earlier prospect of six hours alone with Thomas Cooper seemed a pleasure by comparison.

'So Mr Cooper is known to you only since this morning?' Father Duggan raised a fluttering hand from his knees. 'Then it's as well I joined you. I'm sure Mr Cooper is an exemplary person and a gentleman but he's still a stranger, to all intents and purposes, and you are a young girl and must be . . .'

'I'm a woman, Father Duggan.' I liked the sound of the words as I said them. 'I've passed my majority, as you well know, and will make decisions for myself as to the company I keep. Furthermore, Father,' desperation made me rash, 'I will take myself out of this carriage and spend the rest of the journey in the corridor if you persist in tormenting me.'

My angry haste almost landed me there.

'As you please. Perhaps standing in the corridor would give you time to repent your behaviour towards your priest.' Father Duggan, if he'd been God Himself, could not have been more imperious. 'You have had too few controls and far too much excess in your life. With your misfortunate father gone you're in dire need of a controlling hand. Your mother would thank me for watching over you for the journey. It's my duty, the least I can do.'

He took a breviary from his black bag and settled more comfortably into his seat. Reading, his face was as still and blank as an iced-over pond.

I saw that he actually expected me to get up, leave, and stand like a bold child in the corridor. That way he could keep an eye on me without having to put up with my company. He would also have the satisfaction of observing my discomfort.

I contemplated opening the window wider, lifting the belt and letting the frame fall with a crash. We'd be caught in a whirlwind and there would be the great fuss of getting the window up again. Father Duggan might just leave for another carriage. I put my hand on the belt.

It wouldn't work, I decided, withdrawing my hand. Father Duggan was more likely to devote the journey to praying loudly for my soul.

I felt Thomas Cooper watching me and, when I turned, caught his eye. He shook his head, looking at the window, then brought his eyebrows together in comic reproof and discreetly wagged a finger. I pulled a grimace of my own, shrugged and glanced resignedly at the priest. He was still reading, and waiting for me to leave.

'Will you join me in the saloon car, Miss O'Grady?' Thomas Cooper issued the invitation in a friendly, off-hand manner. 'I'm told it's excellent and roomy and that they serve coffee and tea from an early hour.'

He might as well have set off a cannon as far as the priest was concerned. His head shot up as he began protesting in a cracked and disbelieving voice.

'Miss O'Grady is not at liberty to go with you to the saloon car. She is in my charge and I forbid it.'

'I'm in charge of myself, Father Duggan,' I tucked the trailing hair back under my hat, 'and it's probably best to leave you to read your prayers in peace.' The hair, in retribution for my spite perhaps, refused to stay pinned and fell to my shoulders.

'I forbid it!' Father Duggan held the prayer book in front of him like a shield. 'I am your priest and I forbid it.' He hesitated then said again, 'Absolutely forbid it.'

'My invitation is by way of a thank you to Miss O'Grady for her kindness earlier this morning.' Thomas Cooper stood up with a brusqueness that wasn't wasted on the priest. 'I assure you, Father, she will be quite safe in my company.'

The breviary's pages crackled as Father Duggan ran a flustered hand through them. 'She is inexperienced in the ways of the world, it's not right to expose her to places and occasions of sin. As her priest I am bound to . . .'

'There will be no sin committed, Father, I assure you.' Thomas Cooper sounded sharp. 'Not by me and certainly not by Miss O'Grady. I have every faith in her virtue.'

He picked up his hat and stepped towards the door. He stopped, because he had to, when Father Duggan stretched his long legs in front of it.

'I hope, Father,' said Cooper calmly, two fingers gently smoothing his moustache, 'this doesn't mean you are now questioning my intentions or, God forbid, *my* virtue?'

'I'm sure you are virtuous enough in your own way,' the priest temporised, 'but you are a man, nevertheless, and Miss O'Grady is a young woman and must be protected. At this moment in time she has only me to look after her . . .'

'She has her God, surely,' Thomas Cooper spoke very softly, 'and what is very obviously a strong and resourceful character.' He leaned across and slid open the door. 'Perhaps, Father, you should put more trust in both of those yourself.'

He stepped over the priest's black-shod feet, brushing against them as he did so, and stood facing him from the corridor. His hands were by his sides again, the way they'd been when he'd stood in the middle of the road earlier in the day.

'I think, Miss O'Grady, that Father Duggan is now in agreement that a visit to the saloon car will not damn you to hell's external fires. You will accompany me there, I take it?'

I was already on my feet. The train swayed and I clutched

the back of the seat to steady myself. Thomas Cooper held out his hand to me. Father Duggan's black shoes didn't move as I took the hand and stepped over them.

'If you go with this man to that that den of iniquity, I cannot be responsible for you.' Father Duggan blessed himself. 'I have told you, as your priest, not to go there. On your own soul be it.'

I followed Thomas Cooper's square back until he stopped at the passage between two cars to wait for me.

'I really am lost now,' I said as I came up, 'I'm on the road to hell, for certain.'

'In Father Duggan's book we all are, more than likely. A road paved with stops in saloon cars and cities such as Dublin.'

I laughed and felt liberated. If I had to have company on the journey to Dublin, then at least Thomas Cooper's promised to be a lot more entertaining than Father Duggan's.

IO

The saloon car was stately and sumptuous, with a great deal of draped wine-coloured velvet and men playing cards, even at that hour of the day. There were two other women and they were stately, too, and quite old.

Thomas Cooper gave money to an attendant to find us seating. We sat with a table between us and had potted beef, buttered eggs and oatcakes. The table was laid with silver and white linen, and with glassware which I worried about constantly.

'The Midland and Great Western Railway has too great a confidence in its smooth running,' I said as the train lurched and I clutched at a goblet.

'And in its passengers.' Thomas Cooper poured us both water when I'd repositioned the glasses.

'What has the Midland and Great Western Railway to gain by giving us fine glassware?' I said. 'Surely tin would be more serviceable?'

'It has its reputation for refinement and passengers willing to pay for such to think about.' Thomas Cooper gave his half-smile. 'Tell me,' he helped himself to the beef, 'what do you think you've gained by venturing from the grasp of your Father Duggan?'

'Freedom from him for the rest of the journey, though I'm sure he'll resume the battle for my soul when I return home.'

I tasted the buttered egg and realised I'd also gained a grander breakfast than the milk and soda bread Ellie had packed for me. The milk was probably curdling in the carriage now, in keeping with Father Duggan's mood.

'They're the same wherever you go in the world,' Thomas Cooper said, surprising me with his vehemence, 'priests or witch doctors – all the same. Interfering with the lives and rights of people, always in the name of one god or the other. There's nothing special about your Father Duggan, believe me. He's just one of a universal tribe of madmen and women who need to be kept in their place.'

'My brother Hugh would agree with you,' I said. 'He believes the Church and the priests have too much power over the people and should hand over some of their wealth to the poor.'

'Does he indeed?'

Thomas Cooper shrugged himself out of his jacket and hung it carefully over the back of his chair. He was wearing a pair of trouser braces over a white linen shirt. The shirt was well-filled by his shoulders and he was altogether bulkier than he'd seemed in the jacket. I thought he'd forgotten our conversation when he said, 'Your brother Hugh sounds both wise and unwise. Better surely to give work to the poor, so that they may support themselves? Work is man's lot. Work sets us free. Do you not think so?'

'Surely that depends on a lot of things,' I said.

'On what, for instance?' He looked curious. His hands, breaking bread on the plate, were blunt and capable. The hands of a man used to work.

'Well . . .' I tried remembering Hugh's arguments with my father. 'It's said there isn't enough work for all of the poor, and that what there is is often badly paid and unsuitable . . .'

'Unsuitable? Work is work, Miss O'Grady. It's what we're born to. Doesn't the Bible itself say that if any man would not work then neither should he eat?'

'The Bible also says the labourer is worthy of his hire,' I

said, more confident as I moved to something I'd a knowledge of, 'and I can't accept that the malnourished poor should be made to work when they haven't the strength. Nor that children should be made to work before they've had a childhood.' Both were injustices I'd seen for myself in Co. Sligo.

Thomas Cooper was silent so long that I was about to explain myself further when he said, 'Do *you* work, Miss O'Grady?'

'I do. Though like most women my work is concerned with my home and family. What do you work at yourself, Mr Cooper, when you're not holidaying in the West of Ireland?'

All I knew about him, after all, was that he'd been driven to the station by a fretful man and his belligerent wife.

'I work a rubber plantation in Africa, and have charge of a station outpost.'

I was unprepared for this. Any one of half a dozen roles – farmer, seaman, bridge builder – would have fitted with the notion I had of him in my head. Africa and a rubber plantation were beyond my imagining.

'A rubber plantation,' I repeated. And then, because I couldn't think of anything else, said, 'What part of Africa is it in?'

'In the Congo Free State – *l'État Indépendant du Congo* to give it its proper Belgian name.' He smiled, amused by my surprise. 'Do you know Africa?'

'Not at all, Mr Cooper, no more than I know Europe. I'm completely untravelled, by choice. I *can* read an atlas, however, and even the newspaper.'

I was deliberately cool. Freeing me from the company of Father Duggan didn't give him the right to treat me like a child, and an illiterate one at that.

'Your Congo Free State is in Central Africa and is owned by King Leopold of Belgium,' I said. 'Am I right?'

He took his time about answering, waving away the waiter when he came to clear the table, leaning forward with arms folded when the man was gone.

He spoke quickly and passionately then, bringing a faraway African world, with steaming jungles and boiling skies, into the saloon car. I didn't once interrupt. Short of banging the table I didn't see how I could, but in any event, was completely fascinated.

'I congratulate you, Miss O'Grady,' he began, 'it's been my experience that most people in this country, or indeed in England, know very little about the Congo Free State and the good work being carried out there for its African peoples. Since you have read about it, however, you will know that King Leopold has opened up the territories at the heart of Africa to the world. He has liberated its peoples, sent in his troops to quell the Arab slave traders who had plagued them for centuries, sent his country's Catholic missionaries to educate and civilise, as well as allowing in other Christian missionaries.

'More than all of this, however, he has invested his own personal fortune in developing the Congo Free State. He has helped its people take their place in the world's economy, first by helping them trade in ivory, now in assisting them to become leaders in the world's rubber market. The African had no previous knowledge of the value of the wild rubber vines, seeing them simply as snake vines, wrapping themselves around the giant jungle trees covering their land. And such vines as they are!'

He spread his hands and looked around for something to equal or compare to their enormous size. Finding nothing, he went on.

'They climb as high as one hundred feet in search of the African sun, a burning demon in a sky so blue you cannot look at it without a reeling in the head. Once the rubber vine finds the sun it spreads out, winding its way for hundreds of feet across the topmost limbs of more and more trees.' He tapped the table with two fingers to make his point. 'The great miracle of this plant is that it produces a thick, milky sap called rubber. The result of that miracle is that the Congo Free State has become the most profitable colony in Africa.'

'How do you bear the African sun? That heat?'

'It's like a wall at first, an unseen wall pushing against you, making it difficult to breathe. But you learn to deal with it, as with all things African.' He paused. 'Africa is a miraculous place.'

'And your work is on a plantation of these rubber vines?'

'Yes. Though we are always in search of new growth, more rubber to harvest. I manage a station outpost for a company to which the king has given concession rights for the harvesting of rubber. It's hard work but the people are willing.'

'The Belgian king seems to have a great interest in Africa?'

'The *État Indépendant du Congo* is his passion. He has made it what it is through wholehearted investment and good-heartedness. You're not aware of this?'

I tried to remember what I'd read. Nothing came to mind and I wished I'd paid more attention.

'I am,' I said, 'now that you've so eloquently explained. How long have you been there?'

'Almost five years.'

'Will you stay there? Or will you come back to Ireland?'

'I never plan my life, Miss O'Grady.' He smiled. 'I've learned the African way of trusting that life itself will show a way. The Congo is one of the world's great rivers, as you no doubt know . . .' I didn't know, but would make it my business to look it up '. . . and its basin one of the places on this earth where nature truly *does* conspire against man. It's steaming, dark and poisonous. It is also rich and magnificent. I am excited by it, and by the work I do there, and convinced of the good the king is doing for Africa. I'm privileged to be a part of it . . .' he paused '. . . for now. I may have other needs in a few years.' He sat back with a small, apologetic smile. 'I'm sorry, all this talk about myself. It's unpardonable that a man my age should bore a young woman of *yours*.'

'I'm interested,' I said. That smile made him look younger. The sun, catching his face at an angle, helped make him look younger still, even attractive in a way. 'I've met few people with lives so interesting as yours. Does your wife live with you in Africa?'

'I am alone in life *because* of Africa,' he said. 'I chose to go there rather than marry.'

'You chose Africa?'

'I chose Africa,' he echoed.

If he felt regret it didn't show. If relief was what he felt that didn't show either. He was a boy in man's clothing, an adventurer. He would probably never marry.

'Your complexion is not very bronzed-looking,' I said, and he laughed loudly enough to turn the heads of several people in the saloon.

'You want to know how long I've been out of Africa, Miss O'Grady,' he raised a beckoning hand to the waiter, standing inside the door in uncomfortably buttoned-up blue serge, 'and you'd probably like to know, too, what I was doing in the West of Ireland and now on this train to Dublin?'

'We can talk of other things, if you'd prefer,' I said, 'or not at all, as the case may be.' I didn't like to be treated like a child, or laughed at. I didn't like the vanity of his notion that I was fascinated by his comings and goings either.

'I've offended you. My apologies.' He didn't look sorry.

'I'll have tea, please,' I said to the waiting boy, 'and my companion, I think, will have coffee.' I raised an eyebrow at Thomas Cooper who nodded, rubbing two fingers across his moustache in that way he had. He'd stopped smiling.

The boy went away and we sat in silence, me looking out of the window and thinking how green and pleasant the countryside was but how terrifyingly far from the sea. The Atlantic horizon, where the mood changed every day, was my own favourite view at home.

Thomas Cooper cleared his throat. 'To answer your question, Miss O'Grady, I've been out of Africa since the month of January, and have been three weeks visiting in the West with my friends the Redmonds.'

'I didn't ask how long you'd been out of Africa, Mr Cooper,' I reminded him, 'but five months does seem a long time to be away from a job and country you care so much about.'

'I hadn't intended staying away so long.' He stared out of the window, his face a blank. 'Business affairs have kept me busy.' He turned to me. 'If it's not an intrusion, Miss O'Grady, was I right in supposing the priest to say that your father has recently died?'

'At the end of March.'

'I'm sorry, I wouldn't have intruded myself on your grieving had I known.'

'I'm glad you rescued me from the priest,' I said.

'I'm glad I rescued us both from the priest,' he replied, so seriously that I laughed.

'Father Duggan is a rigid and misguided man of God,' I said, 'he's not actually the devil.'

'I dislike men of God, or women of God, for that matter, who abuse their calling by dictating how others should live their lives.'

This defence of my position made me look at him anew. He wasn't insensitive, and was certainly kind. I'd always been too hasty in my judgments.

'Father Duggan refused to bury my father,' I said, though God knows why. It seemed relevant at the time.

'Why was that?'

'Because my father took his own life and died in a state of mortal sin. He couldn't therefore be buried on consecrated ground.'

Thomas Cooper looked thoughtful. 'Whereas a man who commits murder or a thief *can* be buried in God's holy ground?'

I hadn't thought of this and was confused. 'Yes,' I said after a minute, 'I suppose that's the case. If they repent.'

'That must be a great relief to the world's thieves and murderers,' said Thomas Cooper dryly. 'Why did your father end his life?'

'Because of melancholy and drink,' I said, 'and because the life he knew had changed too much.'

'It must be hard for you, and for your family?'

'I miss him. We all do. But I'm to be married and am meeting my fiancé in Dublin. There is light at the end of every tunnel.'

I blurted out all of this as much to reassure myself as to present him with an image of me as a young woman with a future to look forward to.

We were silent for a long time after that.

I was tired and the train, beating a rhythmic 'going to Dublin, going to Dublin' on its tracks, lulled me asleep. I woke when we stopped at Mullingar, where the station clock said it was just after ten o'clock. Unless we were derailed or had some disaster befall us, we would be in Dublin at the scheduled time of noon.

It wasn't until I was fully awake that I remembered Thomas Cooper. Embarrassed, I looked across at him to find him watching me.

'Are you rested?' he said.

'I am, thank you.' I sat up, straightening my back and then my hat, which had fallen forward. I intended buying myself a new one in Dublin. A dress, too, and shoes. A shawl. Some novels. I would buy Theo a handmade shirt.

'I hope you didn't stay in the saloon car because of me,' I said, aware Thomas Cooper was still watching me.

'Your company, even while asleep, is infinitely preferable to that of the righteous Father Duggan.' He smiled his half-smile. He really was a serious man.

'Thank you.' I smiled back at him. 'Though I'm sure the company of almost anyone on the train would be easier than that of Father Duggan.'

'You do yourself an injustice, Miss O'Grady. I find you interesting company and wouldn't have chosen to travel with anyone else on this train.' He stared directly into my eyes. 'You're not so naive, surely, as to imagine it an accident I found my way to your carriage in Sligo station?'

I was embarrased. I was also startled. 'Your binoculars . . .' I began.

He waved a dismissive hand. 'Binoculars are easily replaced, whereas the opportunity to get to know a young woman such as yourself is rare.' He leaned forward. I was glad of the table between us. 'You're a singular young woman, Miss O'Grady, I'm privileged to enjoy your company.'

The whistle was blowing outside, doors banging shut. The platform had emptied to a few people waving to those who'd got on to the train.

'We're leaving the station,' I let out a relieved breath as the saloon door opened, 'and we're both going to have the privilege of more company.'

Two men in striped trousers and stand-up shirt collars settled beside us. They were old, in their seventies I'd have said, and full of talk.

'Good day to ye,' the man opposite me said, 'it's a warm enough day for travelling.'

'It is,' I agreed eagerly, encouraging him.

I needn't have bothered. He and his companion started up about the state of the country and world and the disgraceful cost of rail fares. When they asked Thomas Cooper for his views he said he'd been out of Ireland too long to have any.

'A lack of information never stopped anyone in this country having an opinion,' said the older of the two. I sat back and closed my eyes again and let them at it. This time the train rattled out 'going to Theo, going to Theo, going to Theo', which made the journey pass far more quickly.

I waited until we were drawing into the Broadstone in Dublin before making my way, with Thomas Cooper, back to the carriage for my bags. Father Duggan was still bundled into his coat but took his nose out of his breviary when we came in.

'I trust your journey was a pleasant one, Miss O'Grady?' He ignored my companion.

'Indeed it was, Father. I hope yours was just as pleasant?'

'I passed the time in prayer.'

The door was pulled open by an attendant and the three of us climbed down silently with our bags to the platform. The priest hovered as I said goodbye to Thomas Cooper.

'My brother Hugh will be here to meet me at any minute,' I lied loudly for Father Duggan's benefit.

'There's no point my offering you a lift to your lodgings then.' Thomas Cooper was wearing the top hat again and looked every inch the city man.

'No. Thank you. Hugh will look after everything,' I said. He took my hand and held it lightly.

'I've enjoyed meeting you,' he said. 'When we meet again I hope we won't be strangers to one another.'

'I'll remember you as the man from Africa.' I took back my hand and lifted it to summon a porter.

'I'm staying in the Imperial Hotel in Sackville Street,'

he said. 'If you're in the vicinity we might take tea some afternoon?'

'Perhaps.' I was short. Father Duggan, also looking for a porter, was too close for comfort.

'I won't delay you then.' Thomas Cooper raised his hat. I lost sight of him in the crowd almost immediately.

A porter came and took me and my bags to a carriage. I could feel Father Duggan's eyes on my back, following me until I, too, was swallowed by the crowd.

11

Dublin glowered. I missed home and the countryside as soon as I stepped out of the station and into its streets. Even the morsels of sky visible between the high buildings were a duller blue than the western skies. The air was duller, too, as well as heavier and a lot less sweet-smelling.

The carman was too friendly.

'You arrived on the Sligo train?' he said.

He had a red, whiskery face and the round, watery eyes of a frog. The hair coming down under his cap could have done with a wash. When I agreed I'd come from Sligo this wasn't information enough for him.

'You travelled alone?' he said and I nodded. 'Don't know what kind of parents you have.' He threw my bags into the carriage and gave me his hand. He wasn't young, about sixty I'd have said. 'It's not right. If you were my child I'd not let you cross the country on your own.' I climbed into the car. 'This city's a dangerous place. There's all types in it these days. Still,' he beamed and grew philosophical, 'you're a fine, big girl and you're a country girl to boot. You're probably well enough able to look out for yourself.' He leaned through the door as I sat down. 'Don't trust anyone. That's the only bit of advice I'll give you but it's worth its weight in gold. Don't trust anyone.'

He proved trustworthy enough himself.

Hugh lived, with Theo, in lodgings in Arnott Street. I'd visited him there with my mother a year before. The house was small, made of red brick and owned by a widow-woman called Sheridan who made the most money she could from it. The 'rooms' she rented to Hugh and Theo were in fact one room divided down the middle; she'd even managed to divide the window in two.

Not that either Hugh or Theo was missing great views: the window looked on to a mean back yard where there was a privy and where the widow did washing in a tub. Arnott Street was a good distance from their studies at the King's Inns but the rent suited Hugh. Arthur Howard would have paid for more salubrious accommodation for his son but Theo preferred to be with Hugh.

My plan was to ask Theo and Hugh, if they were at home, to come to Bewley's Café with me. If they weren't then I would ask the widow to allow me to leave my bag in her parlour while I found myself a place to stay. I might even stay in a hotel, if there was one near by.

'I'll wait here until you're safely inside the door.' The carman looked doubtfully at number 55 Arnott Street as I paid him.

'There's no need,' I said.

'I wouldn't feel easy with myself if I didn't,' he said.

The widow's house was a lot less genteel than it had been the year before. The curtains needed washing. The front door needed painting. But the same could be said of the curtains and doors at Kilraven so I could hardly be judgemental. The door knocker was a cast-iron hand holding a ball. There was no reply the first time I used it.

'Give her a good bang,' the carman shouted, 'you'd want to have you ear against the door to hear that timid bit of a knock.'

To stop him shouting I knocked again, three times, and so hard that a shower of peeling paint fell from the door to my feet. The door to number 53 opened.

'You'll be knocking a long time before that door opens.' The fat woman at number 53 had a grey cat in her arms. 'There's no one at home.'

'When will Mrs Sheridan be back?' I asked politely. The woman looked me up and down.

'You're the sister of one of them, aren't you? You've got the dark lad's eyes. I recall you being here before, with your mother.' She looked at the bag at my feet. This must be the neighbour Hugh said was so nosy she counted the coat buttons on passers by. 'You've travelled from the West, looks like,' she said. 'It's unfortunate your brother didn't tell you – but that's men for you. You can't trust them, even the best of them.'

'Tell me what?' I said.

'I'll answer your first question.' She leaned against the side of the door. 'Mollie Sheridan won't be back for a week or more.' She stroked the cat. It moved its tail, slowly. 'She's on her honeymoon.'

'She married again?' I said.

'She married again,' the fat neighbour agreed. 'It's amazing the appeal a woman with a house of her own has for a certain kind of man. When the lads didn't come back she thought it better to make a more permanent arrangement for herself.'

'When they didn't come back . . . ?'

'That brings us to your second question.' She squinted behind me at the carman, sniffed loudly and went on. 'They didn't come back after the Christmas, neither of the two of them. Gave her notice and all of that but the result was the same in the end of the day. She'd an empty house and no heart for finding strangers to replace the lads. They were five years coming and going to her and she'd got used to them. So she married her fancy man and had done with it.'

'Where did they go?' I said.

'They went to Bray. Mollie Sheridan has a friend with a lodging house there.'

'I meant my brother and his friend. Where are they staying now?'

'How would I know where they are?' The woman was irritable. The cat squirmed and she tightened her grip. 'What's certain is that they've given up their studies.'

'How do you know that . . .' I began but was interrupted by the carman.

'There's one of you on every street corner,' he said rudely to the woman. He'd climbed down from his seat and was standing beside me. 'You're the kind's mindful of everybody's business but your own. Tell the girl where her brother's gone and don't be wasting her time.'

'Are you calling me a scandal-monger? Who're you? Only a carman doesn't know his place and could do with a wash.' The woman loosened her grip on the cat. It jumped free and was gone. 'My husband's in the DMT and he'll have you in the courts for slander . . .'

'Now there's a remarkable coincidence.' The carman, cutting her short, drew himself up and rubbed a red, veiny hand across his whiskers. 'I've a son a member of the Dublin Metropolitan too. Could be I'll have to ask him to help in an enquiry into the whereabouts of two missing young men if this girl can't find them. That'll mean questioning next-door neighbours . . .'

'I'm a busy person.' The woman moved back into her hallway. 'My time is valuable . . .'

The carman put his boot in the doorway. 'You know where they're gone and, by Christ, you'll not get a penny out of this girl here for what you know.' He folded his arms. 'Because that's what you're after, I know your kind. You're like the newspapers – making money out of everyone's misery. Do your Christian duty and tell the girl or I'll have my lad in the police over here to discuss an obstruction case with you. It won't go well with your husband, if you have one at all . . .'

'I'd like to know what business it is of yours . . .'

'Just tell the girl what you know about her brother,' he said, 'or it'll be the police you'll be talking to.'

The woman gave the carman a venomous glare before turning an equally poisonous look my way.

'I'm not surprised your brother didn't tell you,' she said, 'though he was brazen enough about the life he was living, and his friend too. You'll find out all you need to know about your brother if you take yourself to the Queen's Theatre tonight. Keep your eyes peeled and you're sure to see him.' She turned back to the carman. 'More than that I can't tell you, no matter if you were to bring the entire Metropolitan Police Force down on top of me.'

'That'll do to be going on with.' The carman picked up my bags and threw them back in the carriage. He opened the door. 'You'd best get back in,' he said to me.

'My time's worth something,' the fat woman called, 'and so's the information I gave you. Ye'd be searching the town but for me.'

'We'll be searching the town anyway.' The carman climbed up to his seat.

'Where are we going?' I called, but he put a thick finger to his lips.

'We won't burden this poor woman with any more information,' he indicated that I should close the door, 'and an even worse thing to take any more of her time.' He mopped his face with a large brown handkerchief, put it back in his pocket and lifted the reins.

We were in the maelstrom of the city proper in no time, sights I could only barely have imagined passing the window. I trusted the carman by now so let him get on with the driving while I tried to work out what had happened to

Theo and Hugh, why they'd moved without telling anyone. No immediate answers came to mind so I gave in to the distractions outside.

There were drunken men and bargaining women with stalls of fruit by the road, and shop boys roaring the praise of barrels full of pigs' cheeks. A street singer singing in a high, whining voice about O'Donovan Rossa was almost drowned by the noise of the tram gongs, like a background drum beat there all the time.

When we slowed down to avoid running over a crowd of ragged, fighting children I called to the carman, 'Where are we? Where are we going?'

'We're in Camden Street,' he said, 'and I'm taking you back to the Broadstone. There's a train leaves at four o'clock that you might be lucky enough to get.'

I opened the door, threw out my bag and jumped down after it, holding on to the door to stop myself from falling over my skirts as I hit the ground.

'You'll do nothing of the kind! You can leave me here,' I shouted, as much in anger as to make myself heard. 'I'll find myself a boarding house.'

'Jesus, Mary and St Joseph!' The carman reined in the horse and mopped his face again, looking down from his seat. 'Haven't you given me enough trouble already? You're the kind won't listen to anyone. Your unfortunate parents . . .' he mopped furiously '. . . couldn't keep you at home, I suppose.' He stopped mopping and gestured with the whip. 'Get back inside and I'll take you to a respectable boarding house. I can do no more for you after that.'

The street children swarmed and pulled at my skirts as I climbed back in. They were thin and rickety and their hot hands grabbed the door as I tried to shut it.

'Get out of it!' the carman roared and raised his whip. 'Or as God is my judge I'll get down and use this whip across

124

yer backs.' He cracked the whip in the air, twice, and they disappeared.

He brought me to a three-sided square with a small green park in the middle. There were railings about the houses and another lot of children fighting in the street but it was cleaner and not so smelly as the majority of the streets we'd passed through. I got out when we stopped in front of a house with shining brasses on a blue door.

'Where are we?' I said.

'You're in Queen's Square, off Great Brunswick Street, not far from the Queen's Theatre.' He began mopping his face again. 'By Jesus but it's hot!' he sighed, then became businesslike. 'I'm known to the woman of the house here. Known to her for years. She's a Mrs Rita Burke and gives board to the theatrical kind of person. You'll be set up if she's a room and bed free for you.'

He rapped once with the shining knocker. We waited. He didn't knock again. After a minute the door opened and the carman took off his hat and bowed.

'You're looking well, Rita,' he said, 'haven't seen you looking so well in a long time.'

'You haven't seen me in a long time, Ambrose.' Mrs Rita Burke had a piping girlish voice. 'You look well enough yourself.'

She was tall. Her black dress had collar tips which came up under her ears. Her peppery grey hair was scraped tightly back, her eyebrows were painted in red pencil and her eyes hard to see behind small, round spectacles.

'I've a room free if you're looking for one,' she said to me.

I gave the carman one-and-a-half times what he asked for and we shook hands. 'Keep an eye out behind you as you go,' he said. I was sorry, in a way, to see him leave. He'd become familiar in an uncertain situation.

Mrs Rita Burke was fond of the colour yellow. My room

had a black iron bedstead and a washstand but the cretonne curtains were yellow and so were the papered walls, the cushions in a cane chair, the shaded gas-lamp. A large crucifix over the bed was black.

I sat on the yellow bed and looked out at the grassy patch in the centre of the square. I took off my hat and shook my hair free. I splashed cold water on to my face at the wash stand. This last calmed my racing thoughts a little.

I checked the time on my father's watch and went in search of Mrs Burke. I found her in her kitchen, standing by a hot range stirring a boiling mixture smelling of soap. The walls were covered in music hall and theatre posters. The one nearest Mrs Burke showed Miss Marie Lloyd hitching up a yellow dress to show black stockings.

'I suppose you're hungry?' Mrs Burke said.

'A cup of tea would be nice.' I studied the posters. 'Do you know where I can find the Queen's Theatre?'

'I do.'

'Is there a performance there this evening?'

'There is.' She gestured to a cane chair by the table and I sat down. A dresser against the wall was filled with porcelain vases and a flowered tea-set.

'What time should I be there?' I said. When she didn't answer immediately I didn't press her. Something told me she wasn't the kind of woman you took liberties with. She stopped stirring and put tea and a plate of arrowroot biscuits in front of me. She watched me eat and drink for a minute.

'You're hungry.' She removed the plate and what was left of the arrowroots and put a plate of cold corned beef and cabbage in its place. She went back to her stirring while I ate that too.

'Seven o'clock is time enough to be at the Queen's,' she answered my question at last. 'It's a ten-minute walk from here. It's *The Countess Cathleen* tonight.'

'So I've been told,' I lied. I didn't want her asking me questions.

For my night at the theatre I wore a white linen dress with lace insertions that Ellie had helped me make the summer before. I put my mother's combs in my hair and Bella Mulligan's earrings in my ears.

'You've no one to walk with you?' Mrs Burke frowned when I came downstairs.

'I'm to meet someone at the theatre,' I said. She raised disbelieving eyebrows.

The Queen's Theatre was very big and very grand, though it didn't look it from the outside. The shiny grandeur began when you stepped inside. The foyer was all gilded, with chandeliers and mirrors and a wine-coloured carpet underfoot. The walls were covered in jewel-coloured plasterwork.

I was the only one not wearing silk or satin and looked ridiculous in my white linen. Like a postulant, or a girl on her confirmation day. The men wore velvet-collared evening dress and the women, when they took off their cloaks, had bare shoulders. A lot of them had pearls in their hair. Everyone spoke at the top of their voice and laughed as if it was their last chance on earth to enjoy a joke.

I'd never been to the theatre before so did as the person in front of me did and bought a ticket for the front row of the balcony. I stood on the stairs then, with my eyes peeled, as the woman in Arnott Street had advised. If Theo were to appear in the foyer, or Hugh or Bella, there would be no chance of my not noticing. But when the bells for the beginning of the performance stopped ringing, and I was the last person being ushered by an impatient fellow in braid and buttons into the auditorium, I was still alone.

I took my seat as the music grew louder, the audience came to its feet, the curtain rose and the stage filled with players. They were a hungry-looking lot and, when they spoke, it was in very flowery language. The Countess Cathleen herself was dressed in radiant green with gold and had a burning red plait of hair hanging over her shoulder. She was easily recognisable as Bella Mulligan.

Her part was that of a woman foolish enough to believe that by selling her soul to a pair of devils she could save the poor and starving. She was convincing, even if the story wasn't. The poor would not be saved and nor, so far as I could see, would the Countess herself. The devils, one of them a man and one a woman, had been declaiming for several minutes when I saw Theo.

He was in a box to the side of the stage decorated with leering cherubs. Hugh was in the box, too, in evening dress and looking every inch the man about town.

Theo was leaning forward, his face eager. His moustache had grown and drooped at the sides in a way that made him look quite the sophisticate. I stared hard at the box, first at Theo then at Hugh. But the principle that a fixed stare will make itself felt didn't work and the interval arrived without either one of them so much as glancing in my direction.

When the curtain fell and the applause died I stood and waved and called to them. This was a waste of time, as well as an annoyance to those around me. Theo and Hugh sat on, smoking cigarettes and chatting. Short of appearing on the stage myself, I didn't see how I was going to attract their attention. I would have to make my way to the box. If I didn't, I might lose them in the crowd at the end of the performance.

It wasn't difficult. Following signs, I came to a set of stone steps leading to a corridor along the back of the boxes. I knocked, called out their names, 'Hugh! Theo!' and opened the door to the box nearest the stage.

My entrance had as dramatic an effect as anything on the

stage. Theo turned with a cigarette halfway to his mouth and stayed like that, staring in disbelief. Hugh jumped up, knocked over his chair and was by my side in a flash.

'God in heaven, Nessa, what's wrong?' He had his hands on my shoulders and was looking at me as if he expected me to grow a second head. 'What are you doing here? What's happened to Mama?'

'Mama's well, Hugh, and nothing's wrong. I've come visiting, that's all.' As the only one of the three of us who knew what was going on I felt quite cool, even superior. This would not last. 'I've had a terrible job finding the pair of you,' I added.

Hugh was shaking his head as if to waken himself. 'You're sure everything's all right? You came on your own?'

'If I'd known I'd be so unwelcome, I'd have stayed at home.' I looked at Theo, still sitting and staring in his seat. Hugh gave him a quick look too.

'We can't talk here,' he took my arm, 'the performance is due to start again and we'd be a distraction . . .'

'I looked for you in the foyer,' I said.

'We came early with Bella . . .' Hugh paused. 'We can talk more easily outside.' Theo didn't stand even as we left. I knew then that I should have listened to Ellie about the advisability of surprise visits.

'Ellie and Manus are to be married,' I said as we stood on the other side of the door. Some news was obviously expected of me and it might as well be good.

Hugh gave a low whoop and lifted me by the waist from the ground. 'I'd a feeling she might get him in time. Sound woman, Ellie Hope.' He put me back on my feet. 'How's Mama taking it?'

'She's coming round. She knows she'll have to, though I suppose she'll always wish he'd married someone with money.'

'When did you arrive in the city?' Hugh ran a hand through his hair, smiling and devising a plan in his head to deal with me. I knew him.

'This afternoon. On the train. You've left your lodgings.' I looked him in the eye, very firmly.

'I have,' he agreed.

'Theo's left too.'

'He has,' Hugh was even more agreeable, 'but now's not the time to discuss all of that. There's the rest of the play to see . . .'

'I'm not the child you think I am, Hugh.'

'You are,' he sighed, 'you're every bit the child I think you are. But let's go back inside the box. I must see the end of the play.' He paused, then amended, '*We* must see the end of the play.'

The curtain was rising as Hugh put a chair between himself and Theo for me to sit on.

'You should have sent word you were coming,' Theo, wits gathered, whispered to me as I sat. 'I could have met you at the station.'

We watched the rest of the play in silence. Up close, the cherubs around the box were a lot less leering, and a great deal less cherubic.

The play had lost what appeal it had held for me. I found the story even more improbable, the characters more ridiculous, the words overly extravagant and obscure. I was alone in my view. When it ended the audience rose to its feet and applauded and called the players back to the stage and applauded again. Bella in particular was clapped and in return graciously blew kisses and bowed. Theo was so enthusiastic he looked in danger of both blistering his hands and falling out of the box.

'I thought it improbable,' I said, clapping more moderately, 'though Bella was fine.'

'Keep your voice down,' Theo hissed, 'you've been privileged to see what is destined to become one of the classics of Irish theatre.' His moustache trembled.

'May God help the Irish theatre then,' I said.

Hugh came between us, putting his cloak about my shoulders and telling us we should be going. The cloak, old and familiar, was comforting to be wrapped in.

'I'll go backstage and hurry Bella along.' He put a silver-topped cane under his arm and a top hat on his head. 'You two wait for us at the front door. It'll give you a chance to talk together. There's a dining room booked for the night.'

Theo preferred to wait in the laneway by the stage door. It was where everyone came out, he said, and we would be more certain of seeing Hugh and Bella immediately they appeared.

We had plenty of company as we stood in the spluttering gaslight. Most of those around us in the narrow laneway were beery menservants, clumsily holding flowers and gifts and invitations for the actresses. Theo said the same lot were to be found every night at stage doors across the city, procuring for their employers.

'Why did you leave your room in Arnott Street?' I said.

'It didn't suit me any longer.' Theo was smoking a cigarette and leaning against the wall as he kept an eye on the stage door. His top hat was set at a rakish angle which was new to him; I thought he looked very fine.

'Did the room change or did you?' I said, knowing the answer. Theo had changed. In the long minute it took him to answer I wished I hadn't asked the question at all. It was the sort of thing a mother or sister or old friend would ask. A lover would know already.

'It was a dark room,' Theo said at last, 'I didn't like it.'

'It took you long enough to notice the darkness.'

'I'm a man of twenty-five years, Nessa.' Theo sounded

impatient. He lit another cigarette and pulled deeply on it. His eyes never once left the stage door. 'I'm the same age as Hugh. You don't treat him like a boy. No one does.'

Maybe not. But Hugh had been grown up all his life and Theo, all *his* life, had been in need of being cared for.

'I was worried,' I said, 'when I couldn't find you. I wanted to surprise you.'

'You've surprised me all right.'

'You've given up the law, haven't you?'

'I have. I am devoting my time to becoming a playwright.'

'I'd no idea you were so fond of words,' I said. When he didn't answer I continued, 'Has Hugh given up the law too?'

'No. Just the room in Arnott Street. He'll be starting his exams in two days.'

We stood in silence after that, enclosed in our separately miserable worlds, the trust and loyalty and intimacy of years gone in minutes. Or maybe it had been going for years and I hadn't noticed. Without thinking I touched an earring with a finger, hoping it would catch the flickering light. But it was far, far too late for me to play the coquette with Theo Howard.

The players who'd acted as starving people came out first and there was a scramble as bouquets were presented and arms offered.

'I've changed, Nessa,' Theo said, and the words were between us at last.

'I can see that,' I said. The years of waiting were over and, in the oddest of ways, I felt relief. There would be a resolution at last. Even so, I felt dizzy, as if my legs were about to stop supporting me.

'I didn't wish for it to happen.' Theo's eyes wouldn't meet mine. 'You were all I knew, once, and all I wanted for a long time. But the truth of it is that I've met a woman who is everything to me. I don't mind telling you, Nessa,' but his expression had become strained and he clearly did mind, 'that

I'm bewitched. It might have happened to either of us, being apart all the time as we were.' He took a deep breath. 'I hope you'll understand, in time if not tonight.'

He dropped the cigarette and it rolled, sparks flying, then died in the drain. I kept looking at him. It was all I could do. He touched my hair and kissed me on the forehead. His breath smelled of cigarette smoke.

'What we had between us was a childish thing.' He stood very straight, like an actor on a stage delivering a speech. 'You'll see that in time, too. I hope we will always be friends, Nessa, because I care for and love you as a friend, a sister. I don't feel passion for you, and I'm sorry about that. The love between a grown man and woman is something altogether different, as you will some day learn . . .' He stopped and put an arm about my shoulders. I wanted to tell him not to say anything more but I didn't and he did, shaking his head as he reflected on the great passion I was as yet denied. 'It brings with it an agony of pain but a glorious uplifting too. You will wonder how you lived before it.'

'I can see you've joined the ranks of the country's poets. I wonder you're able to talk to me at all, given you're in such an uplifted state,' I said pointedly.

Theo gave me time to consider my lack of grace as he lit another cigarette. Even in the gaslight I could see him flushing slightly.

'I'll put it in plainer language then, if you prefer.' He spoke round the cigarette in his mouth. 'Celestine is, and will always be, the only woman I want.'

'Does this Celestine know she's the woman you want?' I said, the words making a bitter taste in my mouth. 'Does she want you?'

'Those are things between Celestine and me.' He shook his head. 'I'm sorry, Nessa, to have hurt you. I'm sorry to have to say, too, that I don't feel it would be right to discuss her with you any further.' He paused. 'Hugh knows how things are.'

'Hugh knows?' I repeated. I wanted to walk away.

'He does,' Theo said.

Hugh knowing clearly made everything all right, so far as Theo was concerned. Not quite everything had changed then.

12

Bella, when she appeared, was the Bella of old, though a bit tired-looking after her time on stage. She hugged me and admired the earrings, my hair, myself. She was the first person to ask if I'd a place to stay and clapped her hands and laughed when I told her where I'd got myself a bed.

'You found Rita Burke's place! How clever you are, Nessa. You'll be safe staying with Rita, she's an upright woman these days.' She laughed, shaking her head. 'Just keep on her right side.'

Hugh took her arm and mine, and hurried the three of us to a waiting carriage. The driver, caught in the urgency of the night, drove quickly to the Shelbourne Hotel and a dining room set aside for those involved with the play. All of this happened with much talk and laughter.

None of it hid the fact that Theo had remained behind to escort his new love.

'Tell me about Theo's Celestine?' I said to Bella in the carriage, but she shook her head.

'Tomorrow,' she said gaily. 'Tonight we're going to celebrate *The Countess Cathleen* and your visit to Dublin.' She had moonstones in her ears and a free-flowing silk cloak with poppies all over it. She looked lovely.

'Why does everyone treat me like a child?' I said. 'Please tell me her full name at least?' Hugh tapped the floor with his cane and looked out of the window.

'It won't do you any good, knowing her name,' Bella said,

'but she's called Celestine Lowry.' She folded a lock of hair behind my ear. 'And now you really must forget about her until tomorrow. We'll talk then.'

Celestine Lowry. It was a musical name, and exotic. Nothing as flat and ordinary as Nessa O'Grady about it. I was sorry I'd asked.

In the hotel dining room I was put sitting at a long table and given champagne to toast the play, the players and the rest of the run. It wasn't until I stood, raising my glass along with everyone else, that I noticed a woman staring at me. She was down the table from me, at the opposite side, and was wearing a yellow dress and a long golden feather in black, black hair which gave her away as the woman who'd played one of the devils on stage. Theo was nowhere to be seen but I knew without a doubt that this was Celestine Lowry.

She was older than she'd looked on the stage by seven or eight years. Her staring eyes, which had heavy kohl lines drawn around them, were the dark green of a stinging nettle. A pearl choker disguised a neck past its prime. But she was a handsome woman, I couldn't deny her that.

We drank the toast. Flowery speeches were made about the play, the players, the playwright, the director, the future. My concentration wasn't good and I took in very little of any of it. I took a second glass of champagne and, when we sat down, was poured a glass of red wine.

Celestine Lowry used her hands a lot as she spoke to her table companions. She had an amber ring on her middle finger and a ruby on her little finger. Her eyes kept flickering in my direction. There was an empty place beside her.

When Theo appeared she pretended not to notice him. She wasn't as good an actress as Bella and her childish game was easy to see through. Theo said her name and put a hand on her shoulder and she turned then, in mock surprise.

'Theo! What a bold boy you are!' She had a lovely voice,

dark and musical. 'I waited for you in my dressing room. You didn't come.'

Theo looked confused, then pleased. 'But I did. I went to your room. You'd left . . .'

'We must have missed one another.' She shrugged. 'How very tiresome. But you're here now and I've kept a place for you, so sit beside me. Please.'

My question to Theo was answered too.

Celestine Lowry might not, until now, have wanted him. My arrival had lent him desirability.

'Eat.' Bella, sitting on my right, tapped my arm. 'Food and drink are what you need.'

She was picking half-heartedly at her own food. Plates of lobster, in a buttery sauce smelling strongly of whiskey, had been put in front of us and her face, looking down, paled a little.

Celestine Lowry's dark voice carried down the table. 'Playing the devil has put me in the mood for anything, my dears. For anything and everything that life has to offer.'

The white fish meat in its red shell and whiskey sauce seemed all at once very unappealing. I had, in any event, eaten Rita Burke's corned beef and cabbage. It had made me thirsty so I had another glass of wine.

'We could leave, if you like,' Bella said abruptly.

'You're the Countess Cathleen,' I said, 'you can't leave your own party.'

'I'm sleepy,' Bella said, yawning to prove it. She didn't need to. Her pale face and tired eyes weren't an act. She sighed and smiled and put her hand over mine as I lifted the wine glass again. 'Hugh won't stay if I leave, Nessa, but he won't allow you to stay here on your own either. Why don't we end the night now? We could all do with some rest, and after all,' her smile was coaxing, 'the best is over. The play was the thing . . .'

'I'm not a child, Bella,' I reminded her again, 'to be coaxed home to bed because of a disappointment.' I finished the glass of wine. When I put it down Bella seemed less clear and further away than she'd been when I lifted it. The room had become a much friendlier place too.

It being a night for speeches, I decided to make one myself.

'I've accepted the situation with regard to Theo and myself,' I said grandly to Bella, pushing back my chair and standing. I tinkled my spoon against a glass for silence, the way earlier speakers had done. Then I tinkled it again. When enough faces had turned my way I began.

'I would like to propose a toast to the happiness of two of the company here tonight. I have known Mr Theobald Howard all my life. He is handsome and amusing and a fine horseman. Of Miss Celestine Lowry I know only that she is talented and beautiful and certainly of an age to be married. I'm sure their liaison will be a happy one. I wish them well.' I lifted my glass. 'I think we should all wish them well.' Nobody moved. I raised my glass to Theo, sitting with his head in his hands.

'To your health and happiness, Theo.' I drank and said, 'Will you not drink with me?' When he didn't I took another long gulp. Celestine Lowry watched me with a wide smile. I smiled back at her. Hugh's voice spoke in my ear.

'You've said enough, Nessa. It's time we were going.' He put one hand around my waist and with the other tried to take the wine glass from me. I held on, spraying red wine over the white tablecloth and yellow flower arrangements. Hugh abandoned his efforts.

'I'm coming to the end of what I have to say.' I sipped at what was left of the wine, mercifully unaware of the heart ache I would feel the next day, and the day after that, and after that again.

'I've believed, all my life, that Theo Howard and I would one day marry. That will not happen now. This woman . . .' I inclined my head Celestine's way '. . . will have his children, not I.' A thought came to me. I stared at Celestine Lowry in consternation. Disastrously, I put the thought into words. 'I hope she is not too old because Theo would like children . . .'

Celestine acted then. In one fluid movement she stood, walked down the table and threw the contents of her wine glass in my face. I can't say I blamed her.

'Since you're so fond of the drink you can have mine as well,' she said 'or maybe, like your father, you can't have enough of it.'

There were titters, a few screams and a scramble as chairs were pushed back, out of the way of anything else which might be thrown.

They were in no danger from me, Hugh saw to that. He caught and pinned my arms by my side before turning and holding me hard against him.

'Enough, Nessa,' his voice in my ear was hard, 'it's over. We're leaving, now. You will walk with me to the door and there will not be another word out of you. When I release you, you will look neither to the right nor the left. Keep your head up and look only at the door. Do as I say, Nessa, and do it now.'

He let my arms go. He turned me so that I was facing the door. He put an arm about me and walked me in its direction. I kept my head high. Wine dripped from my face and hair. Wine churned in my stomach too.

'Go back to where you came from and stay there!' Celestine's voice followed us. 'You're not fit for civilised company and you're certainly not fit to marry a man like Theobald Howard. Or any other man, for that matter . . .'

Voices hushed her. I heard Theo's amongst them. But I

did as Hugh said and kept my head high and didn't turn to look back.

Celestine Lowry wouldn't be silenced. My remark about her age had clearly cut to the quick. 'If you were half-civilised you would apologise,' she called, 'take back your filthy insult. Theo is lucky to have escaped you.'

We were through the door then, walking along a corridor towards a wide, bright staircase.

I've no memory of Bella and Hugh taking me in a carriage back to Mrs Burke's boarding house in Queen's Square. No memory at all.

My next conscious thought was fourteen hours later. At two o'clock the next day my landlady's whisper, a sound like a wind whistling round a corner, woke me. I didn't open my eyes. I felt as if I would roll off the bed if I did. I remembered everything that had happened the night before, everything.

I could also hear every word of Rita Burke's windy whispering.

'A jade, pure and simple, that's all she is and ever was,' she said to a second person in the room. 'And a treacherous, bad-tempered jade at that. I'm sorry I ever gave her a room. I won't again.'

'I doubt you'll have to.' The other woman was Bella.

I opened my eyelids a fraction. I was afraid that if I opened them fully my head might split in two, or the light blind me, but I also wanted to eavesdrop. In any event, from the tone of her whisper, it was likely Mrs Rita Burke would ask me to leave her bed and house as soon as she saw me awake.

Bella spoke again.

'She's found herself a besotted young fool for her bed,' she said, 'and she'll hold on to him for as long as she can. Old age is Celestine Lowry's nightmare and he'll help her believe she's still young.'

'Nightmare or not, she'll betray him in no time. No time at all. She hasn't it in her to be loyal. When she was here she fought with everyone in the house and had a different man in her room every time my back was turned. Her young Sligo man will live to be sorry.'

'He was sorry last night.' Bella gave a low laugh. 'Nessa didn't hand him over without extracting her pound of flesh.'

'Much good it did her, poor creature.' Rita Burke looked down at me. It was hard work to keep my eyelids from fluttering open. 'She'll be good and sick when she wakes. It'll have given her a taste for the drink, that's what the night will have done. Another destined for the gutter.'

'She'll be looked after,' Bella said, hastily, 'you don't need to worry.'

'I suppose she'll be sent back to the West of Ireland to marry some lump of a farmer on horseback?' There was disgust in Mrs Rita Burke's whisper.

'Her brother will take charge of the situation.' Bella's answer was cool.

'That makes two situations he has to look after.' Mrs Burke sighed.

There was silence after this, and a shuffling. I opened my eyes a fraction. Bella had moved to the window and was standing there, staring down.

'You can't keep your own condition to yourself for much longer,' Mrs Burke said. 'You'll have more turns like the one you had downstairs. You need looking after.'

'Be quiet, Rita. In the name of God, be quiet,' Bella groaned. 'Don't you think I know well enough what's ahead of me?' She put her hands in her hair and rocked from side to side. 'I'm my mother all over again. I took such care not to be like her, and now look at me.'

'Whingeing won't solve anything.' Rita Burke's whisper rose. 'You're not the first woman to be destroyed by a man and neither was your mother. Mind you . . .' She got out of her chair and bent to straighten the bedclothes at the end of the bed. I stopped breathing, but she didn't look at me in any event. 'I thought the father a bit full of himself last night,' bending made her voice croaky, 'but that's no crime. He didn't seem to me a scoundrel. He looked after his drunken sister well enough.'

'It's me doesn't want the baby,' Bella said. 'It's me, Rita, me, me, me! And until today no one but me knew about it either. And no one will . . .' White-faced and hugging herself, she faced the other woman. 'I don't want you talking to anyone about what happened downstairs. Do you hear me?'

'Jesus, Mary and Saint Joseph look down on us!' Rita Burke sat back in the cane chair. She blessed herself over and over and stared at Bella. 'You can't be thinking of harming it!'

'You can leave your Holy Family out of this.' Bella stood over her. 'Do I have your word?'

'I can't be party to wrongdoing, to a mortal sin against God.' Rita Burke rubbed her hands together like a caterpillar.

'Keeping your mouth shut and minding your own business doesn't make you a party to anything.'

'Knowing and doing nothing will make me as guilty as you'll be guilty, will condemn me to the same eternal fires . . .'

'Keeping my secret will be the least of your sins, Rita Burke.' Bella's voice was harsh. 'And it's a bit late in the day for you to be playing the saint. You're upstanding and righteous today because myself and others keep the worst of *your* secrets to ourselves. Now, have I your word?'

Rita Burke went on rubbing her hands together. 'It's a terrible thing you're contemplating. A sin against God and man. Is there no way out of it?'

'None,' Bella said.

'Mary, Mother of good heaven, look down on us,' said Mrs Burke.

Bella's skirts rustled as she fell on her knees in front of her. It was a pose she'd taken on stage the night before with Celestine the devil.

'You had your chance once, Rita, in the music halls. You know how you felt when it ended for you. The same thing's happening to me now. My chance has come but I'll lose everything if I have this baby . . .'

I opened my eyes fully and found, by making a great effort, that I could move my lips and speak.

'I'll take your baby.' I lifted my head an inch from the pillow. 'I'll look after it for you.'

The heaviness of the silence out of which Bella and Rita Burke stared made me afraid that speaking had affected my hearing. I saw Bella's mouth move but heard nothing. Not a sound.

'I've gone deaf,' I said, and eased my head back on to the pillow.

'You're alcohol sick, child of grace.' Rita Burke swooped, plumped my pillows and raised my head in her hand. She put a glass of noxious brown liquid to my lips and made me drink most of it. 'You'll feel worse before you feel better,' she said, and she was right. Within minutes I was vomiting into a bucket. But I did feel better afterwards.

'Are you cured?' Mrs Burke gave me a glass of clear water.

'I am,' I nodded. My head ached and so did my stomach, arms and legs. The smell from the bucket filled the room. Bella opened the window and stood with a hand over her mouth.

'I meant, cured of the drink.' Mrs Burke sounded impatient. 'Are you cured of wanting to drink when the world throws a spot of bother your way? Are you disabused of the notion that alcohol is what you need to gather your courage together?'

'I never believed either of those things,' I groaned and closed my eyes, 'and I don't believe them now. What happened last night was . . .' I thought about what it was '. . . an accident.' I mopped my damp forehead with the sleeve of the long cotton nightgown I was wearing. Not my own, so it must be Rita Burke's.

'You'll have to take the pledge.' Mrs Burke lifted the bucket and put it outside the door. She was back immediately. 'The pledge will keep you from the machinations of the devil and the evils of strong drink. Temperance will save you, not regrets. Temperance and Father Cullen and the Pioneer Movement were what saved me. You can be saved, too, delivered from the depravity of drink. I'll take you to a meeting this very night. There's one in St Francis Xavier's Church. It'll set you on the right road.'

She stared down at me, a fiery messenger with her glasses glinting in the sunlight through the window. I slid slowly from the bed.

'I'm cured,' I said again, 'you've cured me yourself.'

It was true. It would be a long time before I could take an alcoholic drink without smelling the contents of that bucket and seeing Mrs Burke's black shape in my mind's eye.

'A meeting won't be necessary,' I said, and stepped away from the bed and closer to Bella, still by the window but looking out now.

'Don't be too hasty making up your mind,' Mrs Burke warned behind me, 'drink is a powerful master.' She hesitated, thought better of whatever it was she was going to add, and said, 'You'll find me in the kitchen if you change your mind.' She left the room quickly, leaving the door open.

'Sit down.' Bella, just as quickly, moved from the window

and closed the door sharply. She stood with her back against it.

'There's a train to Sligo at four o'clock,' she said. 'We'll make it if you gather your things together quickly.'

I said nothing for a minute or two. I was thinking that it wasn't just Theo who had changed. Bella Mulligan had too.

'I'll look after Hugh's baby for you,' I repeated.

Bella was silent for a much longer time than I had been.

'It's not as simple as that, Nessa,' she said in the end. 'I can't go on stage and be the Countess Cathleen with a belly like a swollen cow. I can't *not* go on either. This is a beginning for me in Dublin and I will not give up what I've fought hard for . . .' She moved from the door and stood closer to me. 'It's not the end of the world, Nessa. There will be other babies for Hugh and me. Try to understand.'

I went on looking at my hands, thinking about the day in March when I'd killed Kilgallen's dog; about the grief it had caused me, the grief it had caused Mossie and even old Kilgallen, too, when Mossie had gone to tell him. All that for a dog. Bella didn't seem to have any grief in her for the life she was thinking of ending.

'You could wear corsets,' I said.

'Not for long.' She paused. 'And corsets wouldn't keep it from Hugh.'

'He wouldn't want you to do this thing.'

'Look at me, Nessa,' Bella said, pleading.

But I'd had enough of her acting and didn't want to look into a face I could no longer trust. I went to the window and stared over Mrs Burke's whitewashed yard, to the festering hovels and unwashed children in the laneways behind.

'I'll tell him,' I said, 'he won't let you do it.'

'Hugh cannot stop me,' Bella's voice was light and sure, 'and you will not tell him unless you want to ruin him.'

I turned to look at her at last. She was rouging her cheeks at the mirror, fingers deft and quick, eye critical. Her face, when she met my eye in the glass, was a mask of joyless determination.

'I've made the arrangements, Nessa. There'll be an end to this thing growing in me by tomorrow evening. You're telling Hugh will not stop me doing what has to be done, but it *will*, most definitely, fearfully upset him. He'd be distraught, in fact, and that would not help him pass his examinations. He'd feel about this thing just the way you do, poor lamb. Why do you think I haven't told him myself?'

When I didn't answer she shrugged and put the rouge away and sat on the bed. She was wearing blue, and it suited her.

'You're a sensible person, Nessa.' She put her head to one side. 'So consider. Do you want to have Hugh distracted just now? He's worked hard and long at learning the law. There's no money for him to keep going if he fails, you know that.' She opened a blue velvet bag and took out a phial of perfume. She dabbed her wrists and the sweet scent of lily of the valley floated my way.

'Have some.' She held out the phial. I shook my head and she put it back in the bag.

She was matter-of-fact when she went on.

'Hugh wants two things in life. He wants to be a fine lawyer and he wants me by his side. It's entirely within your power, Nessa, to take both of those things away from him.' She smiled with her mouth. 'I love your brother, as he does me. We suit one another very well. But I will not be owned, the possession of any man. And you shouldn't allow yourself to be owned either, my angel.'

She leaned forward and touched my hand. When she looked up our eyes met and for quick, elusive seconds I felt again the intimacy we'd shared in March. But there was no trust this time and Bella knew it as well as I did. She said quickly, 'You must make up your own mind about what you will do, Nessa. But I think, when you reconsider, that you will realise I am right and see the wisdom of keeping my secret.'

'Only it's not so secret as it was,' I said, 'Mrs Burke knows. She'll tell . . .' Bella's laugh stopped me going any further.

'My poor, innocent angel.' She seemed genuinely amused. 'Rita Burke's a card and a darling but her word's not worth a fiddler's curse. Her own story's too well known for that.'

'Tell me her story?' I said, playing for time, not ready yet to say what I would have to, eventually.

'Oh, it's just that Rita was a passable singer before a jealous lover nearly squeezed the life and voice out of her.' Bella's amusement had turned to impatience. 'She took to drink and the streets of Dublin and London after that, until she found temperance. She's got plenty of secrets herself, our Rita, that she wouldn't want told. They'll help keep her mouth shut. But even if they don't, Hugh is not going to believe anything Rita Burke tells him, or even listen much to her.'

She stood up and took a step closer to the window. The sun on her hair made a golden halo. 'So what, my angel, are you going to tell him?'

I turned away from her, back to the window and the hungry children outside. Bella was right about one thing at least. I was a sensible person. My brother could do without me destroying the happiness he wanted for himself. He could have done without Bella destroying their baby, too. I saw no choice but to keep silent and hope he never found out.

But I would know and would think about it every time I saw them together. It was a secret I would have to carry alone. I couldn't share it with Ellie and I certainly couldn't tell my mother. They would never understand.

They wouldn't keep it a secret either.

All I understood myself, and even that not too well, was *why* Bella was determined to do it. I couldn't even begin to understand *how* she could do it.

· 'Are you not afraid for yourself?' I faced her again. 'That you might be hurt inside? That you might die?'

'Of course I'm afraid,' Bella snapped, 'I've simply chosen the lesser of two evils.'

13

Notions of what might have been came back to haunt me.

If I hadn't gone to Dublin. If I'd listened, for once, and followed Ellie's advice about not surprising Theo. If I hadn't got drunk. If I hadn't heard Bella's conversation with Mrs Burke.

The ifs were so imponderable and there were so many of them that I was filled with a sense of life leading me somewhere. I decided to follow. I would no longer make plans.

Another mistake.

Hugh called to see me at Mrs Burke's house next morning. We sat in her front parlour, surrounded by small tables crammed with framed pictures of a young Rita Burke wearing everything from peacock feathers to rabbit fur. She gave us raspberry lemonade and another plate of arrowroot biscuits and left the room without once looking at Hugh.

'She was a darling of the gods in her time,' Hugh picked up a picture of Mrs Burke taken with Mrs Patrick Campbell, 'and of the pit. She's a card with a good a heart, they say. Has she looked after you all right?'

'Yes,' I said, 'very well, in fact.'

'Pity about her fall from grace.' Hugh replaced the picture. 'She was as famous for her drinking as her singing, by all accounts. Gossip has it that drink's addled her brain.' He shrugged. 'In the way that it does.'

We were silent for a minute, Hugh thinking about our

father, me thinking that Bella had been busy making sure he wouldn't believe anything Rita Burke might tell him.

'You gave a fine performance yourself two nights ago, little sister,' Hugh said at last, 'we wouldn't want too many reruns of that particular show, though.'

'Don't lecture me, Hugh, please,' I said. 'I don't need reminding how stupid I've been.'

He looked at me, and changed the subject. 'Bella's gone to London. An old aunt, the only relative she has in the world, is dying. She's gone to be with her.'

'Her aunt's illness must have come as a shock,' I said; 'happening so soon after the play opening?'

'The shock came last week when she first heard the old lady wasn't well,' he said. 'But Bella's not one to be defeated. She persuaded the Queen's to let her open the play, hand over her role for a few days, and be back on stage for the beginning of next week. The woman's nobility sublime.' He grinned. 'I'm not sure I'd have been so self-sacrificing myself. Unless, of course, the object of compassionate need was my sister.'

'I'm relieved to hear you'll be at my death-bed,' I said.

'You're lucky to have escaped mortal injury that night.' He threw back a glass of the lemonade, pulled a foul face and began nibbling an arrowoot. The cuffs of his jacket were frayed. 'Celestine Lowry's been known to attack the enemy.'

'She can save herself the bother,' I said, 'she's won the war.'

'I wouldn't be too sure of that.' He stood and moved restlessly between the tables. 'Theo's a fool but he's a Howard fool. Blood and religion will out, as they say. Celestine might not have him in the end.'

I got up too. At the fireplace I straightened the fender and irons. The action hid my face and the reddening in my cheeks.

'You think not?' I tried for a casual tone.

'Look at me, Nessa,' Hugh took my arm and turned me to face him, 'and listen to me as well. Theo Howard is not for you. He never was, though I never saw the point of saying so before. You deserve the best. Theo might be my friend but I'm bound to say he's not the best of men. There's a better one for you somewhere.'

'There are birds without wings somewhere, too,' I said, 'and pigs flying.'

'You should go home,' Hugh adopted a firm pose and tone, 'you've plenty of time to catch the afternoon train. There's no good you staying on here with Bella gone. I've work to do for my exams and no time to spare. I don't want you hanging around Dublin on your own.'

I pulled away from him. 'I don't want to go home, not yet.'

Not until Bella got back, not until I was sure she was all right. I would keep her secret, but I would be useful and on hand to help Hugh if anything happened to her.

So I stayed on in Dublin, unwelcome and unwanted by everyone I'd come to visit. The days were endless and I grew no fonder of the city as they went on, walking the hard pavements and sitting in cakeshops taking tea. Travelling on foot made the city's poverty hard to avoid. There were spindly-legged children everywhere, half-starved pet dogs following them. You saw the poverty, too, in the faces of harried, shifty-looking men and thin, fierce women. I passed endless numbers of the tenement buildings they lived in and glimpsed through their dark doorways rancid interiors full of racking coughs and shouting. I'd never before seen poverty of that kind so close.

Most days, too, I spent some time in Cleary & Co. in Sackville Street, in the Ladies' Outfitting Department, trying to decide between everyday frocks and blouses and in the end not buying anything at all. I'd never gone shopping on my own before and my money, at any rate, was going faster than I'd imagined. I would need all I had if anything happened to Bella and I had to stay on in Dublin.

Once I took the little tram to Sandymount and walked on the strand there. That was the best day. But in the end it reminded me too much of Rosses Point and days I'd spent with Theo and the boys there when we were all younger and not in love with other people. So I went back to walking the city pavements and tried not to think what was happening to Bella in London.

I spent a part of every day with Hugh in the rooms he shared with Bella. These were in Rathmines, in a red-brick house with high-ceilinged rooms and rattling windows. It was much grander than Arnott Street but a lot colder in the winter – a price they were willing to pay, Hugh said, for its relatively cheap splendour and more convivial setting. Theo had two rooms in the basement and spent a great part of every day struggling with a play he was writing. That and avoiding me in Hugh's rooms.

'You know where she is and what she's up to, I suppose?' Rita Burke said to me on the third day.

I saw no point in pretence or useless discretion so I nodded agreement. She put a bowl of porridge in front of me. Her other guests had taken their breakfast earlier and gone to their work.

'God will have his revenge.' Rita Burke moved boiling pots around the top of the range. 'A life for a life, that's His way. An eye for an eye and a tooth for a tooth and a mother's life for a babby's . . .'

'Please don't talk like that! Please . . .' I said. I poked at the porridge with a spoon. It was thick and sticky. 'I don't believe in a vengeful God.'

'What kind of a God do you believe in then?' she said, momentarily side-tracked.

I had to think about this. Rita Burke waited, stirring her pots while I did. She was making pearl water, for the face, by boiling Spanish oil soap in water and adding rectified spirit of wine and oil of rosemary. She would put the compound liquid in phials and sell it outside the theatres. She had many ways of making money and I suspected she had amassed quite a lot. I'd had to pay her for my lodgings in advance.

'I believe in a God who helps those who help themselves,' I finally decided, 'but looks after the poor and needy too.'

'God help your innocence!' She gave a laugh like a dog yelping. 'Tell me, Miss O'Grady, in all honesty – is that what you've observed of life so far? Do you see the poor being cared for, the infirm mended?'

'There are good and bad times in everyone's life . . .' I could hear how feeble I sounded even before she cut me short.

'There are those, Miss O'Grady, for whom life is bad all the time and no amount of praying or calling on God makes a whit of difference. But you'll learn. Life will teach you.' She turned and stabbed my shoulder with a bony finger. 'There is only one God and He is a God of vengeance and He will be avenged on Bella Mulligan for taking a life. Your porridge is going cold.'

'I'm not hungry,' I said. Along with being thick and sticky the porridge had too much salt in it.

'There are plenty of your God's creatures would be glad of that bowl of porridge,' Rita Burke said. 'Pour some sweet milk over it and eat up.'

'I'm not hungry,' I said again and pushed the bowl away. 'I must go.'

I was at the kitchen door when she said, 'She has the devil's luck, that Bella Mulligan, and the devil looking after her. I've watched her for years now. She's just the kind to get rid of a child and get away with it. Your brother's the one to be pitied, to my way of thinking. She'll get rid of him, too, you'll see, when the time comes.' She poured milk over my porridge and sat down to eat it. 'Waste not, want not,' she said, 'so the good Lord tells us.'

'What do you mean, get rid of him?' I said.

'She'll leave him for another when it suits her.' Rita lifted a spoon of porridge to her mouth. 'She's done it before. You're keeping her secret to no avail. She'll break his heart anyway, whether or which. You might as well go home for yourself and leave him to his illusions when she gets back. If you're going to stay around and worry about him then you might as well tell him the truth about her and be done with it. You'd be doing him a favour and yourself one as well.'

She put the porridge in her mouth and masticated like a cow. She looked at me all the time in the steady way that a cow does, too, painted eyebrows unwaveringly arched. I hadn't told Rita why I'd decided to stay on in Dublin. I hadn't told her about keeping Bella's secret from Hugh either. She was a woman with the sensitivity and perception of the half-mad.

'Why would I be doing the both of us a favour by telling him?' I asked the question reluctantly. I didn't really want to know the answer. She swallowed the porridge and lifted another spoonful before answering.

'You'd be taking the veil from your brother's eyes,' she said at last, 'helping him to see straight.' Her eyebrows came together. 'And you'd be saving yourself a lot of torment and grief. You'll not find it easy to live with the knowledge of Bella Mulligan's deed. You're the sort will be tortured with keeping it secret.'

'Is clairvoyance another of your accomplishments?' I was not proud of this remark, but I was confused and angry with her for adding to my trouble. She bent over the porridge bowl and sighed and waved me away.

'You're full of vexation and uneasiness already. What'll you be like in the months and years to come?' She spoke in a whining, sing-song voice. 'When you have to watch her leading him by the nose and looking about her for a richer lover? You'll have no peace. Ever. You may as well tell him now.'

But I couldn't tell Hugh. I would keep Bella's secret because I had to. I'd gone too far now to go back; Hugh would never forgive me if I told him now, too late. I would learn to live with it. I would have to.

All of this I told myself as I walked out of Queen's Square and turned for the city. By the time I was halfway to Sackville Street I'd managed to put most of what Rita had said out of my mind. But the brooding had distracted me and I'd taken a wrong turn. I found myself in the middle of the sagging tenements of Townsend Street. It was a warm day and the smells, of cabbage and urine and God knows what else, went to work on the single spoon of porridge I'd swallowed.

Life can turn on the flick of a coin, they say. In my case it turned on the rounding of a corner. It was finding myself in the jungle of those tenements, as well as the sight of a small girl begging from a box-cart on wheels, that made me decide to buy the spotted lace blouse in Cleary & Co. I couldn't think of a single other cheerful thing to do in Dublin that morning.

I gave the girl sixpence and asked her the way. Following her directions brought me into Sackville Street at a different point from usual. For the first time, facing the store's huge windows and first-floor balconies, I saw that the Imperial Hotel was a part of the same building.

In Cleary & Co. the assistant brought me several spotted net blouses as well as a cheaper one in cream delaine. I decided on the most expensive and lovely of them all, in net with beading for 17/6d. I bought a lace-trimmed camiskirt, too, for 9/6d. For Ellie I bought a white underskirt trimmed with lace, and yellow gloves to the elbow. For my mother I bought a brocaded silk shawl. I crossed to where they were selling footwear and bought myself a pair of shoes with two-inch heels in the palest of blue leathers. They had small bows at the back of the ankle and I'd never owned anything even remotely like them. I wore them leaving the store, sailing down the stairs with my bags swinging from my arms and my feet elegantly picking out the steps.

I felt as drunk leaving Cleary & Co. as if I'd been drinking champagne again. It didn't cost me a thought to go into the Imperial Hotel and ask for Mr Thomas Cooper at the reception desk.

'Who will I say is looking for him?' The clerk, pale and polite, beckoned a boy in uniform and cap.

'Vanessa O'Grady,' I said, and the boy left to fetch their guest.

My mood calmed while I sat waiting. The foyer was busy and plush, the walls exhausting to look at with their green velvet drapes and gilt-framed gloomy oils. I was there long enough to have second thoughts about the venture, and to begin questioning my motives.

Curiosity had brought me here, I decided, that and the fact of having hours to kill before I saw Hugh in the afternoon. I would say hello, make five minutes' polite conversation, and leave. Anything more would only encourage the man.

The more honest part of me knew that the real reason I was in the foyer of the Imperial Hotel had to do with the way Theo's rejection had stripped me of my unsteady sense of my own womanhood, my even less secure sense of my allure to men. Thomas Cooper's attentions had flattered and reassured me. I wanted to experience that flattery and reassurance again. Nothing more.

He arrived without my being aware of it. One minute I was uneasily sitting alone, noticing how the dust from the street had already marked my new shoes, the next he was sitting opposite, leaning forward on a cane and smiling.

'I hadn't expected to see you so soon,' he said.

'I *could* go away,' I said tartly, 'and come back in a week or two.'

He laughed, loudly enough for a woman in widow's weeds to turn stiffly in her chair. 'Please don't do that,' he said, 'I'm more than pleased to see you. More than. I should have made that clear at the outset.'

'It's simply that I was in the vicinity and saw the hotel,' I said, refusing to be mollified, feeling my ears beginning to burn. 'I was next-door, in fact, in Cleary's.' I stopped. He went on smiling at me. 'Shopping. For clothes.' I decided the expression on his face was smug. Or at least self-satisfied. I stood up. 'I called on impulse. I should have left a note. I'm actually very busy and should be going . . .'

'Please give me a few minutes of your time at least.' He stood too. Without his hat, and with me in my new shoes, I was a couple of inches taller than him. It was suddenly a lot easier to be pleasant.

'Do they serve a good cup of tea here?' I sat down again. 'Tea would be nice.'

'I'm no tea expert,' he said, 'but the trade in morning coffees seems brisk.'

He signalled a boy and ordered coffee, black and strong and with a jug of hot milk.

He didn't check with me or ask either when he ordered some Turkish Delight.

'That I can vouch for,' he said, sitting down and gesturing for me to do so as well, 'I've tried it.'

'Thank you.' I sat. 'I'm sure I will enjoy it.' He was beaming and pleased and I hadn't the heart to tell him how much I loathed its sticky sweetness.

'Your brother is well?' he said.

'Very well, thank you.'

'And your fiancé?'

'He's well too.'

'You're enjoying your visit to the capital then?'

'Yes and no. I went to the theatre. To see *The Countess Cathleen*. At the Queen's.'

'And did you enjoy it?'

'It was an experience.'

'Experience can be a good thing,' he said, 'or a waste of valuable time.'

'Have your business meetings been successful?'

'Very,' he said, 'their success will keep me in the city for another week or more. Then I return to the West.' He paused. 'Perhaps I might call on you and your family over the summer?'

'I'm glad to hear your business was successful,' I said, 'and we'd be delighted to have you visit. Kilraven is at its best at this time of year.'

This ended our conversation for a while. We were like strangers, which was exactly what we were. He wasn't interested in the theatre and I wasn't interested in business. I could hardly talk to him about Theo, or Bella, and didn't know him well enough to ask anything personal. He looked better than he had on the train, more relaxed in a pale-grey morning suit with darker-grey neck tie. It was a relief when the coffee arrived.

He took his black, I took milk in mine. The Turkish Delight was predictably sticky.

'I dislike cities,' he spoke quickly, 'I feel uncomfortable and imprisoned by the buildings, the crush of people, the traffic, the stench, the rush and pointless hysteria of it all.'

'I don't like them much myself,' I said, 'and for most of the reasons you've given. Also, I don't like not being able to properly see the sky, and not being free to run when I want to. I've been walking in the slumlands and have seen the terrible poverty of so many. There's a lack of humanity about city living.'

'Aren't we told that the Lord raised the poor out of the dunghill and the needy out of the dust? Don't you trust Him to look after them?'

'A week ago I might have answered yes,' I said, 'but I haven't seen much evidence these last few days of His goodness.' I stopped. The conversation had become more personal than I wanted. 'The woman of the house I'm staying in believes some people are destined to live unhappy lives.' I meant this to divert him. It didn't.

'Is your life an unhappy one, Miss O'Grady?'

His eyes were unblinking but not, I thought, unkind. I looked around the foyer. It had become noisier and more crowded. The widow-woman had been joined by a young girl in a straw hat. It was like one I'd had myself when I was her age. I'd worn it for six summers, until Theo had thrown it out of the boat on the lake one day and ruined it for ever.

'My fiancé is my fiancé no longer,' I admitted.

'Ah,' he said, and handed me the Turkish Delight. I took a piece. It was sticky as Mrs Burke's porridge. I put it down.

'I don't like Turkish Delight,' I said. 'I'm sorry you've wasted your money.'

'I should have asked you . . .' He smoothed his moustache with two fingers in the way he had. 'Perhaps, Miss O'Grady, now that you've discarded your fiancé, you would allow me escort you to a performance by the D'Oyly Carte tomorrow night?' He smiled. 'We could both have an experience together.'

'My fiancé discarded *me*,' I said.

'Then the man is a fool and was clearly unworthy of you.'

'I'm inclined to agree with you,' I said, and did, for a while, that morning.

'You will come to the theatre with me then?'

'I will, and thank you for asking me.'

14

Hugh was not pleased. You would think, the way he carried on, that I'd agreed to move into the Imperial Hotel with Thomas Cooper.

'You know nothing about him. I know nothing about him. You met him on a train . . .'

'I met him first on the road outside Sligo. Mossie was with me.'

'Don't quibble with me, Nessa. He's a stranger. He's twice your age. What sort of man imposes himself on a young girl on a train? Takes advantage of her alone in a Dublin hotel?'

He looked ridiculous and was being ridiculous. He'd thumped the table when I told him, scattering books and writing things, and was torn now between picking them up and roaring at me. The room was a mess anyway, without Bella's touch. He only ever half-opened the drapes, which were burgundy-coloured and blocked all daylight. His hair needed to be cut and washed. His eyes were dark-circled and tired.

'You're being ridiculous,' I said. 'I suppose you've been up all the night studying?'

'I told you not to quibble with me.' His voice rose. 'I forbid you to go anywhere with this man.'

'*You* forbid *me!*' It was all I could do to get the words out. 'Who are you to forbid me anything?' I did a bit of scattering myself, taking hold of and throwing a small inkpot across the room. 'You live a life that would outrage most of society, you're in no position to tell me what to do, Hugh. You've been gone from us as a family for years. Summers and Christmastime are all Mama and myself and Manus have seen of you. I might have been lying in ditches with every reprobate in the county for all you knew . . .'

I stopped. The inkpot had smashed against the wall, the splashed ink dripping inevitably downwards to the carpeted floor. I grabbed the first cloth that came to hand and ran.

'I'm twenty-three years old,' I said, rubbing at the wall in a fury, 'I'm a woman. I've been making my own decisions for years and neither you nor Manus has paid the slightest heed . . .'

'You were at home,' Hugh crouched beside me and took the cloth from my hand, 'you were safe.'

'Safely promised to a man who'd no intention of ever marrying me.' I sank to my knees, resentment and my realisation of the true position pouring out, 'that's how safe I was. Safely looking after a father drinking himself to oblivion and a brother following close behind. Well, that's all over, Hugh, that life. There'll be no place for me at Kilraven once Manus and Ellie marry. I'll be one of the county's unmarried spinsters, an extra mouth to feed, growing old and crabbed and bitter and with no one to care about me. I want something more than that.'

'You *deserve* something more than that.' He took my hands and helped me to my feet. He was shaking, his face white as paper. 'Sit down.'

He led me to a wing-backed chair by the empty fireplace. The springs were gone. Even through my petticoats I could feel them as Hugh, at the sideboard, poured brandy into two glasses. Everything I'd said was true, but also unfair. My brother had escaped and made his own way. It didn't make him evil, or to blame for my situation.

'I'm sorry,' I said when he handed me a very small glass

of brandy with lemonade in it. 'None of it's your fault. But you could have told me about Theo . . .'

'I thought he'd grow out of it.' He sat on the corner of the table, holding own, bigger, glass of brandy. 'I hoped you'd grow out of him.'

'I had nothing and no one to divert me, as he had.' I was sour. The brandy helped, though I couldn't have taken it without the lemonade. My sense of smell was too acute for that.

'Is that what this man is, this Cooper – a diversion?' Hugh swung a leg casually as he sat on the table. I wasn't fooled.

'He might be,' I said.

'He's a stranger to us, Nessa. We don't know him . . .'

'*You* don't know him.'

'He lives in Africa, for God's sake, that's all I need to know. He's an adventurer. An opportunist. There are bad reports of the Belgian king's Congo. It's said slaving abounds and that white traders and state officials kidnap and use African women as concubines . . .'

'It's also reported that King Leopold is responsible for civilising and uplifting work in the Congo. There are missionaries everywhere, and schools.'

'He told you this?'

'His name is Thomas Cooper, and yes, he's talked to me about Africa. I encouraged him. It's more interesting than forever talking about the money we owe and the next bit of land or *objet d'art* we might sell and whether or not . . .'

'That I'll grant you,' Hugh cut me short and finished his brandy, 'but you still don't know him and Africa is a long way for an honest man to travel to make a living.'

'I suppose you knew everything of Bella Mulligan's seed, breed and generation before you made love to her?' I was on sure ground now, and made my points firmly. 'Who are you, Hugh, to act the hypocrite and tell me what to do? You live as you like, and do as you like. Why should it be any different for me? Why should I be bound by respectability when you're not?'

'Hypocrite I may well be, Nessa, but I'm a realist too. The reality is that as a young woman you'll not be so quickly forgiven transgressions as a man.'

'Bella is a woman.'

'Bella's is a different world from the one you'll have to live in.'

'What world is that?' My blood had begun to boil again. 'Have you planned a life for me, Hugh, to replace the one I've lost?'

'You're strong, Nessa. You'll build a life for yourself.'

'I will. I am. I may even go to Africa.'

I didn't mean this. The very idea was preposterous but it had the desired effect on Hugh. He stopped pontificating and sat at the table with his head in his hands.

'God's curse and a sudden end to your Cooper,' he groaned. 'I should never have allowed you to ramble the city alone.' He looked at me. 'I worry about you.'

'I worry about you,' I said, 'but I don't interfere with your life.'

'I'd like to meet this Cooper,' he said, 'you can't deny me that. It's only fair that someone in the family should meet him.'

'I've invited him to visit Kilraven in the summer. You'll meet him then. Everyone will.' It seemed a better bet to tell a small lie here. To admit Thomas Cooper had invited himself would have fuelled Hugh's antagonism to him.

'Where will you go with him tomorrow night?' my brother asked.

'To see the D'Oyly Carte Company at the Gaiety Theatre.'

'I'll meet you afterwards.' Hugh began to gather the

164

scattered papers. 'We'll have supper together, the three of us.'

I didn't object. I found I wanted to observe him and Thomas Cooper together. It would be interesting to see how they got on and would allow me to see Thomas Cooper in a different light. Also, and this was definitely a *good thing*, Theo would hear I'd been to the theatre with *another man*.

All of which planning went awry and reminded me, again, that I'd decided to follow life's lead.

I arrived to visit Hugh next day to find that Bella had come back.

'Nessa, darling!' her voice called to me from the open bedroom door as I came into the parlour with Hugh. 'Come and sit with me. I want to hear all that you've been doing with yourself.'

I hadn't been in the bedroom before. Even with the high ceiling it was so dark it took my eyes a minute or two to adjust. The air smelled of rosewater and of something else, musk maybe. I was aware of mirrors – a standing tailor's mirror and another over the fire mantel – and of trunks overflowing with clothes.

'It was good of you to stay with Hugh . . .'

I followed Bella's voice to the end of a high, brass bed. She lay, in the roseate glow from a small table-lamp, against a bank of velvet cushions and lace pillows. Her hair was loose, a pale silk camisole showed off her shoulders and she had a tea cup in her hands. I'd never seen her look so pretty.

'Are you all right?' I said, my tone not as neutral as I'd intended it to be.

'I'm fine, thank you.' Bella sipped delicately at the cup of tea. 'The trip was more tiring than I'd expected so I won't be going on stage until tomorrow night. Still, I'm glad I went. It was a journey had to be made. But enough of me.' She put the cup aside and leaned forward, patting the bed. 'Sit, angel

Nessa, and tell me all your news. Hugh tells me you've got a man friend. My, but that was quick.'

I stayed where I was and she sank back against the pillows and cushions, one eyebrow raised, saying nothing.

'Your aunt has recovered then?' I said.

'Oh, yes. She's a hardy one and I knew she'd come through. I hope you weren't worried about her?'

'I wasn't as certain as you were that she would be all right.'

'Well, now that I've reassured you, darling,' Bella's voice became coaxing, 'tell me your news?' Without waiting for an answer she lifted her hair off her shoulders and stretched her arms wide. Earrings like miniature chandeliers swung sparkling from her ears. 'It's so good to be back. I missed Hugh so – and I missed you, too, my angel. Now, tell all, do.'

My hands, wrapped around the brass bed rail, had become clammy. 'There isn't a lot to tell,' I said. 'I travelled here on the train with a man called Thomas Cooper. I met him again at his hotel yesterday. That's all.'

'Not quite all, my pet. Hugh tells me you're to go with him to see the D'Oyly Carte this evening. I'm so pleased for you.' Bella clapped her hands and the chandeliers glittered. 'The Nessa O'Grady I left was bereft, lonely, heartbroken. I come back to find her with a new and exciting lover . . .'

'Thomas Cooper is *not* my lover.' I spoke loudly, my knuckles whitening as my clammy grip tightened on the bed rail. 'And he's not exciting either. He's old . . .'

'But he lives in Africa, darling!' Bella sat up with her arms about her knees. 'He's probably rich as Croesus from mining or plantation-owning or selling ivory. I've never met a man who went to Africa, or to any of the colonies, without becoming rich. And what age is he, for God's sake? He can't be *that* old.'

'He's about forty.' I stopped, considering. 'Maybe less. He has lines from the sun and a moustache so it's hard to tell. And he's losing his hair and trying to pretend he's not . . .'

'Is he married?' Bella was businesslike.

'No. Or maybe he lied, how would I know?'

'You're so *grumpy*, darling. Why would he lie? It's too easy to find out the truth. Is he handsome?'

'He's not a tall as I am.'

Bella, with a sigh, dampened a finger and ran it over an eyebrow. 'He doesn't have a peg leg, darling,' she said, firmly, 'nor a glass eye. It looks as if I'll have to view this Thomas Cooper for myself.'

'What do you mean?' My stomach gave a great lurch of misgiving.

'Just that we'll all four of us have supper tonight after the Gaiety, you, me, Hugh and Thomas Cooper.' Bella gave a tinkling laugh. 'Won't that be nice? It'll be fun, too, and God knows I need a night out.'

'It wouldn't be fun at all. It would be embarrassing.'

It would also make me look a clodhopping girl in the face of Bella's womanly dazzle and beauty. It would be my birthday dinner all over again. Only this time I didn't trust Bella, had no idea what her real motives were.

'Embarrassing?' Bella laughed again. 'Embarrassing for whom, my pet? I won't be embarrassed, and nor will Hugh. Mr Cooper . . .'

'*I* will be embarrassed, Bella.' I felt panicky and hot, the night ahead looming as another mortifying episode in my social life. 'I'll cancel the arrangement . . . it's too soon . . . I don't want all of this . . . Theo is still . . .'

Bella cut me short with a wagging finger and a loud shushing sound. 'Listen to me, Nessa my pet, and remember what I'm going to tell you.' Her eyes held mine. She was in her mothering role again, and enjoying it. 'There isn't a man in

167

this world worth pining over. Not one, anywhere. If that's the only wisdom you learn from me then it'll be enough. Forget Theo Howard. He's a boy. He'll always be a boy. You've met a man, from the sound of things. Give him a chance. He may not be the love of your life but he's an *experience*.'

She lay back and smiled, not very happily, I thought. I wanted to tell her that Thomas Cooper would have agreed with her about the value of experience, that the two of them seemed to have a lot in common. But she was too well established in her role to hear me.

'Experience is something you don't have much of, my pet,' she lowered her voice, 'and something I have in bucketsful. It's why you don't understand my trip to London. But you will, in time.' She stopped, took off the earrings and held them in the palm of her hand. 'Hugh bought these for me while I was away. He's a darling man.' When she looked up there was a frost in her violet eyes. 'I do love your brother, Nessa, make no mistake about that. Every bit as much as you love him.'

'There isn't a man in the world worth pining over,' I repeated her phrase, slowly. 'Please don't compare my feelings to yours, Bella. We've too little in common for that.'

She watched without a word while I took the earrings she'd given me out of my bag and left them on the dressing table. It was a while before she spoke and when she did she was off-hand.

'Have you said anything to him?'

'About why you went to London? No.'

'Oh, dear, dear me,' Bella sighed, 'so glacial. So sure and pure and righteous.' She was suddenly impatient. 'I need rest. Leave me, Nessa, and tell Hugh I want to see him.'

My brother had his head in his books. He'd changed while I was in the bedroom and was wearing a brocade waistcoat. It gave him a look of my father.

'Nice waistcoat.' I touched the gold of a brocade peacock's head. 'Bella would like you to go to her.'

'Bella brought it from London.' He patted the waistcoat, a proud grin on his face. I despaired for his judgement, his future, his intelligence. 'You're leaving?' he said.

'I am. I'm going to take the late-afternoon train for Sligo.' I walked towards the door. 'Everyone keeps telling me it's the one to go for and I've decided to listen to everyone, for once.'

'What in the name of God's wrong with you, Nessa?' Hugh's exasperated voice followed me as I pulled open the door. 'You've an arrangement for tonight . . .'

'I had,' I said, 'it's cancelled.'

He followed me down the steps and into the street. I didn't speak or answer any of his questions until we were well clear of the house. When I was sure my voice wouldn't betray me I said, 'It's a woman's privilege to change her mind. I want to go home instead.'

'I'm glad you saw sense,' Hugh said, 'it was a bad idea from start to finish. A man you didn't know, that none of us knew. Better to let him go.'

He had more sense than to say more, or to follow me further.

I took two trams to Queen's Square. Mrs Burke said she was glad to see me go, that the city was no place for me, and helped me into a carriage with my bags. I looked back as we left the square. She stood with arm raised, like a soldier saluting. There was a certain nobility about her.

At the Imperial Hotel I asked the driver to stop. He was a far cry from Ambrose and said a wait would cost me extra. I told him to earn his money and be there when I got back. I'd lost all patience with Dublin and everyone in it.

The same pale man stood behind the reception desk in the

169

hotel. I gave him the letter I'd written to Thomas Cooper and told him to see he got it before six o'clock.

'Mr Cooper is in his room,' he said, 'you could give it to him yourself.'

'I'm afraid I can't wait,' I said and left without looking back.

In Cleary's I bought three bales of dress fabric: two in dyed linen (pale lemon for me, pale blue for Ellie) and the third of watered and ribbed wine-coloured poplin for my mother. I spent £2 on trimmings and £1.2s 6d on a straw hat trimmed with tulle, satin, ribbon and a curling mauve feather. There would be no Theo to throw this one across the lake.

At the Broadstone I refused to pay the driver his money until he'd helped me to the platform with my bags and then waited with them while I bought a newspaper from a screeching boy. I chose the *Irish Times* because it seemed to me the thickest, and when I got on the train I opened it wide and hid behind its pages. If God Himself were to sit opposite I would not speak to him. I would at least travel back across Ireland in peace.

But not even the *Irish Times* brought me that. A news item jumped out at me almost at once, a long column of detailed writing about a three-storey tenement in Townsend Street which had collapsed the day before. The writer said this had happened 'with an awful suddenness' and 'buried alive two families who had inhabited the rooms in the upper portion'. He went on to castigate those who had 'allowed the two houses to stand until they gave magic proof of their dangerous character by killing seven people' and declared that the city would 'never be safe from its tenement slums until they became an evil memory'. Abolition, he declared, 'was the only cure'. I wondered if the begging girl I'd given the sixpence to had belonged to either of the buried families, and if so whether she'd seen death coming. I swore never to visit Dublin again.

I closed the paper and took my chances with the people sharing my carriage. They were a miserable young boy, who got out at Mullingar, and a matronly woman who slept all the way to Sligo. Neither of them spoke a word to me and I gave thanks for small mercies.

15

Around midday, on the longest day of the year, Ellie Hope told me she was pregnant. We were walking under a sweltering sun towards the estuary. The grass was high, the wandering line of distant mountains a hazy blue, the road dusty. My response, born of Bella's way of dealing with Hugh's child, was less than gracious.

'Does Manus know?'

Clear as a bell I heard the ring of dread in the words. Ellie did too. She quickened her pace, forcing me to do the same to keep up with her.

'He was the first to know,' she said, 'you're the second. I told him I'd be telling you today. We'll be giving your mother the news before the end of the week.' She gave me a sharp look. It didn't hide her hurt. 'You don't sound to be all that pleased. Is it that you don't want to become an aunt? Or is the shame of it bothering you? Or maybe it's that you're worried people will say Manus married the servant girl after she snared him with an heir?'

'Ellie!' I shouted her name. It didn't stop her ranting.

'Maybe you're worried they'll say I got myself with child to stop him changing his mind about marrying me?'

I caught and gripped her arm, hard, and turned her to face me. She lifted her chin and then her eyebrows, questioningly. A bird in a bush near by began a high, lilting tune.

'That's a linnet,' Ellie said, 'there's a lot of them around this summer.' She pulled her arm free and walked on again.

'Mossie says they bring joy with them, that they're a bird of life.' I followed, slowly, knowing better than to interrupt when she had something to say. 'It's all fairy tales and nonsense. He made it up because he guessed my secret. I thought about telling him but held back because I wanted to tell you first.' She stopped and broke a piece from the hedgerow and began to use it as a fan. 'I thought you'd be glad for us,' she said, 'for myself and Manus.'

I cursed Bella Mulligan. Then I passed Ellie by and stood in the road in front of her. She stopped walking and fanned herself.

'My, but it's hot today.' She closed her eyes.

'I'm more pleased than you can know,' I declared loudly, 'it's the best thing to happen this miserable year. It was the shock made me ask about Manus, that's all. I'm glad, Ellie, glad, glad . . .'

'That'll do, I believe you.' She began walking again. 'It's just that I'm fierce sensitive since I found myself with child.' She fluttered the branch as I fell into step beside her. 'The smallest thing offends me and you seemed to be doubtful at first.'

'Surprised. I was surprised. You'll have to give me a few minutes to get used to the notion of Mother Ellie.'

'Take all the time you want.' Ellie opened the front of her dress and fanned her freckled breasts. 'I'm three months gone, so that's another thing for you to think about and calculate as we go along.'

We walked on towards the sea. It was blue-green and sparkling with a couple of basking sharks in the far distance. As we came closer a small breeze gusted in and cooled us a little. Ellie's happiness hung about her like gauze, a protection from the slings and arrows and all that was ahead of her. It was the very best of days and I would remember it.

We walked to the end of the Mass path and sat on a flat

rock at the edge of the sand. The sharks seemed a lot closer than they actually were, like a couple of friendly black sailboats lazing in the sun.

'There'll be hell to pay with Father Duggan,' Ellie said.

The priest had called twice while I was in Dublin, both times demanding Ellie live in the village until after the wedding. She had told him sharply to look after his own soul and my mother had given him tea.

'He might not marry you,' I said, 'he'll likely send for an outside priest to give you a blessing in the church porch, nothing more.'

'That'll do us and the the loss will be his,' Ellie said. 'We're planning a wedding party the likes of which the county hasn't seen in a century. Manus and myself will be man and wife whether Father Duggan consents to bind us together or not. We'll be answerable to God and not to any black crow of a priest.'

She was fearless. I wondered if Manus knew just how fearless.

'This is the only thing I want, Nessa.' She drew her legs up and wrapped her arms about them and her skirts. She was wearing shoes but no stockings. 'I never wanted any other man and I never gave a thought to having babies until I met Manus. When I did meet him it was all I could think about.'

'So you weren't even a small bit worried when you found you were pregnant?'

'I'd be a liar if I said I didn't have a quiver or two on my way to tell Manus. But before he'd opened his mouth I'd decided on names and I told them to him. Pearl if it's a girl, Humphrey if it's a boy. He disagrees about Humphrey . . .'

'Did it ever occur to you, even for a second,' I spoke slowly, looking out to sea, avoiding Ellie's eye, 'not to have the baby? To wait maybe a year or two until things had settled?'

'What're you talking about?' Ellie's head turned sharply my

174

way. I still didn't look at her. After a minute she answered the question. 'Why would I do that, Nessa? It's as I told you: I want Manus's babies more than anything, no matter the circumstances. And how would I go about doing such a thing, even if I wanted to? And how would I live with myself after?'

'How indeed,' I agreed.

She'd told me more than she knew and, for the first time, I accepted something of Bella's situation. Her passion was for the theatre, not babies and family, and her love for Hugh was of a different kind from Ellie's for Manus.

But I hated keeping her secret and was tormented by a notion that Hugh would find out. I felt disloyal and treacherous all the time I was with him. Still, Ellie had put her finger on something that made all the difference: Bella knew how to go about ending a pregnancy and could live with herself afterwards. Her secret might eat into my soul, but it was something I would just have to live with.

Ellie took off the shoes and stretched out her bare feet and laughed. 'We'll fill Kilraven with babies, myself and Manus. We'll have ten of them.'

'There'll plenty of room for them anyway.'

I could have said food to feed them was another matter, as well as heating and a sound roof. But it wasn't the day to raise such worries.

The signs, such as frogs lying low in the ponds, were good for a long, fine summer. Ellie and Manus, with my mother's agreement because she was still officially in mourning, decided to announce their engagement at a garden party at Kilraven on the last day of July. They would announce their wedding date, too, and settle the details about a priest and church later. My mother insisted they invite Father Duggan. It might soften his heart, she said. I doubted it.

Hugh would be home then, and Bella with him. Theo would

be home, too, though no one knew whether or not he'd be accompanied.

Thomas Cooper would also be a guest. He'd written a reply to the note I'd left at the Imperial Hotel, and I'd written back inviting him. My motives were anything but pure. He would be a salve to my pride if Theo turned up with Celestine Lowry.

I felt a little bit guilty, too, about not going to hear the D'Oyly Carte with him. In his letter he was very flattering and regretful about not seeing me – but he also made it clear that he'd already bought the tickets.

I'm sorry we weren't able to use the tickets, but am hopeful that we will meet again. I very much enjoyed the occasions we spent together. I will be away in London and Brussels for the next while but will be back in the West of Ireland with my friends the Mansfields in or about the middle of July. I will write to you again from there and make an arrangement to visit you. You are a unique and lovely young woman and you greatly impressed me. I do not want to go back to Africa without seeing you again.

He signed himself 'Thomas Cooper, Esq.', which seemed rather formal, given the contents of the letter.

Preparing for the party took up most of the days until the end of July, which suited me fine. It meant I'd little time to think and less time to mope.

'I don't know that I want Theo Howard here at all,' Ellie said, early on in the planning. 'I've lost the small regard I had for him. He's a fool and a swine. *You* might think it civilised to behave as if nothing had happened but *I* think it's a feeble way of going on. Let him feel the cold wind of rejection himself.'

She kicked at the weeds creeping along the garden walk in

front of us and made a note on the pad she carried everywhere with her. Most of the walks were invisible but Ellie had a plan for clearing them. She had plans for everything.

'No, rejection's too good for him. He should be made an example of,' she continued.

'How would you do that?' I said, curious to see how far Ellie's loyalty to me would go, how horrible might be its manifestation.

'I'd denounce him, if it was me. I'd post signs about him around the county and town. I'd see that his hussy of an actress got short shrift at mealtimes, or any other time a servant might be attending on her here or in the Howard house. And . . .' she looked gleeful '. . . I'd plan a surprise for him, in the dark of night in a field somewhere, that would leave him sore and sorry he'd ever betrayed you. I'd leave it so's he wouldn't come home again in a hurry. I'd . . .'

'Enough!' I stopped her, laughing. 'You wouldn't do half those things but I appreciate the intention anyway.'

'The thing of it is, though,' Ellie began noting something else on her pad, 'that you don't know which half I *would* carry out.'

'Theo's mother and father will be coming,' I said, 'and I wouldn't hurt Arthur Howard for the world. And I've asked Thomas Cooper. He'll help me put a face on things.'

'I suppose a fancy man from Africa's a bit of a social trophy all right,' said Ellie, and sniffed. She was piqued that I'd had an adventure involving a man all on my own. She'd questioned Mossie endlessly about him and, without ever seeing Thomas Cooper, already disapproved of him strongly.

She'd slipped with the greatest of ease into the role of an O'Grady wife, even if she wasn't one yet. We'd opened and dried out another bedroom and for the sake of appearances she slept there, alone. In every other way, more and more every day, she was already looking after Manus and Kilraven.

She saw to the kitchen and food, to the rooms and linen and washing. She brought in a girl from the village three times a week and paid her half of what she'd once been paid herself to help with the heaviest work. She put Manus to work with Mossie, not very successfully, in the stables and outhouses. She conferred endlessly with my mother about what she was doing and about which pieces of the least-loved artwork should be sold to raise money. Every week saw a new empty space on a wall, a gap in a display cabinet, a piece of furniture missing.

I sacrificed the chaise-longue (in its case much loved) from my own room to buy wine and champagne just the week before the party.

My mother, smiling through the days and still living in the past with my father, was happy enough to let Ellie at it. So was I. We were both glad to see some sort of shape for a life to come being put on Kilraven, and on Manus. We helped where we could but neither of us had anything like Ellie Hope's energy for work. Even pregnant she was tireless.

The last day of July, as promised by the signs, dawned bright and cloudless. Ellie, who was growing larger by the day, appeared in my room in the late morning.

'You'll have to help me.' She was half-buttoned into a dress she'd made from the blue linen I'd bought in Dublin. 'I'll wear it if I have to stop breathing to do so.'

We left the back open and draped a light shawl from her shoulders. She put her hair in a plait at the nape of her neck and looked, in the end, almost respectable and very pretty. I wore a dress I'd had made from the lemon linen and put wild flowers in my hair. My mother wore grey. No one tried to persuade her to do otherwise.

'"Such beauty! It makes the bright world dim",' said Manus, quoting some poet or other as we came into the hall.

He took my mother's arm and the four of us went outside as the first guests came up the avenue.

The party was an hour old when Father Duggan came and stood with me on the steps.

'It saddens me that you don't spent more time in the church,' he said. His heart, far from softening, seemed set in stone. 'It's an even greater sadness that Eleanor Hope hasn't seen fit to confide her difficulties to me.' He looked out over the gathering with a sniff.

'I don't think she sees her marriage to Manus as a difficulty,' I said. I'd retreated to the steps to avoid Theo, and to take photographs with Hugh's camera.

'Maybe you'd like to sit at a table, Father?' I said, hopefully, and took a trial look through the view finder.

Some people were already sitting at the two long tables Mossie and Manus had made and laid out together. It was the last thing Mossie had done before taking himself and Finn off for the day with a fishing rod. He'd a passionate dislike of crowds.

'I would not.' Father Duggan was affronted. 'I'm here for your mother's sake, and her sake alone. The poor woman must be demented at the turn in events.' He was wearing a black frock coat and looked more than ever like a doom-laden crow.

'What turn is that, Father?' I said.

'Eleanor Hope's condition is no secret. It's a sad thing to see a great family brought low. Your unfortunate father must be turning in his grave.'

'My father will be saluting them from his grave, if he's doing anything,' I said. 'He was the one brought the family low in the first place. We're all hopeful that Ellie and Manus's marriage will be a new beginning. Will you marry them?'

He stared at me before turning away, speechless, to look again at the growing crowd. We'd invited one-time tenants, villagers, friends of my parents', Manus's Gaelic Leagers. Most had turned up. Theo, home for the summer, had come with his parents.

Celestine Lowry, telling Bella she was afraid of wild animals and too much daylight, had remained in Dublin. God knows what she'd told Theo. He was still in love with her, by all accounts.

Hugh and Bella had appeared from the house and were being attentive to my mother. 'Your trip to Dublin didn't do you much good,' Father Duggan said, 'you're as insolent as ever you were.' He sighed. 'You are constantly in my prayers, Vanessa.'

'You won't marry them then?'

'I couldn't in conscience . . .'

'Then I'll write to the bishop,' I said, 'he'll find a solution.'

I'll never know where this bit of bravado would have got me because at that moment, with a noise like a small thunder-clap, a motor car appeared along the avenue.

I went slowly to meet Thomas Cooper.

He was wearing a silk tie with a gold and diamond pin. Much too overdressed for a garden party. He climbed down and gave me his hand.

'I'm very glad you could come,' I said, aware of Ellie and Manus coming across the gravel behind me. 'You drove here without trouble?' His hand felt surprisingly big, and warm. The car was the same one which had broken down on the road outside Sligo.

'I made sure beforehand that all would be well.' He let my hand go and hit the motor car's bonnet with his palm. 'These contraptions need to know who's master, that's all it takes.' He smiled at me. 'You look lovely, Vanessa, very lovely.'

My ears tingled and my cheeks flushed. I stepped back a pace.

'My brother and his fiancée are anxious to meet you,' I said as Ellie and Manus, on cue, appeared to either side of me. I introduced them.

'Nessa's told us about you.' Ellie sounded accusing. 'You live in Africa.'

'In the Congo Free State,' Thomas Cooper agreed with a nod and, I was glad to see, a loosening of the neck tie. 'In Central Africa,' he added. He wasn't quite so confident as he looked then, a fact which made him seem more human.

'Why do you live there?' Ellie said. 'I would think Africa hot and very foreign to the habits of a man reared in the West of Ireland.'

'The world is wide and I was born curious,' he said. 'Africa is a fascinating country, and an exciting one.'

'The land of rubber and ivory, butterflies and gorillas,' Manus said. 'What keeps you there, Mr Cooper? Are you a trader in Africa's produce or an exploring scientist?'

Thomas Cooper laughed. 'A bit of both,' he said. 'The rubber trade pays my wage, the continent's beauty keeps me there.'

'You have no family in Africa then?' said Ellie. She had her head to one side, watching him closely. I frowned but she ignored me. I would have pinched her arm but she moved away.

'None.' He sounded regretful. 'It's a brave and adventurous woman would make her life in Africa and I haven't been lucky enough to persuade such a woman to marry me. Yet.'

'It's a witless and misguided woman you need,' Ellie chided. 'Why would any person in her right mind choose to live and have children among snakes and savages in the boiling heat?'

'Sadly, Miss Hope, that is a view held by enough women to have kept me a bachelor. I'm told by Vanessa, however, that I must congratulate you and Mr O'Grady on your forthcoming nuptials.' He smiled. 'I wish you every happiness and prosperity in your lives together.' His manners were really quite polished.

'Thank you,' Ellie said, with noticeably less grace than him.

'We should sit to eat,' Manus prompted.

'I'm sure you're hungry after your drive,' I said.

'Famished,' Thomas Cooper agreed.

'Stop your carry-on,' I hissed in Ellie's ear as we made our way to the tables, 'he's my guest, so be polite.'

'I'll be polite when I've made up my mind about him. I haven't done that yet.'

The Western Orchestra, two fiddles, two flutes and a bodhran, struck up a lively air to encourage everyone to their seats. I introduced Thomas Cooper to my mother, Hugh and Bella, then took him to sit as far from Ellie as I could.

He ate as if he was, indeed, famished, and was surprisingly good company.

'I feel we are friends by now,' he said at one point and I nodded. Sitting with him among my people, in the corner of the world that owned me, made him feel somehow familiar. And safe.

Safe enough to tell him about Kilraven and our difficulties. And about Ellie's pregnancy. Telling him was in a way superfluous; he was unashamedly curious and could see well enough for himself how things were.

'Your mother is a beautiful woman.' He studied her, sitting at the next table, hardly eating a thing. 'Will she marry again?'

'Never.' I was shocked. 'She and my father were . . .' I couldn't finish.

'I understand.' He was silent for a moment. Then he said, 'Will you remain living at Kilraven after your brother and Miss Hope marry?'

I looked at him in astonishment.

'Where else would I live?' I said. 'This is not Africa, Thomas. You're in Ireland now and in Ireland, or England or Scotland or Wales for that matter, an unmarried woman by custom remains in her home. Customs are no doubt different in Africa but can you really have forgotten how things are here?'

'Things seem to me to have changed a great deal.' He had finished the cold meat on his plate and was signalling for more. 'I hear people talking about a new Irish Ireland and about the march of a nation forward. I see new freedoms. You seemed to me a part of this, an independent young woman with a mind of her own.'

Peg Mahony from the village trotted up to him with a platter, simpering and bobbing. Peg was always like that, at least to people's faces. I had to stop myself sending her away when she called him 'Sir' for the seventh time and tipped almost the entire contents of the platter on to his plate. Thomas didn't even look at her, so her slavering was entirely wasted on him.

'A mind of my own won't keep a roof over my head,' I said when Peg had backed away, 'and I'm untrained for anything but the country life.'

'What will you do with yourself?'

'I suppose I'll fill in odd nooks and corners in family life.' I heard myself sounding angry and lightened my tone. 'I'll help with bringing up the children. Ellie says she and Manus hope to have ten or more . . .'

'But you'll marry, surely?' He raised one eyebrow and sipped at a glass of the summer punch Ellie and I had made using blackberry wine from the year before. He didn't seem to like it very much. 'Do you not want to have children of your own?'

'The answer to your first question is that I had hoped to until recently,' I reminded him sharply. 'The answer to your second question is the same.'

'Things past cannot be recalled, my mother always said.' He kept his head down, eating away, ignoring my tone. 'It's your future I was asking about.'

'I've given up imagining myself married.' My ears flamed and I was sorry I'd tied my hair back. 'And Ellie's ten children will be quite enough for Kilraven, big as it is. There'll be room enough for us all, though God knows how we'll keep it going.'

He was not to be diverted. 'Surely there are dozens of young men eager to court you?'

'None who interest me,' I said.

None who were interested *in* me either, but I didn't say this. It was too sad a fact to put into words.

'I wonder if I'd be of interest to you as a suitor, if I wasn't going back to Africa?'

He was smiling and half-mocking and I had no idea how serious he was. I didn't want to think about it.

'Who's to say how friendly we might become if things were different?' I said. 'If is a word with great possibilities.' I smiled back at him, then looked away and spread the smile in a general way on those around.

'Thank you, Vanessa, for not altogether dismissing me. You've given me the courage to say my piece anyway.' He spoke softly, close to my ear. So close I was afraid to turn my head for fear of our faces touching when he went on. 'I'm not young, and I can't offer you the life of a county gentlewoman that you aspired to. But I'm not old either and am in excellent health and not without resources.'

He paused. I stared resolutely at the people opposite. To this day I can't remember who they were.

'I have never in my life before been so impressed by a woman as I am by you.' He said this in a matter-of-fact way, then sat upright again. I still couldn't look at him.

'You're very . . . flattering,' I said.

'It's not my intention to flatter you, Vanessa, I'm too simple a man for that. My intentions are far more straightforward. I am . . .' He cleared his throat, dabbed his mouth with his napkin, picked up his glass and put it down again. 'I'm wooing you, Vanessa. In my most awkward fashion, that is what I'm doing.'

He was quiet after this, picking at his food and sipping from his water glass. He left the summer punch where it was, unfinished. I myself went on smiling and looking straight ahead. I felt like my mother, though her smile hid grief and mine acute embarrassment.

A friend of Manus's stood and read a poem with the terrible lines, 'They will carry their love into a lighted room. And live there in joy for ever'. Manus himself made a small speech about how glad he was to see everyone and how happy he was to have Ellie share his 'numberless dreams'.

When all of this was over the dancing began, the dry weather having left a patch of lawn just about hard enough. When Hugh came and asked me to dance I made my excuses and left Thomas with relief.

'He's pleasant enough to look at,' Hugh said. The Western Orchestra was playing some sort of a waltz and we circled the lawn slowly.

'Did you expect him to have a cloven hoof?' I said.

'I didn't expect to see him here at all.'

'Why not? He's become a friend,' I said, echoing Thomas's own phrase. 'We've been corresponding,' I added.

'If he diverts you, why not?' Hugh said. 'Though what you've in common with a man his age is hard to see.'

'Maybe it's because we've so little in common that he diverts me. I'd everything in the world in common with Theo and all it did was divert him away from me.'

'*Touché*,' my brother said. 'Just be careful, little sister. He's . . .'

'He's what?' I prompted when he hesitated.

'Travelled.'

'Meaning he's worldly and I'm not.' I watched Thomas Cooper through the crowd. He'd moved away from the table and was standing in the shade of a goat willow, lighting a cigar. 'Meaning he's sophisticated and I'm not.' The Western Orchestra moved on to a quicker tune and I stopped dancing. 'Maybe it's time I changed, Hugh. Maybe it's time *I* became more worldly and sophisticated.'

'You're all right as you are.'

'Being what I am hasn't got me very far in life, has it?'

'You're cared for, Nessa.' Hugh looked embarrassed and pained. 'You're greatly loved by all of us.'

'And I love all of you but it's not enough. I want to *use* my life. Do something with it. *Live* it.' We walked to the edge of the lawn. Theo, dancing with his mother, waved at us. We ignored him.

'You've plenty of time yet to start living,' said Hugh, 'you're only twenty-three.' He sounded like an old nun we'd had at school and I told him so. Theo and Hermione Howard began making their way towards us.

'I don't see anyone else around here waiting to start living their lives,' I said, 'not you and Bella, not Ellie and Manus, not Theo . . .'

'What're you planning?' He looked suspicious, and worried.

'It's too soon to tell you,' I said, to torment him and just as Theo and his mother joined us.

'How pretty you look with those blossoms in your hair.' Hermione straightened a flower over my ear. 'Doesn't she look nice, Theo? Like a child of nature.' It was plain he had told her nothing of Celestine Lowry.

'She looks lovely.' Theo beamed at me. It was a beam which said, 'I can be nice to you now because it's safe, now you know my heart's with another.'

'I've left a friend alone for too long,' I said. 'Perhaps you'd like to come and meet him?'

Thomas took the cigar from his mouth as we came up to him. I stood by his side as I made the introductions.

'Are you holidaying in the locality, Mr Cooper?' Theo asked and I knew Hugh hadn't told him anything of my earlier meetings with Thomas.

How certain they all were that he meant nothing, how sure that I would pine indefinitely for Theo. How well they thought they knew me.

I put my arm through Thomas's. He put his hand over mine. Hermione looked from one to the other of us, shock turning to a realisation that things had changed without her knowing it.

'I'm staying with friends out near Rosses Point,' Thomas said, 'but now that I've seen Kilraven and this corner of the county, I'll be spending more time here.'

'You like it so very much?' Hermione Howard cleared her throat and turned a puzzled face in the direction of the mountains. Her voice was faint. 'Don't you find it all rather savage?' She paused. 'I did at first. I still do, sometimes.'

'Not at all.' Thomas smiled. 'I've experienced savage terrain and believe me, madam, what you have here is civilised beauty.'

'No one better than Nessa to show you the ups and downs of it all,' Theo said. 'She knows every rock on the mountainsides and every tree in the fields.'

His beam was still in place but now there was relief in it too. He'd no need to feel guilty; he hadn't left me broken and lonely. It was a final, telling indication of how frail a thing his affection for me had been.

'Will you be among us for a while, Mr Cooper?' Hugh said. He sounded cool. The contrast with Theo's enthusiasm was stark enough to bring a chill to proceedings.

'I've got a few months before I return to Africa,' answered

Thomas. 'I intend making good use of them. I've been away from Ireland a long time. Too long a time, in many ways.'

My mother joined us, with Bella. They both carried parasols but couldn't have looked more different. My mother had a gaunt elegance to her. Bella, in pink, was full of a summery, ethereal prettiness. She linked my mother's arm and said, 'What a wonderful party! It can only mean good beginnings and luck for Ellie and Manus. But we should be dancing, all of us. Will you dance with me, Mr Cooper?'

'I have a pair of left feet when it comes to dancing, I'm afraid,' said Thomas.

'Such modesty.' Bella left my mother's side and clicked shut her parasol. 'Come,' she held out her hand, 'you'll be surprised what you can do with me as a teacher.'

'Thank you, but no.' Thomas didn't move. 'I doubt even your charming guidance would help.'

'How can you say that,' Bella was teasing, her head to one side, 'without at least giving it a try? I warn you, Mr Cooper, I'm not used to being refused.'

'I can well believe that life rarely says no to you,' he conceded, 'but in this instance you must accept that neither of us would enjoy the experience.'

Bella, with a shrug and a playful pout, turned to Theo. 'You'll dance with me, Theo, surely?'

'I will, surely.' Adopting a similar tone, Theo whirled her away from the company on to the hard-packed grass. My mother and Hermione moved away, talking together. Not knowing what to do I stood with my hand still on Thomas's arm. I was also feeling very hot, and trying not to admit to myself that I felt bothered.

'How do you find King Leopold's Congo, Mr Cooper?' Hugh lit a cigarette without offering one to Thomas.

'Difficult and rewarding.' Thomas looked thoughtful. 'It's a land in transition. King Leopold is a philanthropic monarch.

His troops have defeated the Arab slave traders who preyed on the people there. He's also invested a personal fortune in public works to benefit the African population.'

The problem of my hand on his arm was resolved when, seeming to forget it was there, he plunged arm and hand into a breast pocket, produced another cigar, clipped the end and put it unlit into his mouth. He went on speaking all the while, even with the cigar in his mouth.

'Europeans such as myself can live a civilised life there now. There's the railroad and regular ship traffic to Europe to keep us supplied with the foods and other essentials we're used to. There is, on the other hand, a lot to be done in the way of educating the African.'

'Questions have been asked in the newspapers about the treatment of African workers.' Hugh was laconic. 'Words like oppression and exploitation have been used. References have been made to slavery and torture. I wonder why that is, Mr Cooper?'

I was shocked, but even so felt sure that Hugh was merely being provocative and that what he was suggesting was simply scandal. If he'd had facts, or any certain knowledge, he'd have taken pleasure in throwing them at Thomas. That he didn't like him was plain.

'Politics, Mr O'Grady, it's all to do with politics. Britain and France and Germany, as well as the mighty United States of America, would have liked to make a colony of the territory that is the Congo Free State. But King Leopold worked tirelessly and quietly with Henry Morgan Stanley to take the land and people into his care. He has done civilising and uplifting work . . .'

'So *some* of the papers would have us believe.' Hugh, cutting him short, was irritable. 'But others of them, as I've said, have also carried reports of the murder of an Irishman, a Charles Stokes. They say he was hanged without trial by a Congo state officer, his "crime" to marry an African woman and build a trade in ivory which threatened the king's monopoly. If a white man can be so casually put to death, Mr Cooper, then what chance has the poor African of a fair hearing at the hands of King Leopold's troops?'

'A most regrettable, and rare, incident, and one which happened several years ago.' Thomas examined the unlit end of his cigar, a frown between his eyes. 'The Congo government was as outraged as you are by Mr Stokes' death. All of us who worked and lived in the colony were outraged. The government made indemnity payments and took steps to ensure such a thing wouldn't happen again. In addition,' he looked up sharply when Hugh would have interrupted, 'in addition, and as a direct result of Mr Stokes' death, the king appointed the Commission for the Protection of the Natives. It surprises me, Mr O'Grady, that you aren't as aware of these facts as you are of the killing.'

'Oh, I heard that the government reacted at the time. It had to because of the outcry. But there's been no word of the work of the commission . . .'

'The commission reports to the king.' Interrupting Hugh, Thomas was briskly matter-of-fact. 'And the king, as you must also know, is the most highly regarded monarch in all of Europe. He deals with things in a quiet way. There have been no more unlawful killings.'

'Or none that we've heard of,' Hugh said. 'I suppose, Mr Cooper, that a man can remain unaware of atrocities if his own motives are suspect.' He held out his hand to me. 'We'll dance, Nessa,' he said. It was a command. But it was a plea as well so I gave him my hand.

'Why are you so rude to Thomas?' I said as we moved in slow circles amongst the other dancers. The Western Orchestra were playing what they said was a polka. My brother didn't care much for dancing and moved awkwardly.

'I don't know enough about him,' Hugh said, 'and neither do you. I'm surprised to see him here, that's all. I thought we'd heard the last of him when you left Dublin.'

'How can I get to know him unless I meet with him?' I said. 'How can you and mother and Manus get to know him unless you meet with him?'

'*Touché*.' Hugh was curt. His attitude, as he stared ahead with a tight, serious expression, exasperated me.

'*Why* don't you want me to get to know him? Tell me what your objections are? It's only fair that you should.'

'He seems . . . shifty,' Hugh said reluctantly.

'No, he doesn't. He looks you straight in the eye and gives direct answers.'

'He's an adventurer.'

'He may well be, but why is that such a bad thing? He has chosen to work in Africa and make money. He could have stayed at home in Galway and remained poor but where is the virtue in that? We are poor. Most of our neighbours are poor. Does that make us better people than he is?'

'It hasn't to do with money . . .'

'What has it to do with then?'

'With a way of life, a view of the world as a place to exploit for personal gain.'

'You don't know that he's like that.'

'I do. I know him. I've met his type before. He's an exploiter and an opportunist.'

'You don't know that he's either of those things . . .'

'I know that he exploited the fact of your being a woman travelling alone, that he seized on it as an opportunity to . . .'

'He did nothing of the sort, Hugh. We'd already met on the road outside the town. You're condemning him on the basis of your own prejudices.'

'Not prejudices, Nessa, more a knowledge of the world coupled with instinct. I don't trust him. There are stories going about of horrific forced labour on the African continent, about corrupt Irishmen and Europeans willing to benefit from it. Your friend may not be of their number but I'm not convinced.'

'It seems to me, Hugh, that you've heard a lot of stories but have very few facts about Africa or the Congo.'

'I'll get them. Or perhaps you can give me some? What do *you* know of the Congo?'

'Only what Thomas has told me. But I've at least listened and given him a fair hearing.'

'Why are you defending him so?'

'Why not? He's done nothing to offend me. He's been pleasant and attentive. Why are you attacking him?'

'Because I'm worried about you. You're special and beloved of all of us, Nessa, and I don't want this man, with his diamond tie-pin and shady life, to take you from us.'

'You're being ridiculous, Hugh.' I was sharp. 'There's no question of his taking me anywhere.'

'Oh, yes, there is, Nessa. Yes, there is.' Hugh put an arm around my shoulders and held me against him for a brief moment. He spoke quickly, close against my ear. 'Thomas Cooper is a man who gets what he wants, and he wants you. You must believe that I've met his type before. He wouldn't be here otherwise. He wouldn't have made himself available in Dublin otherwise.'

He let me go and looked at me, steadily and seriously. And altogether too worried. 'Please think about everything he says to you. Be wary. Be watchful. Please, Nessa.' He took my hand and began leading me from the 'dance floor'. 'You aren't dealing with a boy this time.' He looked thoughtfully at Thomas, waiting for us in a cloud of cigar smoke by the goat willow. 'I very much doubt your new friend ever *was* a boy,' he gave a short, low laugh, 'in the same way I doubt Theo will ever make a man.'

He was right, my brother Hugh, about so many things. But he'd been telling me what to do all my life so of course I didn't listen to him.

The summer went on. Hugh and Bella went back to Dublin at the end of August and Theo went with them. I'd seen very little of him anyway and too much of Hugh and Bella. The love between them was a daily reminder of what I might have had with Theo – and of what Bella had done.

16

Thomas drove from Rosses Point three times a week to visit me. I grew to like him, and to feel easy in his company.

He brought me presents: a book of poems, a pair of crocheted gloves, a single rose from his friends' gardens. He took me for drives in the motor car, into and around Sligo town, and once, disastrously, to visit his friends the Mansfields. Mrs Mansfield's character hadn't improved and my patience hadn't increased so we didn't repeat the experience.

He visited my father's grave with me. Walked with me all over the grounds of Kilraven, as well as to the beach and through the woods. I had the photographs I'd taken at the party developed and we enjoyed an afternoon going through them and laughing with Ellie and Manus and my mother. He walked with me through Kilraven, too, quietly admiring, ignoring the disrepair and empty spaces.

We went with Manus and Ellie to a party once and he danced with me, quite well too.

'I like to choose who I will dance with,' he said when I reminded him how he'd told Bella he couldn't dance.

As I grew to like him, so did my mother. He talked to her about fetishism in Africa and about exotic animals. He brought a change to our lives and was a diversion at a time when we were very glad to be diverted. He never once attempted to make love to me, though he did hold my arm as we walked and once, sitting in the garden, put an arm around my waist and kissed my neck.

Even so, or maybe because of this, by the end of the summer I'd agreed to marry him.

Mossie didn't much like him and Ellie refused even to try to. But since neither of them had ever cared much for Theo either this didn't bother me one bit, not even on the day Thomas turned to me as we came up the steps from the garden and said he would like to marry me.

'Why?' I said.

'Because you're beautiful and you are not a fool. It's time I had a wife. I'll be forty in a few years and will leave Africa and retire to Ireland. I intend buying land and will farm and raise a family. I want you to be the mother of my children.'

He stopped talking. I said nothing. It wasn't that his plan was repulsive to me, just that I was surprised by its clarity and simplicity. He cleared his throat and began talking again.

'I'm afraid that if I go now, leaving you behind me, I will lose you. So I want you to come back to Africa with me, help me run my station outpost at Pongara until it is time for me to come home. I want to show you places and a world you've never seen . . .'

'It would be easy enough to show me places I haven't seen,' I said, interrupting because I felt it was time I said *something*, 'I've seen very little.' I'd no real practice at accepting, or rejecting, offers of marriage.

'You agree then?' He didn't often betray emotion but on this occasion he looked shocked.

'That is *not* what I said.' I walked on quickly. It was another hot, dusty day and I was wearing an old sprigged cotton dress. 'I'd have worn something more suitable if I'd known you were going to talk to me like this.' I took a deep breath. 'Africa's a long way from here and it's nothing like this place.'

'You're not saying no then?'

'I'm not saying anything at all.' I was trying to decide whether to run for the house and leave him there, or stay and discuss what I'd known in my heart, all summer, was coming.

Knowing was one thing. Facing it was another.

'If you will be my wife,' Thomas spoke softly behind me, 'I will give you whatever you need to make you happy Tell me what you want, Vanessa?'

'I want Kilraven to be as it once was,' I said. Standing there, looking up at the ivy-clad walls and staring windows and remembering its shining days, it was all I could think of. I'd never wanted it so much. 'I want it to have a sound roof and dry rooms . . .'

The way it had been when I was a child, when my father was well, before the Land Acts left us without tenants or an income.

'Money will restore the house,' he said, 'I have money.'

'I want other things too.' I turned to face him. He was standing very still, the straw hat he was wearing shadowing his eyes. His moustache in the sun was like bristling gold. He was single-minded and reliable, and knowing he loved me made me feel powerful in a way I never had before. And he did love me: it was in the way he looked at me and in his desire to please me.

Hugh was the same with Bella, and Ellie with Manus. I'd recognised, over the months, that love between two people was anything but evenly balanced. My new philosophy recognised that people did what they could with the friends and lovers who came their way in life.

Also, it seemed to me that marriage was all things to all men, and all women. The marriages I knew – that of my parents, of Mossie and Julia, of the Howards – were as varied in their texture and qualities as life itself. Who was to say a marriage based on the one side on love and the other on need wouldn't, in its own way, be as comforting and companionable as any other?

'Perhaps we should go inside,' Thomas suggested.

'No. I'd prefer us to talk here.'

I had to discuss things in the sun on the steps where I felt free. If we'd delayed, even to go inside the house, I might have weakened and run and never made the commitment I did.

Because not only had I known all summer that Thomas would ask me to marry him, I'd known, too, that I would say yes. Given certain conditions. It was time to do so.

'Should I buy a ring?' His mouth smiled. I still couldn't see his eyes.

'You're proposing, of course, that we would marry very soon and leave for Africa immediately?'

'That's what I'm hoping will happen.'

'And how long would we live there?'

'For as long as my work keeps me there.' He spoke slowly. Even without seeing his eyes I knew that he was watching me closely.

'How long would that be?'

'Five years, no more.'

'No less either? I'd hoped you would say two, or perhaps three. Five years is a very long time to live in that climate.' I paused. 'It's a very long time for me to be away from . . .' I looked about me '. . . everything and everyone.'

'I can arrange a three-year contract,' he said, 'or for you to come back ahead of me to set up a home for us. Whichever you prefer.'

I thought about this. 'Whichever is best at the time would be the thing to do,' I said at last, 'as long as we're agreed that I will be in Africa no longer than three years.'

I looked away from him, across the mountains and down to the estuary. I drew no help from any of it.

'The rest of what I have to say is less easy but must be said.' I walked to the edge of the steps, putting him behind me. But he took a couple of quick steps and came alongside and took my hand. I still didn't look at him.

'I'm fond of you, Thomas, but you must know that I don't care for you in the way I did for Theo Howard. You . . .'

He cut me short, quite coolly. He still held my hand. 'I accepted that would be the situation before putting the question to you. I'm convinced, however, that we will grow closer as we live and share a life together in the Congo. I live in a comfortable enough house but will see that it is made even more comfortable for you. You will have everything you want – much more than you have here. Even so, it's a rough and ready life, Vanessa, you're intelligent enough to know that. But it's a pioneering life. Civilising Africa will benefit mankind. You're made for the adventure of it, for a life that's more exciting than the one you've known here.'

'If I am to marry without love I must have other assurances.' I was as cool as he was. For my part, there was a sense of the inevitable about it all.

This was my escape, a timely, God-given chance of a new life. It wasn't perfect but he was right – it had an excitement to it. It was also an appealing alternative to living on as a spare spinster with Ellie, Manus and my mother. Thomas would be good to me, and kind. It was enough to be going on with.

Going away held another, not inconsiderable, charm for me. I would be putting a distance between myself and Bella and Hugh. Africa would bring new experiences and a better knowledge of the world; living there would equip me to live better with what Bella had done.

Being fond of, rather than loving, my husband would give

me freedom too. I wouldn't be tossed about and uncertain the way I'd been when I loved Theo.

'Tell me what assurances you need?' Thomas said.

'The ones we've already agreed to: money for Kilraven. I will repay this by working at your side, helping at your station in Pongara in every way I can. And there's our agreement, too, that I, at least, will return home in three years.' I paused. 'I'd like these things in writing, Thomas.'

If he was hurt he didn't show it.

'I've never in my life seen a black man or woman,' I said as we went back inside the house, 'except in drawings and photographs.'

'You'll have no need to fear the African black.' Thomas sounded grim.

'I wasn't speaking out of fear,' I said, 'merely stating a fact.'

I was also wondering how it would be living in a land where to be black-skinned was normal, where the white of my own skin would make me stand out as different.

'I hope the Africans won't see me as an intruder,' I said, only too aware of such feelings against strangers who came to live in the West of Ireland.

'There'll no question of that,' Thomas said.

Agreements were drawn up for our marriage, to very mixed reactions from my mother and Ellie, Manus and Mossie. Hugh came from Dublin and did the legal business with tight lips and a stiff politeness towards Thomas.

The other thing agreed was that we would share a double wedding with Ellie and Manus in the village church in the middle of November. After a visit from Thomas, Father Duggan said he would perform a joint ceremony. The prospect of a new church roof had, it seemed, greatly alleviated his conscience.

As weddings in that part of the country went it would be

a small and quiet one. My father, after all, would be dead only a short eight months and Ellie almost the same length of time with child. It suited me very well to be married without great fanfare. It made it easier.

17

It snowed the day I got married.

The first flakes fell in the dark hours of the very early morning. Sitting by the window in my bedroom I watched them grow from gentle to fierce until the air was thick and the ground white. Brighter than any moon, their whiteness shone through the window on to the ivory satin of my wedding dress, hanging by the wall. Ellie had made it for me and, though I looked at its ghostly, waiting outline for a long time, it told me nothing of what I might expect from marriage.

Nor did the still, white, waiting countryside.

That was at five o'clock. By eleven my mother helped me button myself into the ivory dress. My veil was the one she'd been married in herself.

At exactly half an hour before midday Mossie set off driving myself and Hugh to the church. My brother was not in the best of humours and to break the silence I remarked on the bitterness of the easterly wind and on the snow scurries over the fields. Hugh, who was to give me away in place of my father, agreed the change in the weather was sudden and fell silent for the rest of the journey.

Ellie, to ward off bad luck, had spent the night before with Julia in the house in which she'd grown up in the village. She'd got the dressmaker there to make her dress, too, because she was afraid that walking up the aisle in her own handiwork would also invite bad luck. It was a lovely dress, pale lemon in colour and trimmed with ribbons, and she looked beautiful wearing it, in spite of her being big enough for triplets.

I was sorry to be leaving before the birth but there was no way around it. Thomas had to get back to his work in Africa.

Ellie was already outside the church, waiting, when we got there. We walked up the aisle behind one another, Ellie first on Mossie's arm, me following on Hugh's, to where Manus and Thomas stood waiting at the foot of the altar.

'We must be glad and pray for those partaking of the holy sacrament of marriage this day,' Father Duggan said in his sermon. 'It is to be hoped that the sacrament will bring them closer to God, that both couples here before us will enjoy His grace and embrace His goodness. We particularly send our prayers with Vanessa and her new husband, Thomas, on their perilous journey across the world. They are destined to toil among the heathen African, to live a life very foreign to our own.

'We are told how enlightened, Catholic Belgium, her king and missionaries, toil ceaselessly for that dark continent. Nevertheless, it's a sad truth that Christianity is unknown to many of those Vanessa and her new husband will live amongst. We must pray that, by example, Vanessa and Thomas will both be enabled to enlighten ignorant minds and save poor, misguided souls. Our prayers go with them, as they do with Eleanor and Manus.'

We were then joined together, to be man and wife, for better, for worse, until death us did part.

Afterwards, Hermione Howard sobbed loudly and clung to my mother outside the church. Mama, who'd at last had a dress and jacket made from the ribbed poplin I'd bought, supported her through the village crowd to the Howard carriage. Theo had been unable to come from Dublin and Arthur was too ill to attend. The gout, he'd said. Hermione was going straight home. With more honesty than either her son or husband she'd admitted she couldn't face my wedding breakfast after the years of hoping she might become my mother-in-law.

My mother stood smiling as Hermione left, accepting good wishes until Hugh came and took her home in a carriage with Bella.

Mossie drove Ellie, Manus, Thomas and me back to the wedding breakfast at Kilraven. We laughed a lot, packed together in all our finery, out of the worst of the snowy cold and glad the solemn part of the day was over.

The meal was of pheasant with celery and cream. The table had been laid out in the great hall and a huge amount of wine went around. There was music and singing and poetry-reciting. Finn sulked, not liking the disturbance one bit, and sat beside me most of the day. It was as if he knew I was going.

My trunks were packed with a modest trousseau of embroidered nightdresses, plain slip bodices, knickers with a double edging of lace, and a frilled, flannel dressing gown. I'd packed a book of Manus's poetry (handwritten for me), and Ellie's camisole, and a pearl choker given me by my mother which had been her mother's. Mossie gave me an ancient dagger, one he said my grandfather had brought home from Italy. It might come in handy, he said, in the event of a wild animal coming too close to me. It had a mother-of-pearl handle so I packed it.

'What will I do without you?' Ellie said to me in the late afternoon. I was changing into the tailored suit I'd bought in Sligo for travelling. It was of peacock-blue serge.

'You have Manus,' I said, 'and you'll have your baby soon.'

'I wish you'd stay, Nessa. Let him come back for you in a few years.'

'I'm Mrs Thomas Cooper now, Ellie, so it's ridiculous to be talking to me like that. Will you help me strap down the trunk?'

'Remember who you are,' her eyes glittered and her breath smelled of wine, 'and remember that you've only married that man, not given him your soul. I'll light a candle to you in this room, every day that you're away from it.' Her hands, holding mine, were like clamps. 'Remember the candles, too, Nessa, and you won't be alone.'

'Be careful you don't burn the house down,' I said.

We hugged then, very hard, but not for long. Thomas was not the kind of man who understood tears and I didn't want to give mine a chance to fall.

I left Kilraven with my husband at five o'clock to catch the late train for Dublin. Everyone stood on the steps in the cold, fresh, falling snow, waving until we rounded the bend in the avenue. Finn ran after us for a while, a mournful sight with his tongue catching snowflakes and paws losing their grip. He didn't stop until we went through the gates. I stayed looking back at him until he was too far away to see any more.

We caught the seven o'clock train to Dublin and began the long journey to Africa.

18

The steamboat which took me upriver to the station outpost at Pongara was called *Le Roi Léopold*. The Africans called it *kutu kutu*, because of the sound it made. It was long and narrow, with two decks. The Africans also called it 'the house that walks on water'.

The water was the River Congo and it was wide and winding, alive with terrors, endless.

Even on the upper deck of *Le Roi Léopold*, where there were cabins for Europeans and Americans and awnings against the tropical sun, the heat was like a leaden weight. It dried in my throat when I breathed in, dried again in the baking barricade of air when I breathed out. The sky, on this second morning of my journey upriver, was the same remorseless blue it had been the day before, and on all of the days before that since my arrival in Africa.

No one had told me about the sky, or the heat. Not really told me. Nothing I'd heard or learned or read before coming had even half-prepared me for the relentless nature of the African sun. Nor for the teeming mayhem, the noise, the colours, the smells.

The cruelties.

The confusion I felt.

The longing for home.

I'd been on *Le Roi Léopold* for an entire twenty-four hours. One day. In another two I would disembark at Pongara. It was just a three-day journey, not long at all. Unless you were the one making it.

There was a house made of brick at Pongara, waiting for me to live in with Thomas. Fifty other people lived at the station, which he had explained was in a clearing between the river and the forest. He'd gone on ahead in a smaller, faster boat to prepare for my arrival. As trading outposts went, Pongara was well established and served regularly by all manner and size of riverboats. Thomas had charge of it, along with supervising the harvesting of rubber in the area. We would spend our three years in Africa there.

That wasn't such a long time.

The wheel of *Le Roi Léopold* was to the stern and it had a shallow draft to allow it clear sandbars. I was learning about such things. The captain was an unpleasantly fat and unctuous Belgian called Hubbert who giggled a great deal and was a friend of Thomas's. At dusk, dinner tables were laid out on the upper deck for Captain Hubbert and the two white ship's officers to eat at with the passengers. I'd refused his invitation to dine. I was glad of some time on my own after the weeks of travelling with Thomas.

Another thing I'd learned was that sea journeys made me sick. I'd been sick between Dublin and Liverpool, between Liverpool and Antwerp, and the motion of the steamship bringing us from Antwerp to the west coast of Africa had forced me to spend most of the two weeks below decks in the cabin.

And now on the river journey I was ill, too, but not in the same way. This time I was simply exhausted from lack of sleep and the draining sun. I couldn't eat without being sick and I couldn't stop thinking of home. I hadn't yet adjusted to aspects of the married state and some of the sights I'd seen along the river had me doubting I could adjust to Africa either.

The Congo river was full of crocodiles and eel-like fish and dark, changing waters. Hippopotamuses reared their heads and opened their jaws like Fardy Quin's traps. Along its banks there were thousands of mud tracks and huts, palm trees, umbrella trees and elephant grass. There were hedges of cacti, wide-leaved banana trees and rope plants hanging like snakes between the high trees. I'd seen beautiful birds and large, shaggy-haired black monkeys with their tails held in the air behind them.

But these weren't the sights which made me worry about adjusting to life in Africa. The line of black men with thin, bandy legs in filthy loincloths, backs broken under the burden of the boxes, bales and ivory tusks they carried on their bare heads, was one of the things which did that.

The men kept their eyes fixed on the ground, their knees bent, their bellies thrust forward. They steadied their load with one arm and used the other to hold on to a walking stick. A white man in a hat walked behind them with a whip.

This, then, was where the ivory which was used to make piano keys came from. Or combs like the one which I could no longer bear to have in my hair. I shook it free and dropped it into the river.

As a gesture it was childish and useless, and seen by a young boy who was paddling a dugout with two others. They'd been calling to the steamboat, and laughing, but when the comb hit the water the boy stood and dived in after it. He was underwater for so long I thought he'd drowned, that the steamboat's churning had sucked him under, that I would have to jump in after him or at least have the boat brought to a halt. But his black head bobbed up, his long brown fingers holding the comb, before any of this had to happen. I waved at him and his white teeth flashed before he turned to swim back to the dugout and his friends.

When I looked towards the riverbank again the men being used as mules had disappeared into the forest.

And now, it seemed, I was witnessing another aspect of Congo life, one which made me worry even more about my ability to adjust to life in Africa.

The steamer had moored at a riverbank the night before, not far from a station outpost. Sentries were posted and the black members of the crew sent to chop down trees to fuel the rest of our journey. They lit huge fires on the riverbank and by their glowing orange light went on cutting trees into logs well into the night. When they finally stopped they slept on the ground in the clearing.

A great screaming and crying brought me out of my cabin just before dawn. On the riverbank, directly in front of where I stood on deck, the wood-chopping crew members had been woken and herded together by a soldier with a gun. In the clearing where they'd slept other soldiers were flogging a child.

Their whips were long strips of sharp-edged leather and every lash opened a red stripe on the flesh of the child's back. He was no more than ten years old. The screaming came from a group of other children, forced to watch as they waited their turn for a whipping.

I closed my eyes. Maybe, when I opened them, the scene would be changed, the soldiers gone, the children playing.

'They're being punished for laughing,' an American-accented woman's voice said in my ear. 'Most people would be glad to hear a child laugh, but not the brave soldiers of the *Force Publique*.'

I turned to see a woman several years older than me and several inches taller. Her shoulders were squared in a grey flannel dressing gown and she wore a long black plait over her shoulder. She had straight black eyebrows. Because I'd been avoiding other passengers, most of whom were government officials and traders, I had no idea who she was.

'Some of those children are as young as nine years.' She didn't take her eyes off the riverbank scene. 'The oldest is no more than twelve. The soldiers ...' She stopped, and shrugged.

We stood together at the rail, silent and sick as more and more children were beaten in front of our eyes. About two dozen in all were flogged that morning. When it was over the soldiers lit cigarettes and walked away. The children huddled in a group, hands held comfortingly to each other's heads, bodies too bloody and sore to be touched.

'They laughed?' I said.

'At a white man. Two of the littler ones. They laughed at a drunken white man.' The woman looked at me. 'The whipping is to remind the rest of the children never to forget that the white man is all-powerful and always right and a cruel master.'

'But nearly all of the soldiers are black themselves ...'

'The soldiers of the *Force Publique* are nothing but a ragbag of mercenaries and criminals trained in terror. They believe what they are paid to believe.' She shrugged. 'It's the monsters who give them their orders who genuinely believe the Africans to be sub-human, fit only to slave for the white man. But the monsters of the world are too few to be really dangerous. They're made dangerous by soldiers like those, men only too ready to act without asking questions.'

'Their parents ... where are the children's parents?' I said.

'My dear young woman,' my companion sounded impatient, 'you are clearly a newcomer to the Congo Free State. If you'd been here any length of time you would know that fear and brutality have made slaves of their parents too. God is mocked in the Congo Free State and so is freedom.'

The bleeding children were being led away by two elderly women. They did this silently and quickly, with frantic gestures, as if afraid the soldiers might come back with their whips at any minute. They disappeared into the trees and the place where they'd been tortured became just another clearing by the riverbank.

'Who allows the army to behave like this?' I said. 'Why aren't they punished?'

'You haven't been listening to me.' The woman sighed. She was standing very still, her eyes on the river. 'The soldiers do what they're told to do by the state's administrators. They're the most powerful army in Central Africa and only the Good Lord knows how much of the state's budget goes to pay for their loyalty. You'll see their garrisons along the river as we go. There's no shortage of soldiers in the Congo.'

'They carried guns,' I said. 'Who do they fight against?'

'Try to understand.' She lifted her head and squinted as if hoping to penetrate the dark mass of the forest. 'The *Force Publique* member is both policeman and soldier. He is at war with and fighting everyone but his superior, and is loyal to him only out of fear. When he fights it is usually against warrior peoples, native tribes who refuse to be subject to a king whose throne is a world away from here.'

She turned, leaned back against the rail and gazed at me with open curiosity. She had a very direct way with her, and was quite unembarrassed. I tried to be the same but was severely handicapped by ignorance and uncertainty.

'The King of the Belgians has never set foot in Africa,' the woman was matter-of-fact, 'but he's nevertheless become rich beyond belief on African ivory and rubber. His great, insatiable greed has become his god, the thing he lives for.'

The way her eyes rested on my peach silk dressing gown you'd have thought it, or the person wearing it, a symbol of that same king's godless greed.

'King Leopold is thought of in Europe as an enlightened monarch,' I said. Tired I might be, as well as confused and homesick, but I could still remember what Thomas had said, what I'd seen for myself in newspapers, and what the world believed about the Congo Free State.

'It's reported that the king rules the Congo well and humanely,' I continued. 'I've read myself how he had the railroad built, and schools set up.'

I'd been trying to inform myself. The newspapers and books I'd read on the steamer from Antwerp had said nothing about a murderous soldiery. I'd read a magazine called *The Truth About the Congo*, too, from cover to cover, and come across nothing vile. In fact, it had reported how King Leopold saw the Congo as his personal responsibility and had set up a 'chain of outposts or hospices, both hospitable and scientific'.

That there was brutality in the Congo I'd seen for myself. To accept, from a woman I'd never met before, that cruelty was a way of life and the country's ruler evil was another matter altogether.

The American woman wound and pinned her plait on top of her head. She was now a great deal taller than me, and resolutely silent.

'The world's view of the Congo is that it's a developing land,' I faltered.

'The world will always believe what it wants to believe.' The woman shook her head, testing, then put a final pin into the plait. 'But the facts are that the king's soldiers are more of a police force than an army and are as corrupt as those who give them their orders.'

I was silent myself then, energy spent. I felt sick and I felt ridiculous dressed in my silk dressing gown, the pearl earrings I hadn't taken out the night before, my blue slippers. All bought in Antwerp, with Thomas, all garish and inappropriate on this boat, against this woman's critical scrutiny.

The sick feeling worsened. The beaten, bloody images of the children wouldn't leave my mind.

'I think I should go to my cabin,' I said. Its long, narrow space with bunk bed, table and armchair had become a sort of haven.

'Are you all right?'

The woman put a concerned hand on my arm and that was all it took; a wild, unreasonable anger seized me then. She'd told me too much, too soon. She'd added to my confusion.

'No, I am not all right.' I shook off her hand. 'I've been a day and a night on this boat, six days altogether in Africa. I can't sleep, I can't eat without vomiting afterwards, and I can't bear the heat without feeling faint. I miss my home and family and, oh, those children . . .' I put my head in my hands and turned away from her.

'I'm sorry, so very sorry. It was thoughtless of me to tell you the things I did so crudely . . .' When the woman put her hand on my arm again I left it there. 'Why don't we sit for a while?' she suggested. 'This is the coolest and most beautiful part of the day and the sunrise is not to be missed. Come.'

She led me like a child to a row of wooden deck chairs. I'd tried sitting in one the day before and found it awkward and uncomfortable. The same chair felt fine that morning, so glad was I to sit down. The woman sat in the one next to me and was mercifully silent.

The sun came up from behind the trees, an orange orb in a purple sky whose exotic beauty made me feel further away than ever from Ireland. Somewhere on the deck below us a whistle blew and the crew, who'd been sitting quietly on the riverbank since the departure of the soldiers and children, pushed out a couple of canoes and made their way back to the boat. They were hardly on board before the paddle wheel at the stern began to slowly push the boat upriver again.

'How did you know the children were whipped for laughing?' I broke the silence myself.

'I was visiting the station last night. I saw what happened.' She stopped and cleared her throat before going on. 'The agent and his men laughed at me when I pleaded with them not to punish the children. Laughter is permissible in some situations, it seems.'

'My name is Vanessa O'Grady.' I held out my hand to her. I wasn't yet in the habit of calling myself by my married name. I wondered if I ever would be.

'I'm Eunice Milton.' Hers was calloused, and large like the rest of her.

'Are you a teacher?' I said.

'I am in a way, I suppose.' She smiled, took away her hand and stared down at its long, blunt fingers.

'Perhaps you're a naturalist?' I prompted.

This time, when she didn't answer immediately, I waited.

'I'm an Episcopal missionary,' she said at last, a half-smile on her face. 'My husband Granville and I came to the Congo from Virginia in the United States nearly four years ago.' She stopped, waiting for me to respond. When I merely nodded she went on. From her tone she might have been telling someone else's story. 'Our mission is based upriver, a little more than two days from here. We came to preach Christ's gospel, and to lead the African peoples away from such practices as polygamy.' She paused. 'The Lord, for His own reasons, did not bless us with children. Africa is our child, Granville's and mine.'

'It must be a fine life,' I said, for want of something better to say, 'serving God.'

But Father Duggan served God and didn't seem very happy about it, I remembered. Maybe the life of an African

213

missionary would have made him happier. 'Have you made a great many new Christians in your four years?' I continued.

'What we mostly do, these days, is give refuge and some education. What we also do, and it makes us more unpopular than any amount of proselytising, is raise our voices against the injustices we see.'

'Are there many?'

'You will see. I pray then your voice will join ours.'

I was in no state even to join my hands. 'Do you miss your home in America?' I said, changing the subject.

'Africa is my home now.'

'And your husband, does he feel as strongly about this country?'

'He does,' she smiled, 'and with more reason.'

'Why is that?'

She gave a small laugh. 'You'll see,' she said again, 'when you meet him.'

She refused to be drawn on what she meant by this, but I was getting used to her deliberately obscure ways and let it go. We sat quietly for a while after that, getting used to one another. Then I told her what I was doing in the Congo.

'I also came to Africa with my husband. We were married, in Ireland where *my* home is, just over five weeks ago. We've been travelling since then. He left me in Matadi and went ahead on a smaller, faster boat to prepare things.' I turned to her. 'I've never been anywhere outside of Ireland before. I've a lot to learn.'

'What is your husband's name?' Eunice Milton asked.

'Thomas Cooper. He has charge of an outpost station called . . .'

'Pongara,' she interrupted. 'I know it. I know your husband too. Our mission at Tonkinese is about two hours further upriver.'

'We're neighbours then.' I was pleased, and relieved. Here

was a woman I could talk to, who might even become a friend.

'We're neighbours,' Eunice Milton agreed. She didn't seem all that pleased about it.

The river had broadened now. We went between wooded islands, Eunice watching with a frowning lack of faith in the navigational powers of the captain and crew.

'Are there many accidents on the river?' I enquired.

If she had more bad news I wanted to hear it now, in the cool of the early morning, while I was sitting in the shade. She didn't reply directly.

'It was thought your husband had left Africa for good.' She lifted both hands to her plait, adjusting pins which were already secure. 'It's a surprise to hear that not only has he returned, he's brought a wife with him.' She cleared her throat. 'I hope you will be happy, my dear, that God will bless your union.'

'Thank you. I'm glad to meet someone who knows Thomas.'

'My husband and I met him soon after we arrived in the Congo.'

'You know him well then?'

'Not well, no. You must know that your husband disagrees with allowing non-Belgian, Protestant missionaries into the Congo? He's not a religious man, nor even, I think,' she raised her black eyebrows, one a little more than the other, 'a Christian?'

'We were married by the Catholic Church,' I said, 'but it's true that Thomas attends neither church nor chapel and that he has not much time for clerics and priests and the like. I know nothing of his views on missionaries. Maybe he feels about them as he does about priests.' I smiled to show I didn't agree with him. 'That they do more harm than good.' I remembered something else I'd read. 'Mary Kingsley feels the same,' Eunice Milton raised an eyebrow and I finished,

215

quickly, 'that missionaries do more harm than good in West Africa.'

'Mary Kingsley did a lot of good and no harm to anyone while she was in Africa. The same is by no means true of others who criticise missionaries.'

'By others you mean Thomas? Are you saying he's done harm?'

'How old are you?' Eunice Milton put her head to one side. 'You seem very young. Not more than twenty-one or two.'

'I'm twenty-three,' I said irritably, 'old enough to know that you've avoided answering my question.'

'Old enough, too, I hope, to know when discretion is the better part of valour.' Eunice Milton leaned forward. 'I've had my differences with your husband, my dear, but think it would be better to keep them for another time. It may be that you and I will have differences too. Do you share his views on many things?'

'We've had no great disagreements yet,' I said.

We'd no great disagreements because Thomas didn't discuss things with me. I'd discouraged him after a discussion about work in which he had opined that those who didn't work did not deserve to eat.

'Have you been trying to bring Thomas to God?' I said, curiosity not allowing me to keep my mouth shut.

'You could say that, yes,' Eunice replied.

'I don't think he's the sort of man can be persuaded of anything,' I said, carefully, 'unless it's to his own advantage.'

'How right you are.' She turned to me again and, this time, something in her unflinching gaze told me she would be better to have as a friend than an enemy. 'You appear to have got to know your husband well in a short time, Vanessa.'

'Not really.' I shook my head. Whatever Thomas's faults he was still my husband and so deserved my loyalty. I'd only just met Eunice Milton and owed her nothing more than civility. 'I'll be spending three years at Pongara with him. I plan to work alongside him and get to know him very well in that time.'

'What do you know of the station at Pongara?'

I hesitated before answering, not sure from her tone what she meant. Then I gave her the bare details of what I knew.

'I know that there are more than fifty people living and working there, both black and white.' I ticked each point off on my fingers as I went. 'That there's a comfortable, brick-built house for myself and Thomas to live in. That the wives of two of Thomas's workers live there, an English woman and a Belgian. That it's four days journey by rail and by steamer from the town of Matadi and the coast.'

'Yes. Pongara is all of those things.' Eunice Milton fanned her face absently with a hand. It was getting warmer, the sun climbing. In no time at all it would be uncomfortable again. I started to say something about this but she made a silencing sound and leaned towards me. Her intensity took me by surprise.

'You should know, too, that our mission is about two hours away by canoe, or dugout, on the same side of the river.' She spoke quickly. 'Don't ever attempt to reach us through the forest, and don't ever try to come alone. If you need to see me, or to come to Tonkinese, there's a man at the station called Lingomo Mongo who will bring you by canoe. Either that or send him with a message and I will come to you. Are you clear about that?'

I stared at her. She held my gaze. 'Are you clear about what I've just said?'

'I'm not a fool,' I said, 'you've made yourself very clear. But if my understanding is clear you're telling me I may want to escape to your mission?'

'Anything's possible, but all of that's for the future. Right now you need some breakfast. We both do. I'll bring it here.'

While she was gone I walked to the end of the deck to watch what we were leaving behind. This was not a good idea. We were moving fast and just looking at the wash from the steamer's paddles made me feel sick again. The sight of the crew having breakfast on the deck below didn't help. They were being given handfuls of rice and stinking dried fish.

My appetite was well and truly gone by the time Eunice came back with a breakfast of tea, bread spread with honey and some pineapple. She'd changed, too, into a black skirt and white blouse with a cross at the neck. She looked Amazonian.

'I can't eat,' I said.

'We must nourish the body as well as the soul.' She was brisk, putting the food on a low table between us and pouring the tea. 'Your system will never resolve itself to Africa if you don't eat.'

She stopped to light a cigarette, sucking in the smoke until it seemed her cheeks would disappear down her throat. As she exhaled the smoke poured from both nostrils and mouth; her hand, holding a cup of tea, appeared through the circling haze.

'Drink,' she said, 'I've sweetened it. This is a country in which you must be strong. Africa will devour you if you don't stand up and fight back.'

I took the tea.

'You smoke cigarettes,' I observed. The tea was like all the other tea I'd had in Africa; not hot enough and tasting as if it was made from dried bay leaves.

'You should smoke too.' Eunice Milton put her head back and drew again on the cigarette. 'Cigarettes keep away disease, especially here on the river. Mosquitoes hate the smoke. So do all sorts of other disease carriers. Here,' she handed me a cigarette, 'try one. You'll be better off drinking wine than water in Africa, too.'

'Which do *you* drink?' I put the cigarette between my lips and she struck a match on the silver box hanging around her neck next to her cross.

'Both.' She put the match to my cigarette and I drew on it. 'St Ambrose tells us that when in Rome we should live as the Romans. The African people smoke any number of substances.'

'They also marry any number of wives.' I coughed and held the cigarette at a distance. My eyes went on watering anyway. 'Some of them eat human flesh.'

'I was speaking loosely, of course.' Eunice Milton sat back into her deck chair, happily inhaling smoke. 'How do you like your first cigarette?'

'I don't like it at all. It's burning my throat more than the hot air ever did.'

'You'll get used to it, believe me. It's worth your while persevering. The day will come when you'll be glad of the comfort and protection of a cigarette. I couldn't survive Africa without them.'

The heat had arrived, the air feeling like weighted-down muslin again. I gave the cigarette another try and thought I would choke. I abandoned it, spluttering, and said, 'Why do you stay here?'

Her ready answer gave Eunice Milton away. She'd been asked the same question before, many times.

'We stay because it would be treachery to leave those who need us,' she said. 'We've chosen to spread God's word, Granville and I, and the mission has become a sanctuary for many. The Lord Jesus directed us to the Congo for a purpose and we're needed here more than anywhere we've ever been.' She continued more slowly, her expression lost to me in the smoke, 'You've no idea how much we are needed here, but you'll know in time. Unless I completely misread you, which is possible. And unless, of course, you don't stay.'

'Where would I go?'

'Home,' she sounded impatient, 'as other young wives before you have done.'

'I can't do that,' I said, 'we've an agreement, Thomas and I. We're to stay for three years and then I'll go back to set up a home for us in Ireland.'

'Whatever possessed you to agree to such a thing?' Her face was still shrouded in smoke.

'It was my idea,' I said, defending myself against her implied criticism. 'Thomas has agreed in return to help rebuild my family home, which is large and in need of repair.'

'You sold yourself.' Eunice shook her head. 'Sold yourself for the sake of a house. You poor, foolish child! And how lucky Thomas Cooper was to come upon you in your need. The devil, they say, looks after his own.'

'I did *not* sell myself.' I stood up, too quickly, cup in hand. The deck dipped and slid away beneath my feet and I grabbed the awning with my free hand. 'I secured myself a new life, an escape. Also, I'm very fond of Thomas and will make him a good wife.' Eunice Milton, it seemed, was nothing but Father Duggan in skirts and smoking a cigarette, every bit as righteous and judgemental.

'You will need to be fond of him,' she said, 'though it would be better still if you could love him. Love can bring about wondrous changes in a man. But so can the presence of good,' she paused, 'or at least the absence of evil.'

I held on more tightly to the awning and said reprovingly, 'You would be better off, Mrs Milton, saying what you have to say more plainly. I hope you don't deliver the word of God to the African peoples in such an obscure fashion?' The boat lurched. I dropped the tea cup and grabbed the awning with both hands. 'It's wrong to judge. "Judge not lest you be judged . . ." Doesn't God tell us that too? You know nothing of me, nor of my life in Ireland.' The broken pieces of the cup and saucer scattered across the deck. 'If you've something to say about my husband, Mrs Milton, then say it. Is it that he's a rogue? Or a scoundrel? Or just that he's a non-believer?'

'You're right about one thing.' She began picking up the broken pieces of china. 'It's not my place to judge so I won't say any more about Thomas Cooper. You'll have to do your own judging.'

The light on the water changed from the skimming kind to dazzling, making me feel dizzy. Eunice Milton stood and stared at me with the broken pieces of china in her hand. She looked concerned.

'I'm going to my cabin,' I said, and let go of the awning.

Eunice Milton's strong arms caught me as I collapsed on to the deck. They held and supported me all the way to my cabin, then helped me into the bed and covered me with extra blankets. These did nothing to stop my uncontrollable shivering. Eunice Milton disappeared from the cabin and came back with a brown-coloured bottle and a spoon.

'You need sleep,' she said, 'it's just a small touch of river fever. It'll pass but you *must* sleep. Knit the ravelled sleeve of care, and all that.' She poured a colourless liquid from the bottle on to the spoon. 'Take it.' She held it to my mouth.

I'd never tasted anything so vile. It was worse even than Mossie's attempts at wine-making, which were many and disgusting.

'Take it,' Eunice Milton said again, and I did. Three spoons of it while she stood over me. When I'd swallowed the last of it she pulled the chair close to the bed and sat down.

'What was in that?' I said.

'Quinine.' She felt my forehead.

'There was more than quinine in it.'

'You're right. There were African herbs and cures added. When in Rome . . .' She smiled. 'How do you feel?'

'Much the same. Dizzy. Confused. Worried about what lies ahead of me.'

'You're exhausted. You're also bewildered and homesick. All very natural. This is a good time to pray together to Our Lord Jesus Christ that He may guide and care for you.' She took both my hands in hers. 'Lighten our darkness, we beseech Thee, O Lord . . .'

I was asleep in minutes, with no idea what else Eunice Milton prayed for.

19

A whole new day of merciless sun went by while I slept. When I woke the cabin was in darkness except for the light from a small, sweet-smelling candle burning on the table.

I lay there, under the mosquito net, and felt a sort of peace. The quinine potion had done whatever it had to do and I'd stopped shivering. Maybe it was the potion, too, that had filled me with lethargy. There was no moving me.

I'd been on *Le Roi Léopold* long enough to recognise its slow, evening momentum, to know that the distant yells of crew members meant they were throwing the last of the day's wood into the stoke-hole furnace. Soon we would stop altogether and the captain would join his passengers for gin and tonics and *apéritifs* on the upper deck. I couldn't imagine Eunice Milton joining them. She was more likely drinking wine in her cabin, happy as I was to be alone.

At peace for the first time in weeks I thought back on all that had happened since I'd left Kilraven a married woman.

We'd crossed Ireland amiably enough, Thomas and I, sitting opposite one another in a first-class carriage. Truly alone for the first time we were awkward together, our conversation the polite exchanges of strangers.

'The rest of the country seems to have more rain than snow,' Thomas said as we came in to Mullingar. The midlands had been awash, mud and water-logged fields glistening in the moonlight as we passed.

'A lot more rain,' I agreed. 'The fields will freeze over in the night. The animals will have a hard time feeding tomorrow.'

'You're a countrywoman at heart, Nessa,' he said. Since I'd never pretended otherwise I saw no point in replying to this. After a while he said, 'You'll suit the station life at Pongara very well.'

'I hope so,' I said. I would have to.

I smiled at Thomas, after which we gave each other peace and silence until we got to Dublin.

The stormy weather delayed the sailing of the ship we were to take for Liverpool. With hours to wait before boarding at the North Wall, Thomas insisted we should go to the Imperial Hotel. Once there, convinced he was going to insist on his rights as a husband, I became slightly frenzied.

'I'd like a cup of cocoa,' I said as we sat in a drawing room off the foyer, 'but only if it's Fry's concentrated kind. I'd like some chocolate almonds with it and butterscotch, too, if they have any.'

The night porter, pale as paper and like an undertaker in his black frock coat, said he would see what he could do. He then put some coal on the smouldering fire and discreetly left us alone.

'Would you not prefer to sleep?' Thomas said, quite gently.

'No, I want to eat.' I tried to keep my voice even. It rose of its own accord anyway. I didn't want us to go to a bedroom. Not yet. 'I'm not at all tired. Travel gives me a hunger, I should have warned you.'

The cocoa, when it came, was too milky and not the concentrated kind at all. The almonds were of sugar, not chocolate, and the pale-faced night porter said there wasn't an ounce of butterscotch in the house.

'We don't have much call for it,' he said, 'especially at this hour of the morning.'

What the Imperial *did* have, he told Thomas, was a fresh consignment of fourteen-year-old Pale Cognac. Thomas ordered a bottle and the porter, when he brought it, also brought some of the Jacob's gingernut biscuits Thomas had liked when he stayed in the summer.

'We value our good customers, sir,' the porter said. He all but fell to his knees when Thomas gave him a florin.

'A man who does his job well is worth his weight.' Thomas poured himself a glass of brandy.

'He's certainly to be valued,' I said, 'though I'm not sure that fellow's toadying has much to recommend it.'

'What you call a toady, I see as a man who knows his place.' Thomas held up the brandy bottle. 'Would you like a shot in your cocoa?'

Afraid it would put me to sleep or, worse still, lower my caution, I said no. It was quiet in the hotel drawing room. A standing clock ticked loudly in the corner. A door banged somewhere deep in the bulding. Thomas put his glass firmly on the table and started to say something.

The porter, coming into the room at a rush, interrupted him.

'Your crossing is delayed further,' he said to Thomas, all but wringing his hands, 'they say it'll be eleven o'clock before it leaves. Will I prepare a room for you, sir?'

'No.' I spoke quickly, and loudly. 'Don't do that, please, not on our account. I've a much better idea.' I turned to Thomas, on fire with energy and nerves. 'I'd like to go shopping. There are things I need that I couldn't get in Sligo . . .'

'Antwerp is the place for that.' Thomas looked annoyed, whether at me or the ship's delay I couldn't say. 'I'll buy you what you need there, you'll find the choice better.'

'But there are things I need before Antwerp.' I heard my voice rise. 'My trousseau is so small, it's pitiful.'

'You don't need a large trousseau,' Thomas was firm, 'and Antwerp caters to the African traveller.'

'It may well do so,' I was equally firm, 'but Dublin is where I would *like* to shop.'

Thomas finished his brandy in silence and at eight o'clock I walked alone through the doors of Messrs Forrest and Sons of Grafton Street. Thomas hadn't suggested he come with me and I hadn't asked him to. If a coolness between us was the alternative to our going to bed, then cool we would be.

In Forrest's I bought a Parisian tea gown in maize-coloured *crêpe de chine* with angel sleeves of soft white lace. I also bought an evening blouse in blue silk, and a velvet Swiss belt to match. In Suffolk Street I bought a walking skirt and circular cloak in crimson with a Capuchin hood. They would be of no use to me at all in Africa but the shopping distracted me and did me no end of good.

It also lightened my purse. My father's bequest was diminishing fast.

On my way back to the hotel, so as to have at least one sensible thing to show Thomas, I bought a copy of the naturalist Mary Kingsley's book on her West African travels.

Thomas, waiting with a carriage in front of the Imperial, was politely impatient. On our way to the North Wall I showed him the book.

'A foolish and naive woman,' he said. 'You should have kept your money in your pocket.'

He didn't ask about my other packages and I didn't tell him their contents either. His mood improved when we reached the ship and he was quite good-humoured by the time we were shown to our cabin. We'd barely cleared the estuary, to face into a heaving Dublin Bay, when I began to feel sick.

I, who had never been sick in my life, thought I was going to die. It was as though I'd been pulled through a mangle and had all the will and strength squeezed out of me. My insides mutinied, my head spun and ached. And the sea, oh, the sea . . . I never wanted to see water again, either to sail on or swim in. If I could have walked on it, however, I'd have headed back for shore and never set foot on a boat again.

I saw little of Liverpool and was sick all over again on the journey between that city and Antwerp. Thomas played a great deal of cards with a group of men who included the captain.

We were four days in Antwerp before sailing for West Africa. We stayed in the Van Dyck Hotel.

It was very grand, with a great many flunkies, electric-lit chandeliers, mirrors and circular staircases painted white with gold. Our private bridal suite included a bedroom, sitting room, and room with bath and water closet. Almost all of the furniture was covered in peacock silk brocade and the window drapes were a dusty pink velvet.

I threw myself on to the bed as soon as the door closed behind the men who'd carried up our trunks. I'd never in my life been so glad to have a still place to lie on.

I didn't know it then, but there are worse things than a heaving bed and turbulent waters and sea-sickness.

I slept while Thomas went to look after some business. When evening came a girl arrived and put on the electric light, fixed to the wall and in the shape of a lamp. All this did was fill the room with a dull yellow glow which turned the moss-green walls brown. I'd have preferred gaslight, or even candlelight from the chandelier on the ceiling.

I was lying in the bed, which was large and canopied, with a feather quilt and silk-covered pillows, when Thomas came in. He sat on a wooden-backed chair filled with silk cushions and looked at me. It was no good pretending to be asleep, not with the electric light on.

'I hope you've had a good rest,' he said, 'that you're feeling better?'

'I have,' I said, 'and I am.' It was no good pretending about this either. I would have to become a wife sometime.

'I will join you so,' he said.

I lay on my side and Thomas lay down facing me. He'd taken off all of his clothes. Everything. I didn't look at him. I didn't want to see him.

I was wearing a nightgown. It was of white handkerchief linen with embroidery across the front and a blue ribbon at the neck. Ellie had been with me when I bought it in Sligo and hadn't been impressed. She'd advised me to buy something silky and yellow coloured, with straps not sleeves. I was glad I hadn't listened to her. I felt naked enough in the linen.

'You've had me tormented these past few weeks,' Thomas said.

He put his hand where my hip curved. It was hot. I held my breath and prayed he wouldn't move his fingers or touch any other part of me. By the electric light his eyes were more grey than blue. I met their gaze as best I could. Which couldn't have been very well because he said to me, 'You're nervous. Don't be,' and moved his hand down my thigh.

'I'm not nervous,' I said, wondering where his other hand was.

'Then you're shaking with excitement, is that it?'

The hand I'd wondered about went round my neck and pulled my face closer to his. He'd been drinking. But I'd known that the minute he came into the room anyway. I was an expert on the look and stance and behaviour of men when they'd been drinking. He wasn't drunk, however, I knew that too. Thomas never allowed anything or anyone to be in control of him. A good thing in a man, I'd always thought, before I knew Thomas.

228

'You're excited, Nessa, I can tell.' His eyes held mine, daring me to deny it, deny him.

'That must be it,' I said.

His eyes went on staring as he pulled my face and body closer and closer until we were touching. My arms were pinioned and I could feel the length of him against me. I felt his man's part, hard and moving and terrifying in its impatience. Though it was true, I knew there was no sense in my telling him I felt sick again. It was too late for that.

And far, far too late to think about what I'd done by getting married.

Thomas's mouth covered mine. My breath choked in my throat as his teeth pushed against mine and his tongue forced itself inside my mouth. His fingers were in my hair, holding my head so tightly against the pillow that I couldn't move it, couldn't do a thing to break free from his mouth on mine, to get away from the disgusting, worming thing filling my mouth.

His other hand went between my legs. The shock of it numbed me for seconds, but then, coming alive again, I closed my legs on his hand, made a clamp of them. What shocked me then, this time into a panic, was the strength he had in his hand and the power he was prepared to use to keep my legs apart, to open me, to force his fingers inside.

His tongue was all the time in my mouth, rough, grunting sounds coming all the time from somewhere low in his throat. Bile rose in my own. I tried to cry out. Tried, again, to pull my head away.

Tried to pray.

He lifted his head and my mouth was free, along with one of my hands. I swallowed and took a breath and said his name, 'Thomas,' and pushed against him with my hand.

I thought my half-formed prayer had been answered, that

he would stop and we might talk. Start our married life another night, another way.

But he tore at my nightdress, ripping it down the middle, then threw himself on top of me, pinning me down and forcing my legs so far apart that I screamed with the pain and fear of it. His mouth was at my ear and he was saying something, over and over. Through my screams and tears I heard what it was.

'Nessa,' he was saying, 'Nessa, my love, Nessa . . .'

When his male part drove into me I thought I would be torn in two, and die. It hammered, hammered, hammered at my insides, impaling me where I lay. When I thought he was finished, that he was taking it out, he jabbed it in once more and started again.

I stopped screaming, and I stopped crying.

Fear and disgust were replaced by the impulse to survive and I went limp, like a trapped animal when it lies as if dead in a last hope of reprieve. There were no words out of Thomas now, only grunts and snorting sounds in between. His sweat covered my body and his beard was hard and rough against the side of my face and neck as he went on ramming himself into me.

He whimpered like a child when the end came. His mewing and snuffling made me bury my head further into the pillow to keep his breath and salivating mouth away from my face. For a full minute he lay gulping like a fish on top of me before he rolled away and lay on his back.

I felt a hot stickiness between my legs and knew I was bleeding.

And that was it. My marriage, such as it was, was over before it began. That I'd entered it without any illusions was a nonsense: I'd fully expected fondness and companionship to grow.

There was little likelihood of that after tonight, and in the face of the many, many nights like it to come.

If I felt bruised and mauled outside then I felt dead inside, leaden and weighted down and horribly resigned. I'd made an agreement, I would stick with it. Africa was only for three years, then I would be home again with some of my dues paid and more mistress of my situation.

I gathered my torn nightdress and held it tight about me and stared at the unlit chandelier. Thomas's breathing was regular and I thought he'd fallen asleep. I waited a few more minutes and made to leave the bed.

His hand shot from his side and seized my arm.

'It will be better for you as time goes on.' There was no apology in his voice. 'You had me driven mad, Nessa, wanting you and being denied. It's not good to deny a man – any normal man anyway. You might as well learn that now as later. And by God I'm a normal man, you can't deny me that.'

He stopped, seeming to think this warranted an answer. Having nothing to say that he would have wanted to hear, I remained silent. His grip on my arm tightened.

'You'll learn to care for me, Nessa, I'll see that you do. My feelings for you are stronger than any I've had for a woman before.' He paused and I knew, without turning, that he was smiling. I didn't want to see his smile. 'I've wanted you since I turned the field glasses on you on the road outside Sligo,' he said. 'I'd never seen a woman move the way you did. It was as if you owned the ground you walked on. And now you're mine.'

'We're married . . .' I began.

'I am your husband,' he cut me short, 'and your provider. We will get along fine together so long as you keep those two things in mind.' He let my arm go. 'You may go to the bathroom now.'

There was not so much blood as I'd feared, but there were

231

plenty of towels and water so I washed myself. Then I washed myself again. I found another nightdress and put it on and went back to lie in bed beside my husband.

I couldn't, after all, stay in the bathroom all night.

It was a long time before I slept. There had been nothing, nothing at all, in our coupling that was in any way like the love making I'd witnessed between Hugh and Bella. As the grey light of another day slivered between the drapes, I knew there never would be.

Next day Thomas brought me shopping in Antwerp.

'You shouldn't have wasted your money in Dublin,' he said. 'From now on I will buy you whatever you need.'

Antwerp had a great many buildings in the elaborate Gothic style. The shops Thomas brought me to were elaborate too. He bought me several large linen hats and a straw one with ribbon and artificial flowers. He bought a white linen suit with a nipped waist and peplum over my hips. He bought me a pale-blue dress with embroidered collar, a peach silk dress with low neckline, and several skirts and blouses for everyday wear. He bought jet and diamond-studded combs for my hair, as well as an ivory one.

'Don't think me ungrateful, Thomas,' I said as we came to an end of the buying, 'or that I don't appreciate your generosity, but are these really the kind of clothes I will need in Africa?'

'They are precisely what you will need.' He took my arm and moved us away from the assistant. 'People like you and me must maintain standards, Nessa. We must be an example to the African, and to others. How we appear is important.' He touched my cheek. 'You will be a queen, my dear, admired and looked up to.'

I'd no desire to be a queen, in Africa or anywhere else. 'I'm sure the African people have their own queens,' I said. 'And their own kings too.'

Thomas didn't reply.

For himself my husband bought a dozen white shirts and a paisley-patterned waistcoat. He bought a white linen suit, too, and several pairs of white linen trousers. Everything else he needed was, he said, in Africa.

He also stocked up with supplies of English marmalade, condiments, canned meats, *foie gras* and other pâtés, as well as a great many cases of wine, mostly red and all French.

The remainder of our nights in Antwerp weren't so bad as the first, simply because I knew what to expect. I learned to lie limp and unprotesting when Thomas joined me in the bed. He then did what he wanted to fairly quickly. We didn't speak again about this aspect of our marriage. He didn't stop me going to the bathroom to wash myself afterwards either.

It was cold and it was bleak waiting on the Antwerp quayside to board the ship for West Africa. While Thomas finished his business with the ship's officers and port officials, and while the steam was got up and hatches battened down on the ship's cargo, I studied our fellow passengers.

This exercise didn't bode well for life in the Congo.

The number of soldiers going on board was a surprise. So was the look of them. They were the rag ends of whatever army they belonged to: young, underfed and trying to look like grown men. Many were drunk and many more looked pale and frightened now that the hour of departure had arrived. A few sobbed beside grim, unrelenting fathers. Older men wore guns across their shoulders and broad tropical felt hats. A few of them were sun-bronzed and indifferent to everything around them.

I counted the women: three or four accompanying husbands like me, and a few lone females plying their trade before boarding.

'The next time you stand on *terra firma* it will be under a blue sky.' Thomas took my gloved hand.

'I look forward to that,' I said.

I went ahead of him up the gangplank. I didn't turn once, not even as I went along the deck and through our cabin door. When the ship began to steam out of the harbour I saw no point either in going up on deck to wave and gawp with the other passengers.

Antwerp was where I'd finally acknowledged to myself the nature of marriage without love. There was nothing much I wanted to look at there.

20

My introduction to Africa was through another port town.

Nearly three weeks after leaving Belgium we tied up at Boma, on the north shore of the River Congo, some fifty miles inland from the Atlantic Ocean. The sky above was every bit as blue as Thomas had said it would be, but the explosive life it shone upon might have belonged to another planet so far as I was concerned.

The quaysides teemed with people of every race, colour and type. White men stood in watchful groups while black and yellow men worked.

It was my first time seeing black-skinned people. Although, as I'd told Thomas, I'd read about them and seen pictures, I'd never imagined black skin would shine so much, nor look so velvety. I found myself wanting to touch the first black man I stood close to and was afraid he would read my mind. But he didn't look at me. A lot of black people didn't look at me when I was with Thomas.

On the quayside there were lines of black porters, with children as young as nine or ten among them, all carrying ivory tusks as well as crates or barrels of wine on their heads. An overseer walked around them cracking a long whip.

Most of the Africans were thin. Some had deep scars on their faces and bodies and I saw two with suppurating wounds which should have had dressings on them. They worked non-stop; never-ending loads on thin shoulders, on fragile heads atop thin necks. They looked anything but happy, rolling their eyes fearfully in the whip's direction.

As soon as our trunks and boxes came off the steamer a line of these men, along with two children, were ordered to carry them from the docks.

'They can't do it!' I said, loudly enough for the overseer to hear. 'You must get some stronger men to take them, Thomas. That man and those children aren't fit for it.'

'They're up to the job all right.' He patted my arm. 'You'll understand soon enough that the African is bred to idleness and must be rescued from himself. Or herself as the case may be. Children, too, must be taught to work. Everyone is the better for it. The king himself has pointed out that, when dealing with a race which practised cannibalism for thousands of years, it's necessary to use methods which will shake their idleness and make them realise the sanctity of work. You must understand and not worry. And you must not interfere. Just accept that there is another way of doing things here.'

'But they look ready to die, some of them.'

'Don't be ridiculous!' Thomas laughed. 'You'll see how hardy they are, how cunningly they try to avoid work. Come . . .'

As we went, a black man fell close by and was prodded to his feet. His skin was worn thin like an old leather bag. We went past white men standing in warehouse doorways, guarding the cavernous darknesses behind them. The air was thick with noise, sweat, strain and intrigue.

And with colour too. Dazed as I was leaving the ship, walking the quayside, getting into the trolley taking us away from the docks, I was still mesmerised by the colours.

There were shining ebony bodies in loincloths, others with swathes of every hue on their heads or wrapped round them. The white men (I saw no women) all wore white, as Thomas did. Compared with the indigenous people of the Congo they were a monochrome lot; bleached but still central to the colour scheme.

We spent the night with a Belgian friend of Thomas's in a large house on a plateau above the docks. The house itself wouldn't have been out of place on the outskirts of Antwerp, with its bay windows and decorated pilasters, pillared porch and canopied balcony.

Thomas's friend, whose name was Eugene Leclerq, wouldn't have been out of place at my father's gambling table. Or in a snake pit. He was long and oily-haired and watchful, and his hand, when he took mine, was cold and clammy. He was a government official and we were barely sitting to dinner before he announced that the downcast black woman serving us was his 'present concubine'.

'Some of the realities of our life here may shock you at first, Mrs Cooper,' he ate busily while he spoke, in perfect English, 'but you'll come to see the wisdom of our ways in time. It's survival of the fittest in the Congo, in every sense, and we must all take good care of ourselves.' He looked up at me then, smiling with his yellow teeth.

To calm myself I mentally counted the long candles standing by the walls. There were five of them, all burning.

'You're quite right, Monsieur Leclerq,' I said, 'it would be foolish of me to pass comment, or make a judgement, about the way you live your life, here or anywhere else. I know nothing of your circumstances. I don't know you at all.'

'That can be easily rectified.' Eugene Leclerq's smile became wide enough to show his bottom teeth as well. 'I am a hospitable person. My home is always open, to the right people.'

'My wife has done very little travelling in her life before now.' Thomas spoke quickly. 'She has not, in fact, even been outside her own land.'

'You are to be congratulated, Monsieur Cooper,' Leclerq

looked at me and away again, 'you have done well. My good wishes for a fruitful marriage.'

Walking about Boma with Thomas I saw that he had a different set of manners for Africa. He was rougher with people here, especially the black people, and had a curtly dismissive way of expressing himself.

I didn't like it. But it was another thing I would have to accept.

If I thought Boma the end of the world as I knew it, then Matadi, where we were taken to board the train for Leopoldville, was the edge of the world I was entering. From Leopoldville we would travel by riverboat to Pongara.

Matadi itself was nothing but a straggle of low huts and corrugated sheet-iron buildings on a hillside overlooking the river. The population that I could see was made up of black and white adventurer types with guns across their shoulders and hard faces. There were any number of drunken sailors and of black women whom Mossie would have dismissed as being 'no better than they should be'.

These women sold themselves openly even to the point where one woman, tall and with painted scars on her cheeks, came up to Thomas as we went together into the railway station. He behaved as if she wasn't there, almost walking through her. She laughed, loudly, and called something after him. He ignored that too.

From Matadi we travelled on the train through a land of high, mysterious jungle forests, mountainous rocks and thundering Congo rapids. The forests had all the tropical beauty I'd ever imagined, with climbing plants everywhere behaving as if they were curtains, hanging from as high as seventy feet sometimes, every other one with scatterings of crimson flowers across them. There were all sorts of trees and red, green, yellow and purple flowers. But in other ways the forests were dark and grim and closed off-looking.

In Leopoldville there were more government officials to be met, a dinner to be attended, and three nights in bed to be endured before Thomas left on the smaller, faster boat to go ahead of me upriver to Pongara.

Alone, at last and for a while, I waited for *Le Roi Léopold*. I boarded her at dawn the next day.

Through all of this I tried not to think of home, especially not of Ellie and the baby she would be giving birth to. Thinking about her made me more lonely than I could bear. I wondered if she'd had a boy or girl and, on nights when my past life and the girl I'd once been seemed unimaginably far away, wondered if I would ever see my niece or nephew.

Sometimes, too, selfishly, I wondered if she'd kept her word about lighting a candle every day in my bedroom. It was comforting to imagine it burning there, to think that I was not forgotten.

Thomas, for his part, never really hurt me again, though he was sometimes rough enough to give me bruises on my thighs and upper arms. But he wasn't unkind and he was, in his own way, generous. He didn't criticise my lack of response. I wasn't sure if this was because it didn't matter to him, or because he believed things would change once we set up home together. I found change hard to imagine myself.

I dozed on and off all of that last day on *Le Roi Léopold* and promised myself, between sleeps, that I would persuade Eunice to give me a supply of her sleeping potion before I left the boat. Better still, I would get her to tell me how to make it. I had plenty of quinine in my bags; it was essential for travel in Africa.

At around eight o'clock in the evening Eunice Milton came knocking at my door. I wasn't asleep. The paddles had stopped some time before and the silence had woken me up.

'I've got some food for you,' she called, 'is it all right to bring it in?'

She came on in without waiting for an answer. I rolled from under the mosquito net and sat at the side of my bunk bed, which was comfortable and covered with a yellow cotton spread. Eunice Milton put a tray on the table. Laid out on a lace cloth there were slices of oatmeal bread, pâté and sliced fruit. There was a tea pot and two cups in saucers.

'There's just enough to keep hunger at bay. No point your eating a heavy meal at this hour of the evening, it'll stop you sleeping.' She began filling both cups with tea.

'I've slept enough,' I said.

I tidied my hair as she lit the oil lamp, then held a cup of tea obediently while she stirred in sugar, two spoonfuls, without asking. I was beginning to see how her forthright, not to say domineering, manner might be at the root of her cool relationship with Thomas. He liked to be in charge, to have things done his way. So did she.

'You'll undo the good the rest did you if you stay awake tonight.' She sat to light a cigarette. 'See how the mosquitoes keep themselves to themselves when there's smoke about?' She waved a hand. 'Better have one yourself if you don't want to get back under the net.'

My second cigarette was a lot easier to smoke than my first had been. Eunice put a small oval tin on the floor between us and we dropped our ash into it as we smoked and talked.

I told her about Ellie.

'I feel sometimes as if I've stepped out of the world. Ellie's been through childbirth, I'm sure of it. My mother is a grandmother, my brother a father and my other brother an uncle.' I stopped, sighing a little before adding, 'And Christmas has come and gone.'

'Letters are a good way to keep in touch,' said Eunice,

'I write a great many, to both friends and family. Every-one does. It greatly helps one's sanity. Riverboats come by nearly every day. They pick up and deliver mail.' Her cheeks hollowed frighteningly as she took a long pull on her cigarette. She fanned the smoke with her hand. 'There may even be mail waiting for you.' She smiled. 'The Lord works in mysterious ways, and so does the Congo mail system.'

I felt hugely cheered up, though a bit dizzy from the ciga-rette. The irritable buzz of a mosquito came from somewhere in the cabin, but it didn't attack.

'Thomas says he's lost all sensitivity to mosquitoes and that I will, too, in time. I'll try smoking his cigars in the meantime.'

'Have these.' Eunice took a cigarette from the box and handed me the rest. 'They're a lot easier to smoke. Ilanga Mongo, whom you'll meet at Pongara, will give you oils to keep all manner of insects away. They are notoriously sensitive to smells. Your husband is right. With luck you'll lose sensitivity and they won't bother you. They don't bother me any more.' She gave a small, surprisingly girlish giggle. 'Truth is, I smoke cigarettes because I like them. Though Granville doesn't know that, so don't you tell him.'

That was when I decided I liked Eunice Milton. She was not so righteous after all.

'Have you met other Irish people in the Congo?' I said.

'Oh, yes, from time to time. The British Consul here is an Irishman.' Her eyebrows had risen. 'Didn't your husband tell you?'

'No. He said nothing.' I broke a piece of bread and spread it with pâté. Eunice sipped her tea. 'He clearly didn't think it important,' I said.

'Clearly.' Eunice Milton's tone was dry. 'The consul's name is Roger Casement and he's a good man, if an odd one. He

241

certainly has the measure of what's happening here. He's visited your husband's station.' She hesitated, coughed, and went on, 'He's called on us at the mission too. He travels a great deal. Sees a great deal.'

'I'll surely meet him then,' I said.

'You can do so this Sunday. We're expecting he'll visit again, though nothing's ever very certain in the Congo.'

'Then I'll come to meet him.' I took another piece of bread, dry this time. The pâté was far too thick and garlicky for my taste. 'I'll travel by river, as you advised.'

'Just so long as you don't travel alone, whether by river or through the forest.'

She stopped talking and drummed her fingertips on the table and I knew that she was trying to prevent herself from saying something. I watched, and waited. I was getting to know her, a little. Eunice Milton liked to say what she thought and wasn't good about keeping her own counsel.

'I want you to bear in mind what I said before. You must come to us at the mission if anything untoward ever happens,' she said at last. 'Don't feel you're alone, or that there's no help for your situation.' She stood. 'I must go now. I have work to do in my cabin.'

'What's likely to happen?' I stood, too, my heart thudding uncomfortably. It was awful to have my fears of the unknown reinforced like this. 'Please tell me what you're talking about?'

'I talk too much,' she touched my hair, gently, with two of her fingers. 'I have no children. You could almost be my daughter.' She hesitated, then sighed and turned away. 'There is an evil here, Vanessa, that I think you will recognise fairly quickly.' She opened the door and was gone.

I wrote long into the night, pages and pages to Ellie and a shorter missive to my mother. I put them together in one envelope, addressed it and delivered it to a ship's officer to take back downriver to be dispatched at Boma.

Then I packed my bags again and lay down, fully dressed in the white linen suit Thomas had bought for me in Antwerp, to wait for morning and our arrival at Pongara.

21

Thomas waved. I couldn't see his face clearly from the deck but knew the white-dressed figure in front of a row of five black men had to be him. The Africans were taller than he was and stood still as stones.

I waved back.

'That's your new home.' Eunice Milton, beside me, pointed to a house on raised land behind the other buildings.

I'd have recognised it anyway by its brick façade and Thomas's description. Its square fortress-look was relieved by a white-painted veranda and windows with white-painted frames. The door, which was closed, had been painted blue. It was by far the grandest building in the compound and if it hadn't been for the veranda would have fitted fine into a Dublin suburb.

This would have comforted me if the rest of Pongara hadn't looked more like a military base than a station outpost.

There were soldiers everywhere, all of them carrying guns. A high wooden wall kept the forest out, and the Congo's blue flag with its gold star hung sadly limp from a flagpole near the riverbank. Around it, in a natural, sun-filled clearing that came right down to the river, there were several thatched-roof houses with verandas shaded by palm trees.

A second man-made clearing had been hacked out of the forest. My new home was in this second part, the hill on which it stood as man-made as the clearing itself and dwarfed by the high, impenetrable wall of the jungle trees beyond. Behind them, no doubt, there were leopards and gorillas in their thousands.

'Most of the trees around here are acacias,' said Eunice, following my gaze, 'though there are a fair number of mango trees and oil palms as well. You'll get to know them.'

'I'm sure I will,' I said, not sure of any such thing as I clicked open my parasol. I held it over both of us, waving again at Thomas. We were a lot closer to shore and the paddles had all but stopped. 'Tell me about the buildings,' I urged. 'Who lives in them? What are they used for?'

The Africans had rushed ahead of Thomas and were launching three dugouts from a row drawn up on the riverbank. When they were in the water Thomas climbed into one and sat very straight, facing the steamer. He was wearing a white hat with a deep brim and cloth at the back to keep the sun off his neck. It was exactly like the one I'd seen in pictures of Henry Morgan Stanley.

'Your husband will tell you everything you want to know,' Eunice covered my hand with hers on the rail, 'but please remember, you're not alone.'

'Forewarned is forearmed,' I said, quickly and sharply. 'I want *you* to tell me what the station buildings are for, Eunice. Please. I want to know.'

'Keep the information to yourself then,' she said, 'and form your own judgements about whatever your husband chooses to tell you.' She took her hand from over mine and went on in a low voice.

'The long, wooden building on the height next to your home is the blockhouse. The tripods on the roof are for rifles, the trapdoors to allow soldiers access. See, there are a couple of men taking up position . . .'

She was right. One of the men was looking through the

sights of a rifle. 'I suppose they need to guard against leopards,' I said.

'Leopards don't attack humans unless provoked or wounded.' Eunice Milton made an impatient sound. 'They're more likely to go for the goats or dogs. But such domestic creatures, as you can see, are corralled near the waterfront. Don't interrupt again, Nessa, please. Your husband is almost alongside so I'll have to be quick and you'll have to listen carefully.'

She looked down as she went on so that the brim of her brown cloth hat hid her face from the canoes and Thomas. But since I had to crane to hear her my posture probably gave away the fact that she was telling me something.

'The blockhouse is a prison, too, and a storehouse for guns and ammunition. Gates in the walls allow workers to bring in the rubber which is stored in the sheds at the bottom of the hill. Tusks are still brought in, too, for the ivory, which is stored mostly in piles like those at the end of the sheds. The armed soldiers are guarding both. They're also making sure the workers don't return to their village homes.'

I would have interrupted at this point but she swore, under her breath, and made a furious, hissing sound. Her God was clearly a lot more tolerant than Father Duggan's.

'The grass-roofed buildings by the river are where your husband's white soldiers and chargehands live, some of them with female companions they will tell you are their wives. The huts in the middle are where the Africans live. The pens in front hold chickens and goats and a little ways off there's a small garden with vegetables such as manioc and sweet potatoes. The cut wood you see piled on the bank is because your husband doesn't encourage riverboats to stay overnight at Pongara.'

'Thank you,' I said, and walked along the deck to meet Thomas as he came up the rope ladder and on to the boat.

'Africa suits you, my dear.' He held me at arm's length. 'You look well, and rested. But we mustn't allow too much of its sun on your skin. You've become a little . . .' his face took on a look of slight distaste '. . . freckled.'

'You look fit and well yourself, Thomas.'

He did, too. He looked stronger, more solid in himself. He looked powerful in a way he hadn't before; like a man in charge. Which of course was what he was. This was Thomas Cooper, Station Master of Pongara, and I was meeting him for the first time. He was wearing polished boots to his knees.

'I'm glad to see you dressed for the occasion.' He smiled, kissed me on the cheek and took my arm. 'First impressions are very important. Everyone here has been waiting impatiently to see you.'

'I'm anxious to meet them too.'

We stood by the rail, close to the steps leading down to the lower deck. Thomas called to the man in the canoe he'd travelled in and he immediately laid a bright cloth over the plank seat. He didn't once look up or acknowledge me in any way. Captain Hubbert, who was easily as broad as he was tall, rolled along the deck towards us. He was followed, as he always was, by an African boy of about fourteen wearing white trousers and a perpetual grin.

'Thomas, *mon ami*, you must stay for a *petit verre* with me. You and your beautiful wife. We have seen so little of her during the journey . . .' He rocked on his heels and looked at me, giggling. His lips, in his brown beard, were very red. 'She is timid, perhaps?' He rubbed his beard.

'I wouldn't call my wife timid.' Thomas gave a short, amused laugh. 'She's not used to the sun, and she's also,' he playfully slapped Hubbert's shoulder, 'most selective about the company she keeps. Rough and ready riverboat captains

247

such as yourself, Hubbert, are not to her taste.'

'Perhaps if she knew me better her tastes might change.' Captain Hubbert giggled. 'I have, as always, the best champagne on board. A crate of Jules Rémy.'

'We must go.' Thomas was suddenly sharp. 'My wife's tastes are unlikely to change. Not even over a bottle of Jules Rémy.'

Captain Hubbert's rosy lips pursed.

'Very well.' He snapped his fingers and the African boy put a folded handkerchief into his hand. 'I will impose no further.' He slowly unfolded the handkerchief.

'You've been gone from us some time and have come back a husband. It is understandable that old friends must take second place in your life.' He wiped his face with the white cotton, expression petulant as a child's.

'You know me better than that, Hubbert.' Thomas put a hand on his arm. 'We've been through too much in this heathen kingdom for you and I ever to be less than the best of friends.' He took my hand and brought me closer. 'But I've been three days apart from Vanessa . . .' He patted my hand and smiled at the captain.

'I'm a doting husband myself.' Hubbert's giggle made me shiver. 'I understand only too well. We'll have that glass on the return trip.'

'You have my crates ready?' Thomas said.

'Absolutely. Your boys can take them straight away.' Hubbert smiled. 'I have mail, too, for your lady wife. I didn't dare interrupt her solitude during the trip.'

He blew a whistle, once, and crew members on the deck below began lowering crates to the men in the canoes.

'I'll take care of my wife's letter,' Thomas said. Captain Hubbert smiled.

'We have the same custom in Belgium,' he said, and took an envelope from an inside breast pocket. As he handed it to Thomas I saw my name in Ellie's handwriting and an Irish stamp.

'Please, Thomas.' I held out my hand.

'Later.' He shook his head in kindly fashion. 'You'll have enough to do balancing yourself and your parasol and skirts as we go ashore.' His eyes looked behind me and his expression changed. It became tight and cold. 'Mrs Milton.' His voice, too, was tight and cold. 'I'd no idea you were downriver.'

'Not only was I downriver, Tom, but I've also been getting to know Vanessa.'

Eunice stood beside me, smiling. 'We're privileged indeed to have her for a neighbour. May I congratulate you on your marriage?'

'You may.' Thomas brought his heels together and inclined his head. 'My thanks to you and goodbye. I must supervise the unloading of my stores. Come, Vanessa.'

He'd gone three steps down the ladder to the lower deck when Eunice called, 'It would be nice, Tom, if you and Vanessa could come to tea on Sunday afternoon.' Her voice was high and cheerful. 'Say about four o'clock? We're entertaining a countryman of yours.'

'Vanessa will be too busy to socialise for a while to come.' Thomas didn't stop and he didn't look round.

Eunice took my hand briefly and squeezed it. 'No matter what he says you are *not* alone,' she said. 'Don't ever think you are.'

I sat with my back to the riverbank on the yellow-covered plank in the canoe. In less than a minute we were far enough away from the boat for me to see the few early-rising passengers gathered around their ship's captain on the upper deck. Eunice Milton stood a little apart. Captain Hubbert waved the white handkerchief and called something. It sounded like 'God speed' but everyone around him laughed so it couldn't have been. Everyone except Eunice. She turned and disappeared into her cabin.

The other two canoes looked as if they would sink from the weight of crates and boxes in them. I felt terribly close to the water myself. Long, jagged shapes moved along the bottom. Or it may have been the reflection of the ripples. The sun was hot through the parasol.

'Are there crocodiles around these parts?' I said to Thomas.

'I cannot bear to be called Tom and that woman knows it.' He ground his teeth. 'She's not a fit companion for you, Vanessa. We will *not* be visiting them this Sunday. Or any other Sunday either.'

'I liked her,' I said, 'she seemed to me a good and decent person.'

'You know nothing about her, nothing! She's unnatural. I forbid you to see her again. I have forbidden her Pongara and will not tolerate your going to the mission at Tonkinese either.'

'What do you mean, she's unnatural? I found her completely unaffected . . .'

'Don't question me, Vanessa. Her deviant way of living need not concern you because she will not be a part of your life.'

I left it at that, for then. Thomas was already working himself into a temper and I was terrified the canoe would overturn and we'd all be devoured by the *things* at the bottom of the river. I remembered how he'd once said Africans had brutish instincts and rough passions and experienced a sickening certainty that he'd been talking about himself, whether he knew it or not.

But he would not stop me going to see Eunice Milton, at the mission or anywhere else. And if she was bold enough to come visiting me at Pongara I would make her welcome, no matter what Thomas said.

I didn't know then that it was what Thomas *did* that mattered.

I ignored his helping hand as I stepped out of the canoe. 'Remember, I'm a country girl,' I said, to take the bad out of it, 'I can get in and out of boats unaided. There's no need for you to fuss over me.'

'You're not in the Irish countryside now,' he said curtly, 'you're in the Congo. One slip and you could perish. Those aren't salmon in the water.'

He strode the couple of yards to where the crates had been landed, spoke loudly to the men as they loaded them on to their heads and watched as they set off. He shouted a last command before coming back to me and crooking his arm.

'Come,' it was a command, 'it's time to meet your new neighbours and servants.'

The performers on stage for *The Countess Cathleen* were as nothing compared to the gathering which awaited us that morning.

The entire population of Pongara had come together in the first clearing. They might have been servants and retainers gathered for the homecoming of a lord and lady of a great house at home. Which was clearly how Thomas wanted it to appear.

In front, kneeling, were the African children. Behind them stood a row of African women and men, very straight and very quiet. The women were wrapped in bright cloth, the men in loincloths or military-style uniforms. Separately, to one side, stood a foursome of white people, two men and two women. One of the men wore a soldier's uniform and hat, the other was dressed in white linen, like Thomas, but was hatless and leaned on a cane. The women wore dresses which might have been worn to dinner in Dublin or Antwerp, in bright satins and lace. One of them had orange hair, the other's was brown.

All of the black people were clapping.

I wanted to laugh. It welled inside me, the sort of laughter that could only end in tears. I'd never in my life felt so foolish, standing there with my parasol in my white linen suit beside a man who thought the spectacle in front of us wonderful. A man who was my husband and who had ordered the whole ridiculous performance. I hoped the lined-up people wouldn't hate me for ever as the cause of their humiliation.

'See how welcome you are, Vanessa,' Thomas said. 'In Pongara you're a queen.'

He was serious.

The two white couples came towards us. Thomas waved a hand and everyone else dispersed.

'We're delighted to have you here, Mrs Cooper.' The tallest of the men, the one with the cane, saluted with two fingers to his forehead. He had thin, bleached hair and eyes the same colour. 'We need the civilising influence of an elegant woman at Pongara.' His smile was pleasant and his accent of the cultured English kind. His skin was stretched thin and yellowy-brown over a bony face.

'Thank you,' I said.

The woman with the orange hair studied me with open curiosity, from my head to the hem of my skirts. Her eyes were like a cat's, with kohl lines drawn to make them even more so. It was hard to read anything friendly in their expression.

'We hope you will be happy,' she said. She sounded foreign and looked about my mother's age.

Thomas made the introductions. The tall Englishman was Charles Beckett and the orange-haired woman, whose name was Blanche, was Belgian and the wife of the second man, who was called Leon Klein and was also Belgian. Klein wore a gun on his shoulder, military trousers and an open shirt. He had a nude woman tattooed on his bared, hairless chest. The second woman was English and introduced as Charles Beckett's wife. Her name was Muriel and she had small black eyes in a pale, powdered face.

'You're welcome,' she said, 'though if you take my advice you won't stand about out here. Night's the only time for a white woman to put her head out of doors in Africa. Stay indoors when you can.'

'The sun takes some getting used to,' I agreed. Thomas took my arm again.

'You'll want to see your new home,' he said, and to the others, 'come up to the house at about eleven o'clock. We'll have some celebratory champagne together.'

I felt their eyes on my back, and their whispers in my ears, all the time it took to walk through first one dusty compound, then the other, to the blue-doored brick house on its hill.

An African woman opened the door to us.

Thomas walked us past her, straight to the cool of a bedroom with tightly closed blue velvet drapes. An oil-lamp and cut-glass bottle of lavender water stood on a dressing table. The bed was a large four-poster with a mosquito net hanging in folds from the canopy.

'I had it especially made.' He parted the netting.

What followed didn't take long. He asked me to remove my clothes but became impatient with my slowness and threw us on to the bed, himself on top of me. He had my skirts and petticoats over my head before he had his trousers opened. I thought I would smother and die as he drove into me but it was over too quickly for that.

'I've lain in this bed for three nights thinking about you,' he said afterwards, 'I'm obsessed with you. You must be very, very careful, Vanessa, how you go with me.'

He said this softly. I had never been so frightened in my life.

22

The stores which had come with me on *Le Roi Léopold* were carried into the house and unpacked by the man called Lingomo Mongo. He was, and would be, the only black man allowed over the threshold.

When Lingomo Mongo had laid everything in the kitchen his wife, Ilanga, put the things away in the cupboards and cool boxes lining the pantry. She was, and would be, the only black woman allowed in the house.

When I tried to help she grabbed things from me so I watched instead, and followed her. She worked quickly, without a word, her long, strong fingers seeming to do three things at once. She didn't smile and she didn't look at me.

'I'll need to know where things are,' I said, wanting to know if she spoke English.

'No, you will not.' Thomas spoke from the doorway. 'Ilanga looks after the household. All you need do is give her orders.'

'I'd at least like to know what there is to eat.'

'There is everything you could want. The king doesn't like those who work for him to be without. Show her, Ilanga,' Thomas didn't come into the kitchen, 'and be quick.' His boots clumped along the wooden floor to the front of the house.

'Here are the bottles and tins,' Ilanga Mongo said in English, pointing to one cupboard before opening another. 'In here is yams, plantain, sweet potato, maize,' she ticked these off on her fingers, 'all are in the cool boxes. Milk comes from the goat each day. When you wish for such as chicken, pig or fish you will tell me. There is plenty food. There will be no problem.'

When I stood beside her, looking at the packed shelves, she moved away from me, back into the kitchen. I felt her eyes on my back, and the silence between us, as I studied the tins of Astrakhan caviar, mock-turtle soup, sauce Hollandaise, corned beef and brawn, *pâté de foie gras*, oysters, apricots, cocoa, Assam Pekoe tea and crystallised sugar.

In glass jars there were syrups, oils for cooking, jams, honey, marmalade. In another cupboard there were bottles of port, Amoroso sherry, French wines, gin and whiskey. In a cool box there was champagne. There was enough food to see us through a war or drought or famine, or all three. It was unbearably dispiriting.

'We'll certainly have enough to eat,' I said, 'and drink.'

'Never a problem.' Ilanga left the kitchen, beckoning. I followed her bare, soundless feet along the hallway until she stopped at a velvet-curtained doorway. 'Your husband is here.'

Thomas was smoking a cigar by a window leading to the veranda. It was a long window and, because of the hill on which the house stood, gave views of the station right down to the wide, wide river. A blue, blue sky shone over it all.

I stood beside Thomas's chair, looking down at my new life. He didn't take my hand, or touch me in any way.

I hadn't expected him to. Holding hands, fond kisses, the occasional embrace, were gestures Thomas didn't even think about. Making love, for him, was what he did to me in bed. His reticence about touching me all summer hadn't been because of any regard for my person. It was just that he hadn't seen the point.

'It's so peaceful,' I said, 'with the sun on the river like that, the green of the forest ringing the station.'

'You sound surprised?'

'That's because I feel, all the time, that there's an Africa I can't begin to imagine hidden behind the darkness of the trees.' Admitting this, I wrapped my arms about myself to stop a shiver. Two men with guns walked along the edge of the forest.

'You give in too much to your imagination.' Thomas looked at the top of the cigar before putting it back in his mouth. He pulled on it and said, 'You're a woman now, Vanessa, and of an age to put childishness behind you.'

I think that if Thomas, on that first morning in Pongara, had reached out and touched me gently I might, somehow, have been able to reach *him* in another sense. I would have tried, even then, to explain that I needed him as a friend as well as a husband. But he moved away, shuttered as ever, and the moment was lost.

'You're safe here,' he said, 'safer than anywhere else in the Congo. I've my own sentries rimming the forest and there's a *Force Publique* garrison near by. They keep us supplied with guns and ammunition.'

'Are so many guns and soldiers necessary?'

'The dangers in Africa far outnumber the guns,' Thomas said.

The room had been got ready for us to receive our first guests. Glasses and champagne stood on a low table, the bottle in a clay holder. Another filled with water stood beside it. A propeller fan hung from the centre of the ceiling.

'Did you find all you'll need in the food cupboards?' Thomas asked.

'They're better stocked than those at Kilraven,' I said, with some truth.

'Yes.' He put a weight of distaste into the word. 'I promised

257

you a better life than the one you've left. I ordered everything you see to be shipped out the day after you agreed to marry me.'

The room was packed with armchairs and footrests. There were a couple of sideboards, too, and, on the walls, drawings of rosy-cheeked children feeding robin redbreasts.

'You've thought of everything,' I said. I would have preferred some of the comfortably low African seating I'd seen in houses in Boma.

'I have.' Thomas pulled a cord on the propeller fan and it whirred slowly into action.

'Sit, Vanessa.' He gestured towards an armchair before sitting down himself once more.

I sat in the red velvet, wingbacked chair. The fan whirred over our heads. I'd put on a loose cotton dress and left my feet blessedly bare but my hands, folded in my lap, were sticky and hot and the dress already clinging to my back and arms.

'There are things you need to know, Vanessa.' Thomas crossed his legs and relit his cigar.

Something moved on the floor behind his chair. I tried not to stare as the biggest ants I'd ever seen walked in a line by the wall, then turned and formed into another line and walked out across the floor. I lifted my feet up and under me.

Thomas was frowning. 'The Mongos, husband, wife and children, will attend to your needs, as they do mine, and to the order and maintenance of the house.' He spoke sharply as you would to an inattentive child. 'You will keep a distance from them at all times, telling them what you want done and engaging in no further talk than that. They know their place. You must learn yours.'

'I can't imagine my place is so very different than it was at home,' I said. 'I'd be happier with a more informal arrangement.'

'Your place in Africa is different beyond belief.' His face

flushed, he pushed himself from the chair. He walked to the centre of the room before turning to look at me, his face even more flushed. 'Here you are a member of a superior race. The African is not fully human. He's primitive and idle and, as I've already told you, the white man in Africa must use what methods he can to shake the natives out of their natural laziness and teach them the sanctity of work.' He paused. 'As well as the need for obedience. We are here to harvest rubber and that is what we will do. You must keep your distance and never interfere with that work.'

'I'd like to be useful in some way.'

I concentrated my gaze on the ants, still marching steadily. No sign of them turning. I was afraid that if I looked at Thomas he would see I was keeping from him that I'd seen children whipped and hungry men used as pack horses. I didn't want to hear from him the lie that Africans didn't feel pain as whites did.

'There's nothing you can usefully contribute,' he said, 'other than to put shoes on your feet before our guests arrive. Only Africans walk about unshod. When you're dressed I'll show you the rest of our home.'

Like the sitting and bedrooms the rest of the house had been furnished in varying degrees to look like an Irish or European home. The dining room had table and chairs and a lantern on a wooden stand. The kitchen had a clay oven and cast-iron grate for burning wood. In a study, where there were empty bookshelves, the envelope with Ellie's handwriting lay on a Davenport beside an ivory letter opener. I reached for it.

'You may read it later.' Thomas took it from me and put it back on the desk with a malachite paperweight on top. 'When our guests have gone.'

The guests arrived separately. First Leon Klein and Charles Beckett then, a few minutes later, the two women. Muriel

Beckett's humour hadn't improved. She refused champagne and asked instead for gin. While she waited she took a cigarette from her velvet purse and lit up deftly.

'Gin is the whites' drink in this Godforsaken country.' She blew a great cloud of smoke into the air above her head and threw herself into one of the wingbacked armchairs. 'Keep the champagne for the blacks. They may yet win the day.' She was using her straw hat as a fan. It wafted the smoke in my direction.

'Gin you shall have, m'dear.' Charles Beckett snapped his fingers at Lingomo Mongo, standing inside the door. 'Gin,' he said. Lingomo Mongo left the room. 'I've asked you to be circumspect around the blacks,' Charles Beckett's expression was one of resigned tolerance. 'We sail a leaky ship here, Muriel my dove, and over turbulent waters.'

He laid down his cane and sat on a footstool beside her, arms hugging his legs, knees under his chin. Indoors, he looked older and more wrinkled. He had a stooped back too. All in all, he did not look a well man. For the purpose of the visit he'd put on a brown velvet jacket. It was worn and sad-looking.

'Don't talk to me about turbulent waters,' his wife spat, 'nor about leaky ships, nor being whatever-you-call-it around blacks. I didn't create the situation we find ourselves in. That's of your making, yours and men like you.' Her dark eyes blackened. Her foot tapped the floor. 'You've brought whatever may happen upon yourselves.'

'Oh, dear, oh, dear,' Charles Beckett sighed, 'you're exhausting yourself with bad temper, my dove.'

'Charles is right, Muriel. Better that we all get along today, we want Vanessa to feel at home.' Thomas, standing behind me with a hand on my shoulder, was placatory, very much the host. He'd started on another cigar and its smoke thickened the air still further.

I could see why he was all for keeping the peace. He wanted a civilised gathering, or at least the semblance of one, and Muriel Beckett wasn't the kind who cared about respectability, or who liked to be crossed. None of our four guests would have passed for respectable company at home. A blind man on a donkey would have seen them for the rough and ready lot they were and no amount of pretence or fine trappings would make them any different.

It was hard to tell if Africa had attracted them because of the kind of people they were, or if they'd become what they were because of Africa. I was betting on the latter.

With the possible exception of Charles Beckett, a once and always shady character but an educated one, none of the four of them had ever occupied a respectable place in life. Beckett might have once been upright but wasn't any longer; I'd met too many of his kind playing cards with my father. He was easy to see for what he was and would always be: a game-player, forever taking advantage of situations and people. Not altogether successfully either, from the looks of things.

I wanted to know more about all of them. That knowledge might give me some idea of my own chances in Africa.

The cigar and cigarette smoke slowly circling in the hot, thick air made me cough. Muriel Beckett laughed as I dabbed my smarting eyes and took another pull on her cigarette.

'We might as well start as we intend being with one another,' she said. 'We had peace while you were away, Thomas, and it's as well for the new Mrs Cooper to know how things stand in Pongara from the beginning.'

'I've always appreciated candour,' I said.

'A celebratory glass.' Thomas stood and went to the bottle and glasses. 'That's what we're here for . . .' He began, awkwardly, on the job of opening the champagne bottle. No one made a move to help him.

'All this show of respectability is such a sham!' Muriel Beckett tapped her foot like a lunatic grasshopper. 'What's the point of it?'

'The point,' Thomas said coolly, 'is that my wife and I intend setting certain standards from our lives here.' He put down the bottle.

'Do you, indeed?' Muriel, proving me right about her character, carried on with reckless indifference. 'You may as well stop fooling yourself, Thomas. All the white virginal wives in the world won't make for respectability around here. Won't change what's happened or what's going to happen.' Her eyes were on my face as she spoke. 'You might as well know from the beginning, Mrs Thomas Cooper, that there's nothing and no one civilised in this country. White or black, it's all the same.'

She stopped. Even her foot was still, momentarily. Then she was off again, tapping frantically and speaking too fast.

'And I know uncivilised when I see it, God knows I do . . .'

'Be quiet, Muriel,' Thomas said, loudly.

'Leave her.' Charles Beckett unwound himself and stood, leaning on his cane. His show of tolerance had no amusement in it now. His shirt was moulded damply against his thin torso and his colourless eyes very watchful. I wouldn't have disobeyed him. Thomas didn't either. He glowered and was silent.

'I will give you the only advice worth your while listening to in the Congo, *Mrs* Cooper.' Muriel Beckett gave a laugh that turned into a cough. 'It's this. Keep to yourself. Don't involve yourself with anyone or anything. Keep before you at all times the thought that you will be leaving this place, going home with money to build a new and better life than the one you've known before. That's what we're all doing here and you're no different from the rest of us, no matter what you may think. No different at all. In any way.'

She pulled on her cigarette and blew smoke in a cloud around herself. The propeller fan went on churning the smoke-filled air but did nothing about getting rid of it. The ants, however, had disappeared.

Thomas took a step towards Muriel. Her husband, behind her, raised his eyebrows.

'She has the floor, Thomas old boy,' he said, '*fait accompli*. I think you'd best let her get on with it. Your wife will hear what Muriel has to say sooner or later. Might as well be in your hearing.'

The words, benign and courteous enough in themselves, were heavy with threat. Since there wasn't much Charles Beckett could have done physically, given his enfeebled state, it seemed a fairly safe bet that he had some other power or hold over my husband.

All I could think of was that he knew something about Thomas's affairs which gave him a hold on my husband, something which tied them together whether Thomas liked it or not. Blackmail was the word that came to mind.

My husband went to the sideboard and poured himself a glass of water. The room was so silent it made a sound like rainfall.

'You're too young and too unformed,' Muriel Beckett said to me. 'Thomas should have left you where he found you.' She shrugged. 'But you're here and we may as well know where we stand with one another from the beginning.'

'Could I have a cigarette, please?' I said, naively imagining that smoking with her would make me somehow more acceptable, lessen her animosity towards me. All it did was bring abuse on my head from Thomas.

'You will not smoke!' His voice rose to a roar. I didn't look at him. 'I forbid it. Smoking in a woman is a degenerate habit.

You didn't smoke in Ireland and I'm damned if I'll have you taking up the practice now you're my wife.'

'Only the purest and best for our Thomas.' Muriel Beckett gave a sharp laugh but didn't offer me a cigarette. She leaned forward, her small eyes squinting at me through the smoke. 'He thinks you're better than us, than me and Blanche and others of our kind, because you've gone through a marriage ceremony.'

When I would have said something, she made a hissing sound and stamped her foot. 'Listen! Just listen and save yourself. Even a rat has the sense to save itself.'

She sat back and went on speaking with the cigarette hanging between her moving lips. I don't know how it didn't fall.

'Wives are ten a penny in the Congo. I know that and so does Blanche and every other woman, black or white, in this burnt and blistering hole.' Her eyes drifted and dulled and she seemed to lose the thread of what she was saying. No one uttered a word while she gathered her thoughts.

'The blacks have nine or ten wives, some of them. To be a wife is nothing here. To be rich is all. All that matters. We came here as mail-order brides, Blanche and me. Did you know that? No, of course you didn't. Thomas wouldn't tell you that, he'd wait for you to find out. But there's no shame attached to such things in the Congo. There's not much shame attached to anything in Africa. Brides were what the advertisement asked for and brides were what we came as . . .' she laughed. Blanche giggled. The men were silent.

'Only we never did become brides, or even wives. There was no need, once we were here, and there's still no need. Blanche has a husband already, in Brussels, and I got out of gaol to come here. Escape was all I wanted, I'd had enough of prison. My name is Muriel Sedley. Blanche is Blanche Lacroix. They're the names we came into the world with and the names we'll have on our gravestones.'

264

'My own maiden name was Vanessa Constance O'Grady,' I said, 'people call me Nessa. I'm more used to it than Vanessa.'

'Nessa it'll be then,' Muriel Sedley said.

And then she really surprised me. She turned in her chair and caught Charles Beckett's hand and smiled up at him, wryly and fondly. She held a real affection for him, there was no mistaking it. Against all the odds Muriel Sedley had grown to care for the man she'd come, sight unseen, to live with in Africa.

'There'd be no point in my taking Charles's name anyway, even if I wanted to,' she said. 'He won't make old bones, will you, dear heart?'

Charles Beckett nodded, faintly smiling. 'Oh, I'll stagger on for a while yet, my dove, don't you worry.'

Muriel Sedley fixed her small black eyes on me again. 'I'll be going home a rich woman when he croaks it. Charles has seen to that. Seen to everything, he has.' She stroked his hand. 'I'll let nothing come between me and that day and nor will he. Nothing and no one. We keep very much to ourselves here in Pongara, Nessa, and don't welcome outsiders. It's for the best. That way the work gets done and the money keeps piling up.'

She closed her eyes, let go of Beckett's hand, leaned back and fell silent.

'Now that the introductions are done with perhaps we might celebrate Mrs Cooper's arrival?' Charles Beckett, languid and smiling, took a white handkerchief from a pocket and mopped his brow. 'Some of that champagne would perk us all up, Thomas old man.'

'You'd have been better leaving Muriel at home if she was in this mood.' Thomas irritably picked up the bottle which he'd put down, and began working again on the cork. 'Better still would have been to lock up her supply of gin.'

'Muriel is quite sober,' Charles said.

'I can speak for myself.' She didn't open her eyes. 'I'm not drunk.'

Nor was she, or not on strong drink anyway. Muriel Sedley was half-demented with the bleakness of her situation and drunk with desperation to be gone out of Africa. Looking at her, I wondered if I was seeing my future self.

The door opened as the champagne cork popped. In the flurry of glasses being filled and Lingomo Mongo delivering the gin, then departing, the mood changed to one of mild festivity.

'To my wife,' Thomas raised his glass, 'to Vanessa.'

The others drank with him, all of them standing except Muriel, who sipped her gin where she sat.

'You have bought your gown in Bruxelles?' Blanche Lacroix took a fold of my dress between her fingers, then dropped it with a small moue of distaste. 'I prefer something a little more . . .' Words failed her.

She was wearing green satin with pink lace on the sleeves and in the low, square neckline. It looked unbearably heavy, tight and hot. Her face was streaked with perspiration and her mottled skin matched her orange-coloured hair in places. Her friend Leon Klein paced the room. He'd come without his gun, or his hat, but had brought a fetid smell into the room with him. His head was bald and pale above the red, sweaty ridge where his hat usually sat. On his forearm there was another tattoo of a nude woman. He hadn't said one word since coming in.

'I brought Vanessa shopping in Antwerp,' Thomas confirmed.

Blanche waved her glass, spilling some of her drink. 'I buy only in Bruxelles. I will not touch the shops in Antwerp when I return.'

'And when will that be?' Muriel said. 'Are you planning a

suicide trip? You've a husband waiting to kill you if you set foot again in Belgium.'

'In Bruxelles,' said Blanche, ignoring her, 'there are all of the shops you will find in Paris.'

'Have you been in Africa long?' I said to her.

'Not so very long,' she said, 'just two years.'

'How much longer will you stay?' I said.

'That depends,' she yawned, 'on many things.' She closed her eyes and settled herself as if to sleep.

'How was your journey upriver, Mrs Cooper?' Charles Beckett yawned too. 'Did you observe much of African life?'

'I saw something of it,' I said, 'and heard something of it, too, from Eunice Milton. You know her, I presume? She's a missionary.'

'That disgusting woman . . .' Muriel Sedley's outraged hissing was cut short by Beckett.

'Mrs Milton is well known in Pongara,' he said, 'she's known in many places, in fact. A busy woman.'

'I've explained to my wife that Mrs Milton isn't welcome here and is no friend either of the Congo Free State.' Thomas refilled his own glass. He didn't offer the bottle to anyone else and his look, when he caught my eye, warned me to be quiet.

'But she *is* a friend of the British Consul in the Congo.' I got up and moved behind the armchair, standing where Thomas couldn't catch my eye. 'She tells me he's an Irishman called Roger Casement. Why would the British Consul pay a visit on a person not friendly to the state?'

'Visit?' Beckett's pale eyes took on a gleam of interest. 'Casement is calling at Tonkinese?'

'Yes. On Sunday.'

'Oh, God, I knew it! It's all starting again, just as I was afraid it would.' Muriel closed her eyes and resumed a frenetic fanning with the straw hat. 'He didn't come near this part of

267

the river while you were away, Thomas. We had peace, of a sort, while you were gone. You attract trouble. You should have stayed away.'

'Muriel has a point, old man, as always,' Beckett said. 'It's an unfortunate thing about the Irish, if you'll forgive me for saying so, Mrs Cooper, that they simply do not know how to behave. Given a little power your countrymen, and women, too, for all I know, will, like beggars on horseback, ride straight to hell. Your Mr Casement is woefully abusing the little power he has in this country.'

'What is he doing?' I said.

'He's interfering with the way things are done, and have to be done.' Thomas moved back to the window. 'That is all you need to know, Vanessa.'

Knowledge was power, my father used to say, though without ever himself pursuing the latter. I wasn't going to make his mistake. I needed knowledge if I was to keep my sanity and anything of myself alive in Africa.

'How is Mr Casement interfering by visiting the mission?' I said. 'Is he a religious man?'

There was a small, tense silence before Muriel Sedley laughed.

'If he is then the Lord does indeed work in mysterious ways. He's an African lover, that consul. A crazy man with a dog. A bulldog. No one trusts him.'

'It may be, of course,' Beckett said, 'that the Miltons intend preaching the word of God for a change.'

He moved to stand at the window with Thomas. With his stooped back he looked like a tall crow against the light.

'What did Eunice Milton tell you was the reason for his visit?' Thomas said. I still didn't look his way – but knew him well enough now to know by his tone that he badly wanted an answer to his question.

'She didn't say. Invited me to meet him, nothing more.

Maybe you might change your mind, Thomas, about going there? Perhaps we could all go together? Make an occasion of it?' I said this lightly, with a false innocence.

'Dear, dear, dear me.' Charles Beckett shook his head. 'I do hope, Thomas, that you haven't brought another African lover to live among us. We've had quite enough crusading for the rights of the primitive around these parts already.'

'What do you mean when you say Mr Casement is an African lover?' I said.

'That he doesn't understand certain principles of African life.' Charles Beckett walked slowly to the table and poured himself a glass of water. 'Your countryman fails lamentably to come to terms with the fact that the white man is a necessary evil in the Congo. Without us, and the work we give them, the tribes of this land would be diseased as maggots, sunk in black magic and eating each another as a daily practice.'

He drank the water, leaning heavily on his stick as he did so. Blanche Lacroix gave a snorting snore and settled herself more comfortably in sleep. Charles Beckett looked at me through his empty glass. His forehead was beaded with perspiration.

'The Congo has become one of the world's greatest producers of rubber – more than eleven million pounds of it each year.'

He put the glass on the table so heavily that it cracked, then broke apart. He made no attempt to pick up the pieces.

'Talk to Mr Casement about these things,' he said, 'see what he has to say.'

'Vanessa will not be talking to Mr Casement about anything,' Thomas declared.

'So be it.' Charles Beckett shrugged. 'But be aware yourself, Mrs Cooper, that everything you will see in the Congo is for the greater good of the greater number. Everything.'

'Vanessa has lived a sheltered existence,' Thomas moved

to my side and took my arm, 'she has a lot to learn about the world.' His grip tightened. 'You look tired, my dear, our guests have exhausted you.'

It was not the time to argue; the bruises on my arm would be there for a week. Leon Klein stopped his slow pacing and spoke for the first time.

'I have work to do,' he said and walked from the room. He left the fetid smell behind him.

'Time for all of us to leave.' Muriel Sedley pushed herself out of her chair. The white powder on her face had begun to streak. 'I don't know what your mother was thinking of, letting you come to Africa . . .' She paused. 'Letting you marry.'

She shook herself and tightened her lips, looking, for just a moment, like Julia Hope on one of her angrier days. Then she put her hat on her head and swept from the room with Charles Beckett behind her.

Blanche Lacroix slept on.

23

Ellie gave birth to a baby boy while I was sailing and being sick on the high seas to Africa. He was baptised Jerome, after his dead grandfather. It was all in her letter, when Thomas finally gave it to me.

He had a look of me, Ellie wrote, 'and the same stubborn jaw'. She went on:

He made his demands to come into the world without warning, in the middle of the night. We'd barely time to get the midwife out to the house before he arrived, screaming and healthy. He hasn't stopped making his presence felt since, nor eating, nor being hugged and loved by the lot of us. His father can't stop looking at and admiring him. There hasn't a thing been done in the house, nor outside either, since he was born. Julia has been to see him and brought a fine pair of boots she made herself for when he starts walking. Mossie has his eye on a pony at the Shaughnessys' place for him. The Howards brought over a perambulator. Manus has promised to clear the avenue so as I may wheel Jerome there when springtime comes and the days are longer.

Finn has got used to a baby in the house and lies outside the door of his room, or by the cot when I bring it downstairs. It's as well that dog's got something to occupy him because we were mad with worry about him the weeks after you left. He missed you that bad we thought he

would die with pining. His fur fell out. He got so thin I
was able to carry him up to the house from the gate, where
he'd taken to spending his time waiting and watching
the road for your return. I miss you myself. I miss you
every day.

Your mother is well, very occupied with the baby. She is
putting a letter in with this one. She is lonely for her dead
husband and her faraway daughter – things which cannot be
helped and she knows it and does her best with each day as
it comes. She told me last week, when I went to your father's
grave to bring her in from the rain, that she had an ache in
her. I'm sure she has, poor woman, but there's no cure for it
but to go on living.

Mossie is very busy all the time. I've never seen a man
so intent on working himself into an early grave. No one
can tell him a thing to do, nor even tell what it is he's doing
half the time either. Rebuilding the stables, looks like, and
replanting the kitchen garden. He watches for post from
Africa. We all do.

Hugh and his woman were here for the christening.
I've got to like her a bit better; she's a nice enough
person and keeps him happy. Hugh thinks, too, that
Jerome has your jaw. He says that he has written to you
already.

We are doing well. There is money coming into the bank
every month. It is being spent wisely, tell your husband not
to worry on that score.

But I wish you were here with us, Nessa. I would prefer
that to all the money in all the banks in the world. I suppose
that it is very hot in Africa? Still, you are strong and will
find a way of dealing with it, and with everything else too.
I hope your husband is good to you, and kind. I hope you
are happy.

Manus sends you a poem. I found him in your room

*one day, writing it. He says it will say more to you than any
letter he could write.*

> My arms are holding you, and I hear
> Your voice, while my son
> Cries in his cot, and the late evening, and dark
> Shadows put you further away than ever.

I cried myself when I finished reading it, wishing I was at
Kilraven and could see and hold my nephew. My mother,
who hated writing, had sent a short letter.

*We are all well and so happy to have new life in Kilraven.
He is a beautiful baby, strong and healthy. He will have
Ellie's red hair. Manus is devoted to him. Everyone
is.*

*The winter is long. I'm sure our grey cold seems very
distant to you, Nessa, with blue skies and sunshine every
day in Africa. Distant as you seem to us, my dear, dear
daughter, I pray at your father's grave for you every day.
I pray for your husband. I hope you are happy. We look
forward to news from Africa.*

She signed it 'your loving mother', and put her full name,
Ada Constance O'Grady. As if I could forget who my mother
was!

There was no letter from Hugh, either that day or the next.
When I asked Thomas if one had come he said he would have
given it to me if it had.

'Lingomo meets the riverboats every day,' he assured me,
'and collects mail along with everything else. He'll take your
replies to the ships' captains, too, for dispatching. You needn't
bother yourself with the trip to the river.'

'It's no bother,' I said, 'my days are idle enough.'

They were too. Once I'd unpacked and sorted my clothes,
arranged my books and other belongings where I could see

and be reassured by them, convinced Ilanga Mongo that the house would not fall down around us if I made my own tea, and convinced her children, two boys and a girl, that I was not a ogre, there wasn't an awful lot to do.

I was sorry when the children continued to keep their distance from me and knew that Thomas was behind it. Time, I reminded myself, all things come with time. I would wait.

When I walked to the edge of the forest I was turned back by Thomas's sentries. When I visited Muriel Sedley she was asleep, and when I called on Blanche Lacroix I found her English more limited than I'd thought. Sunday came and went without Thomas changing his mind about us visiting the mission. I didn't bring up the subject myself.

He was busy for most of each day, working in the block-house, or overseeing the loading of harvested rubber on to a barge to be towed by a steamboat downriver or upriver, or checking on the rubber harvesters. He made sure always to be on hand when the rubber-carrying porters arrived on foot along the riverbank. There could be as many as two hundred of them, all carrying the grey lumpy rubber sap in baskets on their heads. Thomas, sitting in a cane chair, watched while it was unloaded and then weighed. Other men then moulded it into slabs which were left to dry in the sun. In that form it would travel downriver to Boma and, eventually, Europe.

Very early one morning, at the end of my first week at Pongara, a man came out of the forest. He crossed the compound until he came to the clearing in front of the house. When he was within a couple of feet he stopped and called Thomas by name, twice.

'Thomas Cooper!' His voice rose and echoed. 'Thomas Cooper!'

From the window I watched him standing there, waiting. He was carrying something wrapped in blue cloth. After a minute he moved closer. When he got as far as the edge of the veranda he leaned forward, opened the cloth and gently laid out two human hands, both of them severed just above the wrist, on the dusty boards.

They were small. Children's hands. The curl of the fingers made them seem to be pleading.

I lifted my own hands to my face. The movement attracted the attention of the man and he lifted his head. His eyes, staring at me, might have been looking into hell. Thomas came out on to the veranda and said something to the man, who gestured at the hands. My husband replied by kicking them from the veranda. He did this with enough force to send them some distance beyond where the man was standing. The man, without a word, walked stiffly to where they lay and returned holding them in front of him. Tears fell in a river down his face.

I went outside and stood behind Thomas.

'Get back into the house.' He didn't turn and his voice was thick. I stayed where I was. The man was looking at me again. I was reminded of the mute pleading in the eyes of Kilgallen's dog and couldn't have moved to save my life.

'Go back inside the house, Vanessa.' Thomas raised his voice slightly.

The man went on looking at me, still weeping. Four soldiers appeared. They stopped several yards away and stood in a row, watching. There was nobody else to be seen anywhere.

I moved sideways, then stepped in front of Thomas. I made sure I was out of his reach. He would have to use force to get me inside; something I knew he wouldn't do in front of his soldiers. It wasn't mere coincidence that had made me recall Kilgallen's dog: this man was being treated worse than any animal I'd ever known.

'What has happened?' I said to the man. 'Please tell me what's happened and what it is you want . . .'

The man laid the hands gently on the wooden boards of the veranda again. He looked to be an old man, thin and tired with knotty fingers and knees and teeth much too big for his sunken face. He began to speak, at first very quickly in an African dialect, then more slowly, putting what English words he knew together.

'My children,' he pointed to the hands, 'my children. Sons. Young boys. The soldiers,' he gestured behind him, 'took off their right hands. One from each of them. My children have only one hand each now.'

Thomas, in swift, sharp dialect, cut him short. When the man tried to speak Thomas made a gesture of disgust towards the severed hands and moved towards them with his whip.

'Don't!' I said. 'If you touch them again I will follow and pick them up myself. You don't want the embarrassment of that, Thomas, I know you don't. Leave them where they are and let the man speak.'

The man spoke. 'One boy is very sick. Your man knows this. My people have gone back into the forest to cut the rubber. Tell your man no more hand cutting, please. No more.'

'What is this about, Thomas?' I said.

'It's about African cunning and lies.' The blood in Thomas's face was so high he might have had a fever. His eyes were fixed on the African's bent head. 'This man's name is Dokombo. He's the chief of a village not far from here. They're a dissolute lot but I gave them work regardless, and treated them well. They repaid me by lying, playing at being sick, lazing in the sun and weighting their rubber baskets with stones and clay to make them seem heavier.'

He stopped to take a breath. His hands clenched and unclenched by his sides. Dokombo was lucky I was there that morning. I wouldn't have given him much chance against my husband's anger otherwise.

'This man is their ringleader.' Thomas slapped the whip

276

against his boot. 'The rest are mindless and do whatever he tells them to.'

'But the severed hands . . .' I felt all of a sudden weak and held on to the veranda rail.

'Are you saying, Thomas, that this man cut the hands from his own children?'

'There is nothing these savages will not do, nothing.' Thomas's face was as rigid as the rest of him. 'They would pluck out their eyes if they thought it would gain them something and save them working for it. You must learn from this incident, Vanessa. You can see for yourself,' he gestured in Dokombo's direction with the whip, 'how primitive they are. Now go inside, leave me to deal with this.'

'But he says the soldiers did it.'

I looked down at the hands, swallowing hard when bile rose in my throat. I saw how they had been preserved by smoking. I'd seen it done at home with fish, or sometimes meat. They'd been being slowly smoked over a wood fire until a sealing coat formed.

Thomas was lying. I didn't know the truth of the matter but I knew a lie when I heard one.

'He says one of the children is sick. Says you knew. He's asking that there be no more cutting of hands . . .' I was interrupted by Dokombo throwing his head back and beginning a high, angry rant which was meaningless for a few minutes until, as before, he broke into hesitant English.

'My people are working. They will go wherever Malu Malu Cooper asks them to go. They will collect all the rubber in the forest for him. They will sleep in the cages. But there must be no more cutting off the hands of our children.'

Without looking at Thomas, or at me, he bent and carefully, ever gentle, wrapped the hands back in the blue cloth.

'No more,' he folded it neatly over them, 'no more.'

He stood then, holding the small bundle in front of him, and looked up at Thomas. He was a brave man. The soldiers had moved closer. Close enough for me to see that one of them had ritual scars on his face, that another had a constant nervous flutter of the eyelid and a third a permanent mad grin on his face. All of them were young, black and impatient.

Thomas was frighteningly still. Not even the whip in his hand made a move. Dokombo, whatever the truth of the matter, was alone and friendless among men who were anything but well disposed towards him. He was a *very* brave man.

When Thomas's anger erupted and he began shouting again in dialect I put a hand on his arm. I did it coaxingly, trying not to aggravate him further. He was tense as a hound waiting to be loosed on a hare.

'Please, Thomas,' I said, 'for my sake, be gentle with him. Those little hands . . . they'll come between me and my sleep, my peace of mind. For my sake, Thomas, please try to find a way out of this that will send Dokombo away a little happier.' I paused, caressed his arm a little and added, 'You're a civilised man, Thomas, and an intelligent one. There must be a dignified way out of this dilemma.'

I was learning. Ellie Hope's belief that flattery would coax a man to do anything had made an impression on me after all. 'Men,' she used to say, 'are much more credulous of a cajoling word than a woman would be.' I prayed this applied to all men.

Thomas looked at me with his slate eyes and I saw, somewhere behind them, a flickering need turn to manipulative hope. The part of Thomas which wanted to be regarded, to belong somewhere, would not die away. It was what had made him want me for his wife. Made him continue to want me. It was the only power I had over him.

'Dignity is not something the African understands.' Thomas spoke slowly, playing for time to decide what he would do. 'You are asking me to apply values they can never understand, your values and mine, to a situation of their making.'

'I am asking for kindness, for compassion.' I held his gaze. 'I am asking that the cause of common humanity be upheld.' I hesitated, wary not to be seen to lecture or hector and so lose my case. I went on with a small smile, 'I am asking as your wife, as the mother of your children to come, that you spare me the terrible distress of sending this man back to the mother of *his* children without comfort and good news of some kind.'

I dropped my eyes as tears of humiliation as much as distress spilled over and ran down my face. Thomas was silent, considering. Whatever he did would have to be face-saving for him as well as appeasing to me. That was the way he was; I'd no doubt he would come up with something.

I turned away from him. Dokombo's eyes, without appearing to move, met mine. His told me that he knew what was going on, understood perfectly the game being played. There was hope somewhere in his eyes too. The rest I couldn't read.

Thomas came up with something.

'In the normal way of things I would have to have had this man flogged for his lies and to show his people that there is a rule of law which must be obeyed,' he spoke slowly and loudly enough for Dokombo to hear, 'but to spare your feelings, Vanessa, I will on this occasion let him go back to his village unpunished. The barbarous practice of severing hands is one for which he and his kind now try to blame the white man. The truth is that it has been going on in the darkness of this continent for centuries. I will – and I must stress that it is for your sake alone – allow Dokombo back to his village with a warning this time. But I will not tolerate him coming here again and will hold him responsible for making his people work. He alone is to blame for whatever hands have been severed or may be in the future.'

'Thank you, Thomas,' I said.

I touched his arm again, holding myself stiffly so that he wouldn't see me shake. I couldn't listen to any more lies, to any more of him telling Dokombo that he was being allowed to go to please me but would not be free from Thomas's future wrath. I didn't want to hear any more either of a 'normal way of doing things' which involved flogging a man.

Dokombo, still without seeming to move his eyes, looked from one to the other of us. He was impassive, a rock of ages. It was impossible to tell what he thought as he stood there but if I'd been Thomas I'd have been afraid. I was too ignorant and arrogant to feel fear myself.

Dokombo turned, at last, and walked slowly back the way he'd come. The soldiers looked questioningly at Thomas as he came up to them and, when Thomas made a slicing gesture, stepped aside and let him pass. Dokombo didn't look back, not even before stepping into the darkness of the forest and disappearing.

Thomas went back inside the house. He didn't order me to follow him. He didn't have to. There was nowhere else for me to go just then. The four soldiers stood watching as I stood there, the grinning one more manic than ever, as if invisible wires were pulling and jerking the sides of his mouth. I was almost glad to turn my back on him and follow Thomas inside the house.

Ilanga Mongo was too busy and far, far too noisily occupied in the kitchen when I got there. I'd never seen her like that before and could tell that she'd heard, and probably seen, everything.

Ilanga Mongo knew, and was silent, about a great deal that went on at Pongara. I was biding my time but planned to get her to talk to me.

The kitchen was the shadiest room in the house and had the smallest window. It was the room I liked best but its cool couldn't calm me that morning.

I went out of the back door, into the small kitchen garden, and vomited. When it was over I covered what had happened with the hard, dry clay. Back in the kitchen I made myself some lukewarm tea and added three spoons of sugar. Ilanga, still fussing about the place, didn't offer to help.

'Your husband is waiting.' She didn't speak until I'd all but finished the tea. I knew he was. He would be by the window on to the veranda. Only when we were in bed did he let go his need to watch over Pongara.

'Why do the soldiers cut off children's hands?' I said.

'The soldiers are not always good men. You must keep away from them,' she said. She was making manioc bread. It tasted to me like mildewed glue and there was already more than enough of it in the house. I wished she would stop.

'The soldiers do it everywhere in Congo,' she went on. 'Not only here and not only the hands of children. Mostly the hands of men.' Her long fingers rolled and kneaded and pulled at the doughy mixture.

'Who tells them to do such things?'

'He is waiting,' she said.

'What does Malu Malu mean?' I said. 'Dokombo called Thomas Malu Malu Cooper. Why?'

'Malu means quickly. Your husband wants men always to move quickly, quickly with the rubber, the gathering, the carrying. Everything.'

'Thank you.' I put my hand on her arm. I didn't mean anything by it. All I wanted was to touch someone who wasn't hostile to me, someone *normal*. But she pulled her arm away, eyes flying to the open door behind us, and said, 'Go, quickly. Malu.'

I went. Thomas didn't turn when I came into the room.

'I must leave tomorrow,' he said, 'I'll be gone for two weeks.'

I stared at him. 'For two weeks?'

My heart did giddy things in my chest, the first faint reminder I'd had in a long time of what it felt like to be light-hearted. I would be free of him for two weeks . . .

'I must go upriver to see to the work on a plantation at Mokala.' Thomas gave me a sharp, sideways look. 'You'll have to get used to my going away every so often, Vanessa. It's my job to see that the quotas are kept up, and to keep up the search for new sources of rubber.'

'Of course,' I said, 'I understand.' My heart had settled down but by now my poor stomach was misbehaving again. I sat and took deep breaths, but shallowly so that he wouldn't notice, suspect my excitement. 'When will you go?'

'Today,' he said. 'Charles will remain behind, and Leon. They've got used to managing things.' He paused. 'My being away will give you time to adjust, to the climate and to life at the station.'

'Yes,' I said, afraid to say anything more, terrified he might not go, that he might change his mind and send someone else.

'Are you with child?' Thomas asked the question suddenly, with a frown. None of it disguised the anxious hope in his voice. 'You spoke outside about being the mother of my children . . .'

I could have told the truth, told him I'd said what I did to arouse any sympathy he might have in him for Dokombo's plight. But I was too afraid. I lied again.

'I could well be,' I said, 'but it's early days yet so I can't be sure. By the time you come back I should know for certain, one way or the other.'

'You'll be careful?' He rubbed his hands together. 'You'll need to stay inside, out of the heat of the day. I'll tell the Mongo woman and Muriel to look after you.' He paused. 'This is good news,' he said, 'good news indeed.'

He was gone within the hour. I saw him off at the riverbank

then went back and walked through the house alone, hugging myself, feeling free. For a while. The heat of the day began to soak through the walls – though it would never be unbearably hot, an advantage of the thick bricks. After a while I lay down and slept.

The dreams which would mark my time in the Congo began that day. They were peopled by black and white giants, men and women, all of them watching and following as I ran through dark forests with Finn at my heels. Sometimes they hung naked from the rope-like plants; sometimes they appeared in clearings with guns and spears and towered over me. Whenever I stopped running Finn would begin to dig small, severed hands out of the ground. I woke, each time, when he picked one up and began to carry it towards me.

Within three days of Thomas's departure the reality of life at Pongara began to equal anything I saw in my dreams.

I'd been delivering letters for home to *Le Roi Léopold*, which had made one of its twice-weekly stops, and was making my way back from the river when I heard a crying out and commotion. I'd hoped to pick up letters as well but there had been none.

I followed the sounds to a clearing in the forest behind the thatched huts of the African workers. They became fainter as I went and had lapsed into weak, occasional whimpers by the time I came on the scene.

Three African men were tied, naked and face down, on the ground. Their legs were spread and tied by the ankles to stakes, their arms stretched in front and tied to similar stakes. Their naked buttocks were a mass of lacerated flesh, oozing blood and ribbons of torn skin.

Punishment had ended for two of the men. They lay semi-conscious and unmoving except for involuntary shudders of their mangled bodies. Leon Klein, stripped to the waist but wearing his military hat, was dancing on his toes as he delivered a lashing to the third man. There was a half-smile on his red pulsating face and his tongue protruded from between his teeth. The victim, each time the long, twisted rope of leather came down on him, gave inhuman contortions and whimpering moans.

I counted a dozen blows while I stood there, clutching the side of a hut to keep myself upright. God knows how many lashes Klein had delivered before my arrival.

I wouldn't have believed it possible to feel cold in Africa, but my blood turned to ice and drained from my head and, hard as I tried, I couldn't stop myself from falling to the ground as the last of the blows lashed down and opened another wound on the man's buttocks.

24

C harles Beckett was standing over me and I was half-sitting, half-lying on a low straw chair when I regained consciousness. He wore braces on his trousers and a white shirt. The shirt was sticking to his cadaverous body and his face had an expression of bored irritation.

'It's unfortunate, Mrs Cooper,' he sighed and signalled to a woman standing near by, 'that you couldn't make a point of avoiding the more unpleasant aspects of our work with the blacks.'

The woman approached with a tin cup of water. As I took it he looked away to where the beaten men were being helped to their feet.

'I'm sorry you've been upset,' he said, 'but you've only yourself to blame. You have no business here. This woman will walk with you back to the house when you've collected yourself.'

I closed my eyes and drank the water. When I'd finished the woman poured me another cupful. I pulled myself to my feet and stood with it in my hand. Beckett had moved a few feet away and was standing with his back to me, watching more closely the scene with the wounded men. I walked towards them myself, holding the cup tight, trying not to shake and spill the water.

I'd just passed Beckett when he said, 'Don't go any further, Mrs Cooper. That's an order. You have no business here. Go back to your home. That's an order too.'

'You have no authority over me, Mr Beckett.' I didn't turn but kept on walking. He was beside me in an instant.

'You are behaving very stupidly.' He took my arm, his fingers like a crab's pincers. 'You must leave, now.' The pincers tightened.

But I knew how to deal with crabs, and he was just another kind of cold-blooded, crawling bully.

I turned, as if acceding, then brought up my other arm and emptied the contents of the mug smartly into his face. As a crab will when shocked, he loosened his hold and fell back. While he rubbed his eyes and shook his head I took the water bowl from the African woman and continued the way I'd been going.

The last of the flogged men was being dragged to his feet by a couple of soldiers as I came near.

They stood, the three of them, like nightmare apparitions which might collapse at any moment. They were naked, silent and bleeding profusely. Blood covered their legs and dripped to the ground around their feet. The drops went on rolling and became covered in dust. Their eyes, glazed with pain, focused on the bleak nothingness they'd been reduced to.

Half a dozen soldiers and Leon Klein stood looking at them. Klein shouted something in dialect. He still held the long, twisted leather whip, running it between his hands. One of the flogged men tried to move forward, then fell to his knees. Klein shouted again. The man tried to get up.

'I want an end to this,' I said.

I walked until I was standing between Klein and the flogged men. The tattoo on Klein's chest was beaded with sweat.

'This is unspeakable barbarism,' I shouted, 'these men need medical help!'

I met Klein's eyes. It was like looking into a freshly dug hole, a grave which would take coffin after coffin without pity or care.

'These men, madame, will get what they deserve.' Klein's English was stilted and precise. He turned his back to me. Even in the open air he stank. 'You, Egaja,' he prodded one of the beaten men in the chest with the whip, 'show this woman who is right here. Show her what you have learned from your beating.'

The man, eyes blank, took a step forward, then another, until he was standing in front of Leon Klein. His movements were like those of a mechanical toy. He looked as likely as a toy to topple over, too. The dull, glazed look in his eyes didn't waver when his arm rose stiffly from his side, when he slowly and carefully lifted his hand to his forehead and saluted Leon Klein. Klein brought his heels together and saluted back. His expression resembled that of a turkey cock getting ready to crow in the morning.

The man Klein had called Egaja stepped back and the man next to him, older and less upright, stumbled forward. He stopped, looking confused, before he got as far as the Belgian and seemed to forget what came next. But, prompted by a snarl and whip-flick, managed a passable salute.

When the third man began to stagger forward I could take no more.

'I want an end to this!' I was shouting again as I stood in the way of the third man. 'It is inhuman and belittles those of us who watch as much as it does the beaten. It must end. I will not have it. Thomas would not have it, if he were here. I order you to stop in his name.'

In the silence an animal screamed in the forest. Another answered. Then there was silence again, ear-splitting this time. Klein broke it, in a voice like a tombstone speaking. 'I carry out your husband's orders, madame.' He flicked the long tail of the whip back and forth in the dust. 'It is not for you to query how he decides to run the station.'

He continued to follow the movements of the whip's tail, not looking at me once.

'My husband is not here.' I held my ground and my temper and kept my eyes on his face. 'In his absence I have only your word for it that he would approve acts of such barbarous cruelty. I want these men looked at by a doctor.'

I turned and held out the bowl of water to the third man. When he looked as if he would drop it, I lifted it to his mouth. He lapped at it like a cat. Apart from the cry of another animal in the forest it was the only sound to be heard.

'You are a very foolish woman,' Charles Beckett said at my side, 'you will go with Muriel back to your home *now*.'

He took the bowl from my hand, and from the mouth of the African man as he drank, and emptied the water on to the ground. He tossed the bowl behind him.

'You have no right . . .' I began.

'I have every right,' he held up a hand for me to be quiet, 'and you have none at all in this instance.' He was breathing hard through his nostrils. 'What you have seen here is as nothing compared to what was and might be again. Don't interrupt!' He spoke through his teeth, his face no more than three inches from mine as he bent over me. 'And don't question what I'm telling you. If you want to spare other men a worse fate than you've seen here today you will ignore what you see in future, and never interfere again.'

He straightened and I felt Muriel Sedley's hand on my arm.

'You won't do any good by staying here,' she said. 'You may in fact do a lot of harm if tempers get any worse. Please come away with me now.'

The wounded men were being helped away by companions, still naked. It would at any rate have been impossible for them to have put on even a loincloth. The soldiers had dispersed but Leon Klein watched the beaten men depart with a brooding expression as he wound the whip into neat coils.

I shook off Muriel Sedley's hand and began walking towards the house I shared with my husband. She fell into step beside me.

'I knew you'd be trouble,' she said. 'Why don't you listen to those who know what's what here? You can't change things. You might as well leave well enough alone and console yourself with the amount of money the man you married is worth. If you *do* leave well enough alone he could be worth a great deal more. You could be a very rich woman when you leave the Congo. Think about that the next time you're tempted to interfere with a *chicotte* beating.'

'I wasn't a poor woman when I decided to come here,' I said. Not so poor anyway that I couldn't distinguish between decent and indecent behaviour, nor between good and evil. 'What will happen to those men?'

'Their people will look after them. They'll recover. It could have been much worse, believe me.'

'Why were they beaten?'

I walked quickly, ploughing through the heat and giving her a job to keep up with me. She disgusted me every bit as much as her lover and Leon Klein. Every bit as much as my husband, who must surely know what went on in the station he had charge of.

'What sin could be so terrible as to warrant flaying them like that, half-killing them?'

'Idleness.' She came abreast of me and dropped the word between us as if spitting a cold, hard pebble from her mouth. 'The black man has no concept of work, nor of time.' She was taking stride for stride with me now, her face fierce and set. 'His principal occupation, and that to which he dedicates the greatest part of his existence, consists of stretching out in the sun like a crocodile.'

She glared at children running alongside us, then shooed them away. 'The rubber must be gathered.' She paused, looked sideways at me under her brow before repeating, 'The rubber must be gathered.'

'You said it could have been worse for them?' I said. It wasn't that I wanted, so much as needed, to know how bad things could be.

'The men you saw got twenty-five lashes each. On the plantations or in other stations they'd have been given between fifty and one hundred lashes each,' she said. 'It's too much. Leads them to fall unconscious and causes problems. More than one hundred and they sometimes die. Twenty-five is the rule in Pongara.'

'Twenty-five? Twenty-five to each man? That Klein monster delivered seventy-five lashes in all. Seventy-five . . .' I stopped, unable to go on.

I'd thought that by putting words to what had happened, and then repeating them, I would come to some sort of acceptance of it. What actually happened was that I had reinforced the enormity and horror of what I'd seen.

'All because of the rubber,' I said, 'all to do with making men work harder at gathering and harvesting it. Who does the rubber make rich? Is it just men like Thomas and Charles and Leon and the companies they work for? Will the men who are beaten . . .' I hesitated '. . . and the parents of children whose hands are chopped off, become rich too? Do the Africans really benefit from the railway, and the sort of towns that are growing up?'

I tried to hold Muriel Sedley's gaze but her eyes grew harder, and more angry, and she walked on ahead of me.

'You can't be completely stupid or Thomas wouldn't have married you.' She had her back to me so I couldn't see her face. 'Make use of whatever intelligence you have. The Africans are primitives, make no mistake about it. They have no idea what the rubber is worth and less idea what to do with it. Even a dog must be beaten to make it obey.'

'Have you ever beaten a dog?' I said. 'Have you ever stood by while the skin was flayed from a dog as he lay stretched and face down?'

'I've never wanted a dog to do anything for me enough,' she said.

We were almost at the house. The day was getting on and shadows beginning to lengthen at the foot of walls and around trees. All at once I wanted very much to be inside the house, to sit for a while and be soothed by Ilanga Mongo's quiet movements as she did her work. I wanted to make her talk to me too. I wanted to know what she knew.

Because I wanted to decide what I would do, and needed her knowledge to help me in whatever that might be.

'Will they be scarred?' I said.

'Those men?' Muriel Sedley sounded surprised.

'Yes.'

'Oh, yes. But it doesn't matter to them. They relish such things. They even cut scars into themselves, some of them.'

I stopped, abruptly, at the steps to the veranda and faced her. She'd left her house without powder or cream and looked younger. She would even have been pretty but for the fact that her mouth was set in a tight pucker and the furrow between her eyes deep enough to plant potatoes in.

'Tell me why you said there was peace while my husband was away?' I held her unwilling gaze. 'What trouble are you afraid of now he's back?'

'The world is watching. This is a time to be discreet in the Congo. Even Leon holds himself in check when he has to. But your husband . . .' she shrugged. 'Thomas will not be told by anyone. He goes too far. He always has.' She looked away. 'I've done what I can for you. I've brought you home and I've tried, God knows I've tried, to make you see sense.

You'll die in this place, Mrs Thomas Cooper, if you go on involving yourself with the blacks. You'll be struck down by malaria. Or by sleeping sickness, or yellow fever, or some other of the diseases the place is ridden with.'

She shaded her eyes with a hand. She wore rings with green stones on two of her fingers.

'Leave well alone. You've made your bed and now you must lie on it. Stay in your house and among your own kind. Another thing . . .' She turned and spoke over her shoulder as she departed. 'If I were you I'd be careful how you go with that husband of yours.'

She walked away quickly, her skirts swirling dust into clouds as she went. She hadn't gone far when she lifted them, showing yellow stockings and a pair of black button boots. Her back was very straight and her small-boned figure very slim. I wondered what in her life had made her so bitterly unhappy in herself.

My mind was calm and surprisingly clear as I climbed on to the veranda. I found myself already deciding what I would do.

One thing I wouldn't do was take Muriel Sedley's advice. I knew that I couldn't live with and condone what I'd seen and heard. To do so would make me less than I was and I would go mad.

My distaste for the conjugal obligations I'd taken on in exchange for Thomas's generosity to my family was one thing. The only person this affected was me and I had been prepared to work out a way of living with it, and without love.

Altogether different was an acceptance, as his wife, of Thomas's conduct and way of behaving towards the people who worked for him. I couldn't, and wouldn't, go along with the inhumanity I'd witnessed. No one in my family would expect me to accept these things either, not for any amount of money.

Neither could I be expected, merely as Thomas's wife, to accept and live by his principles and beliefs. Marriage didn't mean I could no longer decide for myself what was right and what was wrong.

Or if it did, then I would not stay married. Nor would I stay in Africa.

25

Ilanga Mongo was waiting for me, her husband Lingomo standing behind her.

'Your husband will be angry. He said I must watch over you.' She handed me a bowl of palm wine.

As I drank she reached out and helped me hold the bowl. I knew then how agitated she was, that there would be no soothing calm about Ilanga that day. She'd been so very careful not to touch me before. The station was no more than a village, after all. She of course knew where I'd been and what had happened.

'When you go to the river in the future I will come with you,' she said, 'that way you will not have to see such things as you saw this morning. Your husband will not be happy that you have been there when the Belge was at the *chicotte*.' Her eyes rounded to blacker, more frightened pools than they already were and her hold on my hands tightened. 'He will be angry with you and with me. It is bad to make him angry.'

'What is the *chicotte*?' I eased her fingers from mine. When I had them free I held her hand. The palm was calloused and very dry.

'You saw it, Mrs Cooper, you saw the *chicotte* and what it does. You should not have looked at such a thing. Not you.'

One of her children poked his curly head round the kitchen door. Without turning, as if she'd eyes in the back of her own head, Ilanga shouted something at him. He disappeared. I had never heard her shout at her children before.

'I think that we must talk,' Lingomo Mongo said.

They looked at me together, a pair of tall, shiny-black people, stiff and unknowable and not at all the friends I'd hoped they would be to me. They were too afraid for that.

We sat, the three of us, on wooden stools outside the open kitchen door. The sun hadn't yet climbed over the roof so that back part of the house was shaded still. Even away from the house there was shade to be had under the palm-like leaves of a semi-circle of banana trees. In this part of the compound, too, Lingomo had planted a small garden in which he was growing yams and sweet potatoes. The domesticity and peace of it all put a calming distance between us and the grisly happening at the other end of the compound.

'I don't agree with my husband's way of doing things.' I spoke quickly, before Ilanga could jump up and go, before Lingomo could tell me this wasn't what they wanted to hear. 'I knew nothing of the way things were done before I came to Africa . . .'

I hesitated, hearing Hugh's voice in my ear, my own obstinate refusal to listen to him. Then I went on, even more quickly because I wanted the words to be said and over with.

'What I saw this morning was wrong. More than that, it was inhuman. What I saw last week, the severed hands of children, was cruel beyond belief. The fact that my husband condones these things has been a terrible shock to me.'

I hesitated again, not wanting to put into words my awful fear that Thomas himself might have performed such deeds. As a possibility it was unspeakable. As a thought it was unbearable.

'I want to leave the station. I don't want to be here when my husband returns. I want to meet the British Consul, who is a countryman of my own called Roger Casement. I want

295

to talk to him about my position, and about leaving Africa to go home. I suppose he lives at Boma?'

I looked from one to the other of them. Ilanga had her hands folded in her lap and was looking out over the yard to where two of her children were playing with a dog in the sun. I couldn't read her face but I didn't have to. If I'd been her I'd have been afraid of Thomas's anger, too, have had the same fears for my children.

Lingomo got up and walked to the nearest banana tree and stood with his back to us, leaning against it, his hands in the pockets of his green cotton trousers, his head bent. I waited. And waited. Neither of them said a word.

'I know my husband told you to guard me,' I used the word deliberately, 'and I know you're afraid of him. I understand all this. But it's as wrong for you to tolerate what is happening as it would be for me. If you help me to get away, you will at least . . .'

'I would be putting the lives of my children and wife in danger.' Lingomo didn't turn. 'Is that what you want me to do? If you leave here nothing will change and we will suffer.'

He turned at last. He didn't take his hands out of his pockets and still he leaned against the tree, but his voice was lacerating and his eyes full of outrage. 'Are you so very important, Mrs Thomas Cooper?' he said. 'Are your feelings more important than the safety of a black family?'

He might as well have taken the leather whip to me. I stared at him for fully a minute, aware of flies buzzing in the silence, of an animal or bird shrieking in the forest. Anger rescued me.

'My feelings are not the issue, Mr Mongo. The brutally inhumane way this station is run is the issue. What is certain is that nothing will change if I stay here but may if I leave and report on what I've seen. What is equally certain is that your children, growing up with these things happening every day, will very likely join the ranks of the soldiers who take part in the beating of their fellow Africans. Is that what you want for them?'

'No.' Ilanga spoke for the first time. 'All we want is that our children continue to live until they are grown.' Her eyes were filled with the bleakness of the world in which she lived.

'But things must change . . .' I stopped. I sounded futile and knew it.

Two of the Mongo children, a boy and girl whose names were Yoka and Boali, had become bored playing with their dog and moved closer to their parents to play a game with sticks in the dust. The third, a boy called Mola, went on playing with the dog. The sun, coming through the leaves at last, moved back and forth on their skin, on the designs they made on the ground.

Boali was wearing a pink dress and her black curls shone with the perfumed oil her mother rubbed into them every morning. She was about six years old. Her brother cheated at the game and she slapped him smartly on the hand with one of the sticks. He howled and sulked when his father said something to him. They went on playing. Yoka was eight, the oldest of the three children.

'You are right that things must change,' Lingomo said, 'but I will not let my children suffer to make that change.'

'I promise you they will not,' I said. 'I will make a report and bring the consul back to see for himself. Thomas will be forced to change his ways or be replaced . . .'

I stopped when Lingomo gave a short, hard laugh. His wife buried her head in her hands and rocked back and forth.

'Many such reports have already been made.' Her words were hard to hear between her fingers. 'The King of Belgium is all-powerful. No one hears what is said. No one.' I heard Hugh's voice again. He'd said something similar.

'My brother didn't want me to come here. He'd read about an Irishman who was murdered in the Congo. There was a great fuss in the newspapers but my brother Hugh said it was just the tip of the iceberg, that there had been reports, too, of atrocities happening to Africans and that soon something would happen to make the world listen and see. He was right. They will not dare to touch you while you are with me. The Belgian king will not want the outrage and scandal of an Irish woman endangered, or injured. Or worse . . .'

'Why did you come when your brother forbade it?' Ilanga waved a dismissive hand at my story but was genuinely curious about my disobeying a brother.

'Because I didn't want to believe him,' I said. 'Because I believed coming to Africa was the best thing for me to do.'

'Just as you believe now that going to the consul is the best thing.' Lingomo broke the stick in his hand.

'Yes,' I said.

'You were wrong not to listen to your brother,' Ilanga said.

'Yes.'

'You would be wrong now too,' she said.

'I hope not,' I said and there was another silence. When it had become loud as a scream, and as Lingomo made a move to go, I said, 'My husband is afraid of the consul because he's making another report.' I was thinking about and watched Lingomo's face as I spoke. 'Why would he be afraid, and Charles Beckett and the rest of them, too, if reports are of no account?'

Ilanga answered, taking her hands from her face and looking at her children. 'Because the man you speak of is strange and different and travels alone with a dog. There is nothing he fears and nowhere he will not go. He has seen everything. He has the ear of many and people listen to him.'

'Well, then . . .' I began.

'The man you're talking about has seen men die because of Thomas Cooper. Terrible deaths. He has seen the cages. He has seen many, many hands cut off because of Thomas Cooper. It was because of him that Thomas Cooper left. But he came back.' She stopped. Her face was composed, her eyes unreadable again. 'Thomas Cooper will never leave Africa. He is a big man in Africa.'

'You're wrong,' I said.

'I am not wrong.'

'You're wrong, too, about Casement, the consul. My husband is afraid of him. He has power.' I leaned forward and held my hands in front of me, pleading. 'Please help me get to Boma.'

'Going to Boma will do you no good,' said Ilanga, 'better for you and for us if you get on with being a wife. Others will see to the beatings, the hand choppings.'

'I cannot stay here,' I said. 'I will not.'

'Your countryman does not live in Boma,' said Lingomo, 'and he is anyway not so powerful as the King of Belgium. And he is not *of* Belgium.'

'What are the cages?' I said. 'And tell me about the *chicotte*?'

I would go anyway, whether they helped me or not. I might as well find out all that I could before I left.

'The workers must stay in the forest for twenty-four days per month gathering rubber,' Lingomo said, his voice flat. 'They build cages for themselves to spend the nights in, to protect them from leopards. The leopard gets many of them anyway. The *chicotte* is made of raw, sun-dried hippopotamus hide cut into long, sharp-edged strips. It was unknown before the white man came to Africa. Now it is known everywhere.'

I didn't feel well. 'Leave, come away with me,' I said. 'I'll make sure the consul protects you . . .'

'I will tell you how we are here,' Lingomo spoke softly. 'Listen.'

What he told me was this.

Lingomo Mongo was born in the British colony of the Niger Coast Protectorate and became a schoolteacher. Seventeen years before, when it was being set up by King Leopold, he, and others like him, had been persuaded by the king's officials to come and work in Boma, the capital of the Congo Free State. With few Europeans about, educated Africans were of great use to the new state.

He worked as a clerk in the Governor-General's office in Boma. He also, when he was asked, recruited men – including his younger brother, Tswambe – for the new army, the *Force Publique*, from his own country. When he'd been in the Congo three years he sent for Ilanga, to whom he'd been betrothed. They married and went on holiday to Belgium.

'We were well treated there,' Lingomo said. 'When they asked, I gave talks on the good work of the king's regime in the Congo. They liked me very much. A newspaper wrote of me that I was a "striking example of the perfectibility of the Negro race".' He stopped, looking at the ground, then said again, slowly, 'An example of the perfectibility of the Negro race.'

Back in Boma again he worked hard, for longer hours than he had to. Ilanga worked, too, in a shop in the town selling supplies from Europe. She bought a piano and two armchairs. They never went outside the town. They had a home and work and no need to. All would have been well if they'd had children.

But no babies came. Instead there were rumours and rumblings about the mistreatment of African workers gathering first ivory, then rubber. Some were reported by Tswambe, on visits from far-flung postings in the interior. Lingomo listened and went on working, glad of his security and safety in Boma.

He was eight years in the Congo when he decided to leave his government job and open a shop in Boma which he and Ilanga would run together. They'd been selling canned food and other supplies from Europe for more than a year, alongside African cloth and wooden utensils, when Ilanga became pregnant. Their children, Taupo, Yoka, Boali and Mola, were born one after the other, four years in a row.

It was their first-born son, Taupo, who brought the reality of the mistreatment of Congo workers into the Mongo home.

When he was seven years old Taupo went missing. His body was brought home to his parents ten days later by his uncle Tswambe.

Taupo, wanting to find his uncle, had stowed away on a steamboat taking soldiers upriver. The soldiers had taken him to where Tswambe was posted. He was very busy. With their rubber quota down, fearful villagers had severed vines to extract rubber, instead of tapping them as was the rule. The vines died. Examples had to be made to prevent such a thing happening again and Tswambe and his company of soldiers were there to see to it.

So it was that Taupo saw his soldier uncle line up and shoot villagers. He saw the soldiers burn the whole village and cut down the banana trees. He saw women and children taken prisoner and, in the confusion, was taken prisoner himself. As they were marched to the next village, to be kept there, he saw bodies floating in the river with their right hands cut off and other bodies hanging from the branches of trees into the water.

When he saw his uncle Tswambe in the village Taupo broke free and ran towards him. A bullet stopped him not ten feet from where his uncle stood with his companions, drinking palm wine and awaiting orders. The boy lived until the next day; long enough to tell his uncle, over and over, all that he'd seen.

Tswambe Mongo, in the days and nights after he'd brought his nephew's body home, told his brother, over and over, about the unthinkable things he'd done as a soldier of the *Force Publique*.

Most horrifying of all was his time serving under a state official called Fievez, a man who had punished entire villages when they didn't supply his troops with enough fish and manioc. Fievez's principle of war against such villages was a simple one. As he explained it: 'One example was enough: a hundred heads cut off, and there have been plenty of supplies at the station ever since. My goal is ultimately humanitarian. I killed a hundred people . . . but that allows five hundred others to live.'

On the third day after Taupo's funeral Tswambe Mongo shot himself.

Lingomo Mongo, still a British subject, went to the British Consul, Roger Casement, and told him all that he knew of the atrocities committed by the *Force Publique*. Casement, before leaving on his journeys into the interior, added Lingomo's story to a report he was compiling.

The king's officials were not pleased. They didn't kill or imprison Lingomo because he was, after all, a British subject. The repercussions would have been huge and they would have been international.

In the weeks which followed Lingomo couldn't prove the Congo state officials had anything to do with the burning down of his storehouss, nor that the men following his remaining children everywhere they went were anything but friendly. There was nothing he could do either when state employees were forbidden to buy in the Mongo shop.

Since these were the only people around with any real money to spend it destroyed their business. When Lingomo was offered the job of looking after the home and new wife of a station chief in the interior he knew he had to take it. Either

302

that or live in fear of accidents happening to one or all of his children.

The Mongo family had arrived in Pongara in December. Now it looked to them as if I was bringing all they'd fled on top of them, putting their children once again in mortal danger.

All they wanted, Lingomo said, was peace. Peace and no more dead children.

'Now you know why you mustn't ask me again to take you to Boma,' he said. 'My children will be the ones to suffer if I do. In any event,' he gestured his daughter to him then turned her so that she was looking at me before he went on, 'you will not find Mr Casement in Boma. He is never in his house there. He is everywhere else in the Congo, gathering a report for his government about all that he can discover on the cruel mistreatment of people here. He travels in a steamboat obtained from missionaries, alone with his dog and a man who cooks and helps him. He stays by night in the missions, sometimes. Other times he camps by the riverside or on an island. No one can tell where he is and that is how he wishes it to be. You will not find him.'

Lingomo was wrong. I could very easily have found Roger Casement if Thomas hadn't prevented our meeting at the Tonkinese mission. I saw now that it was more than an aversion to Eunice Milton, or even to Casement's principles, that had made him do so.

All the while Lingomo spoke to me his daughter Boali kept her round dark eyes on my face. They said more to me, in many ways, than her father's harrowing words.

Ilanga broke the silence after her husband finished speaking. 'You will do a far better thing if you stay here and please your man,' she said. 'You can make him not want to torment the black people so much.'

'No. It won't be like that,' I said. 'All that will happen is that you will be proven right, Ilanga, about one thing. My husband is a big man in Africa. He will not want to be anything less.'

'If you go, our job here is gone too,' she said. 'We are five people. You are one.'

And this was the core of it. Ilanga and Lingomo Mongo were asking me not to sacrifice them and their children to the dictates of my morality. They were telling me I would serve a greater good by staying.

One life to save five. One hundred lives to save five hundred. The comparison wasn't, of course, valid – but the Congo was a place which turned everything on its head and where too many wrongs were condoned for bad reasons.

The forest edge was very close to where we sat at the back of the house. The Mongo children, all three of them together now, played around the first row of trees, running in circles and clapping their hands as they went.

'I can't stay here,' I kept my voice neutral, 'and neither can you. We'll leave together: the two of you, me, the children.'

'The soldiers will not let us leave.' Lingomo spoke with quiet exasperation. 'Your husband will not allow *you* to leave. It would make him look a fool. He's a big man in the Congo. He has power here. You have none.'

If he was losing patience then I was losing the opportunity to make something happen.

'We'll find a way to leave,' I said, getting to my feet. 'We'll take the next boat that stops on its way upriver. We'll go to the Tonkinese mission. Eunice Milton will give us shelter. She knows the British Consul. You are British subjects and have rights so he will *have* to help you. That's as much his job as the writing of reports. We'll send out word that we want a meeting and wait there for him.' I paused. 'I will make sure that he takes up your case, I give you my word.'

I crossed my fingers in the pocket of my skirt and prayed

Roger Casement was a decent, caring and brave man as well as the odd one he sounded.

'You speak as if you were in your own country.' Lingomo Mongo turned away. 'As if things were *normal*. The Americans at Tonkinese live by their own rules and many people are not sure of them . . .' He stopped, thinking better of something he'd been about to say. His arm muscles rippled as he clenched and unclenched his fists. 'You must understand that death is everywhere in the Congo,' he went on. 'The deaths of black children mean nothing.' He clicked his fingers in the air. 'The deaths of a black man and woman would mean nothing. Black blood keeps the rubber tree growing and the white man rich.'

I was losing him. In a minute he would be too angry to listen to me, or to reason. I spoke quickly, looking from one to the other of the Mongos.

'I want to think overnight about what you've told me. In the morning I'll tell you what I've decided.'

Lingomo, without a word, walked out of the shade and across the sun-baked space to where the goats were tethered. The two boys ran to him. Boali came and stood with her mother.

'If that is what you wish.' Ilanga shrugged. 'But maybe you should think on this too.' She covered her daughter's ears and went on, very softly, 'The cans of meat in the boxes you brought with you on the riverboat? The ones you wanted me to put on shelves?' She stopped, waited until she was sure I knew what she was talking about, then went on. 'They do not hold what it says on the outside. They are filled with the severed, chopped up hands of children. Black people all know this. But white people still eat what is in those cans.' She took Boali by the hand and went back inside the house.

The Mongo family, parents and children, didn't talk to me any more that day. No one else in Pongara did either. I was completely alone with my thoughts and fears and imaginings, for all of the day and through the long, dark, noisy and wakeful night which followed. The forest had never been filled with so many shrieks, drumbeats or, as morning came, whispers.

All of which loneliness helped me decide as I did. For better, for worse.

It was sometime around seven o'clock when I left my bed, put on a navy-blue and white linen dress, tied my hair back in a scarf (something Thomas hated me to do), made a mug of mint tea and went and sat with it at the back of the house. I sipped and watched the Mongos' house, waiting for the door to be pulled back and one or both of the adults to come to me.

They let me wait. Or maybe it was that they were putting off hearing what I'd decided.

Whatever the cause, I sat for fully half an hour before Ilanga came out of the house and walked quickly towards me. She had a bright-yellow cloth wrapped round her body and a turban of darker yellow around her head. She carried a wooden bowl and studied me as she came, trying to read my face. The children were nowhere to be seen.

'You are going.' She sat and looked at me, the bowl in her lap.

'I am,' I said.

'I had a dream,' she said, 'it was not a good one. I knew you would go.'

'What did you dream?' I said, knowing I shouldn't ask.

'Bad things. You were on water and in water. You were . . .' she hesitated '. . . you were alone and separated from your people. You were holding a child's hand. There was no body attached to it. Blood dripped from the trees.'

I stared at her. 'It was a dream, that's all,' I said at last, 'only a dream.'

But my mother believed in dreams. So had all belonging to me, except for Hugh. And except, too, for Ellie, who was now my sister. Ellie Hope-O'Grady had no time for dreams and nor had Mossie. I clung to this thought.

'Lingomo will not speak with you this morning,' Ilanga said, 'he is sick in his heart and in his head.'

It was quiet everywhere. A bird, very beautiful with its black body and white wings, swooped low but didn't land before swooping off again. I drank the mint tea and found it had lost its taste.

'I'm leaving, Ilanga, because my staying here will not change things,' I said. 'If I stay Thomas will see it as condoning his barbarities for the sake of my family, who are beholden to him. He'll be encouraged to feel more powerful than ever. If I go there are things which can be done. I can speak out against what I've seen happen here. I can give evidence to the consul for his report on the people's mistreatment. I can have the consul arrange for your protection as British subjects, most likely at the mission. You can be gone from there before Thomas gets back. You and your children can't stay here any more than I can.'

I willed her to look at me but she kept her head stubbornly averted, eyes fixed on the bark house with her children inside. She kept her counsel, too, and was silent. Her long fingers played with the bowl, turning and turning it, taking comfort from the smooth wood.

I told her my plan.

'I've thought of a way that will not leave blame for my going attached to yourself or Lingomo,' I said. 'Tomorrow I'll go down to the riverboat, as I always do, to deliver and collect letters. I'll leave a letter here for Thomas saying that my decision to leave was my own and that I've lied to you, that you're no part of my going. When the boat arrives I'll find a way of going on board without being seen – I'm well able to paddle a canoe if I have to. With the usual commotion of people coming and going, I'll be able to . . .'

'Your husband will say I should have been with you. That Lingomo should have been with you.' Ilanga stood. 'I am going now to make manioc bread.'

She put the bowl under her arm and went past me into the kitchen. Ellie, when faced with a difficulty, used to make bread too.

I wrote five letters that day. My only dread as I wrote, and one I tried to put to the back of my head, was that I might be carrying Thomas Cooper's child. A child was a child, and innocent of its parentage, but I was filled with an unholy apprehension about carrying Thomas's baby.

I would never be able to do as Bella had done and our child would be, for the rest of my life, a living reminder of its father. I worried both that I might not love it and that I might lose it, travelling home.

Writing, I put the worry out of my mind, for a while. I wrote first to my brother Hugh, telling him all that I'd seen and that I was leaving my husband. I asked him to send what money he could care of the British Consul, Roger Casement, at Boma, for my passage home. I also asked him to go to London, if necessary, and have the Foreign Office there instruct its consul in the Congo to act on my behalf, since I was a British subject, and on behalf of the Lingomo family.

'Life is cheaper than you can imagine in Africa,' I wrote, 'about this you were certainly right. I want to be sure of seeing you and my home again.'

I wrote to Ellie, telling her I would be home within a month and that Thomas would be stopping the money orders to the bank. I was sorry about this, I said, but trusted her to understand all when it came to light. I wrote to my mother, telling her not to worry, and to Manus, telling him to spend all of Thomas's money they had so as to ensure he couldn't reclaim any of it. Blood cannot be extracted from a turnip, any more than money from an empty account.

Last of all I wrote to Thomas. A short letter, which ended:

I blame myself as much as you for the failure of our marriage. I saw you as a means of escape from the unhappiness of my life in Sligo. I should not have used you in this way, any more than you should have misrepresented yourself to me as you did. To follow me would be pointless. To punish Ilanga or Lingomo Mongo, who are in no way assisting my escape, would be both unwise and stupid. You are unwise, Thomas, but not stupid.

In the morning, on account of its voluminous pockets, I again put on my navy-blue and white linen dress. Into the pockets I packed all of the English money I could find in the house, as well as the brass rods which were the local currency and which Thomas kept in a special drawer.

I took what money I had left of my own, as well as my mother's pearls, Bella's earrings and Ellie's chemise.

I walked to the boat slowly, a long blue challis shawl further covering my hips and bulging pockets, a straw hat with ribbons and flowers on my head. Slowly was how I always walked, on account of the heat and in the interests of killing time in the long days. No one stopped or spoke to me.

No one came ashore from the riverboat either. A single canoe was paddled out to deliver my letters and, for the first day since I'd arrived, there were no supplies sent ashore. Muriel Sedley stood beside me on the shore, chatting amiably enough about Charles having had a night of 'botheration with his lungs'. Two soldiers stood close behind us. There wasn't a chance in the world of my pushing out a canoe unnoticed to paddle myself over the stretch of water to the boat.

Things were even worse the next day. The boat which

called was small and the captain a fierce popinjay who harassed his crew for all of the half-hour it took to unload two boxes.

The boat which called two days later was long and narrow and low in the water. I didn't like the look of it at all as it came close and began off-loading supplies. There was a great deal of shouting and derisive laughter on shore when the captain, who was English and young, shouted over that they'd run short of chopped wood for the engine room. Pongara's soldiers helped the crew with the chopping, the river suddenly filled with busy canoes and the chaos became all that I'd prayed for.

I sat in a canoe and was rowed out with two African women delivering fresh yams and plantain to the ship's cook.

When I told the captain that I was going to visit the Tonkinese mission he merely nodded and said there was a cabin I could use to be away from flying insects and mosquitoes. He didn't question me, just took my money as if I was an everyday traveller and ordered a crewman to show me to the cabin. I sat in its cramped, hot confines until we were well under way.

26

The river narrowed beyond Pongara and small beaches of white sand appeared in places along the bank. The current became wilder, too, and the boat, which was called *L'Oracle* and had seen much better days, was hard put to make anything but slow headway.

The riverbanks became higher as we went and were lined by great black weathered rocks. Trees without leaves hung over them into the water.

When I paced the deck I was thrown about for my trouble. I'd have gone on pacing though, glad of the distraction, if an insect hadn't stung my face and caused it to bleed. After that I took myself back to the cabin. I paced there too.

L'Oracle's slow pace and decrepit state meant that night had fallen and the river had broadened into a glittering, mysterious, moonlit strait by the time the houses of Eunice Granville's mission station came into view. It was pleasantly cool as we drew in to a ghostly, wooded island and tied up to a tree. I was helped down into a canoe and taken to a white beach on the riverbank.

A low-sized man in a black suit of clothes and brimmed hat was waiting to help me ashore.

'My name is Henry Reynolds,' he said, politely letting my hand go as soon as I'd steadied myself, 'and you're welcome to Tonkinese Mission. We're always delighted to receive visitors.' He paused. 'Whatever the hour.'

He wore heavy black boots and spoke as if he was welcoming me at the door of his home, which from his accent was somewhere in England. His smiling curiosity, as he waited for me to answer, was equally polite.

'I've come to see Eunice Milton,' I said.

'Of course you have,' he fluttered tiny hands in the air between us, 'and she'll be delighted to see you too.'

Still he didn't move. His smile didn't waver either. Delight and warm welcomes might be the thing at Tonkinese Mission but they didn't get you any further than the riverbank.

'Maybe you could take me to Eunice?' I said.

Tonkinese Mission would never need the army of sentries Thomas employed at Pongara as long as it had Henry Reynolds. He waited on, silent and pleasant and inoffensive, for me to say who I was, and what I wanted. As guard dogs went, he might look like a poodle, but was really a terrier, a breed to be respected for its tenacity and fierce territorial instincts.

'My name is Vanessa O'Grady,' I said at last. 'Mrs Milton may remember me as Mrs Thomas Cooper. We met when we travelled together on the riverboat *Le Roi Léopold* some weeks ago.'

'Ah, yes, of course you did,' he said, and took a firm grip on my elbow. The top of his hat came barely to my shoulder. 'You must be in need of a cup of tea after your journey.'

The moon had risen high enough to make the mission and its surroundings easy to see as we went forward. The forest was not so close to the river here and the terrain low enough to see hills in the distance. The mission itself covered a lot less ground than the station at Pongara and its buildings were more closely packed together. The sense of community made it as different from Pongara as night from day.

A wooden church, small and white-painted, held centre place. A path edged with white-painted stones wound between several white-painted wooden houses mounted on poles. There was a shop, a school and a long building where, I later learned, children from the school both ate and slept. Beyond them, close to a clump of trees and high grasses, were a number of African-style huts with thatched roofs. A fire burned in the middle of these and three or four Africans stood in its glow, watching our approach.

It was all very quiet. Even the forest was quieter than it had been around Pongara. The sheer peace of the place set up a new anxiety in me.

Lingomo was right. Thomas would not let me go easily. He would not let the Mongo family go easily either. My going, and theirs, would be a matter of pride, possession and terrible anger to him. If he came with his soldiers to Tonkinese there might be no way of fighting him off.

I was framing a mental apology for the trouble I was bringing on the mission when a door ahead of us opened and Eunice Milton stepped out. Her hair, in its plait, twisted long and dark down the front of her white nightgown.

'I've been expecting you,' she said, 'though not at this hour of the night.'

'Your plait . . .' I stopped a few feet from her. 'I've seen the *chicotte*,' I said.

She ran her hand along the coils of hair, frowning. 'I suppose you had to,' she said, 'to understand the Congo.' She held out her hand. 'Come on in. You may as well come inside too, Henry.'

'I'm sorry to have said what I did about your hair,' I said, in the middle of her sitting room. 'I suppose the *chicotte* was playing on my mind.'

'It has a way of doing that,' she touched the side of my face, 'but there is no *chicotte* here. This is my husband, Granville.'

A middle-sized black man with greying hair came and stood

beside her. The shock made a staring idiot of me, even as Thomas's word about Eunice's 'deviant' behaviour began to make sense.

But why shouldn't she be married to a black man? There were black as well as white Americans and of course they must marry one another sometimes. I was mortified by my reaction, how shaken I was, how confused and embarrassed by unwanted images of them in bed, a white and a black body side by side. Holding my hand out to Granville Milton, I felt sure my smile had a lunatic look to it.

He was shorter than Eunice and wore a loose grey robe. A large crucifix hung from his neck on a leather cord. *His* smile was calm and pleasant and his hand, shaking mine, firm and reassuring. I liked him immediately. My confusion eased.

'This is the young Irishwoman who married Thomas Cooper,' Eunice told him.

'Glad you decided to call on us at last,' Granville Milton said. 'You'll be staying a while, I presume?'

'I'm not sure . . .' I stopped as waves of weakness came over me and Granville began to weave to and fro, to and fro.

Eunice helped me into a low chair when I grabbed at her for support.

'I'm making a practice of this.' I attempted a smile.

'You are indeed,' she agreed.

Her husband brought me sweet tea.

They had the grace then to let me be while I wept, Eunice sitting wordlessly beside me, her husband smoking a pipe and reading. Henry Reynolds made himself busy with some paperwork at a corner desk.

I wept silently for a while, then abandoned myself to sobs. I felt free and I felt safe in that room, my noisy, bitter tears no great surprise to people who'd too often seen the work of the *chicotte*, too many severed hands, countless beaten children.

I did a lifetime's weeping that night. I wept for my home

and dreams gone, for the sad, bad, twisted white people at Pongara, for my dead father and lonely, living mother, for the nephew I'd not seen and for Theo Howard, so beloved for so long. I wept most of all for the dreadful marriage I'd made and, when I was through with all of that, wept for the part of me I'd lost for ever, the part that had believed all men and women were intrinsically good and that evil was a rare aberration.

I hadn't eaten for two days so when I was through with weeping Eunice brought me a wooden bowl of stewed fowl with rice, the remains of what they'd had for dinner that evening, and some toasted manioc bread. She put it on a small table beside me, with a glass of goat's milk, and gave me a spoon.

'Your husband is away,' she said, as I began on the stewed fowl.

It was a statement, not a question, and a reminder that news travelled as fast up and down the River Congo as it did between villages at home in Ireland. I nodded, picking up and nibbling the bread, discovering I liked it better as toast.

'So he doesn't know you're here?' Eunice said, persistent as ever.

'She'll be better able to explain herself after she's eaten.' Her husband closed his book and leaned forward with it on his knees. He'd been reading from the psalms. 'Maybe you'd like a glass of wine?' he said.

I nodded and he got up to pour a small amount of dark blood-red wine into a stemmed glass. It tasted like cough mixture.

'Thank you,' I said, glad of the way it burned raw in my throat, glad of anything that jolted me out of myself.

Granville Milton seemed to me older than Eunice. It wasn't that his skin was more lined, though I'd no knowledge anyway of how black skin aged. It was more that he had the air of someone with an acceptance and wisdom of the way people were. Mossie had the same thing, though he could be fierce and impatient in a way I doubted this man could ever be.

Granville was gentler than his wife in every way, and that was how they complemented one another. Though I'd never come across a black man and a white woman together before, in the case of Eunice and Granville Milton it seemed, in a very short time, to be not at all out of the ordinary. I supposed, anyway, that it was a common enough thing in America.

'I would like you to make room for the Mongo family to come here,' I said, 'all of them. For a while at least. And I would like you to help me make contact with the British Consul . . .'

'Begin at the beginning,' Eunice suggested.

I told them everything. How annoyed and forbidding Thomas had been about the idea of my being friendly with Eunice. How annoyed and forbidding the other whites at Pongara had been about the idea of my going to the mission to meet Casement. How worried they were about the consul ever coming to Pongara. The one thing I didn't talk about was my dread that I was carrying Thomas's child. In the face of everything else it seemed unimportant. I put it out of my head again.

I told them then about the children's severed hands. About the father's distress and Thomas's denial of Dokombo's story. There was no need to give any great detail when it came to telling them about the *chicotte* flayings. All of them had seen many such beatings and had too often had to deal with the consequences.

'I must see Mr Casement,' I insisted. 'Both I and the Mongo family need his protection.'

'A lot of people want to see Mr Casement,' said Granville Milton. 'He's a good man, but unpredictable. He didn't arrive the Sunday we expected him but should do so fairly soon. We've heard he's not far from here, though we're not sure which village he's staying in.' He smiled. 'We'll get a message to him, don't worry.'

I needed to know more and drew breath to ask.

'Enough for now,' Eunice said sharply, 'tomorrow's another day.' She held her hand out for my empty bowl and I gave it to her. 'I'll get you warm milk and honey and then it's bed for you.'

I stood. The Miltons' furniture was functional and hand-made of wood and bamboo. The room was mostly white, with rugs of bright orange. There was a large black crucifix on one wall, a bible on a lectern was crossed with a long ribbon of purple and gold, and the curtains were orange. I wanted to stay there for ever.

'The Mongos . . .' I began but Granville, standing, shook his head firmly.

'We can do nothing until tomorrow,' he said. 'You must pray and place your trust in the Lord.'

Henry Reynolds, who hadn't said a word since meeting me on the riverbank, spoke as Eunice came back with the honeyed milk. His voice was full of reproach.

'We should safeguard our people.' He drew himself up. 'We need a man, or men, on guard along the riverbank. We should light more fires.'

'You'd have made a fine army commander,' Granville Milton said. The irony was wasted on Henry Reynolds who stiffened his narrow back and looked gratified. 'I think for tonight we will trust in God and common sense,' Granville went on. 'None but a madman would come upriver in the black of night.' He gave a small shrug. 'Mr Cooper is a day's travel away at any rate, and doesn't yet know his wife is here.'

If Granville Milton implicitly believed my husband a mad-man then Thomas very likely was one. I found I couldn't drink the honeyed milk.

317

'Come,' said Eunice, 'you're fit only to sleep.'

I said my goodnights and went with her.

But the house was small and the walls thin, and as I lay in the narrow bed in a cotton shift that filled me with illusions of childhood security I couldn't help overhearing Henry Reynolds's parting conversation with Granville Milton.

'We should tell your countryman immediately,' he said, 'he would want to know of a situation like this. He may offer protection too. Cooper and his kind are not fond of people in his line of business.'

'I see no sense in disturbing Mr Addison at this hour of night,' Granville Milton said.

'He's not asleep,' said Reynolds, 'he reads until the small hours. He's reading now. I saw him on the way here.'

'We'll leave him to his reading then. Its outcome is likely to profit the world more than anything else he can do at this hour. Goodnight, Henry, and may God go with you.'

Henry Reynolds's response was muffled but the sound of the front door shutting immediately afterwards was distinct enough.

It seemed impossible that I would sleep, but I did. And very quickly too. When I woke, from another dream in which rivers flowed with blood and skin blew in white and black ribbons from bare trees growing out of bare rocks, it was still dark outside. I got up and went looking for the privy and found Eunice waiting for me when I came back inside.

'How long have I been asleep?' It was cool and I shivered.

'An hour. Take this milk, it'll help.'

I took the wooden vessel she handed me. She watched while I drank. I would sleep afterwards, I knew. Eunice was in many ways like the women at home who practised a sort of witchcraft and had a cure for everything. She probably had a lot in common, too, with the African women who gave her their cures and potions.

*   *   *

I saw David Addison for the first time at eleven minutes past ten the next morning.

I'd slept long and dreamlessly and woken to an empty house. I got up, dressed quickly, checked the time and rushed outside, full of a panicky confusion and fear that something had happened.

He was standing in the shadow of a mango tree with two small boys, showing them how to make a cat's cradle with a length of green yarn. His hands moved with dizzying speed while the children watched, wide-eyed. There was the smallest of breezes that morning and the sunlight flickering through the moving leaves made it look as if the three of them were dancing. In Ireland David Addison would have been a person apart; black, unknowable and frightening to many. Here he shone like an ebony African god.

But I had hoped to see Eunice or her husband, and the sight of this man – tall, dark and a stranger – made me unsure.

'Do you want to learn how to do this too?' he called without turning.

'Would you teach your grandmother to suck eggs?' I said and, when he spun round with the yarn between his hands and a look of amusement on his face, added, 'Those children will never learn if you don't stop showing off.'

'You're wrong,' he said and beckoned me closer with a jerk of his head. 'Do it for me.' He handed the yarn to the nearest child, a boy of about eight years old. The boy made a quick, and very expert, cat's cradle. Grinning like a small devil, he held it up to me for inspection.

'It's very, very good,' I said to him, 'you've been taught well.'

As if to prove my point, and further enhance his hero's standing, the boy dismantled the structure and made another, more complicated one. His smaller companion watched me with a grin wide as an open gate. Their teacher was, without a doubt, their god. For that morning, at any rate.

'My apologies,' I said to David Addison, 'there is clearly method to the madness of your teaching.' I felt ungracious, and sounded it. His smile, as he looked down at me, was both gracious and lordly.

'Small boys learn best when they learn quickly,' he said.

He had a neatly trimmed moustache. His hair, too, was trimmed very close to his head. I decided he was patronising me.

'Nonsense,' I said, 'we *all* learn best, young and old, when we're curious.'

He went on grinning at me, his white teeth shining, black eyes curious. I was goaded beyond caution.

'In this instance,' I said, 'the pupils are clearly encouraged by the fact that their teacher is still attached to boyhood himself.'

'Ah . . .' He sighed and looked down at the boys. He ran his hands through the tight helmet of curls on one child's head. 'I won't disagree with you,' he said. 'Since it's said we all carry something of the child within us.' He made a growling sound at the boys and they jumped back in mock fear. 'Go,' he said to them, 'I want to talk to Mrs Cooper. Go.'

'You're Mr David Addison, I presume.' I held out my hand as the boys ran off, ashamed of my tetchiness, hoping we could begin again. 'You have the advantage of knowing more about me than I do about you.'

'Granville told me your story,' he agreed, 'earlier this morning. I hope you're feeling rested, at least.'

He stood with his hands in the pockets of his loose beige cotton trousers. His manner was polite, more distant now the children were gone. He didn't look anything like a missionary should, or might. But then he was an American and Americans were different in every way from the rest of us.

'I'm very rested,' I said, awkwardly, 'thank you. Perhaps too rested. I'm worried at the lateness of the hour. There are things I must arrange. Can you tell me where Eunice is to be found?'

I could feel the nearly noonday sun begin to burn through to my scalp and wished I had a hat. David Addison was standing in the shade.

'She's in the schoolroom,' he said, 'I doubt she can talk to you right now.'

'She must . . .' Panicked, I began to turn in the direction of the low building I'd seen the night before.

'Your friends are safe enough for the moment.' He fell into step beside me. 'You may not even have been missed yet. If they've any sense they'll be keeping your escape a secret for as long as possible. Granville tells me they were your main contacts at the station, that you'd little to do with the whites there.'

'You're very well informed.' I didn't stop.

'It's my business to be informed,' he said, 'as it's Eunice's business to teach. I wouldn't advise interrupting her class.'

'That's all very well for you to say,' I heard my voice rising as my pace quickened, 'the Mongo family are not your responsibility. I've left them in a terrible situation.'

'You have.' He caught my arm at the elbow. His grip was strong, insistent. The shock brought me to a dust-swirling standstill. 'Creating an awkward situation for Eunice won't improve things.' He didn't let go of my arm. 'Especially since she and Granville have already acted on behalf of your friends.'

'What do you mean?'

'A man left for Pongara on foot at daybreak.'

He guided me out of the blazing sun and into the thin shade offered by the side of the schoolhouse. He dropped my arm and took a box of short, narrow cigars from the pocket of his immaculate white shirt and extracted one, slowly. Part of me envied him the smoke that calmed and the occupation that gave him something to do with his hands. I would have asked for one but didn't want to risk his amusement if I had a fit of coughing and spluttering.

'On foot?' It was all I could think to say.

'It's shorter through the forest.' He lit and drew on the cigar.

The smoke had a sweet, noxious smell and I wouldn't have given local insects or flies much chance in its presence.

'He's carrying an official letter from the mission telling Charles Beckett that you've been given protection here, that the British Consul is on his way and that should any harm be done to the Mongos he'll be answerable for it in court.'

'It's not enough,' I said. 'They need to be brought here now.'

'Your husband won't be back for a week or more. Long before that the consul will have arrived here and he and I will have gone to the station together and brought the Mongo family back to the mission with us. It will all be done legally, under the consul's protection and the implicit threat that Pongara's station's wrongdoing will be exposed in print if they try to prevent us. It's the only way to do this thing, Mrs Cooper, believe me. I've met many like your husband in the Congo. The Mongo family's removal must have all the weight of officialdom behind it if our actions are to stand up in court. We must be seen to be right, in law and in the eyes of the world. People like your husband have great power in the Congo and will use every means to justify what they do . . .'

'Stop!' I held my hands over my ears and shook my head. 'I don't understand half of what it is you're telling me!' I shouted. 'What court of law? Why should the world have any idea about this? Who are you that you can expose Thomas?'

I stopped. He was looking surprised, and a little puzzled.

'I'd like one of your cigars,' I added shakily, 'please.'

'I thought, when you knew my name, that you knew what I was doing here.' He clipped a cigar, then lit it as I put it to my mouth.

'I heard your name mentioned, that's all,' I said, puffed on the cigar and spluttered. He looked away.

'I'm a journalist,' he rubbed the back of his neck as if the act would help him think, 'my newspaper is called the *Washington Sentinel*. I'm here because of the stories of atrocities and horrors which have been seeping out of the Congo Free State for several years now. A cousin of mine came here more then ten years ago and exposed the king and what he was doing then. His investigative work here was a landmark in the reporting of human rights abuses but it was ignored. It changed nothing. I came in hope of achieving greater success.' He shrugged. 'And because I'm black, as he was.'

I watched the cigar burn and go out, unsmoked, between my fingers. 'You've set yourself a big task.'

'I have,' he agreed. 'And now it's your turn. Would it be impertinent of me to ask how you came to marry a man like Thomas Cooper?' He leaned against the side of the school house, studying me.

'It would,' I said, 'under normal circumstances.' A journalist, an American and a black man. He was three things I knew little or nothing about. 'You know my husband then?' I said.

'I've met him.' He looked at the end of his cigar, frowning. 'Twice. He made quite an impression.'

'Not a good one, I can see. You didn't like him.'

'No, I didn't.' He stared down at me, quite motionless. 'I thought the man I met morally bankrupt, capable of only two emotions: greed and anger.' He paused, shrugged again. 'I may have been mistaken. You haven't answered my question. How did you come to marry him?'

I told him, as briefly as I could. When he asked me about Kilraven I answered those questions too. I'd been fifteen minutes in the sun being interrogated by him before I came to my senses. In his view, clearly, I'd married a monster. I wondered where that left *me* in his view.

'It's your business to ask questions,' I said finally, 'but I can't say I enjoy standing in the heat while answering them.'

He crushed the remains of his cigar into the dust under his heel. 'My apologies. I've a lot to learn, Mrs Cooper, and not half enough time in which to do it.'

'I doubt there's much I can teach you.'

'Let me be the judge of that.'

'The sun hasn't affected my mind, Mr Addison. I can still think, and make my own judgements.' I was having to tilt my head back to look up at him. This put me at a disadvantage and added to my irritation. 'Nor am I, so far as I know, morally impaired. When I met my husband I accepted him as the apparently kind and somewhat lonely person he appeared to be. Our personal situations at the time made marriage both reasonable and timely. That, quite simply, is the story of my life and marriage.'

'It doesn't sound simple at all, Mrs Cooper.' He kept his eyes on mine. 'But it is a simple truth that we all marry for different reasons. Of course you're not morally impaired. I'm sorry if I seemed to imply such a thing.' He smiled. 'I doubt you even know what morally impaired means.'

'You're patronising me, Mr Addison,' I said. 'Why wouldn't I know what morally impaired means? What right have you to think me a fool?'

He stepped back, startled, and raised a hand in protest. But

I was glad to have found a target for my frustration and anger with events and my life, and went on.

'You've no idea what I know or don't, what I believe in or don't, what I've experienced or lost.' I was tapping my foot in the dust. 'It's grossly insulting of you to imply that I've lived a life removed from any appreciation of right and wrong.' I ran out of steam then, and stopped. The noonday sun was stealing our precious bit of shade and the heat's terrible lethargy taking over. David Addison ran a finger round the inside of his immaculate collar and cleared his throat.

'You're right,' he looked and sounded reasonably contrite, 'I don't know a great deal about you.' He glanced away, showing me his profile, standing in the motionless way he had. 'I will be honest and admit that I made a judgement based on your colour and class. My remark was meant to imply that you had never come up against moral impairment, nothing more. It was a stupid thing to say, and unfair.' He shrugged. 'As an excuse, I can only say that my experience has been that this is true of a great many white women. I was obviously wrong in your case and I apologise again, most sincerely.'

A thin trickle of perspiration rolling from his forehead to his chin might have been caused by the heat, or by discomfort.

'I accept your apology,' I said. And then, wanting to make things easier between us, asked, 'Are you married, Mr Addison?'

'I am.'

'Do you have children?'

'I have two girls.'

'You must miss them, being so far away?'

'I've got used to missing them. My job frequently takes me away.'

This line of conversation was making things between us

harder, if anything. I went back to the subject of my unease, and the one thing we had in common.

'Have you witnessed many of the atrocities being committed in the Congo?'

'Not yet. Not the *chicotte* in use, and none of the infamous severed hands. I did come upon a hanging, however.' He shrugged. 'It's the practice in parts of my own country to hang black men, too, whether guilty of a crime or not. Of course, I've only been in the Congo for ten days. But I've read the reports and hope to persuade your consul to allow me accompany him on his investigations.'

He made it sound like a business venture. I couldn't quite see it like that, so I changed the subject again.

'I'm uneasy about leaving the Mongo family at Pongara for even a few days,' I said. 'Do you know the men who run the place with my husband?'

'Only by repute,' he said. 'An Englishman and a Belgian, I believe?'

'An Englishman and a Belgian,' I echoed, envying him the fact that he didn't know either of them, 'Charles Beckett and Leon Klein are their names. Mr Beckett is unwell, though his suffering doesn't seem to have given him any sympathy for the pain of others. Mr Klein is unwell, too, though in his case it's in the head. He enjoys inflicting pain.' I hesitated. 'He's repulsive. A hippopotamus has more to recommend him, while Mr Beckett's character has more in common with that of a hungry dog. The Mongo family won't be safe with either of them.'

'Things will not be easy for them,' David Addison agreed, 'but there's no point in us going to remove station employees without the power and protection of the proper authorities.'

'There's every point.' I could feel hysteria rise in my throat again. 'You don't know the people at Pongara, you said it yourself. The Mongos can just leave, they're not slaves.'

'Slaves are exactly what they are,' he argued. 'Black Africa is enslaved to the whites who're exploiting the wealth of their land. You know it too. What else do you think you've been seeing these last weeks?'

'When will Mr Casement arrive?'

'Soon. He's on his way.'

'How do you know that? Has he written to you?'

'The drums have mentioned him. And he's a man of his word, so I'm told.'

The drums I'd heard in the night, every night since arriving at Pongara. They'd some purpose then, other than chilling the spine and keeping one awake at night.

'Why can't he be brought here today?'

'Because no one's sure exactly where he is and because he has work to do.' David Addison was becoming impatient with me again. He didn't even try to keep the exasperation out of his tone. 'His report is for the British Parliament, and will need to be complete and damning. King Leopold is a fox who will not give up his colony unless forced to. The lives of hundreds of thousands of enslaved Congolese people depend on Casement's report . . .' he sliced the air with a hand '. . . millions, even. The world needs to know that the Congo is more than a source of elephant tusks and rubber.'

'I hope the Mongo family doesn't become a sacrifice to this great work,' I said and left him there, keeping in the shadow of the buildings as I walked quickly to the Miltons' home. I glanced back before going through the door. David Addison was where I'd left him, watching me as he lit another cigar. He waved. I nodded.

I found no peace over the next two days. I didn't leave anyone else in peace either.

The mission's messenger, a wiry man named Wiki, returned from Pongara without a reply. He'd delivered Granville Milton's letter into Charles Beckett's hand and been told to leave. When he hesitated he was marched back into the forest and sent on his way, without even a drink of water, by two soldiers.

'There is smoke and burning where Mr Cooper has gone,' Wiki pointed west, 'more villages for rubber. He burns when he is displeased.'

'He won't burn Tonkinese,' Granville Milton said, 'we're not subject to the king and so he must be careful.'

Wiki didn't look convinced and I didn't blame him.

I worried more than ever about the Mongos. The root of my fears lay in my own guilt about leaving them exposed in Pongara. I said as much to Granville.

'The answers you seek are with God, Vanessa,' he said. 'He alone can make good what man does in this world.'

We were sitting watching the children come out of school. There must have been twenty of them, boys and girls, tumbling and laughing their way across the compound. It was the easiest thing in the world then to ask Granville Milton about his marriage to Eunice, and if there was general acceptance of such partnerships in America.

'Anything but. Eunice and I came to Africa partly to be free from public disapproval of our union. Even members of our own church were opposed to it. So we came here, both to bring the word of God and for our own sakes. We thought to make Christians of pagans, to lead people away from their gods of magic and from fetishes and superstitions. But here we found that God is many things and has many faces. We're learning as much as we teach.'

We were sitting where everyone in the mission sat to talk: on flat, white-painted stones beneath the shade of a monkey pod tree. Mossie would have enjoyed those stones, and Manus, too. Once you took up position there you were given peace, and time.

'I'm beginning to see Africa differently,' I said, 'and it's because of you.'

'I'm just a black man you find yourself able to talk to.' He shook his head, smiling. 'You see Africa differently because you yourself are newly open, beginning to look and to listen.'

'Perhaps,' I said, 'but you cannot think cannibalism right, nor that a man should have ten wives?'

'No. These things are against the teaching of God.' He sighed. 'But there are other African ways which don't fly in His face and from which we can learn.'

'Have you made many Christians?'

'Some. But the missionary's job in the Congo has primarily become one of bearing witness to genocide and other barbaric acts. We will not, and cannot, be quiet about what we see, so men like your husband want us out of here. King Leopold would also like the non-Belgian Protestant missionaries to leave.' He smiled again. 'You've thrown in your lot with a not greatly loved species, I'm afraid.'

'But you'll persevere?'

'We will,' he said.

He told me then, unemotionally and so that I might speak up for the Congolese people after I left Africa, about injustices such as the 'children's colonies'.

These were state-funded schools run by Catholic Belgian missionaries with the aim of supplying the army with soldiers. He had seen *Force Publique* soldiers, after raiding villages for workers, bring captured children to such colonies. He'd seen how they were ruled by the *chicotte*, and chain, and by fear. He told me how only two boys survived from a group of 108 forced to march to a state colony at Boma.

And still he believed, this good man. Still he believed.

'Oh, God,' I said.

I thought that day I'd learned all there was to know about

cruelty in the Congo. The reality was that there was no end to it.

'Where was God when Dokombo's children's hands were being cut off?' I demanded. 'How do we know He won't fail the Mongos?'

'We must trust in His goodness,' said Granville.

Ultimately everyone failed the Mongos but I failed them most of all. The Miltons and David Addison failed them, too, but I was the one who put them in danger in the first place. I should never have left them to carry the blame for what I was doing.

Eight-year-old Yoka Mongo's right hand was delivered by one of Thomas's soldiers in the late afternoon of the day I sat talking with Granville Milton. The man carrying it came out of the forest at a trot, refused to speak with anyone but me, and when we met handed me an envelope and a small, cloth-wrapped parcel.

I knew before I opened the cloth what I would find inside.

27

The envelope held a letter from Charles Beckett. What he had to say was as precise as the copperplate hand which formed the words. He wrote:

Your husband has been sent word of your departure and will no doubt return to Pongara within days. The package you will have received along with this note is the unfortunate result of your actions.

Yoka Mongo was, of course, innocent of any wrongdoing but there are those in Pongara, as everywhere in the Congo Free State, who persist with barbaric acts in pursuit of justice. I was unable to prevent what happened and will have no control over other such acts. You are the only person who can prevent Yoka's brother and sister from similar suffering.

Your husband's mood will not be good on his return. A great deal of unpleasantness could be avoided if you could be here to meet him.

Muriel sends her best wishes and hopes to see you very soon. She has discovered a cream which affords the skin great protection against the sun's burning rays.

He offered his best wishes for a pleasant return journey and signed it Charles Mortimer Beckett.

'Sounds to me like the letter of a man covering his rear end in the event of a court case,' David Addison said. 'He's threatening us with another mutilation if Mrs Cooper doesn't go back, while making clear he will not accept blame.'

He was all-knowing, businesslike. I hated him for it.

'It won't happen again,' I said. 'I'm going back to Pongara. Today.'

We'd all wanted so much to believe the Mongos would be safe, to believe Charles Beckett and the rest of them would bow the knee to the British Consul, the power of the press and to missionary witness.

But we'd been stupidly delusional and David Addison, for all his confidence, knew as little as I did myself about how things were done in the Congo.

We were in the empty schoolroom, waiting for Granville Milton to arrive. Eunice was noisily clearing away, banging books on to desktops, slamming cupboard doors, slapping with a wet cloth at holes in the wall close to the ground.

'Termites,' she said, 'they're devouring the place. I told Granville we should have put in a brick foundation.' She straightened and glared at me. 'Do you know that termites are the most numerous of all living creatures in the Congo? That they've been on this continent for at least one hundred million years, all of that time living the same way, in the same underground darkness . . .'

She stopped suddenly and sat into a rush chair by her teacher's table. She picked up and studied a child's drawing of a very black gorilla.

'Eight years old, you say?' she said, and I nodded.

'An eight-year-old boy called Yoka,' I said. 'His brother Mola is five years old and sister Boali six. If you let me have a man, maybe two, I'll go downriver in a dugout and be at the station before nightfall. Hopefully I'll get there before they . . .' I stopped. 'I'll pray but I've never been much good at it. Maybe you could pray, Eunice, and Granville too? You've had more practice than I have.'

332

'There's no point your going back.' David Addison, doodling on a pad, was dismissive. 'The children and their parents will be made to suffer anyway.' He didn't look at me.

'They may not be,' I said, 'it's a chance worth taking . . .'

'It isn't your decision any longer.' He looked up then, his black eyes holding mine but telling me nothing. 'If you go back it will look as if we're giving in to threats and bullying. We'll have conceded the battle and they'll go on to win the war. There'll be no ending their cruelties, ever.'

'This is neither a battle nor a war,' I said. 'It has to do with righting a wrong and preventing another. I *must* go. I will go.'

'Oh, be quiet.' He was sharp with me, and frowning. 'It's time you learned to think before acting, Mrs Cooper. You might save yourself and others a lot of trouble if you did.'

He stood and walked to the open door and waved to Granville Milton, hurrying in our direction wearing a loosened African garment. It flapped about him in a way which made him seem about to take wing. Henry Reynolds puffed by his side, gesticulating like a windmill, his hat shadowing his face.

'I *have* thought about this.' I raised my voice and spoke to David Addison's broad back. Eunice interrupted me almost at once.

'David has another solution in mind, Nessa,' she said. 'This is a situation in which several heads may be better than one.' She paused. 'Or at least helpful.'

I fumed, impotently, the creator of a situation I'd lost control over. It was clear no one at the mission was going to listen to me.

When Granville Milton and Henry Reynolds came into the room David Addison looked at them questioningly.

'You think I'm right then?' he said. He seemed very big in that small room, and took up a great deal of the space. This

333

helped give him an air of being in charge of things. At least until Granville Milton took over.

The missionary gathered the red garment about him and sat on the edge of the table. He gave me a half-smile and said, '"Be ye therefore wise as serpents, and harmless as doves",' before turning to give David Addison his full attention. 'Your plan doesn't quite come up to the Bible's standards, Mr Addison, but it's the best we have. I pray to God it will work.'

'Who will come with me?' David said.

'I will,' Granville Milton said, 'as well as the fearless Lontulu Ibea and my good friend Manou because he knows the forest trail so well.'

'You must intervene, Eunice!' Henry Reynolds's voice was shrill. 'Granville shouldn't go. It's not his place. He's needed here. It's not suitable. I'm younger and fitter.'

'I am *not* too old.' Granville Milton rubbed his chin. He was still smiling a little, and deliberately offhand, but it would have been a foolish man who went against him.

Henry Reynolds was a foolish man.

'You're no longer young,' he said in a milder voice. Even indoors, in that classroom overcrowded with adults, he kept his hat on his head. 'What will become of all that we've done here if something happens to you? Simple prudence dictates that I should be the one to go.'

'Enough, Henry.' Granville Milton brought his hand down hard on a desk. He killed a fly, but he also silenced Reynolds. '"Pride goeth before destruction", and your pride has taken over from wisdom. This task is my responsibility, mine and Eunice's, and she has no wish to go. We hesitated and a child lost a hand. With God's help we can prevent hurt to the other children in the family.' He fixed Reynolds with basilisk stare. 'I cannot go if you will not stay.'

'Go where?' I demanded. 'I'd like to know what's happening, what this plan is. It has more than a little to do with me, after all.'

'When do we leave?' David Addison was impatient. He spoke directly to Granville Milton, ignoring me as he rubbed beads of sweat from his forehead with the back of his hand. He'd the air of a man bent on action who could not bear to be diverted.

'We leave for Pongara within the hour.' Granville Milton, answering, looked at me and took his wife's hand. 'With luck we'll be at the station in time to get the Mongo family on a riverboat late this afternoon. Otherwise we'll have them out of the station early tomorrow morning.' He turned to David Addison. 'Manou will tell you what you need to wear and bring. We'll meet at the church and pray together before setting off.'

'I gave up praying some time ago,' David Addison said.

'Then the Lord will be especially glad to hear from you,' replied Granville Milton. He left the schoolroom with David Addison at his side, Henry Reynolds prancing anxiously behind. Eunice did some further unnecessary and noisy stacking of books.

'Tell me about David's plan?' I said. 'Please, Eunice.'

'Sit down,' she commanded, and I did, at one of the small tables the children used for desks. Eunice looked at me for a minute, then shook her head. 'It's a plan which would doubtless work if we were dealing with reasonable people, whose responses could be relied on to be rational. I'm not so sure those things are true of the people at Pongara, however . . .'

'Tell me.' I spoke with my hands clenched to stop myself from shouting.

'Impatience will be your undoing.' Eunice folded her arms. 'Indeed it already has been. David's plan is this: he'll tell the

335

people in Pongara that he intends making what's happened at the station, especially to the Mongo family, internationally known through his newspaper. Having the finger of opprobrium pointed at them is just what King Leopold's people fear most. Like all bullies, they don't like their actions exposed to the clear light of day. Pray God it works.'

'Pray God,' I echoed fervently.

'Granville will see to it that David behaves responsibly,' Eunice continued. 'There's no sense in raging at the people of Pongara. The Belgian is not well in the head and the Englishman is sick in his body. David Addison has fine ideas, but I'm not sure he's got as fine a grasp of the kind of people we're dealing with here. I sometimes think he confuses the Congo Free State with Alabama.'

'Is that where he comes from?'

'It's where he was born and where he grew up, seeing injustices aplenty against black men and women there. Granville grew up in Alabama, too, but he's a man of peace. These things affect people differently. Some want vengeance for wrongs done, others just want an end to them.'

'Eunice, are you saying David is here to seek vengeance?' I felt a new fear stir in me for the Mongos.

'He might not know it himself but he's been greatly affected by things he saw as a boy. He's a man with a lot of anger in him. It's left him restless, and unsettled.' She paused. 'Driven . . . he seems to me driven.'

She folded then unfolded a small pink pinafore. She wore a white scarf to keep her hair back and, if it hadn't been for the ferocious and unsaintly frown between her brows, could have been a dark-eyed madonna.

'You're afraid he'll endanger Granville, is that it?' I said.

'He'll endanger everyone if he arrives in Pongara station like an avenging angel,' Eunice said. She folded the pinafore again, into a very small square.

'There's more than that worrying you,' I persisted.

She put the squared pinafore on top of others like it, smoothed the pile and said, very slowly, 'Charles Beckett and Leon Klein won't be told what to do by a black man. Or by two black men. Perhaps they *should* take Henry with them . . .' She stopped. For fully two minutes she stood with hands by her sides, studying the scalding blue sky beyond the window. 'The only chance they have,' she said at last, 'is if David keeps his head and remembers he is first a creature of God's making, then an American, and lastly a black man. Grievous words stir up anger and will lose them the day. Maybe even their lives.'

'I think he'll do what has to be done,' I said. 'I think he's willing to learn – that he's aware of the limits of his own experience.' I hadn't known, until I said it, that I knew so much about David Addison.

'You think so?' Eunice's eyebrows shot up.

'I'm certain of it.'

'I hope you're right,' she sighed.

As we left she took the picture of the gorilla and hung it on the outside of the door.

'The children believe his image hanging outside will stop that old gorilla coming in from the forest.'

'Do you believe it?' I said.

'Sometimes. I believe in many things here.'

David answered my knock on the door of the guest hut he was staying in immediately.

'Mrs Cooper,' he nodded, then waited for me to speak. I knew he'd seen me coming.

'May I speak with you, Mr Addison?'

'You may.' He took a watch on a chain from his pocket and studied its face.

'I won't keep you long,' I said, and stepped quickly over the threshold and into the hut's single room.

He stayed where he was at the open door, watching me.

'Eunice is worried that you will become angry with the people at Pongara,' I began.

'She is?'

'They will respond with anger if you do,' I warned. 'These are not civilised men. No one will be safe. Neither you nor the Mongos.'

'"The tigers of wrath are wiser than the horses of instruction",' he said. I held myself in check, but only just. Granville Milton quoting wisdoms was one thing, David Addison doing so another. The missionary meant them; the journalist was merely being clever.

'Quotations won't help you much against the likes of Leon Klein,' I said. 'You'd better be thinking of him as the tiger and keeping on the right side of him.'

'I'll remember what you said.' David looked at his watch again.

'I told Eunice that in my opinion you were open to experience, willing to learn. Was I right?' I pressed him.

'Absolutely. How perceptive you are.' His smile was wry. 'Informing myself is my business. Please don't worry that I'll behave, as Eunice might put it, like a bear in a china shop. I am not so insensitive as that.'

'Of course not,' I agreed, embarrassed now. 'I'll tell Eunice.' I moved past him and out of the hut. I turned at the threshold. 'Good luck, Mr Addison,' I said.

'Thank you, Mrs Cooper,' he said.

Just over an hour later I stood with Eunice as the four men filed into the forest. A small, wiry man called Lontulu Ibea went first. He was followed by Granville, who was in turn followed by his friend Manou, a thin and solemn-faced man with deeply scarred cheeks. David followed behind, the only one wearing white. His shirt was the last we saw of them as the dark of the trees and creepers closed about them.

'We must keep ourselves occupied while we wait,' Eunice said, and put a sweeping brush into my hand.

She meant what she said. For the next two hours we swept and cleaned every pew and corner of the church.

But the four men were gone a lot longer than two hours and the six after that passed in a slow agony of fearful imaginings and panicky thoughts. Time out of number I considered plunging into the forest and following them.

Eunice took recourse in prayer and found endless work to occupy her. I tried prayer, too, but found myself inwardly railing at a God who would allow this to happen. I tried work but the mission was a place where everyone had their way of doing things, and my ways were never right. The vegetables I cleaned weren't clean enough, and the manioc I crushed for flour brought laughter from the watching African women.

So I walked, from the edge of the forest to the banks of the river, as far into the grassy open spaces as I could without losing sight of the mission. A boy of about thirteen followed me everywhere and I knew Eunice had told him to do so. I'd have done the same thing in her place.

Everything she knew of me said I was rash, prone to hasty actions. I'd married Thomas Cooper, hadn't I? And then I'd left him. How was she to know what I might do next when I didn't know myself?

There was a small breeze that day and the whispering of the grasses should have been calming but wasn't. As evening came the burning gold of the sun became darker and darker and sank to become a red lantern at the back of the sky. This didn't last long and, when it went, it left behind a purple sky over a land filled with mysterious shapes. It would not have been hard to imagine it the most beautiful place in the world, if you hadn't known better.

But I remembered the estuary beyond Kilraven on a storm-filled day; how the waves looked when they came crashing over the rocks. I longed for its harsh, and very beautiful, vitality.

Lontulu Ibea was the first to return. He came out of the forest, running hard, just before the real black of darkness settled. The boy who'd been following me, and trying with talk of leopards to lure me back to the mission proper, was the first to see him. He gave a high, thin scream that made me jump a foot in the air. My nerves were not themselves anyway.

Lontulu Ibea wouldn't speak to the boy, nor to me. We ran behind him all the way to the Miltons' house where Eunice, with every appearance of calm, stood in the doorway waiting for him. He moved from one foot to the other at the bottom of the steps and said what he had to say in a loud, sing-song voice, in a language of which I knew not a word.

When he stopped Eunice nodded, replied in the same language and disappeared inside the house. Lontulu Ibea, who hadn't once stopped moving, turned and began running again.

Eunice, coming out of the house with a shawl about her shoulders, almost knocked me over on the top step.

'Forgive me.' She steadied me with both hands on my shoulders, asked if I was all right and, when I nodded, took my arm and said, 'We must pray.'

'What must we pray for?' I found the words hard to say. 'Tell me, Eunice?'

'We must give thanks.' Still she held my arm. 'They are safe, all of them, and we must give thanks.'

It was only then, when I saw that she was unable to say anything more, that I realised how terrible the day had been for her.

I knelt beside her on a wooden pew and pretended not to notice when large, thankful tears rolled down her face and over the hands clasped under her chin. I wanted to put an arm

340

about her but knew she wouldn't thank me for such a display so I moved closer, until my arm was touching hers and she knew I was there if she wanted me. She didn't move away.

Henry Reynolds, whose day had been as busy – if not quite as prayerful – as Eunice's, was coming up to the church when we stepped outside. Two great fires were already being lit in clearings between the African huts and people, old and young, were moving about. A man was singing. There was not much melody to his song and in that way it wasn't unlike the *seanos* music Mossie liked to sing. The mood of it, though, was more joyful.

'Lontulu says they're on a riverboat,' Henry Reynolds announced.

'Captain Preston of *L'Oracle* took them on board,' Eunice explained to me, 'God was with them. Another boat and captain might not have taken them.'

'God seems to be using Captain Preston and *L'Oracle* a lot these days,' I said, and she laughed and nodded her head, full of relief. 'How long before they arrive?' I said.

'Another hour or so, God willing.'

Men lit a second fire on the riverbank and Eunice and I prepared a two-roomed cabin for the Mongo family. They would have nothing with them since, according to Lontulu Ibea, they hadn't been allowed to take any of their belongings. He told us, too, that Yoka had been able to walk to the boat, that his mother had been distraught, that David Addison had done most of the talking and Charles Beckett most of the listening. The decision to let the family go had been reached quickly.

'Lontulu says Beckett asked two questions only, and when he heard the answers said the family should get out of Pongara quickly,' Eunice said.

When *L'Oracle* arrived, coming as close as she possibly could to the shore, three dugouts went out to bring everyone in.

Standing by the riverbank fires with Eunice I could see, by the light of the flames, how Ilanga Mongo stumbled before righting herself and, refusing any help, climbing alone into the canoe. Her son Yoka held his wrapped stump in front of him and climbed down after her. Lingomo rowed his family ashore himself. He pulled into the bank and tied up, looking past me and Eunice at the mission behind us. His eyes had the unfocussed look of the walking wounded.

The full story wasn't quite as Lontulu Ibea had presented it.

Ilanga had been raped by two of Pongara's soldiers after fighting with them when they'd come back to the house for Boali. They'd abandoned their plan to sever her hand and the girl had instead become a witness to the atrocity they committed on her mother.

Ilanga hadn't spoken a word since and Boali hadn't left her mother's side, convinced the soldiers would be back. Lingomo spoke only to relate what had happened, and to say that there would be no life for him or his family in the Congo, or anywhere else, until his wife and mutilated child had been avenged.

28

Ilanga Mongo lay on the bed and turned her face to the wall. When I said her name she pulled her legs up, put her hands between her thighs and began to rock herself backwards and forwards. Afraid she hadn't heard me I said her name again, louder, and when she still didn't answer, put my hand on her shoulder.

She screamed. The sound reverberated from the walls of the narrow bedroom, an anguished keening like the lament for the dead at home.

Boali, sitting beside her on the bed, rubbed her mother's back, then her head. She, too, turned her back on me.

'Her torment is bad enough,' Lingomo said behind me, 'she does not want you with her.' I looked at him as I left the room. He was a man of stone.

The youngest child, the boy named Mola, was sitting on the floor holding in his arms a wooden dog Eunice had given him. The dog had one black eye and one white. I knelt beside him and touched it. I was afraid to touch Mola himself. Afraid and ashamed.

'I have a dog too,' I said, 'he wanted to come with me when I left my home.'

The child watched my face and held more tightly on to the wooden toy. He was small for five years and had the luminous, staring eyes of an infant. Ilanga had told me once that he'd been born 'too soon' and, when the Christian God had failed, had been kept alive by a fetish doctor who'd 'called down a great ju-ju against the sickness'.

When I smiled at Mola he just went on staring at me. In the room behind us his mother went on keening.

Yoka's stump had been treated and bandaged afresh by Eunice, whose doctoring abilities were highly regarded. There was nothing for it now but to wait and watch carefully for signs of gangrene. He half-sat, half-lay on one of the three narrow beds Eunice and I had made up earlier. He blinked when I moved to kneel beside him but otherwise stayed absolutely still. Ilanga's keening had faded to a low moaning sound. I touched his black curls. I couldn't stop myself.

'I told them the leopard had come for you,' he didn't look at me, 'and that my mother and father could not stop him.'

'They asked you where I was?' I said.

'I told them the leopard was really Tantu, the evil god, and that we could do nothing against his magic.' He looked down at his stump. 'One of them said I should call on Tantu to put my hand back on to my body and then he cut it off with the machete.' He frowned. 'But Tantu is a hater and does not fix things. He should have known that.'

'Mrs Milton will fix it,' I said, 'she will make you strong again.'

'She cannot give me back my fingers,' the child said.

'Who said you should call on Tantu?' Lingomo had appeared. He spoke very softly. Hunkering down, he handed his son a piece of bread and honey.

Confusion and pain were plain to see on Yoka's face as he tried instinctively to reach for it with his right hand. His father put it into the other one.

'The picture man.' Yoka bit into the bread. 'The bone man said my hand would bring you back.'

The children called Leon Klein the picture man because

344

of his tattoos. Charles Beckett was the bone man because of his thinness.

'You must have been very frightened,' I said.

'No.' He shook his head. 'I didn't know what he would do until it was done.'

'You're very brave,' I said. 'Very, very brave.'

'No,' he said again, 'I am just waiting for my father to cut a hand from the picture man's body.'

Lingomo stood up and went and covered his younger son for sleep. I helped Yoka lie down and covered him with a blue blanket with embroidered sheep on its edges.

'Sleep,' I said, 'it will help make you strong.'

'You will not go away again?'

'Don't worry, Yoka, you're safe here. There are no men in the mission like the men in Pongara.'

They slept, those two small boys, like the innocents they were and without a whimper. Their mother, too, had become silent. Their father sat at a small table and stared at his hands.

'Yoka would not speak to anyone before now,' he said, 'you have at least released his tongue. I believed myself it was the Belgian who chopped his hand. That the Englishman was so much a part of it surprises me.'

'I'll do anything I can to help you.' I sat at the table too.

'You cannot return my son's hand to his body and you cannot make Ilanga the woman she was before she was destroyed. I am the one who must make justice.'

'What will you do?'

I'd seen a man go out once before to take revenge for a family wronged. He was a tenant farmer and I'd been young then, no more than fourteen, but I'd never forgotten how he'd looked when they brought him back, dead. I'd never forgotten either how little help his deed had been to his family. They'd pined without ceasing.

345

'I will do what has to be done,' Lingomo said, looking at me in the way men the world over sometimes look at women. It's a look which separates, says to a woman that she cannot understand what a man's need dictates.

'Please, Lingomo.' I put my hand over his on the table but he took it away. 'Please don't do anything that might leave Ilanga alone and the children without a father. They will grieve for you for ever and be worse off than before.'

He shook his head in reply.

'I don't blame you for the ruin of my family. I was angry when you left but you were not the one did these things. It was the rubber made the men who did this what they are, and the ivory. The white bosses and black soldiers at Pongara were nothing before the rubber and ivory made them rich. Now the white man believes he is a warrior, a trader, an all-powerful king. His soldiers obey because they fear him and because they want a share of his wealth. It is the same all over the Congo. They are the evil ones, not you. They must know torment for what they have done.'

'But if I'd stayed,' I said, 'they would have had no reason to do what they did to your wife and child.'

'They are evil,' Lingomo said, 'you are merely foolish. You must learn to carry what has happened as a weight with you through life.'

'Yes,' I said. After a while I asked, 'What will you do?' but he didn't reply.

I didn't weep, then. But that was the moment in which I took on and began to carry the burden of my guilt for Yoka Mongo's severed hand, and for the violation of Ilanga Mongo.

The low rise and fall of her moaning stopped quite suddenly.

'Look after my sons,' Lingomo said, and went quickly into the bedroom.

The boys slept on. Their father was gone so long, his and their mother's voices so rhythmic and intimate as they talked and talked, that I almost slept myself. When Lingomo Mongo appeared at last from the bedroom he was beckoning to me.

'Ilanga will speak with you,' he said, 'she is more herself now.' He lay on the floor between his two sons and closed his eyes.

Ilanga Mongo was sitting, a shawl of Eunice's around her shoulders and Boali asleep across her legs. She'd grown thinner in the few terrible days since I'd last seen her and her eyes sat in newly hollowed spaces above blunt cheekbones. Eunice had told me she was bleeding still and would need rest and peace if she was to heal.

Ilanga signalled to me to close the door. I did so and stood with my back against it while she stroked her daughter's shoulders and looked at me with dull, hard eyes.

'You must help us,' she said. 'My son's hand was taken when he lied for you.' She paused. 'I have made a plan and Lingomo agrees.'

'What must I do?' I said.

'Come closer.' She didn't stop stroking Boali. The child sighed in her sleep as I stood at the bottom of the bed. 'My husband has been talking to you?' It was a question and I nodded. 'We are destroyed. Our son is maimed and I am defiled and shamed. We have nothing but ourselves, and for us to go on living – for my children and husband and me – there are two things to be done. We are agreed on this, Lingomo and me.'

She leaned forward, cradling Boali's head against her so as the child couldn't hear what she had to say.

'I know the soldiers who forced themselves into me and now, since Yoka spoke with you, we know for sure who it was took our son's hand. Lingomo cannot live as a man if

347

he doesn't avenge himself for this. That is one thing.' She shook her head as I tried to speak. 'Listen, and then do as I ask.' She took a deep breath and steadied herself in the bed before going on. 'The second thing we need are papers so that we can go back to our own people in the Niger Coast. There is no life any longer for Lingomo and me and our children in the Congo. These are the two things.'

She leaned back against the pillows. When Boali complained about the new position her mother took her and, with obvious difficulty and pain, tried to lift her under the blankets to lie by her side. I went to help.

'You should not exert yourself,' I said, 'and I'm not completely evil.'

She said nothing in reply but didn't stop me either when I tucked the little girl under the blanket. She remained silent when I sat on a stool by the bedside.

'You want me to get you papers from the consul?' I asked.

'Yes.' She looked drained.

I lifted a tin vessel of water from the floor and bathed her lips, then poured her some to drink. Her beautiful hands wrapped themselves around the tumbler.

'You must also go with Lingomo when he goes to avenge us,' she said after a few sips. 'You must go quickly, in the morning, so it is done with and we may all leave the mission. Thomas Cooper will come here soon and we must be gone before he does.' She paused. 'He is not a man to let what is his escape him.'

'I know that,' I said. 'I know what kind of man he is.'

I wanted to tell her my fears about being pregnant but knew how inappropriate it would be. I could have saved myself a lot of worry if I'd gone ahead and done so. But life, as I'd always known, is full of ifs.

Ilanga became detached and withdrawn. Whatever anger,

348

pain or humiliation she was feeling, she hid behind a glazed expression.

'I know where the British government man is and how you must get to him,' she said. 'So does Lingomo. Workers who came to Pongara yesterday with rubber loads said they had seen him in the village of Okyon. He is easy to see and they were not mistaken. It is no accident that he is in Okyon. It's a sign that we must do what has to be done.'

'What is it that has to be done?'

'Firstly, you must bring the consul here, to the mission. Lingomo will take you to him. The consul would not come here for my husband alone but he will not not let a white woman of his own country be endangered and it is certain he will come back with you. You will be at Okyon by mid-morning if you leave before the sun rises.'

'I'll go,' I agreed. Then I asked her about the second part of her plan. 'You said Lingomo would take revenge . . .'

My mouth was dry and my imagination agitated. Cruelty was meted out so casually in this burning land; how did I know whether Lingomo had murder in mind, or flogging, or even planned to burn down the whole of Pongara and everyone in it?

'Lingomo is a Christian.' I leaned forward so that Ilanga had to met my gaze. 'You're a Christian too. Christ tells us we should accept the wrongs done to us, that revenge is wrong.'

'Thomas Cooper is also Christian.' Ilanga closed her eyes. 'Yet he takes revenge for wrongs done to him. Sometimes he kills and sometimes he does worse. The Belgian is a Christian, too, and so is his king. The yellow Englishman is a Christian.' She stopped. I said nothing. She went on. 'Lingomo will do what must be done to make right what was done to me and to our child, and you will go with him.'

She kept her eyes closed while she told me what else she'd been planning in the long, brooding and broken time since she'd been violated.

'In the village of Okyon there is a *féticheuse*,' said Ilanga, 'she is very famous. It is not a coincidence that the *féticheuse* and the government man are in the same place. It is a sign. The *féticheuse*'s charms are all-powerful. Lingomo will go to her for a *suhman* to use against those who have wronged us. They will suffer as my child suffered. As I suffer.'

'What will happen to them?' I asked and she opened her eyes.

'You should know that the *féticheuse* of Okyon has already put a fetish on your husband, on Malu Malu Cooper,' Ilanga said. 'She will tell you. Her power comes from knowing so you must talk with her, tell her what you have done. She will give you a fetish which will heal and protect me and my wounded son.'

'What will it be?'

'I've no way of knowing that, just that it will protect and heal my son, and me as well. It must be given to you because you were the instrument of our ruin.'

I said, yes, I would go with Lingomo and do as she asked.

I could see no harm in bringing back a protective or healing charm for Ilanga and Yoka. Lingomo's discussion with her about a charm against Leon Klein and Charles Beckett was his business. There was enough in my own background to give me a sensitivity to such things.

There were many, many holy wells and miracle-working healers and evil-eye people in Ireland. Plenty who believed in them too. St Ciaran of Donegal was known for raising the dead to life. An eel in a well in Co. Clare brought death within three days, three months or three years to anyone who interfered with it.

Because of these things, and others like them, it would

350

be easy for me to do as Ilanga Mongo asked. It was also why I'd the sense not to tell Eunice or Granville Milton, or David Addison, about the *féticheuse*.

Some things are best left to those who understand them.

29

It began to look as if the gods weren't with us. Neither the African ones nor the Christian God I believed in myself.

Lingomo and I made our plans, confident and clear on what we were about. When he first came to the Congo he'd travelled a great deal and so knew the village of Okyon. He drew a map for me of where we would be going: upriver for an hour, then inland through forest for the best part of another hour. Two hours would get us there, he assured me. I said nothing to him about the fear I nursed of the dark unknown inside the forest.

At around midnight we went to tell Eunice and Granville Milton of our plan to go to the village. That was when the Gods, Christian and pagan, turned against us.

'Ilanga is sleeping,' I said in answer to Eunice's raised eyebrow. 'So are the children. She is more at peace.'

'I'm glad to hear it,' Eunice said, and looked from me to Lingomo and back again. 'What are you planning?' she asked. She was good at sensing things unsaid.

'I leave in the morning for the village of Okyon to get further help,' Lingomo announced. 'Mrs Cooper will come with me. We'll need a canoe or dugout of some sort. We'll be back before nightfall.'

Eunice started to say something but her husband, with a smile and a shake of his head, stopped her. 'I know Okyon.' He turned to David. 'It's not far from here. An interesting village and one you should visit. It survived when others around were burned to the ground.'

He ran a finger along the cross beam of his crucifix. I was so certain of what he would say next that I almost said it for him.

'There is a *féticheuse* in Okyon, a very popular woman, reputed to have great powers.'

'You've met her?' David lit a cigar. His fingers were long, elegant in a man so large.

Eunice was already smoking. A small fan stirred the sluggish air. Smoke-filled rooms were something I would forever after associate with Africa. I never grew to like them. But then neither did the mosquitoes.

'I've seen her. We didn't speak.' Granville rubbed his eyes tiredly. 'Her decision, not mine. There are no Christians among the people of Okyon. Its people are no longer taken away for rubber slaves either.'

'Because of this woman's magic?' said David.

'Because of the *féticheuse*, yes. She's greatly feared.'

'Pity there isn't one of her in every village,' David said, 'the rubber slavers would be out of business in no time.'

Granville shook his head in reproof. '"If ye had not ploughed with my heifer ye had not found out my riddle",' he said. 'Don't make the mistake, David, of applying your limited understanding to Africa. Your readers would benefit from being given such information also.'

'Are you telling me you believe in the ju-ju business?' David looked incredulous. 'You, a man of God, telling me you've been taken in by superstitious magic and spells?'

'I'm a man of God telling you that the Lord works His will in many and mysterious ways. You, David, believe in nothing beyond this life and so are in no position to understand these things. Or to judge.' Granville turned to Lingomo. 'Tell me what you intend?'

Lingomo told him, briefly, that Roger Casement had been seen in Okyon and that we planned, between us, to persuade him to get myself and the Mongos legally out of the Congo. The spectre of the *féticheuse,* unmentioned, hung in the air between us.

'When will you leave?' Granville said.

'Before sunrise.'

'I'll send Manou along with you, he's worth ten others on a journey such as this.'

And that would have been that if David hadn't been there, with his righteous anger and hunger for a story for his newspaper.

'I'll come along too,' he offered, 'I've waited long enough to meet Casement. An extra body's bound to be of help anyway.'

Manou and Lingomo knew Africa and would understand – but I'd no desire to have David Addison around, with his watchful eye and notebook, when I visited the *féticheuse.*

'Mr Casement will be returning with us,' I said, 'it would be more suitable for you to interview him here.'

'I'd like to see how he goes about his work,' David argued, 'and you might even find, Mrs Cooper, that I can be useful.'

'There's a certain safety in numbers,' Granville agreed, ending the debate before it had properly begun.

We took the largest of the mission's boats, a strange vessel that was half-barge, half-canoe, and left before six in the morning.

I knew David Addison's coming would change things. I wasn't prepared for the way they would change, though.

The barge-boat took the four of us comfortably. I wore my fullest skirts and strongest boots. Mary Kingsley, who had travelled all of West Africa, wrote with feeling about 'the blessings of a good, thick skirt' and it had seemed wise to take her advice.

The mist on the river was so heavy as we left that when I turned after a short distance to wave goodbye to Granville he'd already been swallowed up. But the sun quickly dispersed it and opened the way ahead.

'Crocodile.' Manou sniffed and pointed to the brown shining river.

I couldn't see a thing. Manou touched his nose and I sniffed and only then caught the musky crocodile smell. It got stronger and stronger until I saw at least three of them, fifteen or sixteen foot long, half-buried in mud and water and moving hardly at all. I closed my eyes and prayed.

When nothing happened after two or three minutes I knew we were safe, for another while.

We hugged the right bank, avoiding mid-river rocks, for most of the journey. We paddled through low rapids at one point and I got good and wet after leaning too far to the side. We passed several villages whose people came to the riverbank to stare or to wave, depending on their gender. Women waved. Men stared. Children did both.

We pulled in at last to what looked like a sandy beach but which proved muddy and soft enough to drag me and my skirts down by several inches. I came ashore weighed down by at least half a foot of thickly slimed hem.

The heat was coming into the day as we started to walk. I was third, behind Manou and David, as we went into the forest. Lingomo came last.

'It's not so dark,' I said after a few minutes. The sun dappled through leaves, the sky like blue stars shining sporadically between them.

'Not yet,' Lingomo said behind me.

The darkness, when it came, was browny-green and closed about us quickly. The heat was smothering; we might have been walking through thick, hot, clear liquid. And then there were the creepers, the same strangling kind I'd seen from the riverboat on my journey to Pongara. They lay along the ground in serpent coils, and like serpents twisted themselves in slow, insidious spirals up and around trunks or out along branches from where they fell in fat, maggoty loops. They made crocheted patterns in the trees fifty or sixty feet above us. They were what cut out the light and left us to struggle in the dark soggy ground below.

Looking up I saw a monkey, small and black with long hair, walking along a branch with his tail up behind him, his face turned down to look at us. I was so caught up in looking at him that I collided with David when he stopped in response to a warning whistle from Manou.

'No more moving,' the small man cried, 'be still.'

As I bumped into him David caught my arm and pulled me close against him.

'Quiet!' he said. 'Don't make a sound.'

It wasn't the time to argue, and I didn't want to anyway. His bulk was solidly reassuring and I was glad to have him to lean against. Manou was a couple of yards ahead of us and we watched together, silently, as he very slowly lifted his stick and approached a mass of leaves rotting between the creepers at the root of a tree. He'd almost reached the leaves when they moved, rearing up and straightening into a three-foot-long brown and black snake, ready to strike.

I screamed as Manou brought the stick down. The snake went still.

'He will be quiet now,' the small man said, 'he is quick to put his fangs into your leg. He eats and you are poisoned and die.'

'He's a kind of cobra?' David kept an arm about me as he turned the snake over with his boot.

'A forest cobra,' said Manou, 'there are many of him about. Be watchful.'

He left the cobra where it was and walked on ahead of us. I gave silent thanks to Mary Kingsley for my skirts; any cobra, forest or otherwise, would have a problem penetrating their folds.

'We'll be out of here soon. 'David took his arm away and smiled down at me. He'd no earthly way of knowing whether we would or not but I believed him.

'I'm sure you're right,' I said.

His smile widened and I saw that he'd needed reassurance as much as I did myself. I found solace in walking behind him after that, one stranger in Africa following another.

I followed him for another hour or more, pushing my limbs, one in front of the other, pushing out breaths, one after another, trying not to look further than his back, not to look to the side, not to look up or down, all the time glad he was there, just a foot or two ahead of me, and that Lingomo was behind me.

We came out of the forest quite suddenly. One minute we were locked in the darkness with bird cries and animal shrieks; the next the trees were behind us and we were blinking in the scorching intensity of direct sun and light, intense and wonderful, everywhere.

'We're getting places at last.' David took my arm and pointed.

Ahead of us stretched sloping grasslands of green and gold through which a wide, uneven track ran downhill. It stopped at a plateau. On the plateau there stood a village.

'Okyon,' said Lingomo, behind me. It was the first word he'd spoken for about an hour.

Okyon straggled at its outer edges but was dense with huts and shelters in the centre. A stream ran halfway round; we would have to cross it to get into the village proper.

'It looks so peaceful,' I said, 'as if it just grew there.'

'A closer look will reveal all,' David said. 'Do you need a rest or should we go on?' He meant well but not even to save my life could I have taken a rest then.

'I'm fine,' I said, 'we should keep going.'

As we came towards the end of the track we passed palm

trees, cactus hedges and a scattering of palm-thatch huts. We crossed the stream, which was deeper and wider than it had seemed from a distance and reached the top of my skirts. The weight of the water added to the earlier slime around the hems and made them drag like heavy parcels from my waist. I was once again glad of David's strong arm when he helped me out and on to the opposite bank.

I wrung out my skirts as best I could before kneeling on the riverbank to splash water on my face and tidy my hair. When I stood up again villagers were all about us, children and adults both, pressing close. I could smell their hot sweat, feel their bare arms and legs and chests, the small hands of children stroking me, teasing my hair, hear their noisy curiosity, see a blur of loincloths and bright wraparounds.

One of the children, a small, laughing girl in a blue wraparound, took my hand and pulled me forward, into the village. David followed and Lingomo and Manou came close behind with three of the village men, all of them talking as if they'd been released from a vow of silence.

First we came to a corrugated-iron-roofed, plank-sided house in a clearing together with a quadrangle of native huts. Then we were passing a row of thatched wattle-and-daub huts, some with corrugated-iron roofs, all with vegetable gardens behind them. The last of these was a long, open-ended house with a conical roof.

'The Talking House.' Lingomo followed my gaze. 'It's where we'll meet with the government man.'

'He's definitely here then?' David asked.

'He's been here for a week,' Lingomo said, 'but we cannot talk with him until we've greeted the chief.'

The village chief was a small, wiry man, similar in type to Manou but impressively self-important. While the other men in the village wore loincloths, he wore a wraparound and a necklace of feathers.

The children scattered as he came towards us. He spoke first to Manou, then to Lingomo, acknowledged David Addison with a gracious bow. He behaved as if I wasn't there, not even looking at me when I sat with the others outside his hut and joined in the drinking of milky-white palm wine and fish soup.

It was because I was excluded, and looking about me, that I was the first to see Roger Casement.

He came out of a hut about twenty yards away with a bulldog at his heels. The dog was fat and looked aggressively around him as he went. His master was cheerful and brisk, with a black beard and longish black hair about a long, lean face. I was surprised no one had mentioned how handsome he was; it was the first thing struck me about him.

I stood and went to meet him.

'My name is Vanessa O'Grady.' I held out my hand. 'I come from the townland of Ballycoole, in County Sligo.' My maiden name had come to me instinctively and I didn't correct myself.

'Delighted to meet you, Miss O'Grady.' He shook my hand and stepped back to look at me. The dog sniffed the wet hems of my skirts. 'I'm Roger Casement,' he said, 'from Kingstown, outside Dublin.'

'I know who you are,' I said, 'I came here to meet you.' I gestured behind me to the others. 'We're all here to meet you for one reason or another.'

He looked past me, briefly, then looked again at my face and clothing. There was nothing rude about this, just a friendly curiosity.

'You're also known as Mrs Thomas Cooper, unless I'm mistaken,' he said. 'I'd been intending to make your acquaintance. Irishwomen are a rare enough occurrence in *l'État Indépendant du Congo*.' His voice was low and melodious, his accent wonderful to hear. 'I doubt, though, that you've travelled this far from Pongara station to make my acquaintance socially. Would I be right in thinking you want consular assistance?'

'I want your help to leave the Congo and go home, yes,' I said, 'but before that there's an African family, from the Niger Coast, in far more urgent need.'

The dog stopped sniffing and barked at me, a gruff, very foreign sound in the baking turmoil of the village. He was a remarkably ugly dog with large jaws, jelly-like jowls and bloodshot eyes. The sort of dog only an owner could love. When I hunkered down to talk to him he stepped back and looked at me, much as his master had done only not half so friendly.

'He's a sociable creature,' Roger Casement said, 'and doesn't like to be left out of things. His name's John.'

John allowed me to pat his head and feel his ears. His expression didn't change. 'How does he find the heat?' I asked.

'No complaints so far.' There was a clear note of indulgence in his master's voice. 'He seems to like the river best. Sits to the fore of our small steamboat and keeps an alert eye on possibilities ahead. Hippos bathing or pelicans feeding, it's all the same to John. He barks if they come too close. Fearless and loyal, that's my fellow.'

I gave the dog a final tickle between the ears and stood up. His owner made a polite nod in the direction of the chief's hut.

'Unless I'm mistaken one of your companions is my Niger Coast friend Lingomo Mongo. It's his family, I take it, which needs assistance?'

'They want to return home,' I confirmed.

'Manou from the American mission at Tonkinese I also recognise. Would your third companion be an American journalist called Addison, by any chance?'

'David Addison,' I agreed, 'he's here to see you too.'

'I'm not usually so popular,' Roger Casement said, and took my arm as we walked the short distance back to the chief's hut.

The chief, with much grace and an order for more palm wine, left Manou, Lingomo Mongo, David, Roger Casement, John the dog and myself sitting together under the shady canopy of the Talking House. We sat on low rattan benches while the wine was poured and fruit was laid out on a coloured cloth. Beyond the shade of the canopy dried earth cracked in the sun.

'There's an African proverb says a man doesn't go among thorns unless a snake's after him, or he's after a snake,' said Roger Casement. 'I'm after a snake and, please God, I'll scotch it. Why are you in the Congo, Mr Addison?'

'I think we're in pursuit of the same snake, Mr Casement,' he said. 'I think, too, that you know that, and why I'm here.'

'Perhaps I do at that,' Casement agreed. 'You're not the first journalist to come seeking to expose the evil and corruption of King Leopold's African empire. What makes you think your newspaper's readers will be any more interested this time than they were before?'

'Because times have changed. We're in a new century. The world is turning . . .'

David leaned forward and I saw in him a passion he'd carefully not revealed before. It gave a burnished look to his black skin and whitened the knuckles of the hands clenched between his knees.

'I want to write about this investigative trip you're making for your government into the rubber-producing regions of the interior. People will listen now. The time is right. The Belgian king is worried, governments are questioning him. The agents and officials on the ground here are worried too.'

'It's true that I've broken into a thieves' kitchen.' Casement pulled a wry face. 'But it's also true that my life and job here are primarily to do with leaky roofs, mosquitoes, dysentery, and having to get out of my bed to listen to the complaints of drunken sailors. In conjunction with all of this I've been sending reports to my government since arriving here last year. Precious little has changed and precious little attention's been paid to them.'

'Yes. But that was before the Congo Protest Resolution was passed in the House of Commons,' David pointed out. 'The British government will have to make a move now. It's being shamed, too, by British journalist E.D. Morel's reports on slavery and brutality. *Your* report will be a catalyst. I want to write about what you've discovered so far. American sympathy and public support can only strengthen your case.'

'You're a persuasive man, Mr Addison, and you've a desire for justice rare in journalists coming to the Congo. Most tend to support King Leopold and to write about his benign reign over his African subjects . . .'

'Not all of them,' David cut him short, 'not all.'

'True,' agreed Casement, 'there's Morel.'

'Morel is writing for today. There was another, earlier man. An American.'

'That would be George Washington Williams,' said Casement.

David gave a half-smile, a concession which changed everything about him. His air of fierce seriousness melted and he seemed younger and warmer, a man you could imagine had some fun in him.

'Williams was a cousin of mine,' he admitted.

'Aha . . .' said Roger Casement, as if the pieces of a puzzle had fallen into place.

Lingomo, in the middle of this exchange, got up and went to lean against a wooden upright. He stood with his back to us, impatience plain to see in every inch of him, staring at a hut with a veranda which was about two hundred yards away.

It stood alone, apart from the other buildings. Two raggedy-eared goats lay in front of it, legs outstretched on the hot red clay. A couple of oil palms gave it shade. The *féticheuse* was well out of sight, but I'd no doubt it was her house.

Manou, too, had lost interest in the conversation. He got up and gave a smile that added crater-like hollows to his scarred face.

'I have an uncle in the village,' he said, 'I go to talk with him.' He left, running like a child out of school.

'Your cousin was the son of a freed slave, was he not?' said Casement.

'He was,' David agreed. 'You're familiar with his work?'

'Only that he wrote a *History of the Negro Race in America* and came as a journalist to Africa more than ten years ago. Am I right in thinking he was the man who wrote that what he found here made the Congo "the Siberia of the African continent"?'

'That was the phrase he used,' David agreed. 'He also wrote an open letter to the King of Belgium, telling him of the death, destruction and excessive cruelty in his colony. He told how the king's government bought, sold and stole slaves. He was the only one to speak out in those years, and he was vilified for it. He died of tuberculosis in England when he was forty-one years old. I have always wanted to finish the job for him.'

'Well, then you must,' said Casement.

'You'll tell me what you've discovered?'

'I'll do more than that, I'll take you with me on the next part of my trip.'

'Nothing will change . . . nothing!' Lingomo turned, a muscle ticking furiously at the side of his eye. He jabbed a finger at Casement. 'While you talk and write out words black people are dying, being beaten, their villages burned, suffering. I gave you my story for your report, and when I went to you again for help you were gone. My family, myself . . . we are more than names on paper. We *are* the things you write about. Now my wife is destroyed, one child is taken and another dismembered. Now we want to go home, to get away from the hell of this place. We are still British subjects, though we didn't ask to be. Helping us is also your job.'

Roger Casement had stiffened. He stared at Lingomo and rubbed his beard. John the dog whimpered, drawing protectively closer to his master's heels.

'You've good reason to call me to account.' The consul got up, went slowly to where Lingomo stood and put a hand on his shoulder. 'Tell me what's happened and I will do what I can for you.'

I left them at it and walked to the house of the *féticheuse*.

She was waiting for me. When I stood in the open doorway and tried to see through the gloom inside, she called to me from an inner room.

'Sit in front of me,' she said, 'and do not speak.'

'I stepped inside. When my eyes had accustomed themselves, I made my way through another door to where the *féticheuse* sat cross-legged behind a low, wooden table. I sat into the sunken centre of a rattan stool, wondering how many people had sat on it before me to make it so very worn. The only other furniture in the room was a shelf. There were several objects on it. One of them had a face.

'Your womb is empty,' the *féticheuse* said.

'My womb is empty . . .' I repeated the words after her, trying to understand what she meant. 'I'm not with child then?'

'You are not with child,' she confirmed. I knew she was right.

I could see her by the yellow light of a burning torch by the wall. She was a big, gaunt woman, wrapped in swathes of patterned cloth which left only her arms free. Her hair, growing high about her head like a furze bush, had three polished bones set into it. Her eyes were half-closed.

'The child you will have in the future will come from a man not your husband,' she intoned. Her voice was flat and low.

When I would have said something she held up a silencing hand. I was quiet while she opened a small skin bag and tossed a number of polished stones with holes in them on to the smooth top of the table. They rolled and settled into a V-pattern. The *féticheuse* grunted. 'Take one and show it to me,' she said.

I chose the stone nearest. It was white and felt warm in the palm of my hand. The *féticheuse* looked at it, then at me. Then she closed her eyes and rocked where she sat. Her face was without expression.

'You are brave but foolish,' she said, 'and your spirit is restless. You would be unwise to cross over water. You would be unwise to betray another woman.' She opened her eyes. 'To be brave is not enough.'

'I must cross water to return to my home,' I said.

The *féticheuse* shrugged. 'You must also go back down the river, but the stones say you must not cross over water. I can tell you no more.' She paused. 'The stones are never wrong.'

'What else do they say about a child?'

'Your husband cannot father a child. Black woman, white woman, all the same with him.' The *féticheuse* made a sound in her throat like a gate closing. 'He cannot make a child with any woman.' She held out her hand for my stone and I placed it in her palm. 'You were unwise to come to Africa.' She put my stone with the others and moved them about with a long index finger. The top of it was dyed blue.

'I know that,' I said. 'I want to know what the wisest course is now.'

I looked at her with as steady a gaze as I could manage in the face of her hooded, unblinking one. I hadn't come to her to be told how foolish I was. This I already knew. I hadn't come to be told *anything* about myself, and if she was as powerful a *féticheuse* as she was reputed to be she would know that. My faith in whatever healing or protective charm she might give me for Ilanga was not, at that moment, great.

But still . . . Still I wanted her advice. In a world in which I could find no centre she offered the possibility of knowledge. The part of me which had always wanted to believe in my father's plans for Kilraven wanted to believe she could find the centre for me.

The *féticheuse* gathered up the stones.

'Go away from Africa,' she said, 'go alone and quickly. There is nothing for you here. Go back to where you came from. Take nothing away that you did not bring with you. Nothing but what I will give you.'

She put the stones in their skin bag and tied the leather string tight. The stone I'd chosen she took and threaded with a leather cord before handing it to me.

'Keep this,' she said, 'it will protect you. Even when you cross water it will give you some protection.' When I hesitated she took my hand and put the stone and cord into my palm. 'You do not have to believe. Just keep it on you always, somewhere, it doesn't matter where. It is the only thing you must take with you from Africa.'

'I didn't come for myself,' I put the stone into my pocket, 'I came here on behalf of a woman called Ilanga Mongo.'

'I know that too,' the *féticheuse* said, impatiently. 'I knew Lingomo Mongo was coming and I knew you were with him. I saw your spirits long before your bodily forms came into the village this morning. Lingomo Mongo's brother did evil and brought evil upon the family and so they have suffered. Lingomo Mongo seeks to avenge himself through me on those

366

who have done harm to his wife and child.' She paused. 'Tell me about the evil you witnessed.'

She watched me all the while I told her what had happened at Pongara, and later at the mission. When I'd finished she got up and went to a shelf. She stood with her back to me for several minutes, giving me a chance to study the human head at the other end of the shelf.

The yellow gloom hid nothing. The head was a foot high and wrinkled, its lips peeled back from teeth filed into points. It had no hair, just a scalp like polished wood. The eyes were half-shut but its eyelids, smooth and unwrinkled, looked as if they might open at any minute.

There were nails sticking out of the head, or they might have been long, fat pins. They were stuck mostly into the wood-scalp but were in the forehead, eyes and cheeks too. There was even one in the side of the nose.

The *féticheuse* came back and laid a different skin bag on the table. Kneeling, she opened it and took out a child's finger. It was the colour of a fallen leaf and seemed to beckon.

'Look at it,' she commanded. I couldn't look anywhere else. 'Touch it,' she commanded. My hand refused to move. 'Touch it.' She was gentler. I managed to touch the finger. It felt like rubber. I looked at her. She was smiling, quite kindly. 'Yes,' she said, 'like rubber.' She put the finger back in the bag and handed it to me. 'Ilanga Mongo will know what to do,' she said. 'No one but she must see it.'

I stood and looked again at the head. 'Why is it that my husband cannot father a child?'

'You already know the answer to your question.'

'Because you have put a curse on him?'

'He used an African woman badly. Beat her until the child she was carrying for him died. She escaped him and came to me. She knew what to ask for to take his future from him.'

The torch flickered and the eyes in the head moved.

'Go,' said the *féticheuse*.

Outside, Lingomo was standing in the sun, waiting. He didn't even look at me as he passed and went into the hut of the *féticheuse*. From the expression on his face I wouldn't have given Klein and Beckett much chance against whatever curse he'd in mind for them.

30

If I'd done as the *féticheuse* told me to do.

If, knowing there was a reason for her saying it, I'd taken only what I brought with me when I left Africa.

If I'd listened, just once, and tried to understand what she meant. If I hadn't betrayed another woman. If I'd gone directly and not given in to my heart's fretful demands . . .

. . . then the next nine years of my life might have been very different. They mightn't have been half so fulfilled, nor so wonderful. Nor so very lonesome, at times.

We left Okyon by boat later that day. Manou and Lingomo Mongo set off first in the mission barge, David and I went with Casement in his boat – a curiously long, iron single-deck affair he'd been loaned by another American mission.

This way of doing things was decided on because Casement and David Addison wanted to talk together and because Lingomo wanted to get back to Ilanga and the children before nightfall. The iron boat moved more slowly than the barge and would not get to the mission until after dark. I didn't like the fact that part of our journey would be by night but knew I would have to put up with it; David decided I would be safer travelling in the iron boat and I allowed myself to be bullied. I wanted to hear Casement's stories; wanted, too, the reassurance of David Addison's presence.

'As his wife, I understand Thomas Cooper can legally stop you leaving him,' he said to me as we steamed through a calmish stretch.

The consul was consulting with his boatman and the mission barge had long disappeared ahead of us downriver. Daylight wouldn't last much longer; the water was already turning brown in the late sun.

'He won't do that,' I said, 'I know him. I've humiliated him, and rather than risk further humiliation he'll let me go. He'll say I wasn't suited to Africa, couldn't bear the heat or some such. He'll try, of course, to get back the money he's paid my family.'

'He bought you?' David looked startled.

His shock, and the way he pulled away from me, was like a slap in the face. I stared at him, seeing my story as he would when I told him, finding myself unable to defend myself or my actions as I had to Eunice. I looked down into the darkening water and faced the truth. I had sold myself. However I tried to present my story this was the truth of it, plain and simple.

'He bought me,' I agreed, painfully, 'as surely as he bought himself a future built on the slave trade of Africa. He bought himself a wife and an old family name to add to his own. He thought his money would buy him control of that family, too, and a fine house to live in and neighbours to impress. He thought he would have a child, too, but he won't even have that . . .' I paused. 'I never saw it all so clearly as at this minute.'

'It's over now. You've got your life back.' David was brisk. 'Cooper will be exposed for his murderous brutality, like others of his kind. I think you're wrong about him letting you go without any trouble, though. Because you've made him look a fool, he may try to have you harmed physically. I'll stay with you until you get on your ship at Boma. We'll arrange to have someone keep an eye on you on the ship, too, until you get to Liverpool. You should make sure to have someone to meet you there.'

'He's vengeful, it's true,' I said, remembering Thomas's

rages and hoping never to witness one again. 'But there's no need for you to put yourself to any more trouble on my account. Thomas wouldn't be so foolish as to harm me.'

'He was foolish enough to think you the kind of woman who would keep silent and condone his barbaric behaviour,' David argued. 'I've met men like him before, many of them. In America they ride in white, at night, through the southern states, burning and killing as they go. They consider themselves above the law of the land, or of common humanity. They're capable of anything because they're not burdened by any sense of fellow feeling, or of decency.' He put a hand on my shoulder, then quickly took it away. 'You'd better believe it, Nessa. Your only chance of getting home safely is to be prepared, and careful.'

All sorts of emotions kept me quiet for a while: uncertainty, loneliness, fear, aching regret about the mistakes I'd made, the people I'd hurt, the plight of the Congo, and apprehension about my life to come.

'You have a job to do and I'm taking up your time,' I said.

'You're work too.' He smiled. 'Your story will be in my reports.'

I laughed for the first time in months. It wasn't so very hard. 'I'm relieved to be serving some purpose!'

Roger Casement's boatman/helper was a man called Hairy Bill, who wasn't hairy at all and wore a white apron, and a green hat on his bald head. He was English and had been a ship's cook. He hated John the dog, rarely spoke, was fiercely loyal to the consul and made stewed sugar and custard whenever he found himself with time on his hands.

We were eating large bowls of this in the dark, keeping mosquitoes at bay with a burning torch and David's cigars, when Tonkinese Mission came into view. There was a fire on the riverbank and by its glow I could make out Henry Reynolds's wide-brimmed hat.

'Thank God for the Henry Reynoldses of this world,' said David. 'I wonder if he knows what a reassurance his relentless rectitude is for the rest of us?'

I was surprised that he should think like this, and that he should say it to me, too, but I knew exactly what he meant.

'He knows full well,' I said. 'He knows, too, that in many ways we need him more than he needs us. The righteous are bold but they're also solitary and selfish.'

'Harsh words,' David murmured. He gazed full into my face and smiled. 'But true. You're wising up to the world.'

'A little. I've a long way to go yet,' I said, and smiled myself.

As an exchange it was only moderately interesting. But neither of us could know how true, and prophetic, my words were.

There wasn't a lot of sleeping done at Tonkinese that night. Instead there was a great deal of talking, and planning. Roger Casement left before daybreak in his iron boat with Hairy Bill and John. Part of the plan was that he would stop at Pongara for what he called a 'pep talk' with Thomas.

A while after daybreak those of us fleeing *l'État Indépendant du Congo* boarded a riverboat called *The Calibre* which had called on its way to Boma. Ilanga wore the child's finger charm about her neck in its bag. She'd accepted it wordlessly.

David travelled on *The Calibre* with the Mongo family and myself; he would spend a week or more with Casement at the consul's house in Boma. The Mongo family would stay there, too; it would take that length of time at least to sort out their travel arrangements and find a place for them to live in the Niger Protectorate. I would leave Boma as soon as possible, taking the first available ship for England.

I wore African dress, a gift from a woman at the mission, for the journey. There hadn't been time to wash and dry my own clothes and, because I'd lost weight, nothing of Eunice's, even with pinning and tucking, could be made to fit me. The woman, whose name was Gaby, wrapped the swathes of bright cloth around me, leaving my arms and shoulders free. It felt very comfortable.

I'd no great hopes of Casement's being able to retrieve the rest of my clothing from Pongara so decided I would wash and dry my clothes in Boma to wear on the journey home. Beautiful as it was, I wouldn't be taking the African cloth with me; I was too mindful of the *féticheuse*'s warning for that. No point in tempting fate by taking from Africa something I hadn't brought to the continent with me.

Eunice stood by my side as we waited to go aboard *The Calibre*. I took her hand.

'I'm sorry to say goodbye to you,' I said, 'it would be nice to think of you coming to Ireland some day.'

'And *I* would like to think of you telling the world what is happening in the Congo.' She gave me a quick, hard hug. 'Be careful. Be very careful what you do . . .'

'I will,' I said, surprised by her intensity.

'I'll be praying for you, praying you will be guided safely out of Africa,' she said. I hadn't told her but it was almost as if she knew about the *féticheuse*'s warning about crossing water.

But it wasn't water Eunice had spotted as a danger to me. She knew human nature and, with an instinct that equalled that of the *féticheuse*, had seen another kind of danger altogether.

The last I saw of her and Granville they were side by side, waving, Eunice seeming to tower over him more than ever, seen from a distance. They were an oak and a poplar in the African landscape and that was how I would see them in my mind's eye over many years of writing to Eunice. They would stay another six years in the Congo before they went home to America.

Roger Casement's boat was already tied up close to the bank when we anchored in the river beside Pongara. Hairy Bill was still aboard and told our captain, who was a Dutchman called Hans Pieters, that the consul would be along shortly and wanted to come on aboard *The Calibre*.

We waited an hour. Thomas was with the consul when he arrived on the riverbank, as well as Charles Beckett and one of the station soldiers. I was surprised not to see Leon Klein, Thomas's usual ally when presenting a bullying front.

The Mongo family stayed in their cabin. Lingomo had evidently done what he needed to do and was trusting the *féticheuse*'s curse to avenge him. There was nothing he and Ilanga wanted to see of Pongara, or any of the people running it, ever again.

The consul paddled out in a dugout, alone, to the steamer. I stood by myself on the top deck and watched Thomas watching me from the riverbank. I was very glad of the water between us.

'Your husband says you may return to live with him,' Roger Casement said. He looked tired, his eyes less penetrating than usual. But he looked wryly amused too. He was a man going through a formality. 'What will I tell him?' he asked.

I took deep breath. 'That I'm no longer his wife. That he's mad and bad and had better not show his face, ever again, anywhere in the West of Ireland.' I paused, then finished more calmly, 'Tell him my brother Hugh will deal with the legal side of ending our marriage and with the contract we signed.'

Casement took my hand in his and looked at it. John, in the iron boat, began a jealous barking.

'There are times,' he said, 'when this job gives me pleasure.' He looked up and smiled. 'I want you to know, Vanessa O'Grady from Ballycoole, that this is one Congo devil whose murderous career we can cripple, if not end altogether. On the scale of things Thomas Cooper's operation here is small, but it's significant.' He let my hand go. 'What's happened here *does* matter.'

He took the dugout back to shore and *The Calibre* moved on. It was the last I would see of him, apart from pictures in the paper next to news of his triumphant campaign and report against the Congo rubber slavers and, later, when he was knighted and became Sir Roger Casement.

That sighting of Thomas, as *The Calibre* moved off, was the last I had of him in Africa. He had his hat on his head, in the style of Henry Morgan Stanley, but even under the shadow of its peak there was no mistaking the malignancy of his glare. His face was red, his white shirt not over-clean. His boots were muddy. I knew that pride would keep him from following me in Africa at least. He'd lost too much face already. His days, as Roger Casement had said, were numbered.

I never again saw any of the beautiful clothes I'd bought in Dublin with my father's money, or the couture garments Thomas had bought for me in Antwerp. I liked to imagine that Muriel Sedley, for all her faults, might have enjoyed some of them.

It took four days and five nights to get to Boma. The days were a torment of heat and flies which I passed taking a last look at the wonders of Africa. I knew I would never again see the forested islands and striped sandbars, the hornbills – one of the few birds I got to know, black in front, white behind – the hulking hippopotamuses and skulking crocodiles, the fishermen who came alongside in dugouts offering fresh fish, the famished porters along the banks carrying rubber on bent backs, and always and ever the high, dark forests sheltering cries and screams.

'How much longer will you stay in Africa?' I said on the

third night to David. We were watching fires along the riverbank. They lit up the water as well as the villages behind.

'I would like to stay until I know all I need to know,' he said, 'but I doubt my paper will pay for me to stay that long.'

'I doubt it too,' I said. 'I doubt you would ever learn enough to be satisfied.' When he didn't reply to this I added, 'Have you always been driven by an urge to right wrongs?'

He didn't answer at once. 'Not always, but for a long time,' he said then, 'ever since my father was lynched by a white mob. His crime was to take back corn he'd not been paid for from a white man's yard. I was seven years old when they took him from my side and hung him from a tree.'

'Were they punished?'

'There is never any justice for men like them. They hide behind one another. But I know who they are.' He paused. 'And they know who they are.'

'Will you expose them?'

'I have tried. And failed.' His face, lit by the fiery river water, had more sadness than anger in it. Fighting his father's battle had tired him.

'So you came to Africa to write about a wrong which could not be so easily hidden? Do you think to make the world question how white men treat black men?'

He looked at me, and shrugged. 'Simply put, but yes, I suppose that's what I mean to do, right enough.'

'You'll do it too,' I said, 'there's enough horror here to fill a month of newspapers with print.'

'It will go on for a while longer, no matter how much or what I write. Those with power don't give up so easily.' He hesitated then suddenly smiled, teeth white in his dark face. 'The last thing I thought was that I would meet a white woman like you in Africa.'

I was disconcerted, but rallied. 'What sort of woman did

376

you expect to meet?' I raised my brows in the sophisticated way Eunice had, one higher than the other. It was easy.

David stared at me for a minute without answering. He'd stopped smiling. 'I will never forget you,' he said, and turned again to look at the fires burning on the shore. He stood very, very still. Rigid, almost.

I looked away from him and, to stop myself taking his hand, moved a step away from him too. Men on the riverbank threw more wood on to the fire and the flames leaped higher, throwing sparks heavenward as they did. The blaze had died to a few slow-burning embers before I found myself able to speak. David said nothing for all of that time either.

What I said then told him nothing of the confusion his words had caused in me, nothing of the sadness I felt at making a friend I would never see again. I gave only the smallest hint of the wild, unexpected joy which had come with knowing he cared for me.

'I like you too,' I said. 'I'll always be glad we've known one another.'

'Is Cooper all you've known of love?' he said, looking at me sideways.

'I loved a neighbour's son all my life,' I said, 'we were . . .'

'I wasn't talking about childhood dreams,' he interrupted me gently, 'but you've answered my question.'

A night breeze came up the river and blew my hair across my face. He moved closer to lift it behind my ears.

'I like to look at you,' he said.

'It was . . . detestable with Thomas,' I said, and shivered. He put an arm about me and pulled me close.

'It's over now,' he said, 'over for ever. He's the past.'

We stood for a long time in a silence even heavier than the one before. The fires were completely out and there was only the light from the moon in a purple-black sky when I said, 'Tell me about your wife,' I have no idea why I said

377

this, nor why I compounded my discomfort by continuing, 'tell me her name.'

'My wife's name is Chloe. My daughters are called Isabel and Beth. They're seven and nearly three years old.'

I wanted to ask if he missed his wife. What I said was, 'Do you miss your girls?'

'Every day,' he said. 'Beth will be three next week.' He paused. 'I was away last year, too, for her second birthday.'

'You live for what you do,' I said, stating the obvious.

'Yes,' he said, 'a fact which is not easy for my wife and daughters. I sometimes think that I *am* what I do. That it is all that I am and without it there's only the shell of a man. It's that way, too, with your consul, Casement. I've been watching him. He is whatever he's doing, and he *must* be doing. There's a lack in us of some sort.'

'There's a lack in all of us,' I said, 'of some sort.'

'In some more than others,' he said. 'Will you return to your childhood love?'

'He loves an actress now. She's older and experienced in a way I never was.' I hesitated. 'I doubt he ever loved me anyway. Not in the way he loves his actress.'

'Never loved . . .' He touched my cheek, then kissed me lightly on the forehead. 'Let me love you,' he said. 'Let us have this night for us, Nessa. Let's take that much from Africa, at least.'

'I couldn't,' I said.

I moved away from him but didn't say what I should have said, that he was married, that he belonged to another woman, that he wasn't mine. I just shook my head and walked away from him towards my cabin.

When I got to the door he was standing in my way. He put his hand on my arm. A pulse beat in his neck.

'Come on in then,' I said.

The cabin was filled with shadows and light from the moon

slanting through the curtains on the porthole. I dropped the shawl covering my shoulders, then felt his hands there. They were cool, and that surprised me.

'David . . .' I whispered.

'Don't say no to me.' He was whispering too.

We looked at each other like people drowning, people who needed to hold on to one another, go beyond words, so as to be sure they were alive.

He kissed me, holding me against him and putting his lips on my neck and my eyes before covering my mouth. I kissed him back and he opened my mouth with his tongue. I let him do that too. I wanted him to. I wanted him to do everything he wanted because that was what I wanted too.

His hands moved on my back and I shuddered. He pulled at the wraparound, loosening it until it fell to the ground and I stood naked to the waist. The blood pounded in my ears. My breasts were full, reaching towards him. There was nothing in me of the revulsion and recoil I'd felt with Thomas. Nothing.

I wanted to tell him this, to say to him that he was erasing an evil done me, putting something good in its place. But I was afraid to speak in case the moment escaped us, in case what I wanted to happen might not. I was afraid even to think – either about the meaning of what we were doing, of the rights and wrongs of it, or what we might feel tomorrow.

David touched my nipples and I cried out and moulded myself more tightly against him. But he moved back, then lifted and carried me to the bed. Kneeling on the floor beside me, he took his clothes off, pulling and tearing at them, holding my eyes with his as if he was afraid I would dissolve and disappear. Or just get up and run.

I did none of those things. I removed my petticoat and drawers.

379

When he was completely naked I held up my hand for him to be still. He knelt there, beautiful and loving in all his shining black glory. But not for long. After a minute he lifted me from the bed and laid me on the floor beside him. I turned on my hip and buried my face in the velvet feel of his chest and held on to him to stop my trembling.

'It's all right, Nessa,' he said, 'it won't be like before.'

'I know,' I said, 'I know it won't . . .'

His hands were gentle on me, caressing as he held me against him, stroked the length of my arms, my thighs, gentle on my stomach as he turned me on to my back. In the moonlight his black eyes were infinitely tender, his mouth smiling. I reached up and pulled his face down to mine, and put my mouth to his in a kiss.

Everything after that happened with a wonderful, exquisite slowness. We lay mouth to mouth, our limbs wrapped round one another, as he gently entered me. I was wet and ready for him and even as he moved in me, even as I lost myself to the fire and abandon rising in me, one last, aware bit of me knew that *this* was what men and women did together, this was as it was meant to be like, that what had happened with the man I'd married had been an aberration, an affront to the nature of love.

Then I thought no more, just widened my thighs and held David with my hands on the small of his back while he moved in deeper, his head between my breasts. He started to say something but it died in his throat and became a moan as he went even deeper into me, moving faster and faster, and we were together and I cried out and heard him cry, too, and gave him everything of myself and stars burst in a purple-black African sky.

When it was over we lay quietly for a long time.

'You are so black in the moonlight,' I touched the velvet of his shoulder, 'you're not brown at all.'

380

He twisted and stared at me, his eyes burning.

'I love you,' he said, and turned on to his back and lay with his arm over his eyes so that I couldn't tell if they were open or shut.

I touched his shoulder and said 'David . . . ?' and he shuddered and turned to me again and buried his head in my stomach.

We slept like that until morning.

31

L
ate on a Saturday afternoon, during the last week of
April 1903, I drove with Mossie Hope back up the
avenue to Kilraven. A year and a month had passed, almost,
since my father had shot himself. Five months had gone by
since my marriage to Thomas Cooper.

It had been raining and in the damp air I heard a cuckoo
sing. Primroses and cowslips were scattered yellow across
the grass and the hedges were white with blackthorn. The
sea was a distant, cold blue. A pale sun shone on it all. I'd
never seen anywhere so beautiful in my entire life.

Ellie met us halfway down the avenue, running to meet
us with her arms outstretched. She was the same as I'd left
her, freckled and lovely and already rounding with another
child in her.

'It's behind you now,' were the first words she said to me,
'it's all behind you.'

Manus came walking with Jerome in his arms and my
mother stood on the steps with one hand waving and, when
I came closer, tears running down her face.

'I should never have allowed you go.' She held me in her
arms. 'I should have stopped you.'

'How would you have done that?' I stood back to look
at her. We both knew she couldn't have prevented me
from going.

'Your father would have stopped you,' she said. This was
true, something else we both knew. 'I should have found a

382

way.' She took my hand and led me inside. She'd got old, and was thinner than ever. Constant tears had washed the colour from her eyes.

Those first weeks at home I slept, constantly. I had bad dreams and, when I cried out, Ellie or sometimes my mother came and sat with me. In this way the dreams became fewer and fewer and until they were rare and I slept more peacefully, by day as well as night.

It seemed to me, during that time, that if I slept enough I would erase all that had happened, would emerge reborn and ready to live my life anew. But it didn't happen like that. When I began to live my life again I was a different person. Kilraven was different too.

I no longer believed the world had more good than bad in it. I'd no inclination to meet or be with people I didn't know. I was often irritable, suitable company only for myself.

The good thing was that it became easier as time went on not to think about David Addison. He'd never been a part of Kilraven so there was nothing of him there and, because I hadn't told anyone about him, his name was never mentioned.

But for all this he lurked at the edge of all my thoughts. It took only the sighting of something beautiful, or of Ellie and Manus holding hands, to bring memories alive, to feel sad for love lost and what might have been. I wanted to weep for him often, but didn't. As with all grieving, this feeling eased after a while.

The dog noticed my melancholy. He followed me everywhere, but at a distance, keeping me in mournful view. Only when I went to my father's grave did he come close enough to lean against me, and when he did he sighed.

Everyone else noticed, too, but Ellie was the one who confronted me.

'Something's died in you,' she said, 'you're a pale shadow

of the woman you used to be. Africa's over, Nessa. You're safe now and you'll have to put it behind you. The summer's here and we'd best make hay while there's sun. I plan to give a party, a smaller one than last year's. I'll need you to help me.'

'You don't need me, Ellie. You've done great things here, you and Manus. The roof is fixed, the windows are sound.' I shrugged. 'The money's finished. There'll be none coming in for a party. It's none of my business, Ellie, since Kilraven is your home and charge now, but it's plans to make money you should be making.'

'Money plans *are* what I'm talking about,' she said, crisply. We were sitting in the gardens and she turned, eyes narrowed, to where Kilraven stood, large and watchful in the sun. 'My plans for a party are to do with what I have in mind for making that house pay for itself.'

She told me then how she was going to make a 'class of a hotel out of Kilraven'. I listened, heart sick and eyes unable to meet hers, afraid she would see how the idea repelled me.

'We'll take in only the best of people because they'll be the ones who can pay,' Ellie said. 'We'll give them fine food, all of the comforts they would want in their rooms. If they fancy a bit of fishing then Mossie will take them to the river, or out on the sea.'

She looked across the estuary as if assessing the numbers of fish it might yield. She was wearing a plain cotton dress, quite short and showing off her arms. Her hair was piled on top of her head and held there with black lacquered combs. She was the same Ellie who'd married Manus, and determined now as she'd been then.

'Mossie will collect them from the station, too,' she said, 'when they arrive. I was hoping you might take those of them that want to for treks on horseback . . .'

'Mossie agrees?' Interrupting, I couldn't keep the incredulity out of my voice.

'He doesn't like it any more than you do,' Ellie observed, 'but you'll both have to learn to live with it. We'll not be the first big house to turn to inn-keeping to hold body and soul together as well as keep a roof over our heads. Nor will we be the last. The life of the big house is gone, and there's more and more people in business and the like with money to spend on holidays. Your father knew the life he was reared to was gone for ever. Your brother Hugh knows it, and now Manus knows it too. Your mother's lost in the past still but *you* know full well what I'm saying is true, Nessa O'Grady. There's no use you hiding from it, fooling yourself that because we've a roof on the house today it'll still be there in a couple of years' time.'

She stopped talking and sat, plump, pretty, fierce and breathless, on the stone seat beside me. She was everything that Kilraven, every stone a monument to another life and every inch of it resistant to change, was not.

'That house will have to be made to pay its way, like every other living thing on the planet,' Ellie affirmed, 'and believe me, Nessa, that house has a life of its own.'

I knew, in that instant, that in the battle between Kilraven and Ellie my brother's wife would be the one to win.

'I'm only a guest here,' I said, 'a married woman without a husband or a home or rights. Another mouth to feed.'

I sounded cross and self-pitying but facts were facts and what I was saying was the truth. I felt adrift, as if there was nowhere in the world I rightfully belonged any more. But Ellie's face had become pink and her eyes bright and, knowing well the signs of her rising temper, I continued quickly.

'There's no good you telling me I've a home here. I can't live on kindness. There's no *place* for me here, and you'd feel the same if you were me. I'll go to Dublin in the autumn, get myself work and a place to live there. I'll be independent.'

'What will you work at?'

'I'll look after children. Teach them, maybe. Or else find work in an office.' I was airy, and at heart not one bit confident. 'There's any number of things I might do.'

'You must do as you think best.' Ellie was tight-lipped, a sure sign she was hurt. But her hurt didn't change the facts of my life and I was determined to go. Ellie stood.

'Since you're here for now at least, we'll need your help with the party. I'll be making it known to everyone who comes that Kilraven is to take paying guests. I'll be asking Hugh and Bella to bring Dublin friends of the kind who might make future customers. I'll be inviting the owners and cooks from the Victoria and Imperial Hotels in Sligo town. It's always best to have those in the same business as friends.'

'How many bedrooms will you rent out?'

Feeling faint at the speed of the imminent change I took off my hat and fanned myself, to little effect. In my mind's eye Kilraven had already become like the Van Dyck Hotel in Antwerp, with bedrooms painted white and gold and people I'd normally not have given the time of day to sleeping in them.

Then, too, there was the awful, unworthy feeling in me that making a hotel of Kilraven was bringing it down, lowering and humbling a great house, making it common where once it had been grand. But Ellie might, after all, have decided to turn Kilraven into a shebeen or, God forbid, a dance hall. I tried to be grateful for small mercies.

'I'll take people into five of the bedrooms,' she was precise, 'no more. They'll be given breakfast and supper but will have to shift for themselves in between.' She patted her swelling belly. 'I've my children to look after.'

'What does my mother say?'

'She doesn't know yet. Manus is to tell her.'

'And Hugh?'

'Oh, Hugh . . .' she sighed. 'He nods along with Bella, of course. *She* says I'll make a fine *chatelaine*, whatever that is.' Her voice had its old, caustic note. 'She says she'll give after-supper recitals to guests when she's here.' Ellie shrugged. 'The more support the merrier, I say. We're going to need all the help we can get.'

'You certainly are,' I said, ignoring her implication.

But I was glad to hear her being caustic. It meant Ellie was, as ever, unimpressed by anyone until they'd proven themselves in her eyes. Bella, clearly, had a distance to go yet.

'Something's died in you,' Ellie said again as we went back up to the house. She beat at a maverick ragwort with the ash plant in her hand. The yellow heads scattered on the path like confetti. 'I thought you had more courage.'

'It's not my courage I've lost,' I said.

But if something had died in me then something new had taken its place. I was carrying a child.

I was ten weeks gone before it came to me that the absence of menstrual bleeding had nothing to do with the trauma of Africa, and everything do with the precious time I'd spent with David Addison

My mother was distraught.

'You'll never be free of the Cooper man now.' She clenched and unclenched her hands, crossing and recrossing the salon in quick, jerky strides. 'He'll come when he hears and bring distress and trouble with him. He's bad blood. Bad, bad, bad! Your father . . .' She stopped, looking at me from a wilderness of confusion. 'My poor child. My poor Vanessa. To be carrying . . . Oh, Lord God in Heaven . . .'

She put her hands over her mouth to stifle a keening

387

sound, then let them fall to look past me to where the sun shone on preparations for Ellie's summer party. Manus, with Jerome on a rug beside him, was putting the second of two long tables into place. The sky was boundlessly blue.

'What's done cannot be undone,' my mother said, 'and all children are born innocent. All of them . . .' She fell to her knees where I sat by the window and took my hands. 'Your baby may grow up good and decent. The sins of the father should not be visited on the child. Try always to remember this. I will tell the entire household, this very day, that your child is innocent.' She stood, put a hand on my head but took it away quickly to wring her hands together. 'When?' she said.

'Sometime around Christmas.'

'It's unlikely in the circumstances that you'll ever find another husband.' She shook her head. 'Even a Protestant one.'

I'd never in my life seen her so agitated. It was as if something had snapped and the self-control which had always held her together had been replaced by an inner frenzy.

I didn't tell her that an African curse meant my husband couldn't have children; that the father of my baby was a married American, and black, who would never, no matter how much I wished for it, be a part of his child's life.

She was in a bad enough state without telling her all of that.

I was ecstatic myself. My spirit returned at precisely the moment I realised I was pregnant. It never again deserted me.

'You'll be staying here so,' said Ellie when I told her. 'Your child will need a home.'

'I'll help run the hotel business,' I agreed.

'Good.' There was satisfaction in her voice. 'We'll need all the help we can get.' There was triumph in her grin.

388

I let everyone think Thomas Cooper was the father of my child until the end of October. Three lots of paying guests had come and gone by then and Ellie, a month further into her pregnancy than I, was tired. I told her first because she was the only one would truly understand.

'Do you mean to tell me your baby will be black?' She sat down on my bed, her eyes fixed on my stomach.

'Very likely.'

'And was conceived on a boat?'

'A riverboat.'

'May the sweet Lord Jesus and His mother Mary look down on us,' Ellie said, her eyes wide. 'And I thought I knew you!'

I became a mother on 30 December, 1903, to a daughter delivered in my own bed in Kilraven. Father Duggan, with a long-suffering face and the addition of a great many prayers for my soul, christened her Constance Davina O'Grady.

For the first months of her life I spent hours of every day admiring the wonder of my daughter. She was without a doubt the brightest, loveliest and most joy-filled child ever born.

Mossie said she was like me as a child, that I'd been equally full of life. My mother disagreed.

'She's black,' she said. 'The child is black. How could a black child be anything like a child of mine?'

My mother couldn't accept Constance. She said the one thing in life she'd never expected to have was a black grand-daughter. What she said exactly, over and over, was: 'I never thought to see a black child in Kilraven.'

She kept using the word 'black' as if Constance's skin was all and everything that my daughter was. She never held her and she never sang to her in the way I could remember her singing to the boys and me when we were small children.

★   ★   ★

But Constance never knew about her grandmother's lack of love for her because my mother died in February, when my daughter was just two months old. She simply went to bed one night and didn't wake up in the morning. The doctor said it was her heart, and of course he was right.

We buried her beside my father. The truth was that my mother had never really found much point to a life without him. My father would have loved Constance, had he been alive, and my mother would have loved her because he did.

Roger Casement's report on the evil done in the Congo was published a short time before Constance was born. It was in newspapers everywhere, and so was he, and it was hard during that time not to think of David and wonder what he had written for his newspaper in America. I never did find out. I was always too afraid that any enquiry of mine would bring me to the attention of his wife. To have betrayed her once was enough.

'Do you ever think about him?' Ellie said on a day when I was reading a report about the Congo in the *Sligo Champion*.

'It's hard not to when I'm reading his words . . .'

'I'm not talking about Roger Casement,' Ellie whipped the paper from the table and made me look at her. 'You know well who I'm talking about.'

I stared up at her, trying hard not to weep. I was very close to my time. When I felt in control of myself, I said, 'I do . . . on the odd occasion.' I paused. 'But less and less . . .'

The tears fell in spite of me. Ellie rocked me in her arms. 'You'll love again,' she said, 'there's someone else in the world for you.'

But I knew that there wasn't, that I would never love again.

I taught myself to think hardly at all about David and even, in time, not to feel any great anguish when an inadvertent thought of him crossed my mind. He'd given me the gift of love, had shown me in one glorious night what could be between a man and a woman. Now I had his daughter. It was enough. It would have to be.

Roger Casement was given a medal by King Edward and was, for a while, a great hero. He wrote that it was in the 'lonely Congo forests' he'd found himself as an Irishman, and that it was being an Irishman made him able to 'understand *fully* . . . the whole scheme of wrongdoing at work in the Congo'.

His report told of hands and other parts of the body being cut off; how nine hundred men, women and children had in one instance been killed for the sake of adding twenty tons of rubber to a monthly crop; how women and children were routinely taken hostage until the required amount of rubber was brought in; how villages were burned to the ground. He wrote about the thousands who were tortured and hung, about the *chicotte's* daily and terribly use, about bodies floating in rivers and lakes with their right hands cut off.

Just as it had been in my dreams.

I was glad to have known him but was often, in the years after, bitter with anger that his work did not bring down King Leopold of Belgium's *État Indépendant du Congo*. It would be 1912 before atrocities against rubber workers came to an end and Casement could say that 'the break-up of the pirate's stronghold is nearly accomplished'.

Thomas Cooper came once to Kilraven, and once only.

It happened in the spring my mother died, when Constance was four months old, just a year after I'd last seen him on the banks of the River Congo by Pongara Station.

I'd been to Sligo with Mossie, shopping for Constance, and found Thomas sitting outside the house, in a motor car, when I got back. Neither Ellie nor Manus would allow him into the house and he'd been forced to wait outside.

Mossie brought the horse trap to a halt not five yards from where he sat and I climbed down. So did my husband. Facing each other, we were no more than six or seven feet apart.

'There's unfinished business between us,' he said.

He was wearing an overcoat and hat, and looked older. But his eyes were alight with spite and he kept hitting a pair of leather gloves against his open palm. Mossie came and stood so close to me we were touching.

'You're wrong,' I said, 'there is nothing between us and nothing we have to say to one another. You shouldn't have come here and it would be better if you left.'

'There is money owing to me,' he said.

'That money was paid while I was still your wife and living with you. I earned it and Kilraven has used it.'

'The money was paid as part of a contract. You broke that contract,' the gloves made a slapping sound on his palm, 'the money is forfeit.'

'You presented yourself to me under false pretences,' I retaliated, 'you told me I would be the wife of a station manager. In fact, I found myself the wife of a cruelly inhuman slave driver. There's documentary proof of your barbaric wrongdoing in Roger Casement's report.' My voice rose. Mossie gave my arm a warning squeeze. 'You can fight your case against the evidence, if you wish, Thomas, but you won't get a penny piece of your money back from this family.'

'You broke a lawful contract!' He was red in the face and shaking. 'And for that I'll see you in court.'

'You may indeed see me in court,' I said. 'My brother Hugh is arranging for a divorce so it's likely we will *have* to go before a judge. There will be plenty for you to answer for.'

Thomas Cooper took an ill-advised step closer and Mossie,

with the speed of a large cat pouncing, was suddenly in front of me.

'Climb back into your motoring vehicle and get out of here, Cooper.' He didn't raise his voice.

'The ape speaks,' Thomas sneered.

We'll never know what would have happened next if Ellie hadn't appeared. She came through the front door and down the steps with Jerome trundling stoutly behind her and Constance in her arms. She stopped on the bottom step and held the baby out to me.

'Your daughter's been missing you,' she said, 'it's time she was fed.' I took and cradled her.

Thomas Cooper was like a man turned to granite.

But not quite, and not for long. Watching him over Constance's head I saw the skin at the side of his half-open mouth begin to twitch and the hand holding the gloves tighten into a livid knot. His eyes were riveted on the child as disbelief turned to revulsion. When he spoke the words came with spittal and through his teeth.

'Whore!' he said. 'Putrid, depraved whore! May you and your bastard child burn in hell's fire for eternity!'

Finn, too late as always to be of help, appeared as Thomas got into the motor car and turned the starter. There was a great deal of noise, none of it productive, and this time no help forthcoming to get it going. Thomas was forced to climb down.

'I will destroy you and I will destroy your family!' He kept his distance as he shouted at me. 'If I have to devote my life to it, I'll see you in the gutter, and your bastard child with you!'

The last I saw of my husband was his incandescently furious back as he hurried on foot down the avenue, Finn snapping merrily at his heels.

The next I knew of him he was dead, killed within a week

in a brawl in a Dublin public house. It was Hugh found out about it, and Hugh who had him buried. For decency's sake I travelled to Dublin and said a prayer by the graveside as they lowered him down. I'd have done as much for an animal. I'd done it for Kilgallen's lurcher.

For reasons I'll never know, I remembered, as I stood there, the look in the eyes of Dokombo, the man whose sons' hands Thomas had had severed. With the memory came the certainty that more than one curse had been put on Thomas.

32

Mossie didn't like the idea of Kilraven as a hotel any more than I did but, like me, he became used to it in time.

'It was built to house the O'Gradys,' he complained when Ellie laid out her plans, 'not as a boarding house for every dog and divil that comes down the road.'

'My children are O'Gradys,' Ellie reminded him, 'and if they're to have a house to live in we need money to keep it standing. Do you have a better way?'

This quietened him, though only a bit. Mossie's real quandary was his dislike of city people, and of what he called 'jumped-up cottagers'. We got a great many of both. An exchange with one of the former during Kilraven's first season set the tone of Mossie's role in relation to our guests. It took place as he stood looking into the fire in the great hall on a blustery afternoon.

'What're you doing there, my good man?' a male guest, arriving back from a walk, put the question loudly.

'I'm not your good man.' Mossie didn't turn around. The guest wore a monocle. The same man had frightened the horses earlier with his braying and stomping about the stable yard.

'Just a figure of speech,' the guest adjusted the monocle, 'just a figure of speech.' He raised his voice even higher. 'So, tell me, my good man, is fire-gazing a local custom we might all engage in?'

Mossie didn't turn. 'Good manners are the custom in this house,' he said, 'and we prefer plain speaking to figures of speech.'

'You are insolent, sir,' the monocle shivered, 'I doubt Mrs O'Grady would be pleased to hear of your attitude.' The monocle fell. It dangled on its cord over his very new brown tweed jacket.

'You are a paying guest in this house,' Mossie turned, 'and as such will be tolerated for only so long as you remember your place.'

'Do you know who I am?' The man squared his shoulders. 'You're clearly not aware . . .'

'If you were the Pope in Rome I'd tell you the same thing.' Mossie walked from the hall. 'This house has given shelter to your kind before, but never for long.'

Ellie, when the guest complained, told him to leave.

Ever after, when guests arrived, she made their place in Kilraven clear to them. They were welcome. They would be given every hospitality. But the house was home to those of us who lived and worked there and they should never forget this. Impressed by Kilraven and glad to have arrived, guests invariably thought this perfectly reasonable.

Another difference about life at Kilraven was that Theo Howard was no longer a visitor. Celestine Lowry had taken herself to London while I was in Africa and he'd followed her. He was missed for a while and then, surprisingly, not at all. Not even very much by Arthur and Hermione who, being quite well off, took to tripping about the world in search of the sun and sulphur baths. I hardly ever thought of him myself. But then the part of me which had loved him was well and truly erased.

Jerome grew to be like his father, a dreamy child in the way Manus had been. Ellie and Manus's second baby was a girl, Ada. With a bare month between her and Constance they were, happily, firm friends from the start.

Ellie had no more children after Ada. She tried every *pisogue* and practice known to every midwife and wise woman along the western shores but never again became pregnant. When Ada was three years old she accepted her lot.

'We've three beautiful children in the house,' she declared, 'and I'm glad of it. Any more would be a burden.'

My daughter was glorious. She was tall and straight with a high-boned face and long neck. She had her father's searching nature and as many contrary traits as I had myself. I told her the truth: that her father was American, that he and I could not have married. She accepted this because she was a child and happy with her lot. I'd no illusions about such acceptance stretching into her young womanhood.

Growing up with different people coming and going in the house was both a good and a bad thing for Constance. It meant she'd a home that was more open to the world than it might otherwise have been. But it also, since she was universally pandered to by the guests, gave her a false idea of the world's acceptance of people with black skin.

Among friends and neighbours, too, Constance was sheltered and loved and her skin colour went unquestioned. When she was four years old I engaged a friend of Manus's to be tutor to her and her cousins. Andrew McHugh had lost an arm in the Boer War and drank more than was good for him but was as gifted a teacher as Constance was apt as a pupil.

Her fourth year was also the year she pleaded with Mossie, washing his hands at the pump in the yard, to find her a magic soap so she could wash her skin white.

'Why would you want to do that?' he said.

'To be like you,' she said, 'and like Mama and everyone else.'

'But to be different is a fine thing.'

'Would you like to be a brown man then?' said my clever daughter.

397

'I want to be nothing but what I am,' Mossie was a match for her, 'and you must be glad with what you are too.' He picked her up and carried her back inside the house. 'You should be counting your blessings, miss, for there's no soap made that will wash your colour away.'

Ellie, a few years later, started a campaign to get me 'back among the living'. For the most part I ignored her but was occasionally trapped into argument.

'You're still young,' was the way she would invariably begin, 'you should go into the town more often, go calling more often too. Why don't you visit Dublin? There are plenty of . . .'

'I don't want a man, Ellie,' I told her, over and over, 'and in any case I didn't have men running after me before I had Constance, so I'm hardly going to find one in Sligo or Dublin now.'

She just as invariably ignored this. 'You could have a man in Dublin didn't know a thing about Constance. You could visit him to go to the theatre and suchlike. There would be no need, ever, to bring him here.'

'An affair? You're telling me I should have an affair, is that it?'

'I'm trying to tell you that there's more than one way to skin a cat, and more than one way of loving a man too. But you know that so there's no good you pretending to be shocked. It's the twentieth century, Nessa O'Grady, and you've already been out in the world. There's nothing to be served by you making a nun of yourself and a convent of Kilraven.'

I went to Dublin occasionally as Constance grew older. I always took her with me. She loved the city as much as the country, and loved the chance to dress herself in Bella's feathers and jewels.

'You can't bury her in Kilraven for ever,' Bella said on a visit when Constance was eight years old. My daughter was like an ancient dark priestess at the mirror, her black curls weighted with beads, her ears and neck hung with coloured glass.

'The decision will be Constance's,' I said.

'Of course it won't.' Bella, still without children of her own, could see what I could not. 'Constance has no idea what's best for her. No idea at all.'

But it was on that visit to Dublin that my daughter learned a thing or two about life's realities, and on that visit, too, that I began the slow process of coming to a decision. We were walking by St Stephen's Green. Constance was ahead of me, impatient with my slowness and wanting to be inside the park, by the pond with the ducks. I heard a group of boys coming up behind me but thought nothing of it until they rushed past. They had Constance surrounded in seconds.

'You looking for the trees?' said one. 'Want us to show you the way?'

'I know my way, thank you,' said Constance.

'It speaks English,' a second boy tittered.

There were four of them and they were neither poor nor ignorant. Their trousers were pressed and they wore jackets with white shirts underneath. One carried a cane and another a hat under his arm. They looked to be aged between sixteen and eighteen.

'I wonder what else it can do?' The boy with the cane flicked it at Constance's cape. 'Tell us, little ape.' He held the top of the cane against her chest. 'Apart from walking upright and speaking English, what other tricks do you perform?'

'Mama . . .'

Constance, bewildered and frightened, threw herself into my arms as I came between her and the boys.

'Get out of here, you foul, bullying hooligans!' I held her tightly against me, her face turned away from her tormentors. 'Hounding a child! Have you no shame?'

'Is that what it is? A child?' The boy with the cane was

399

tall for his age, and thin. He was greatly amused at his own wit. 'We thought it a monkey or some such, escaped from a circus.'

'Come, Constance,' I loosened my hold on my daughter and took her arm, 'we'll leave these disgusting young men to other amusements.' I gave them my most withering glare. It had little effect. 'I hope', I said, 'that you will come to your senses before you're much older. My daughter is eight years old. Choose a victim of your own size to bully next time, if you've the courage. But you won't do that, of course, because you are cowardly bullies. All cowards are bullies and all bullies are cowards.'

They followed, sniggering, as we walked on. Passers-by, seeing what was happening, turned their heads away. The boys, emboldened by this, turned their sniggers into loud guffaws and lewd comments. Constance held very tightly on to my hand. When we got to the corner of the park we had to wait while a row of carriages passed before crossing the road. The boys crowded around us.

The one with the hat stood very close. I could feel his breath on the side of my face when he said, 'Nigger lover! The only disgusting people here are you and your piglet.' He paused and bowed, acknowledging the applause of his companions.

A gap appeared between the passing carriages and I let go of Constance's hand.

'Run,' I said to her. 'Go inside the hotel and wait for me.'

When she hesitated I gave her a small push. She ran then, like the sensible child she was, her long legs carrying her quickly and safely across the road.

'No decent Irishwoman would give herself to a filthy nigger.' The boy with the cane poked me in the arm. 'You should have stayed with your savage. There's no place in this country for your kind . . .'

He was interrupted by one of his companions. 'Nor for the piglets you breed . . .'

As Constance disappeared inside the hotel I turned on them. I didn't raise my voice.

'May God help Ireland if you're its future for I've seen the desolation your sort of brutish and inhuman behaviour can bring to a country and its blameless people. Inform yourselves, go home . . .'

'You should have stayed in that country then,' one of the boys shouted me down. He had the beginnings of a moustache and his eyes, dangerously angry, reminded me of Leon Klein's. 'Go back to whatever heathens you're so fond of. There's no place for you here.'

He took a step closer. His companions crowded around, pushing him. To keep myself at a safe distance I was forced on to the road.

'You may be right,' I said, 'you may well be right.'

Upright citizens continued to pass, men and women both, while this was going on. No one came to my aid. No one raised a voice in protest. I was halfway across the road when it came to me that my father's doleful vision of the new Ireland might, after all, have been a true one.

A year later, by which time the Congo's atrocities had come to an end and Constance was nine years old, I had come to the unwilling, unavoidable decision that there was no future for either my child or me at Kilraven.

Further, that there was no future for either of us in Ireland.

33

Manus drove Constance and me to Cobh the day we left. Hugh and Bella came from Dublin to say goodbye, which was kind of them though it added to the loneliness of the occasion. Ellie didn't come. She couldn't bear, she said, to travel so far from Kilraven. Mossie didn't come either. He said one trip abroad should have been enough for me and that he wasn't going to encourage a second by playing even the smallest part in an American wake.

Even though we'd heard all about the liner we were to sail in we were nevertheless unprepared for the size of it, and the grandeur.

'We could lose one another, it's that big,' said Constance, at heart a practical child but a bit of a worrier since the episode with the boys in Dublin.

'We'll do nothing of the sort.' I held her close. 'We'll stick together, all of the time and no matter what.'

'We'll be over to visit you next year.' Bella looked speculatively up and along the soaring decks and funnels. 'There's sure to be work for singers and performers on a ship this size.' She turned gaily to Hugh. 'I'll work us a passage to New York.'

'Good idea.' He grinned.

He had one arm about her waist, the other around my shoulders. He and Bella were as fond of one another as they'd ever been.

Manus held Constance's hand and said nothing. There

would be precious little chance of his ever coming to America. God alone knew, too, when I would see Ellie or Mossie again, or when Constance would see the cousins who'd been her closest and lifelong allies.

Accepting all of this was the hardest part of what I'd decided, but there was no going back. Constance was too singular ever to be a full part of the society she'd been born into. She had no father. She was a black child on an island of white people. Soon she would be a young black woman. I'd had too many difficulties as a young white woman myself to be foolish enough to believe that she, so much more obviously different, would have an easy, happy passage in either Irish country or city life.

So I was taking her to America, to her father's country, to experience the other half of her heritage. There would be a life for her there, and acceptance.

Eunice and Granville Milton, who now lived in Philadelphia, had been delighted to offer us lodgings until we were settled. I'd no intention of ever contacting David Addison. Our journey was about going forward, not backwards.

Constance had a dream of going to Africa some day too. I'd told her enough about it over the years to make her good and curious. My stories and reminiscences had been by way of atonement for the fact that I'd brought nothing from that continent to give her. Not even the polished stone on its cord given me by the *féticheuse*. That had come off and been lost, along with everything else, the night I made love to her father.

The gangway was secured in place and the other passengers began to come aboard. Constance and I kissed everyone, one last time, and moved forward with them.

Standing at the rail, we waved until our arms ached, until Manus, Hugh and Bella were lost in the blur of people becoming smaller and smaller on the quayside. The cheering

403

and shouting and music grew quiet and then silent and the *Titanic* was underway at last, moving through the water towards the bright horizon.